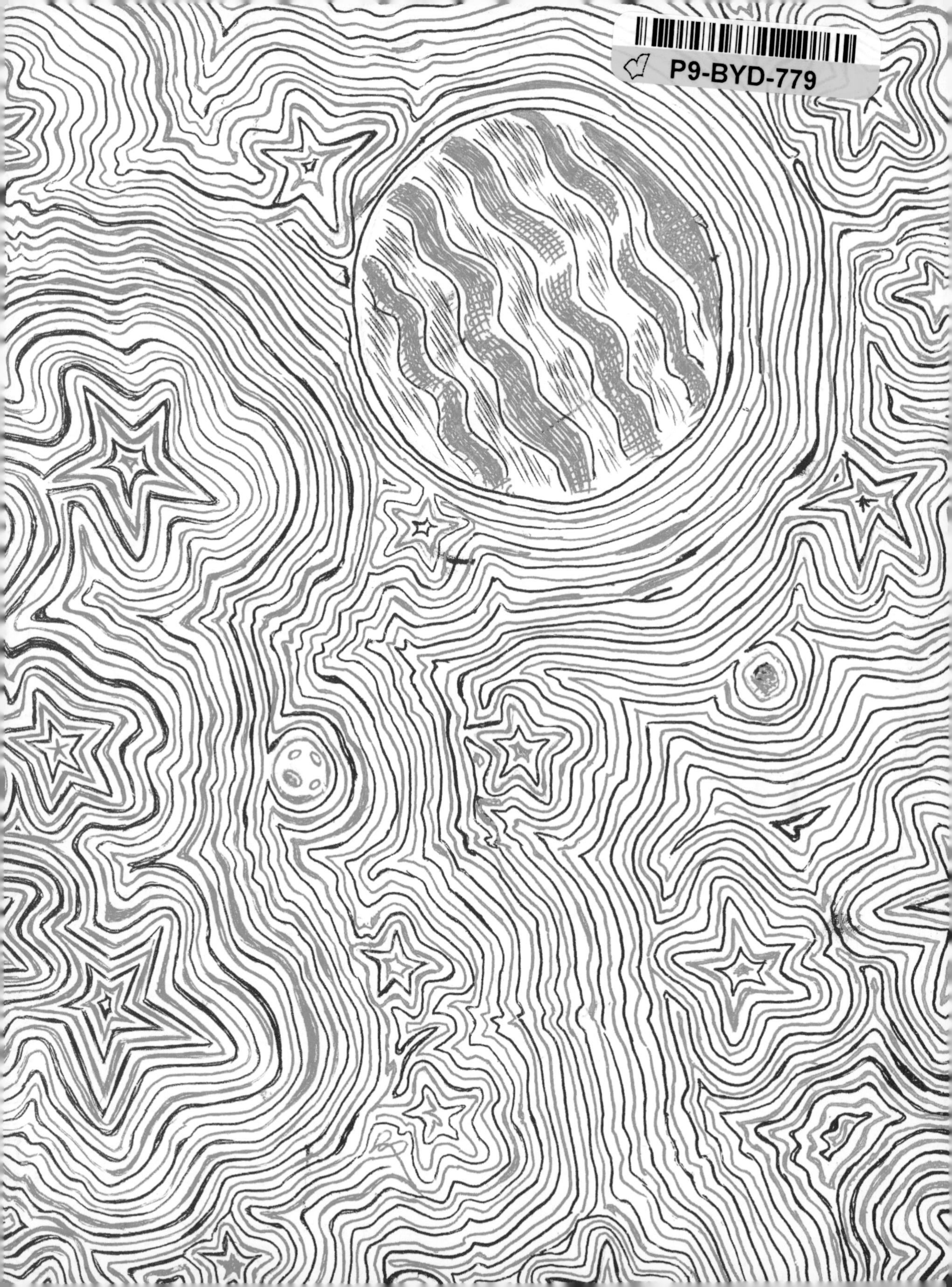

LOWRIDERS in SPACE

BOOK 1

By CATHY CAMPER
Illustrated by RAÚL THE THIRD

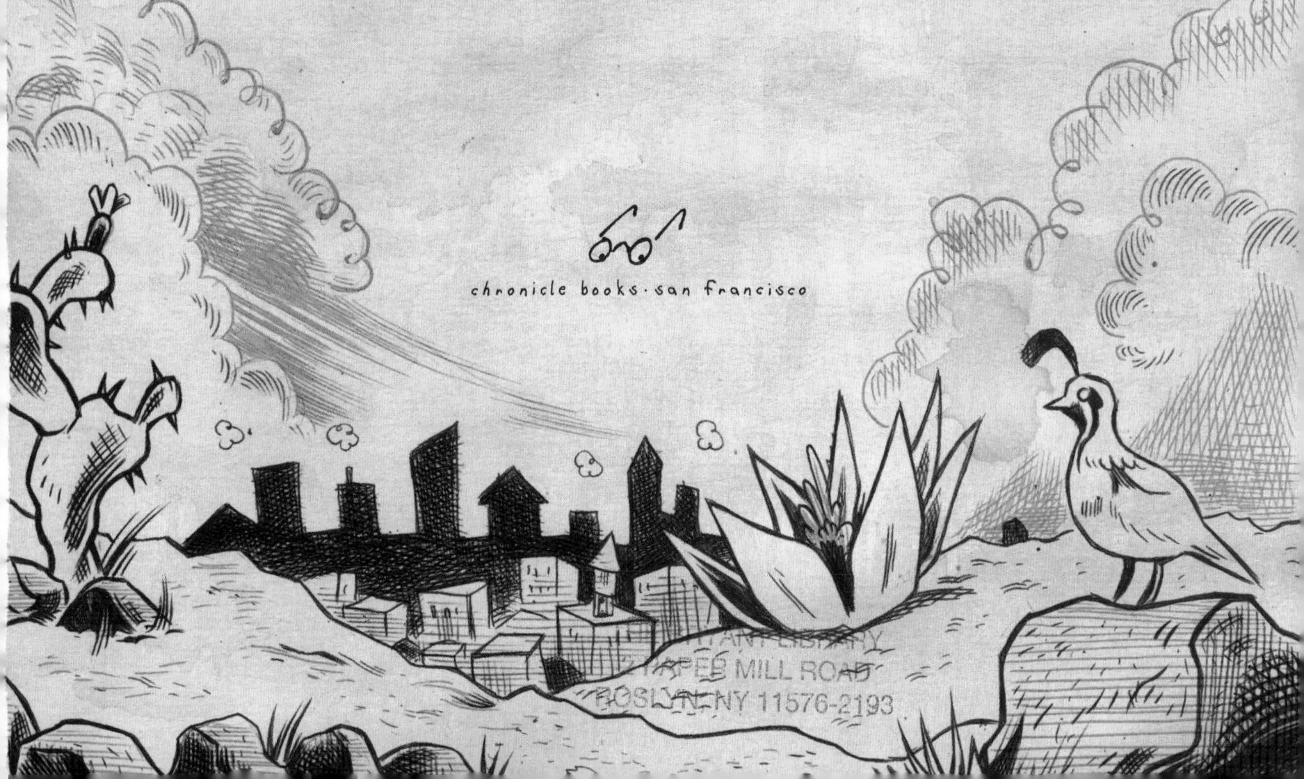

chronicle books · san francisco

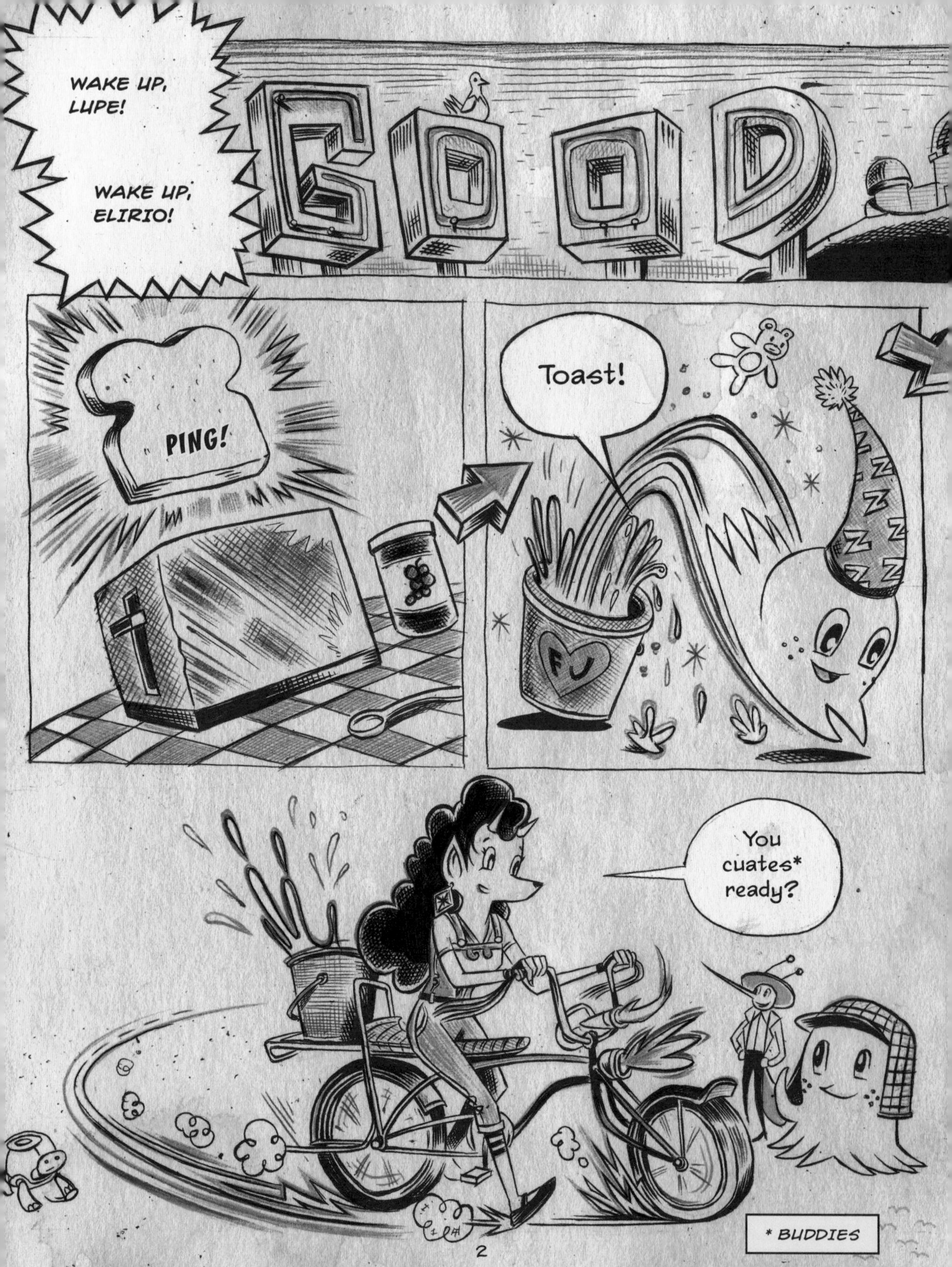
WAKE UP, LUPE!
WAKE UP, ELIRIO!
GOOD
PING!
Toast!
FU
You cuates* ready?
* BUDDIES

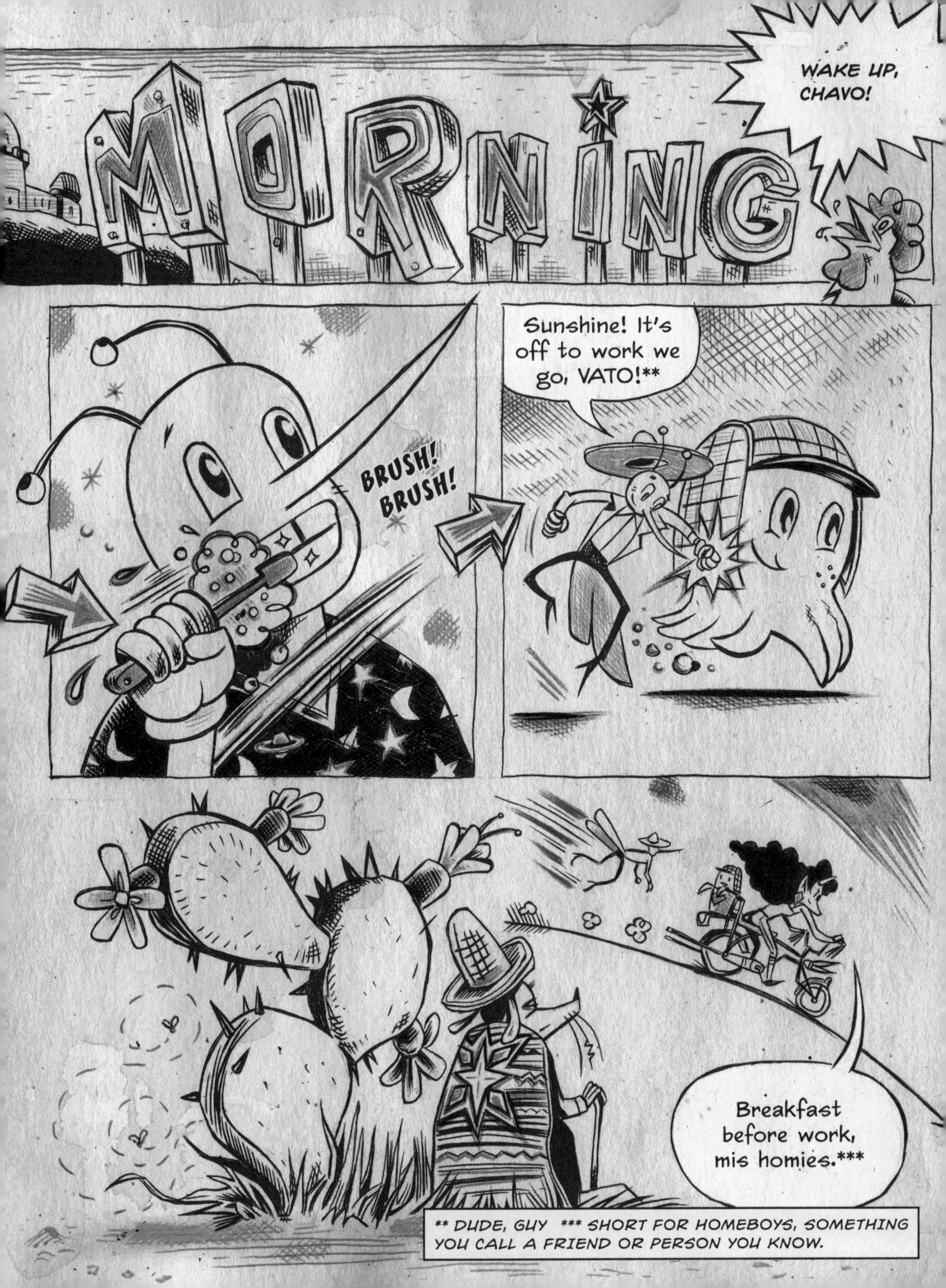
MORNING
WAKE UP, CHAVO!
BRUSH! BRUSH!
Sunshine! It's off to work we go, VATO!**
Breakfast before work, mis homies.***
** DUDE, GUY *** SHORT FOR HOMEBOYS, SOMETHING YOU CALL A FRIEND OR PERSON YOU KNOW.

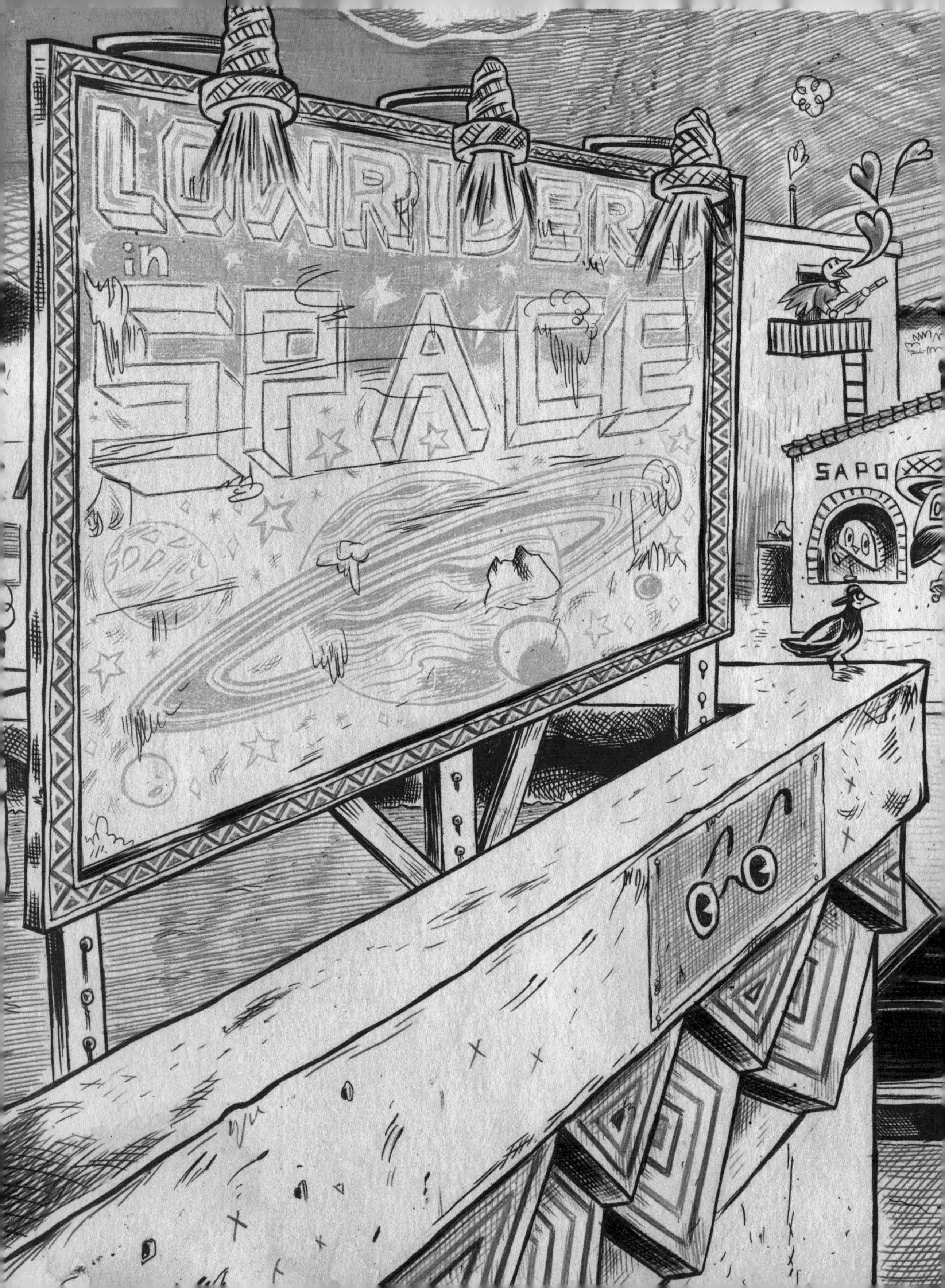
LOWRIDERS
in
SPACE
SAPO

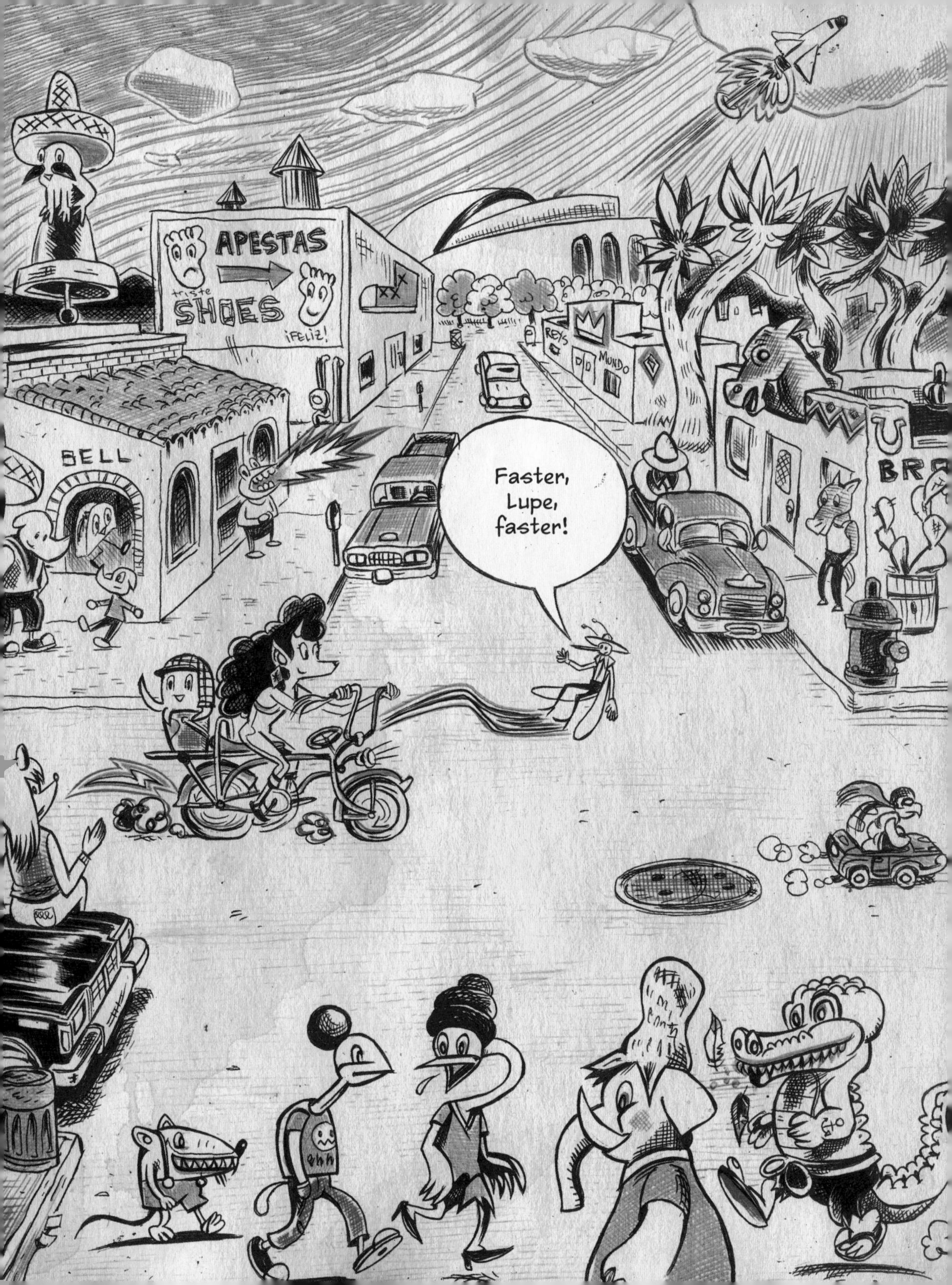
APESTAS
triste
SHOES
¡FELIZ!
BELL
REYS
MUNDO
Faster, Lupe, faster!

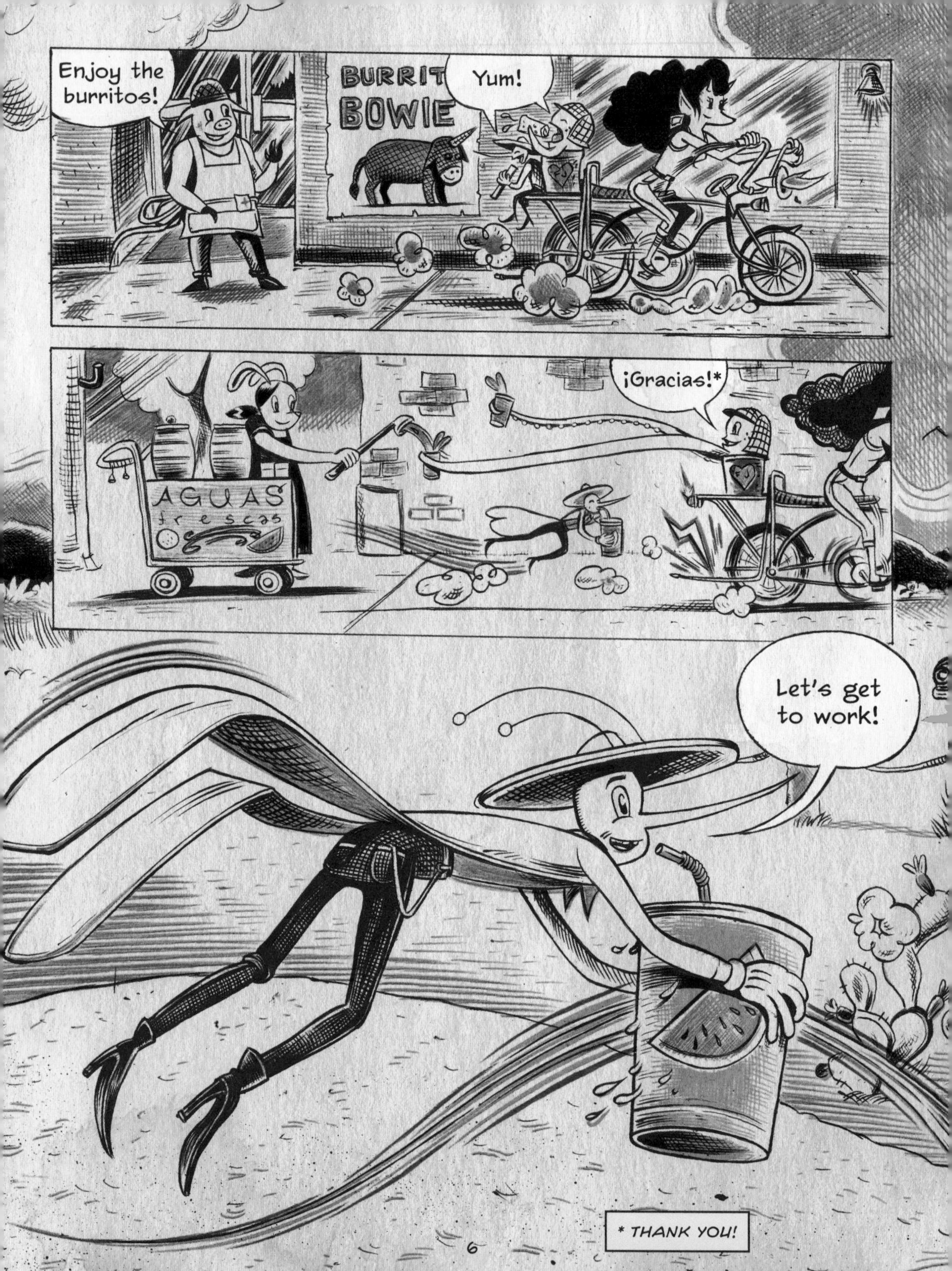
Enjoy the burritos!
BURRITO BOWIE
Yum!
¡Gracias!*
AGUAS frescas
Let's get to work!
* THANK YOU!

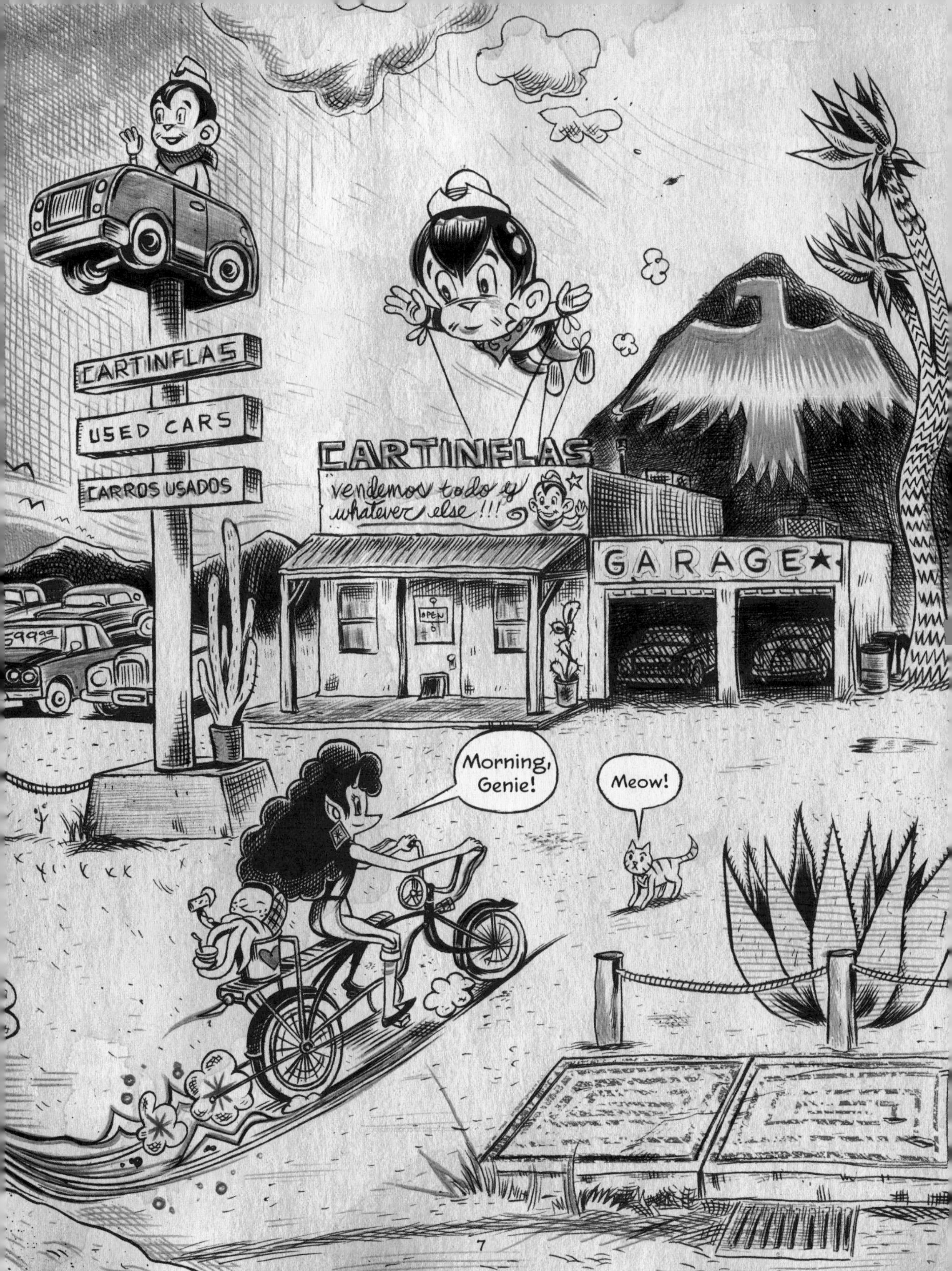
CARTINFLAS
USED CARS
CARROS USADOS
CARTINFLAS
vendemos todo y whatever else!!!
OPEN
GARAGE
Morning, Genie!
Meow!

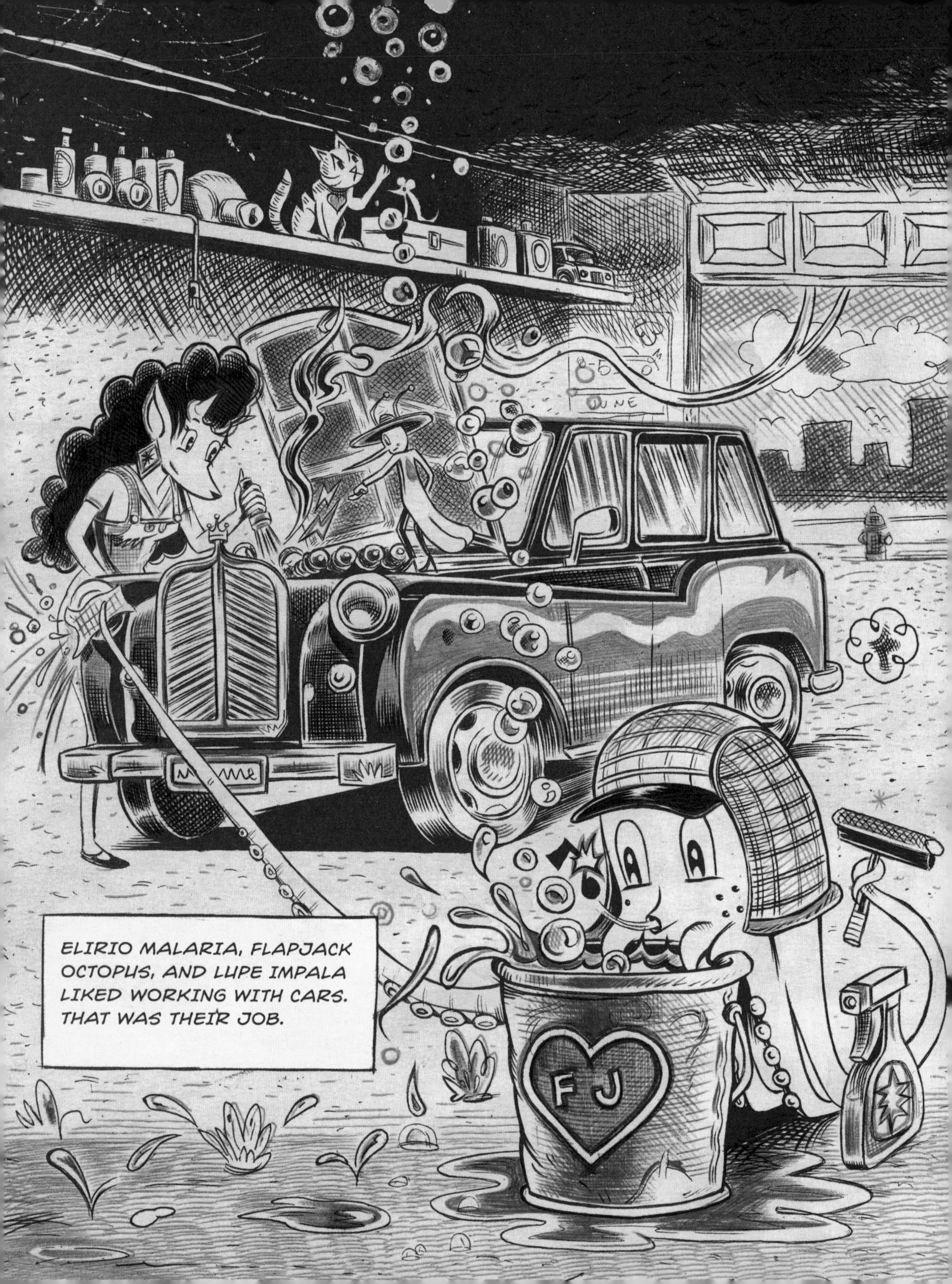
ELIRIO MALARIA, FLAPJACK OCTOPUS, AND LUPE IMPALA LIKED WORKING WITH CARS. THAT WAS THEIR JOB.
FJ

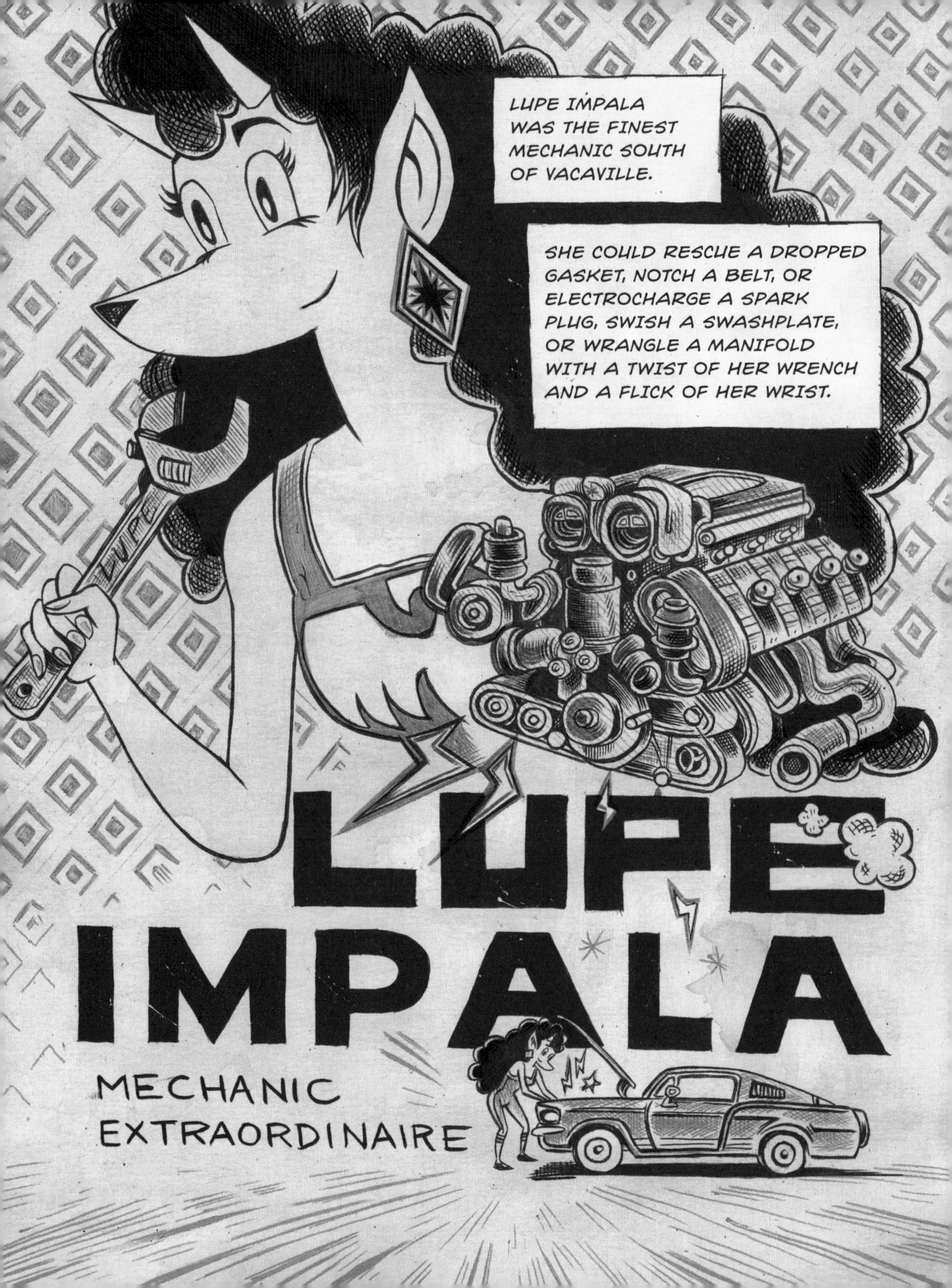
LUPE IMPALA WAS THE FINEST MECHANIC SOUTH OF VACAVILLE.
SHE COULD RESCUE A DROPPED GASKET, NOTCH A BELT, OR ELECTROCHARGE A SPARK PLUG, SWISH A SWASHPLATE, OR WRANGLE A MANIFOLD WITH A TWIST OF HER WRENCH AND A FLICK OF HER WRIST.
LUPE
LUPE IMPALA
MECHANIC EXTRAORDINAIRE

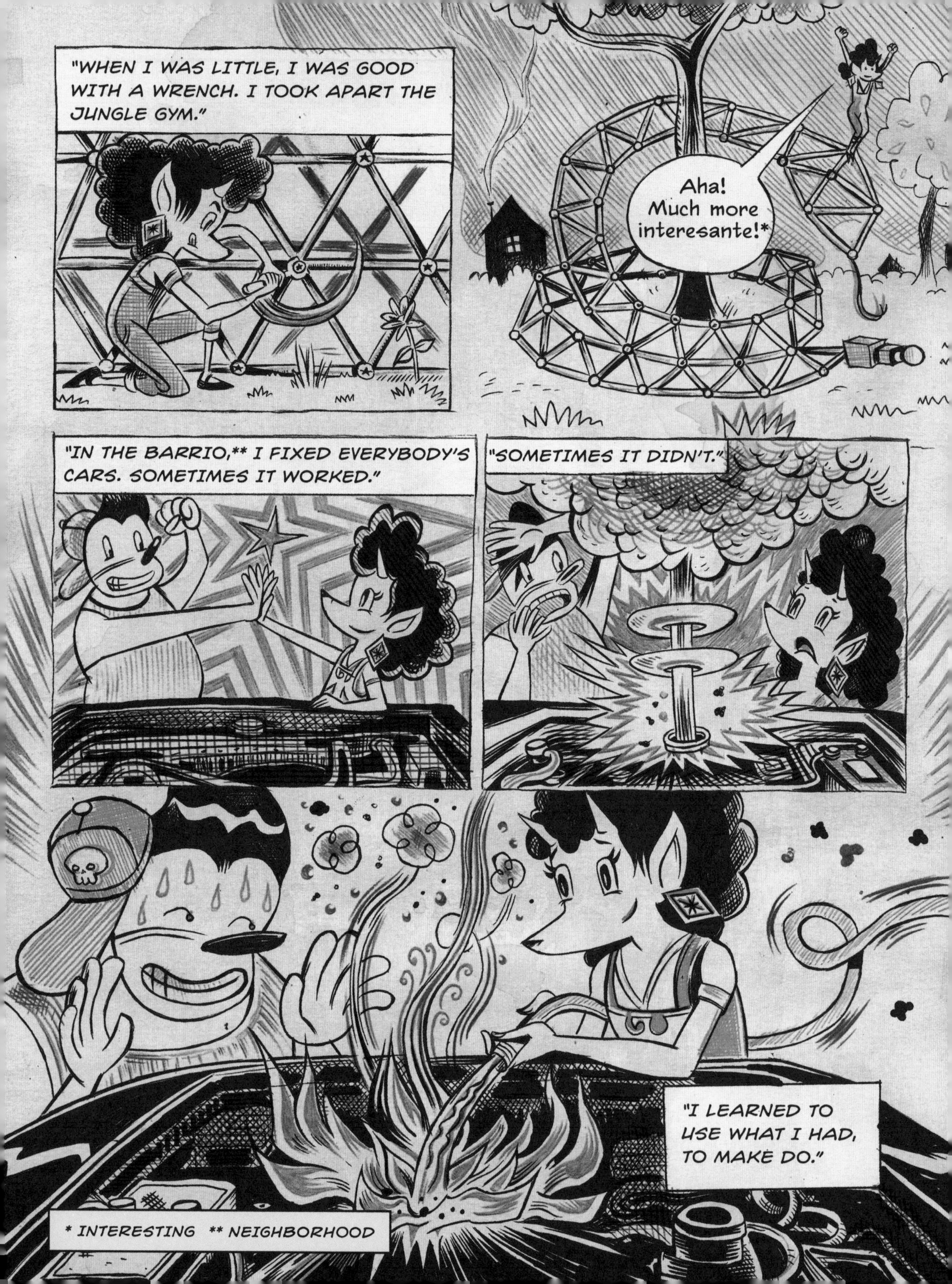
"WHEN I WAS LITTLE, I WAS GOOD WITH A WRENCH. I TOOK APART THE JUNGLE GYM."
Aha! Much more interesante!*
"IN THE BARRIO,** I FIXED EVERYBODY'S CARS. SOMETIMES IT WORKED."
"SOMETIMES IT DIDN'T."
"I LEARNED TO USE WHAT I HAD, TO MAKE DO."
* INTERESTING ** NEIGHBORHOOD

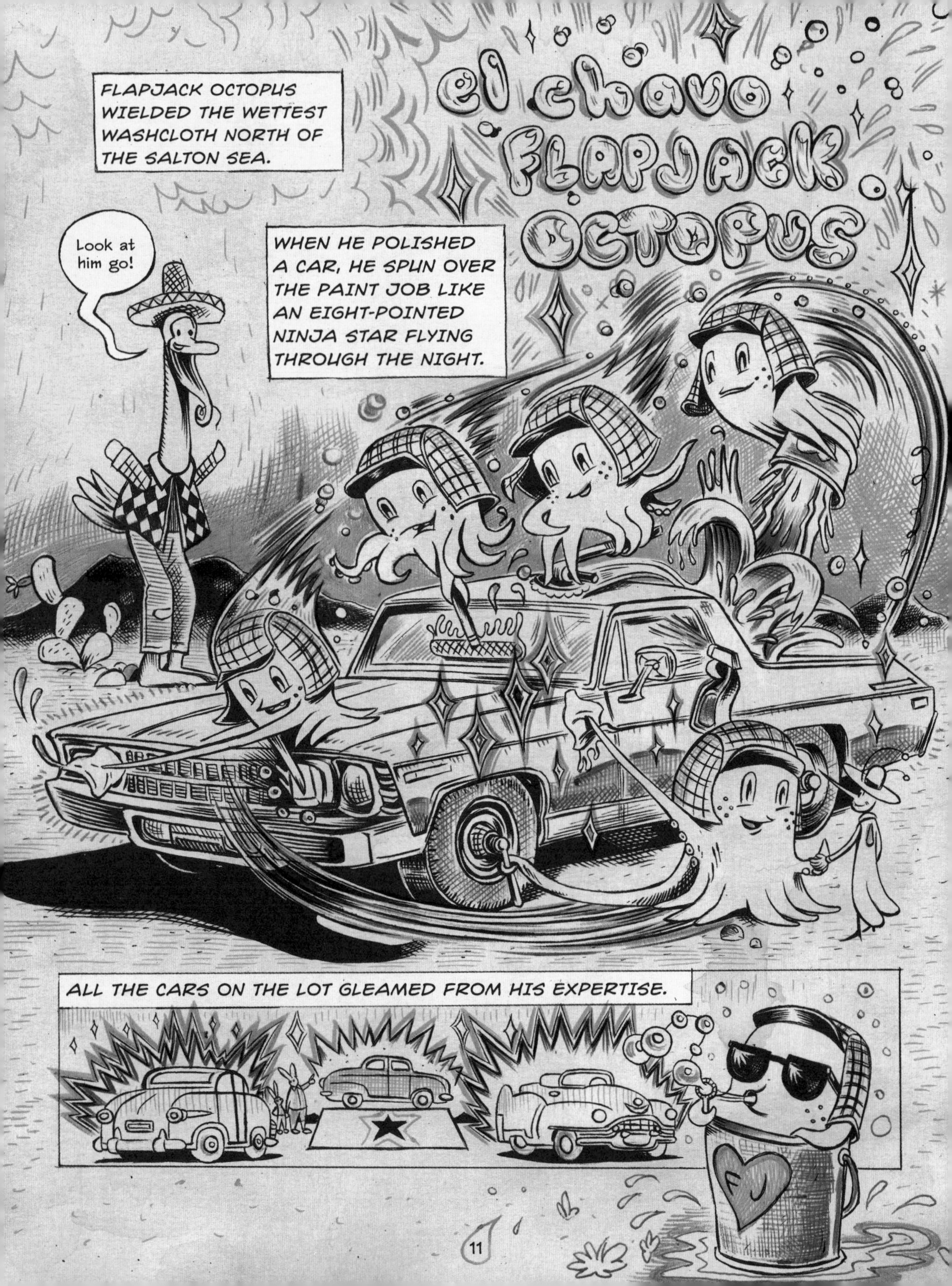
el chavo FLAPJACK OCTOPUS
FLAPJACK OCTOPUS WIELDED THE WETTEST WASHCLOTH NORTH OF THE SALTON SEA.
Look at him go!
WHEN HE POLISHED A CAR, HE SPUN OVER THE PAINT JOB LIKE AN EIGHT-POINTED NINJA STAR FLYING THROUGH THE NIGHT.
ALL THE CARS ON THE LOT GLEAMED FROM HIS EXPERTISE.

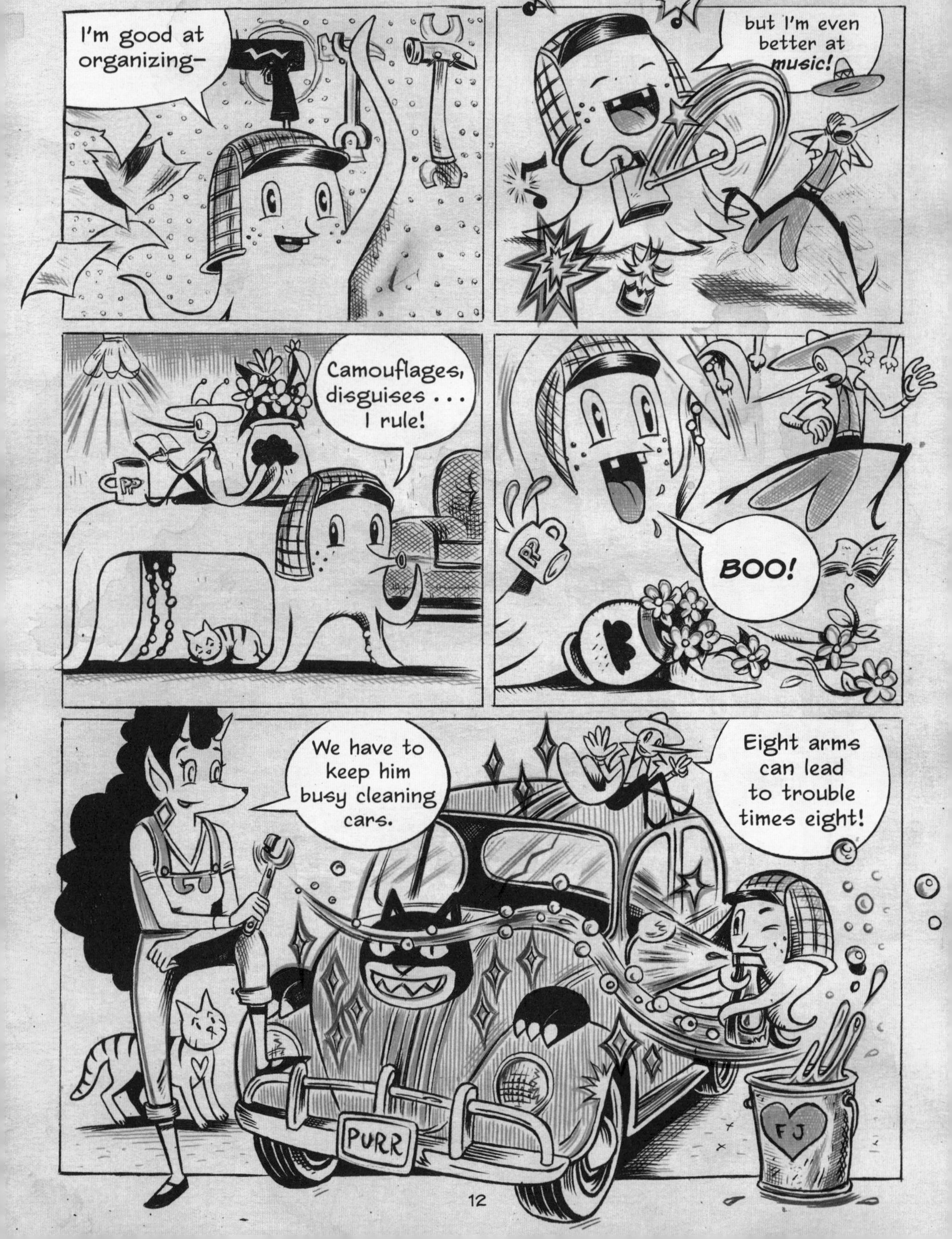
I'm good at organizing–
but I'm even better at music!
Camouflages, disguises . . . I rule!
PP
BOO!
We have to keep him busy cleaning cars.
Eight arms can lead to trouble times eight!
PURR
FJ

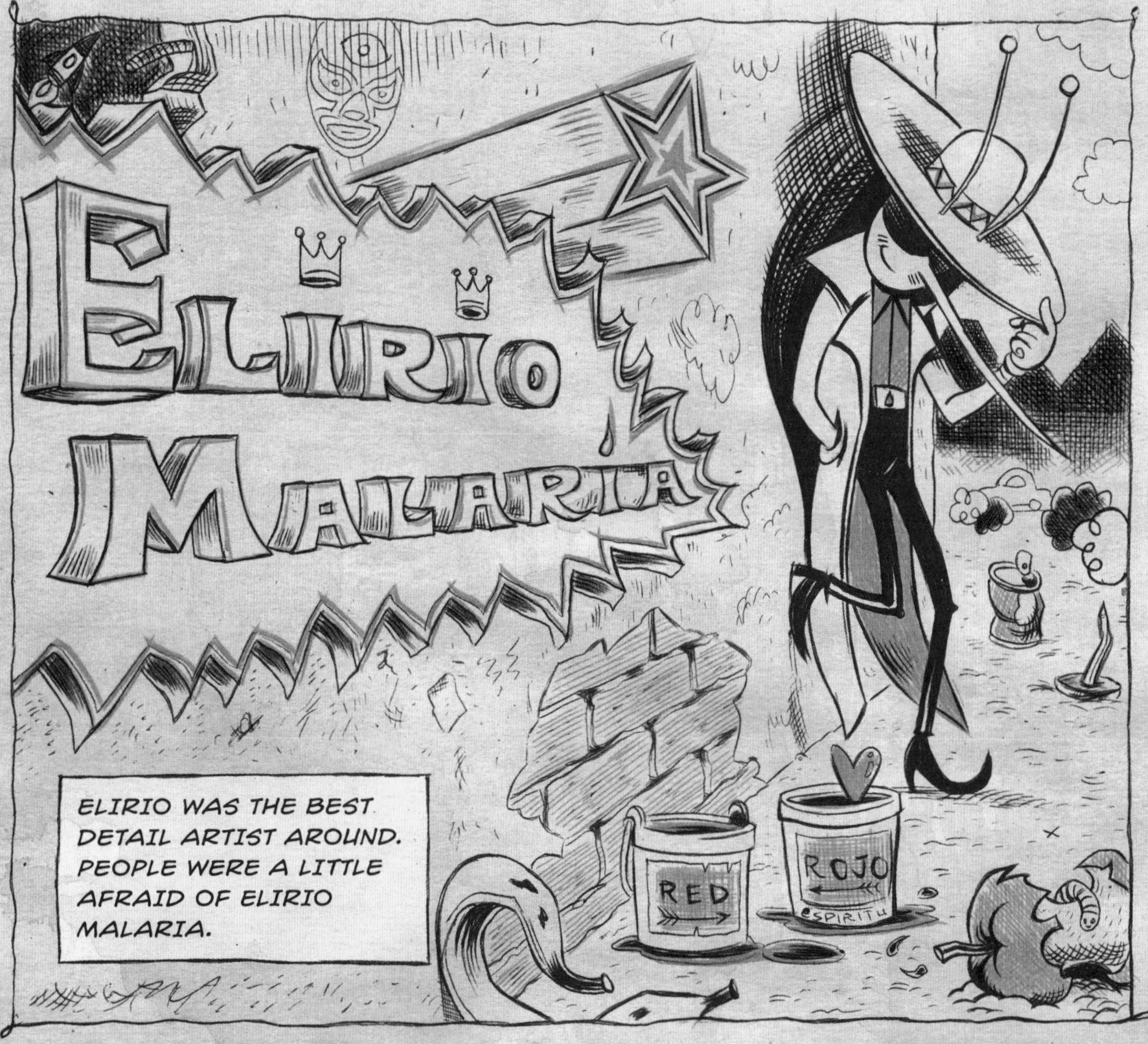
ELIRIO MALARIA
ELIRIO WAS THE BEST DETAIL ARTIST AROUND. PEOPLE WERE A LITTLE AFRAID OF ELIRIO MALARIA.
RED
ROJO
ESPIRITU

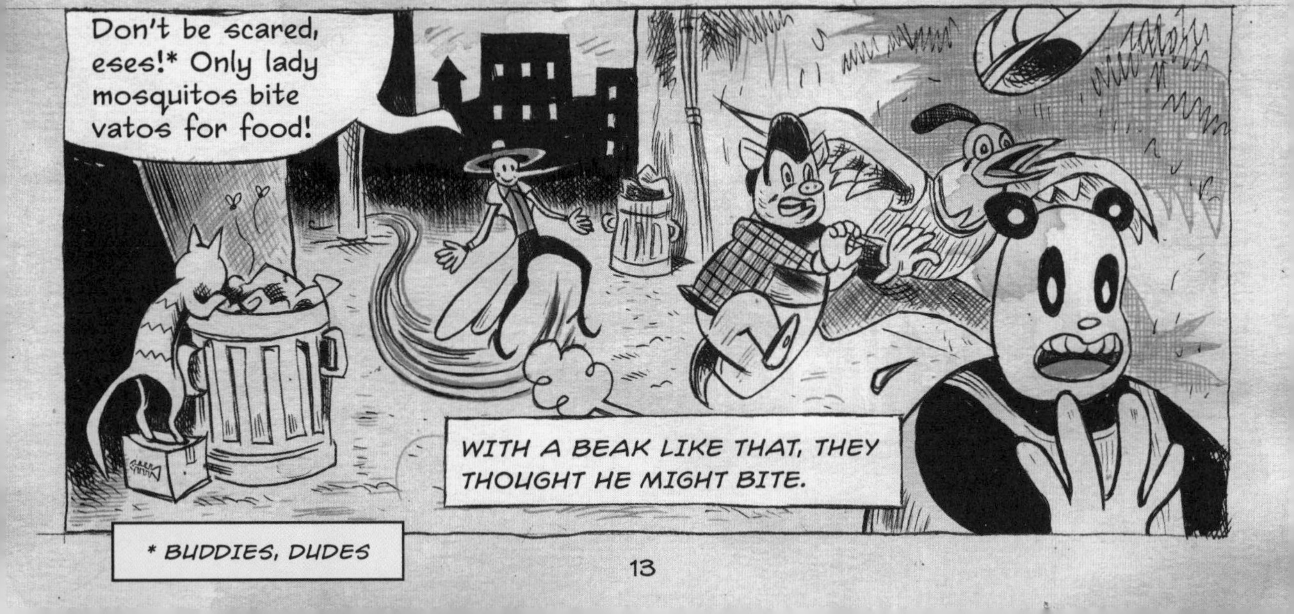
Don't be scared, eses!* Only lady mosquitos bite vatos for food!
WITH A BEAK LIKE THAT, THEY THOUGHT HE MIGHT BITE.

* BUDDIES, DUDES

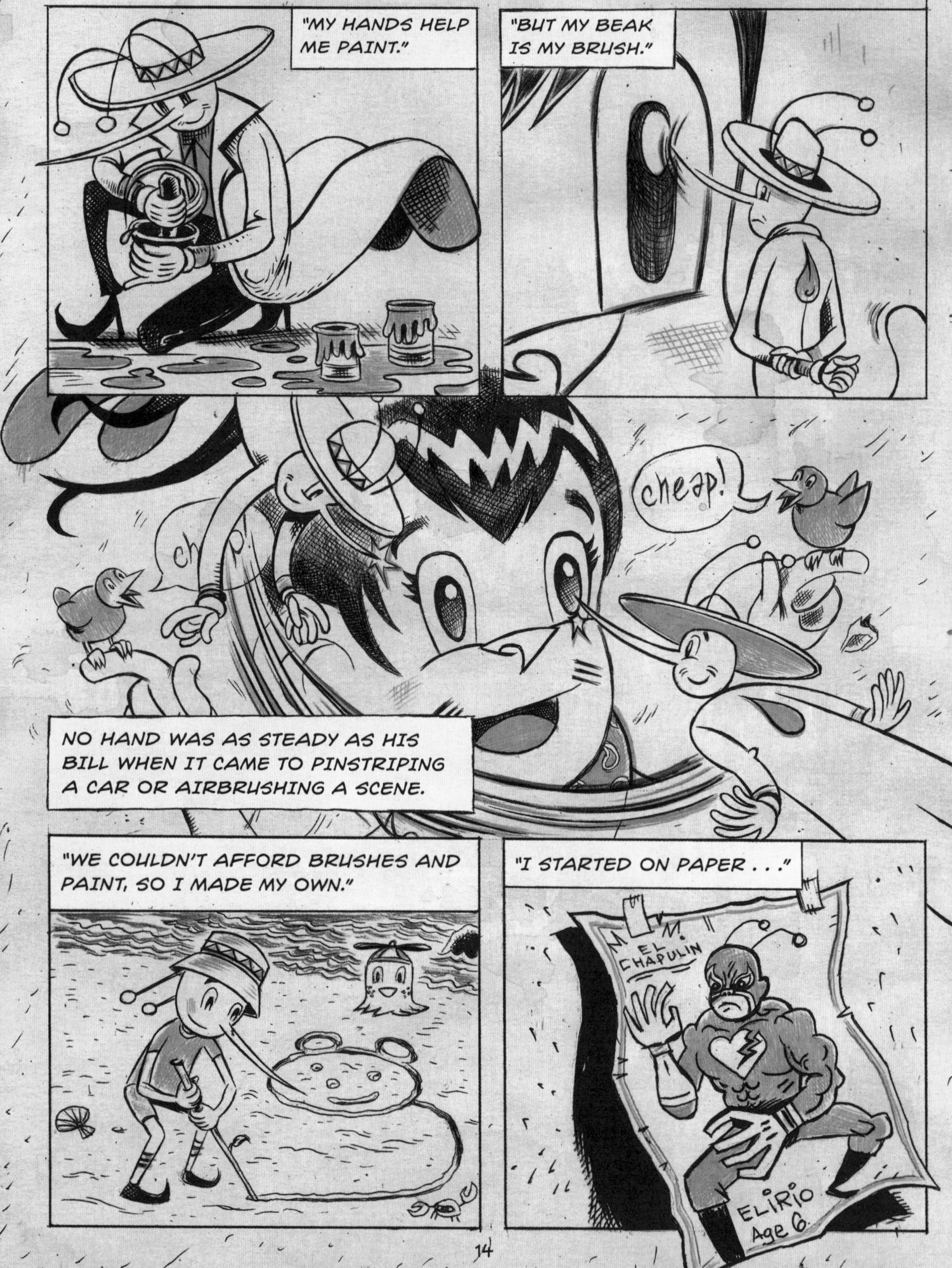
"MY HANDS HELP ME PAINT."
"BUT MY BEAK IS MY BRUSH."
cheap!
cheap!
NO HAND WAS AS STEADY AS HIS BILL WHEN IT CAME TO PINSTRIPING A CAR OR AIRBRUSHING A SCENE.
"WE COULDN'T AFFORD BRUSHES AND PAINT, SO I MADE MY OWN."
"I STARTED ON PAPER . . ."
EL CHAPULIN
ELIRIO Age 6

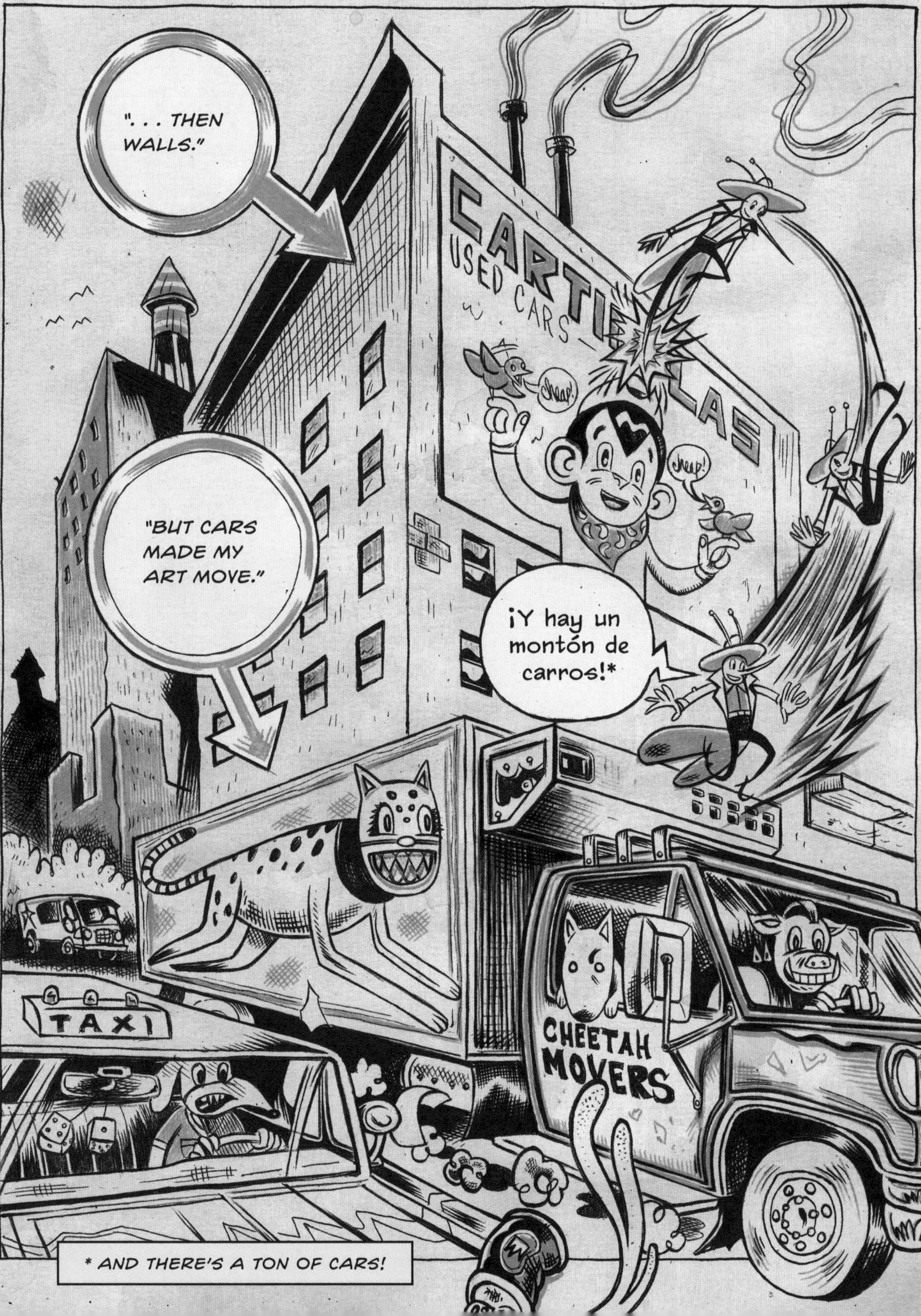
". . . THEN WALLS."
CARTIE LAS USED CARS
"BUT CARS MADE MY ART MOVE."
¡Y hay un montón de carros!*
CHEETAH MOVERS
TAXI
* AND THERE'S A TON OF CARS!

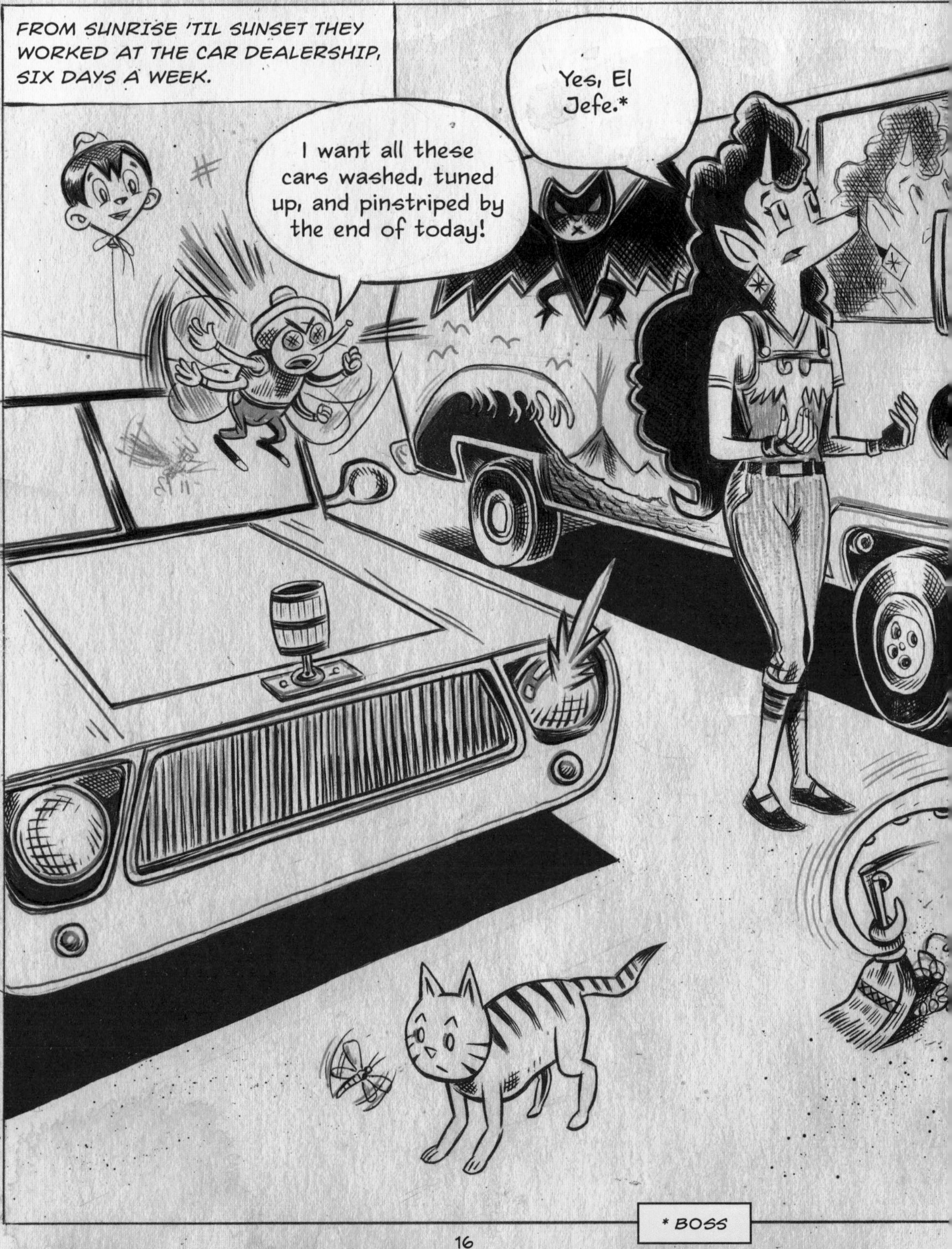
FROM SUNRISE 'TIL SUNSET THEY WORKED AT THE CAR DEALERSHIP, SIX DAYS A WEEK.
I want all these cars washed, tuned up, and pinstriped by the end of today!
Yes, El Jefe.*
* BOSS

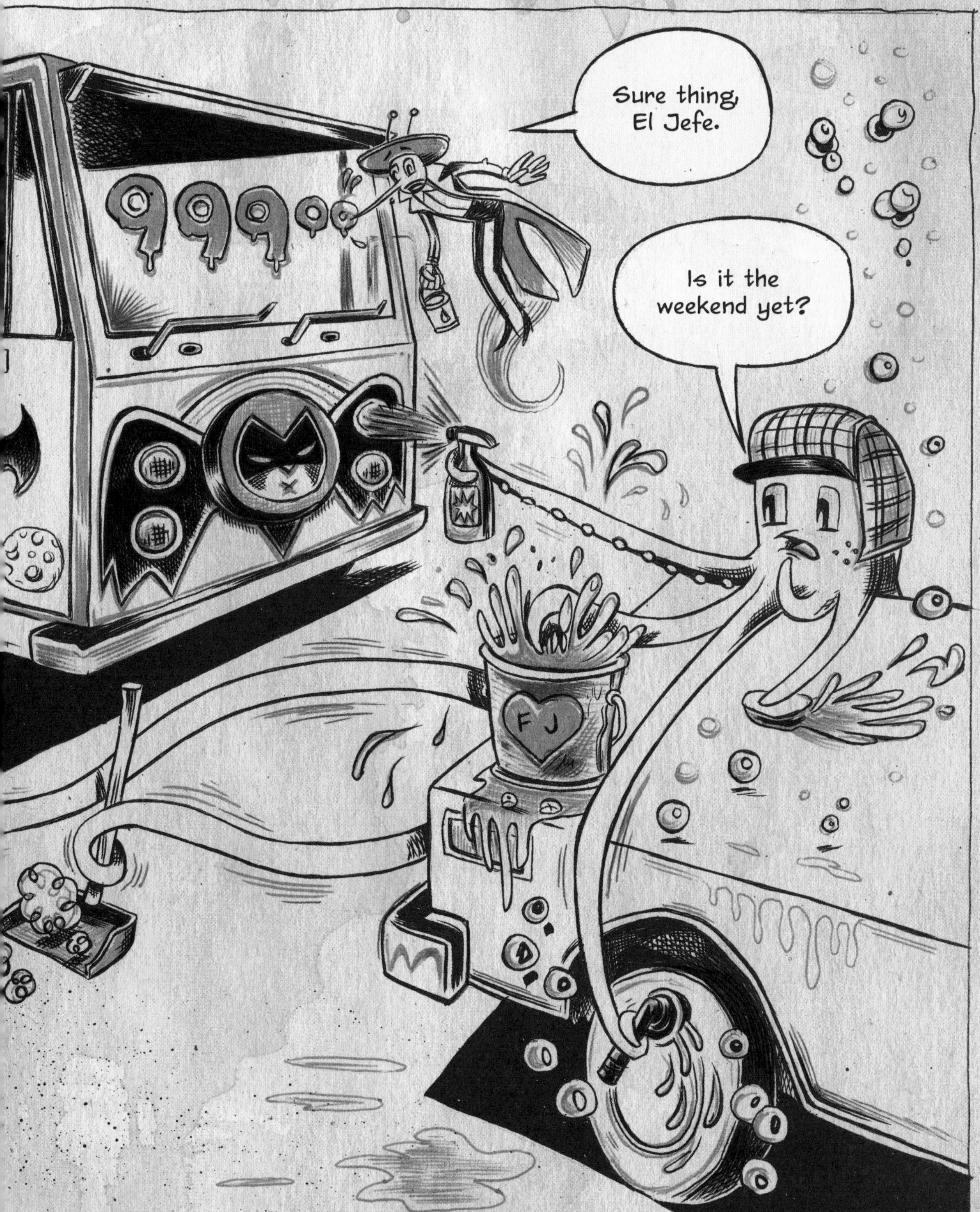
Sure thing, El Jefe.
Is it the weekend yet?

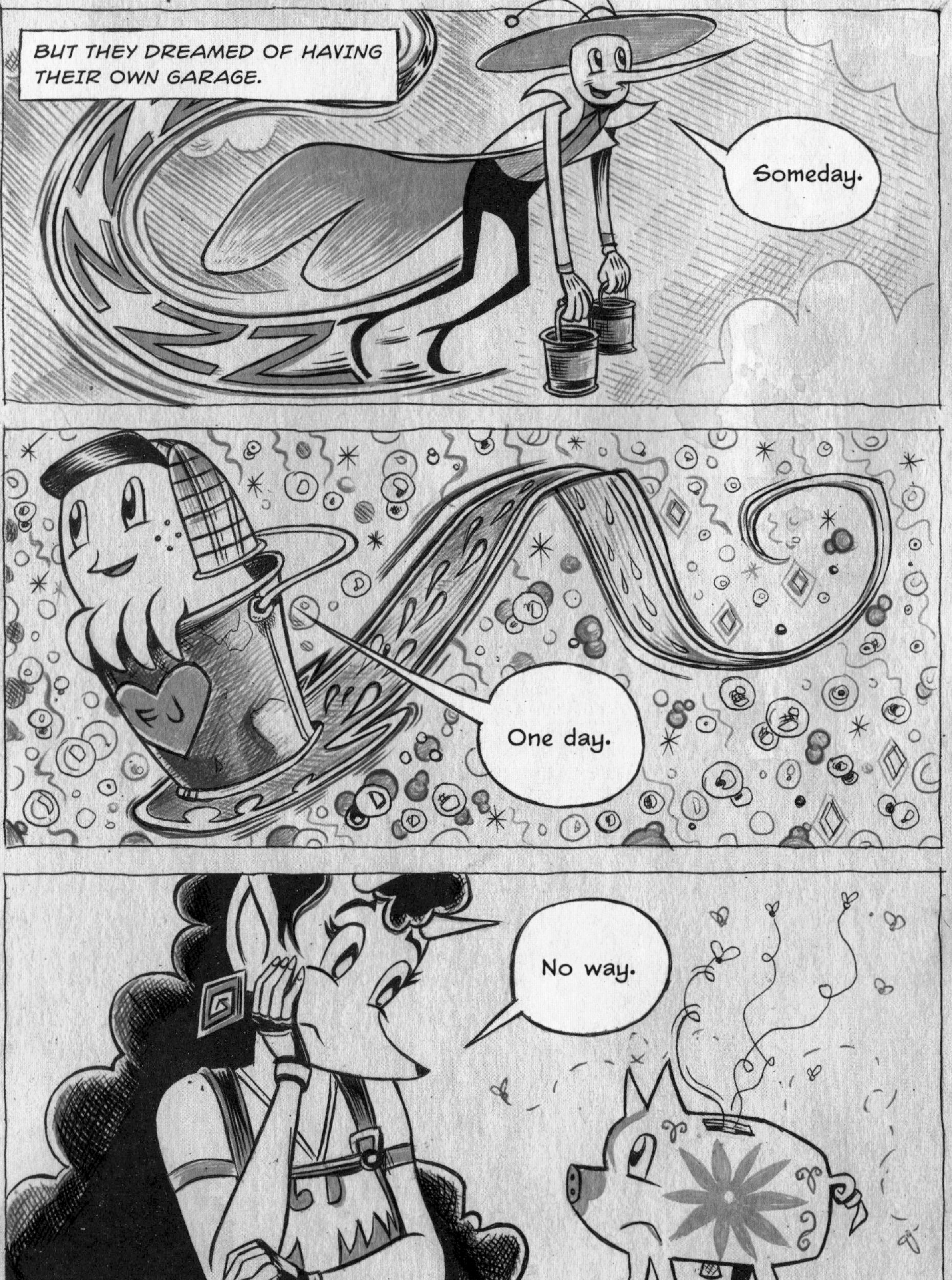
BUT THEY DREAMED OF HAVING THEIR OWN GARAGE.
Someday.
One day.
No way.

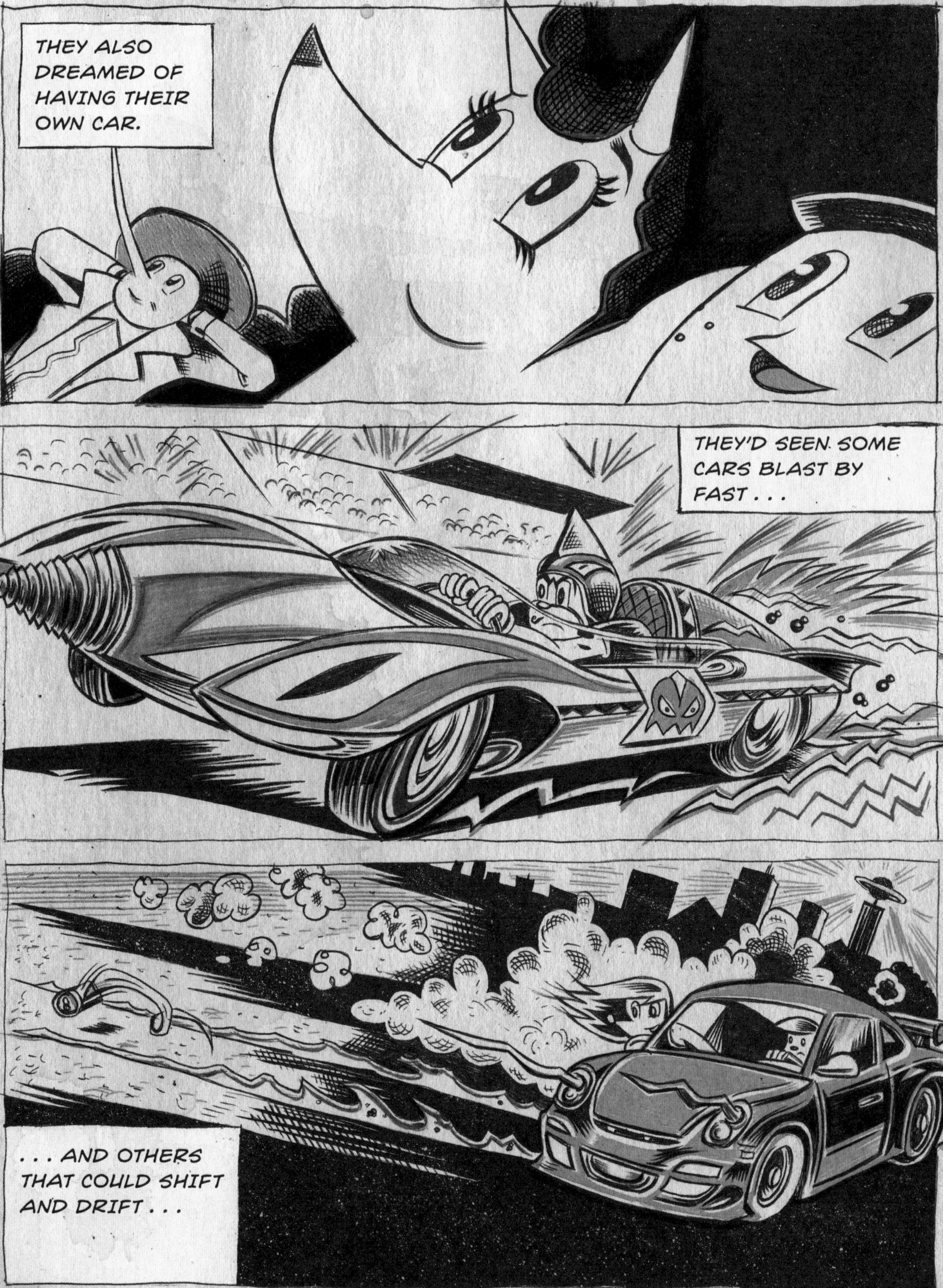
THEY ALSO DREAMED OF HAVING THEIR OWN CAR.
THEY'D SEEN SOME CARS BLAST BY FAST . . .
. . . AND OTHERS THAT COULD SHIFT AND DRIFT . . .

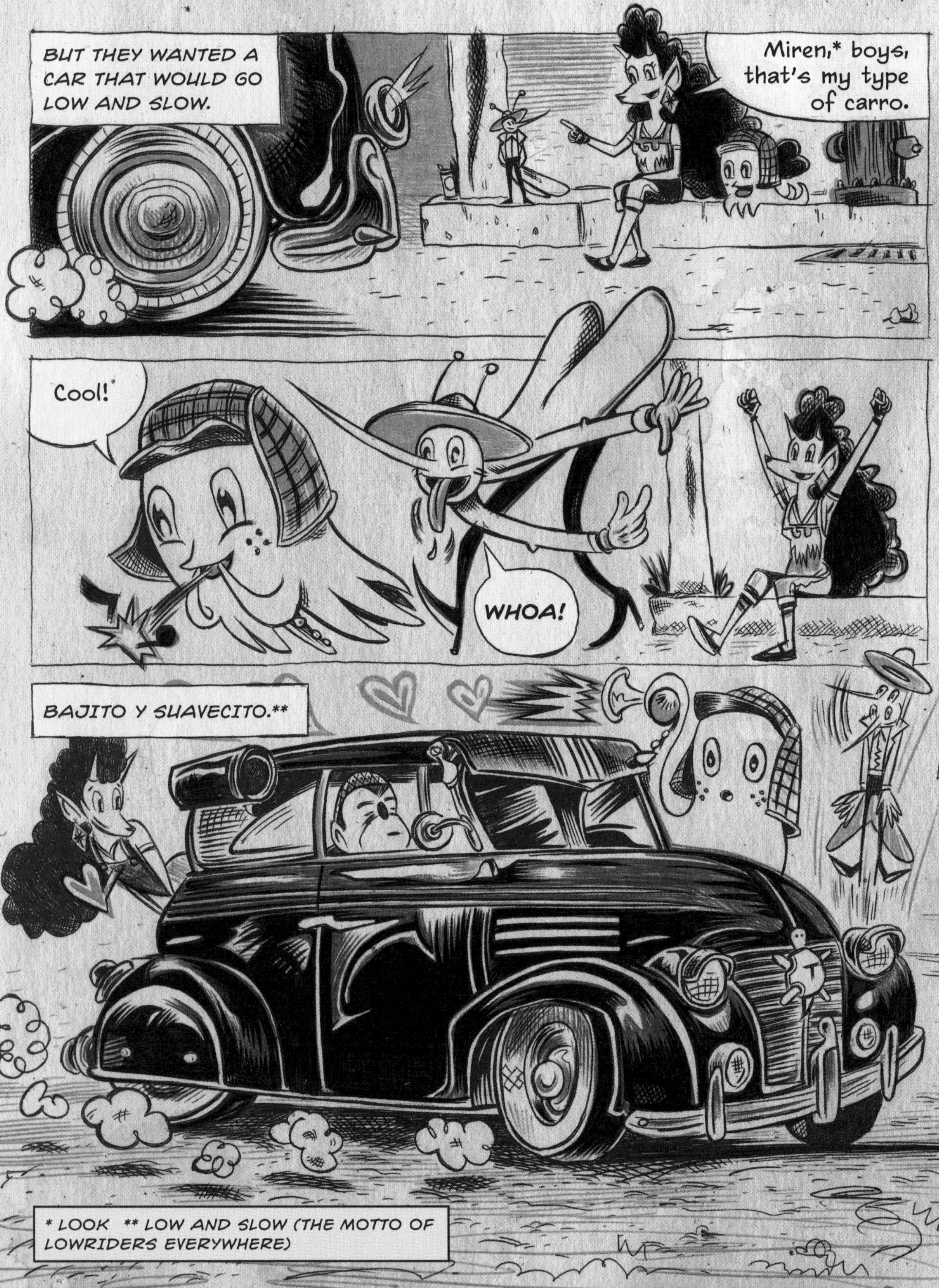
BUT THEY WANTED A CAR THAT WOULD GO LOW AND SLOW.
Miren,* boys, that's my type of carro.
Cool!
WHOA!
BAJITO Y SUAVECITO.**
* LOOK ** LOW AND SLOW (THE MOTTO OF LOWRIDERS EVERYWHERE)

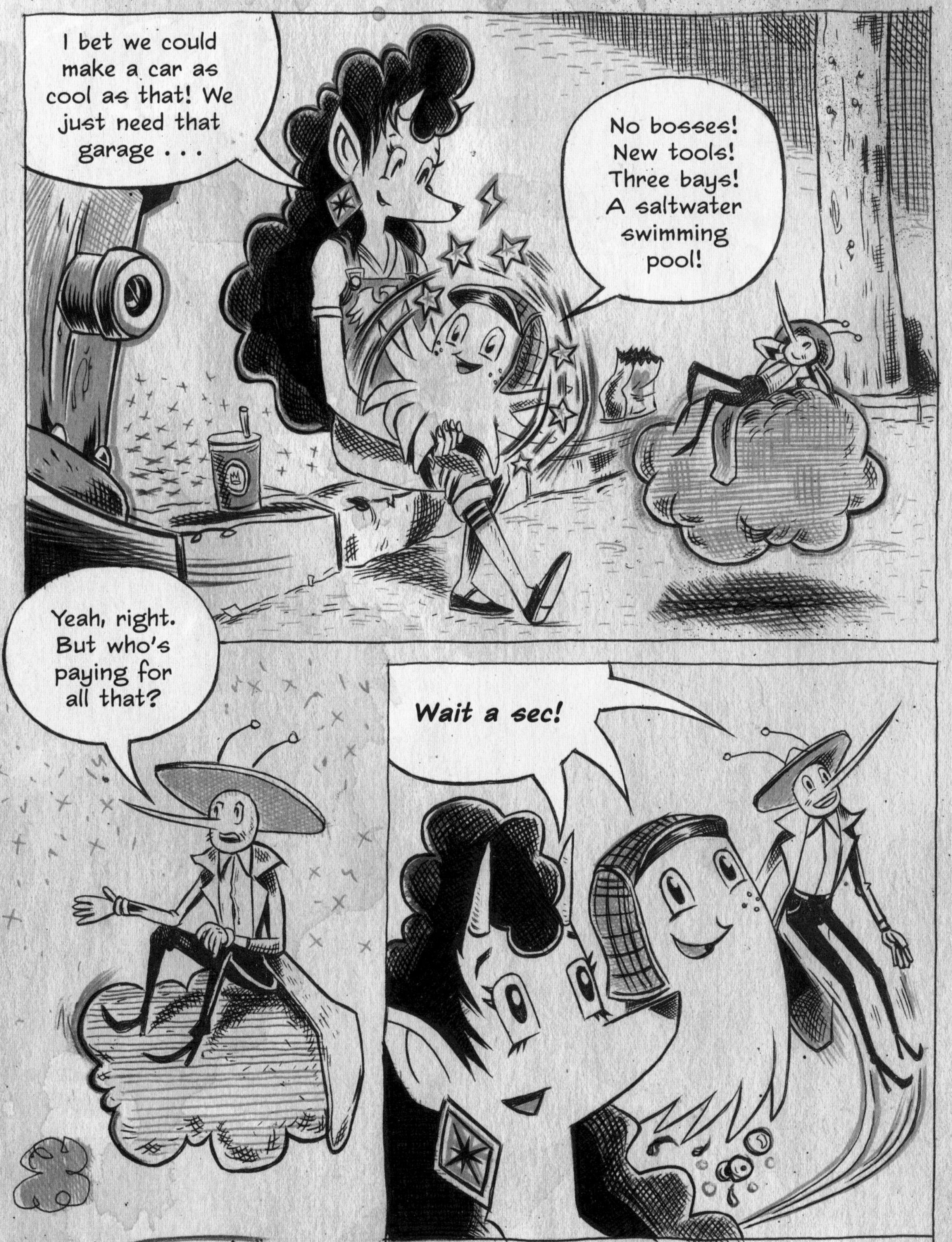
I bet we could make a car as cool as that! We just need that garage . . .
No bosses! New tools! Three bays! A saltwater swimming pool!
Yeah, right. But who's paying for all that?
Wait a sec!

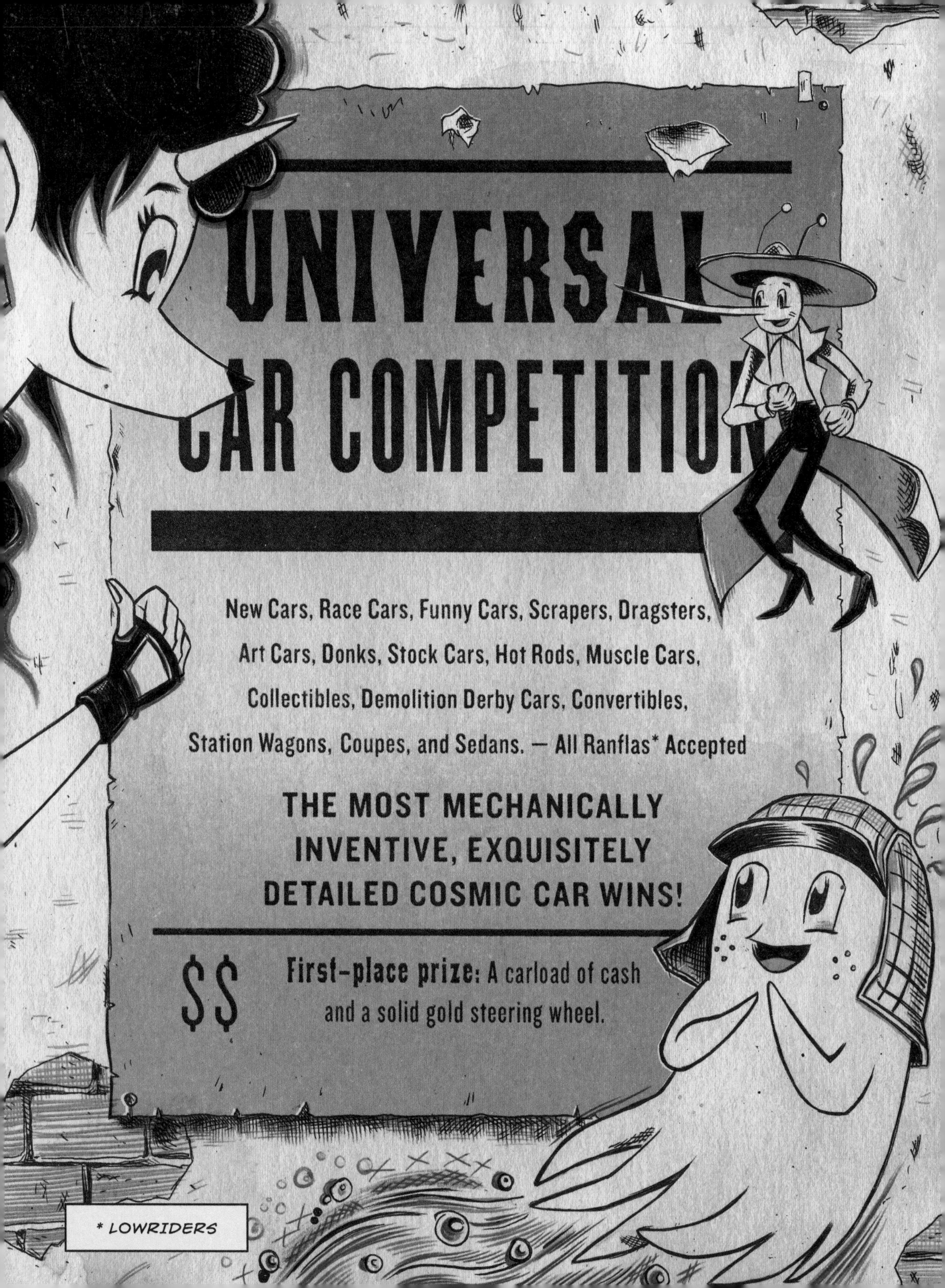

UNIVERSAL CAR COMPETITION
New Cars, Race Cars, Funny Cars, Scrapers, Dragsters, Art Cars, Donks, Stock Cars, Hot Rods, Muscle Cars, Collectibles, Demolition Derby Cars, Convertibles, Station Wagons, Coupes, and Sedans. — All Ranflas* Accepted
THE MOST MECHANICALLY INVENTIVE, EXQUISITELY DETAILED COSMIC CAR WINS!
$$
First-place prize: A carload of cash and a solid gold steering wheel.
* LOWRIDERS

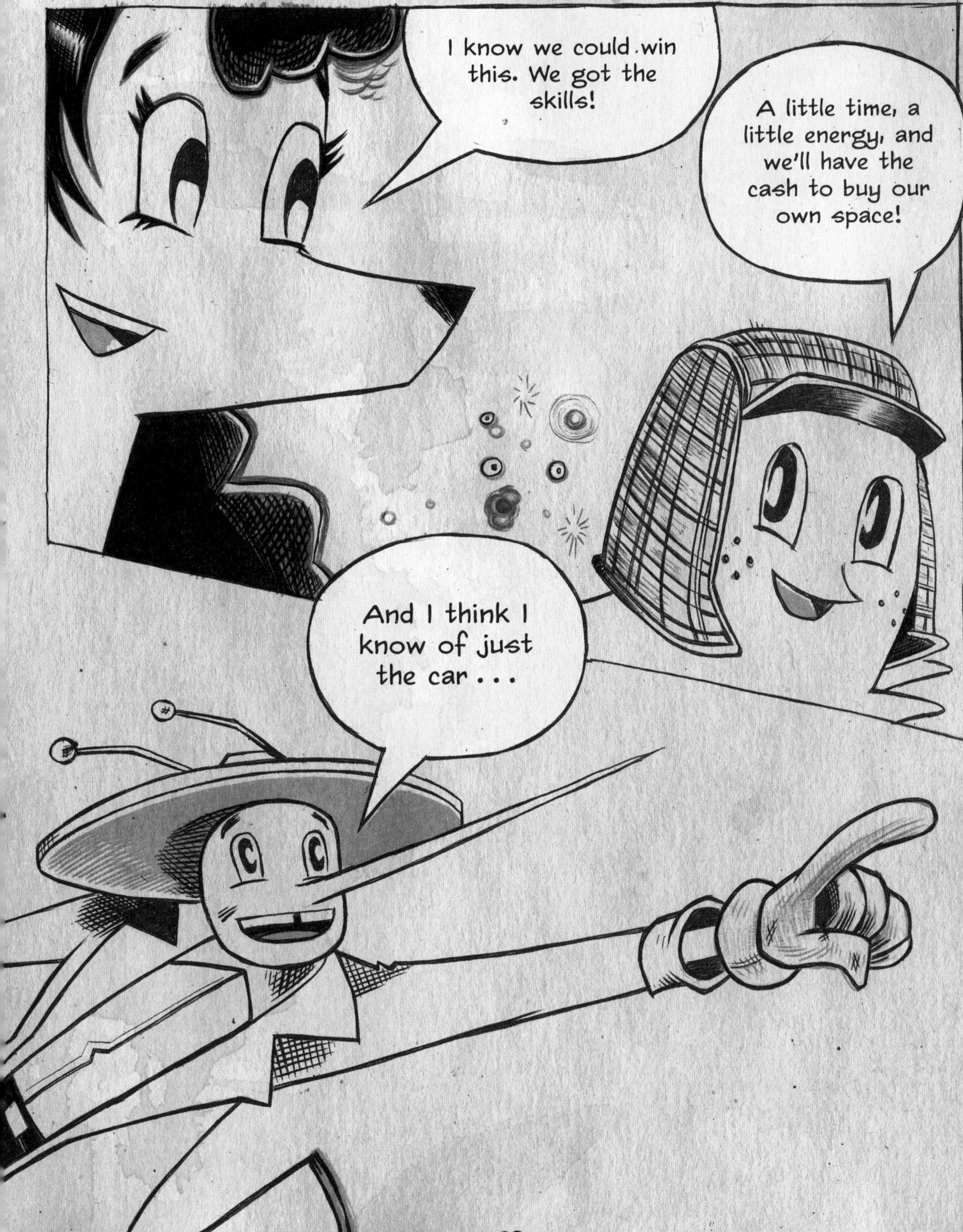
I know we could win this. We got the skills!
A little time, a little energy, and we'll have the cash to buy our own space!
And I think I know of just the car . . .

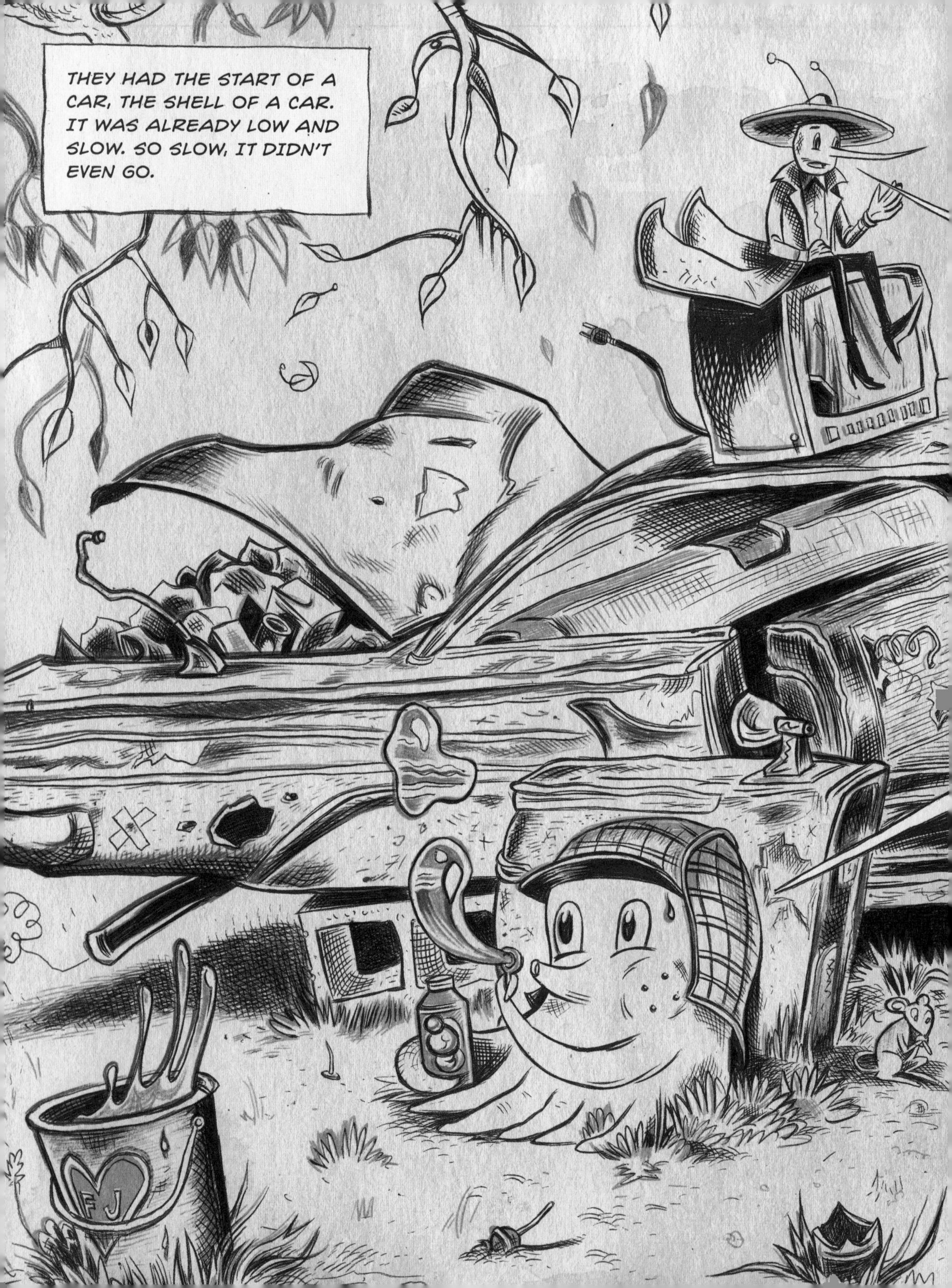
THEY HAD THE START OF A CAR, THE SHELL OF A CAR. IT WAS ALREADY LOW AND SLOW. SO SLOW, IT DIDN'T EVEN GO.
FJ

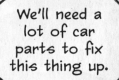

We'll need a lot of car parts to fix this thing up.

And once that's done, we'll need chrome, paint, pinstriping, waxing, buffing . . . ¡Ay! It needs so much work!

¡Y vamos a tener que echarle ganas,* to clean it!

* AND WE WILL HAVE TO GIVE IT OUR BEST!

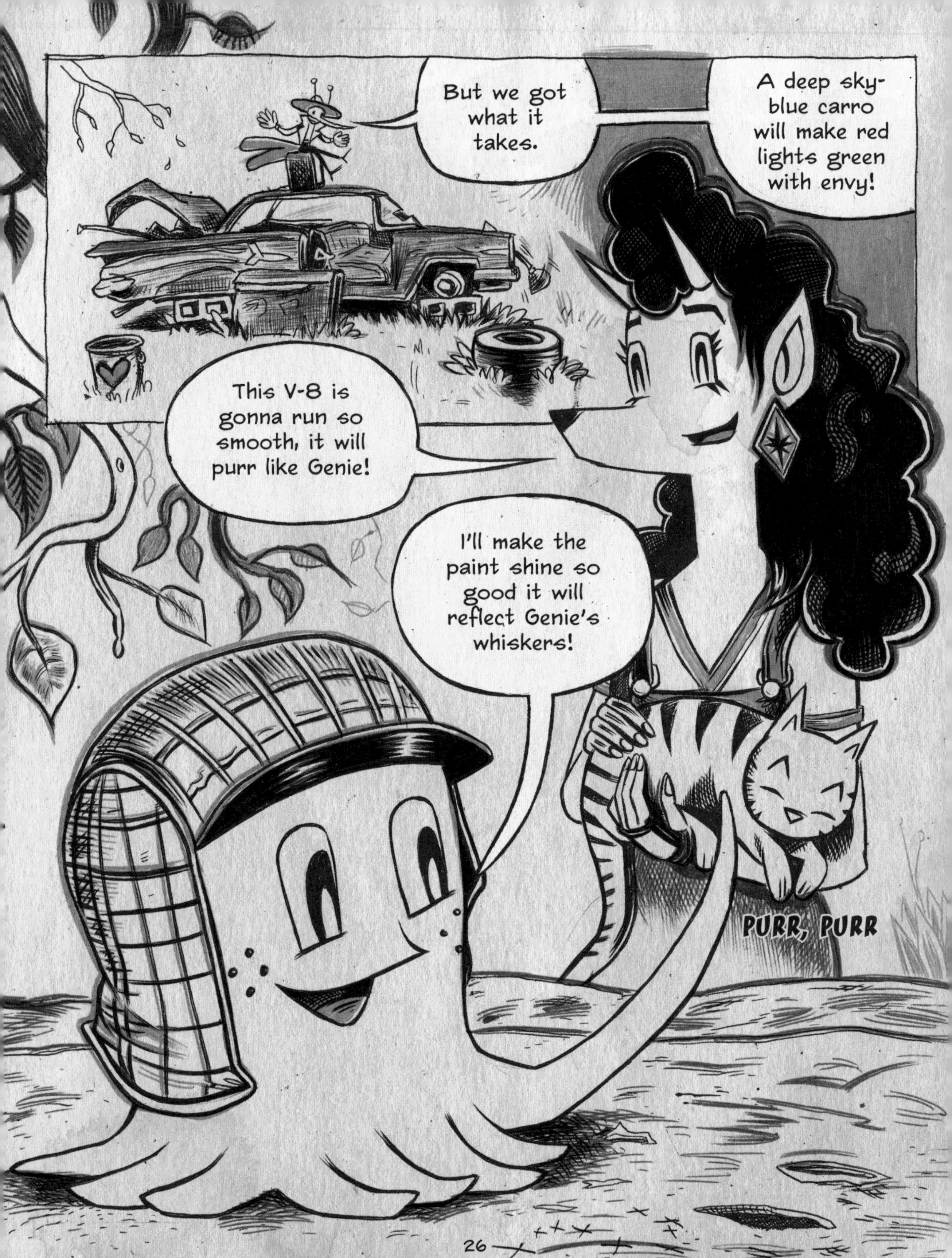
But we got what it takes.
A deep sky-blue carro will make red lights green with envy!
This V-8 is gonna run so smooth, it will purr like Genie!
I'll make the paint shine so good it will reflect Genie's whiskers!
PURR, PURR

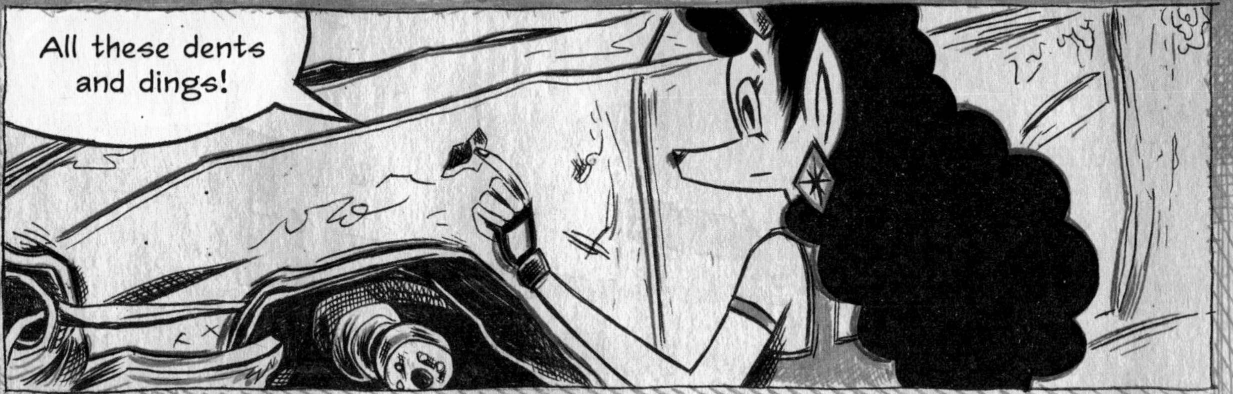
All these dents and dings!

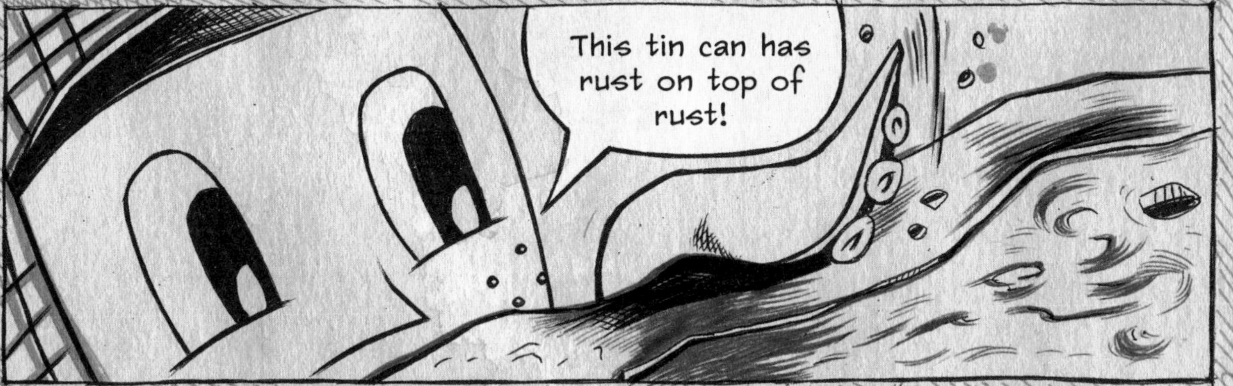
This tin can has rust on top of rust!

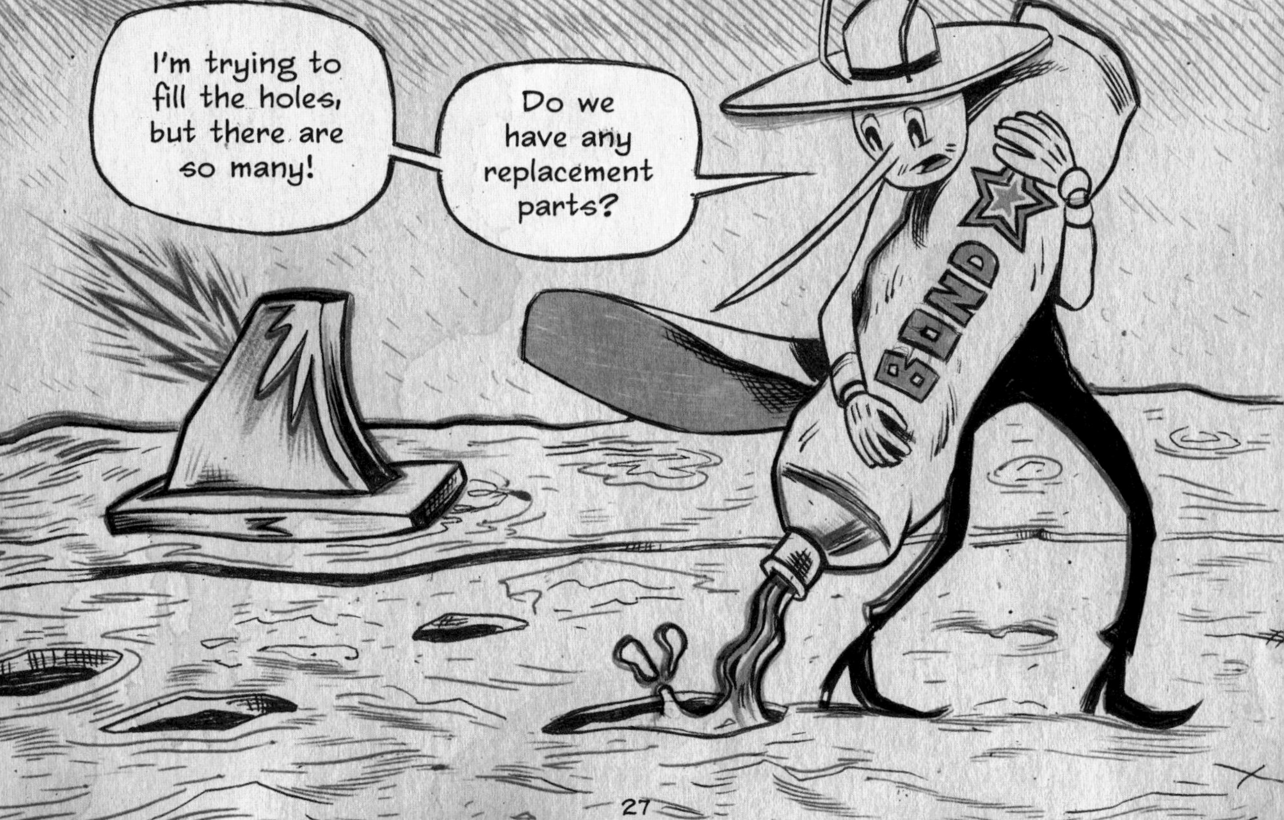
I'm trying to fill the holes, but there are so many!
Do we have any replacement parts?
BOND

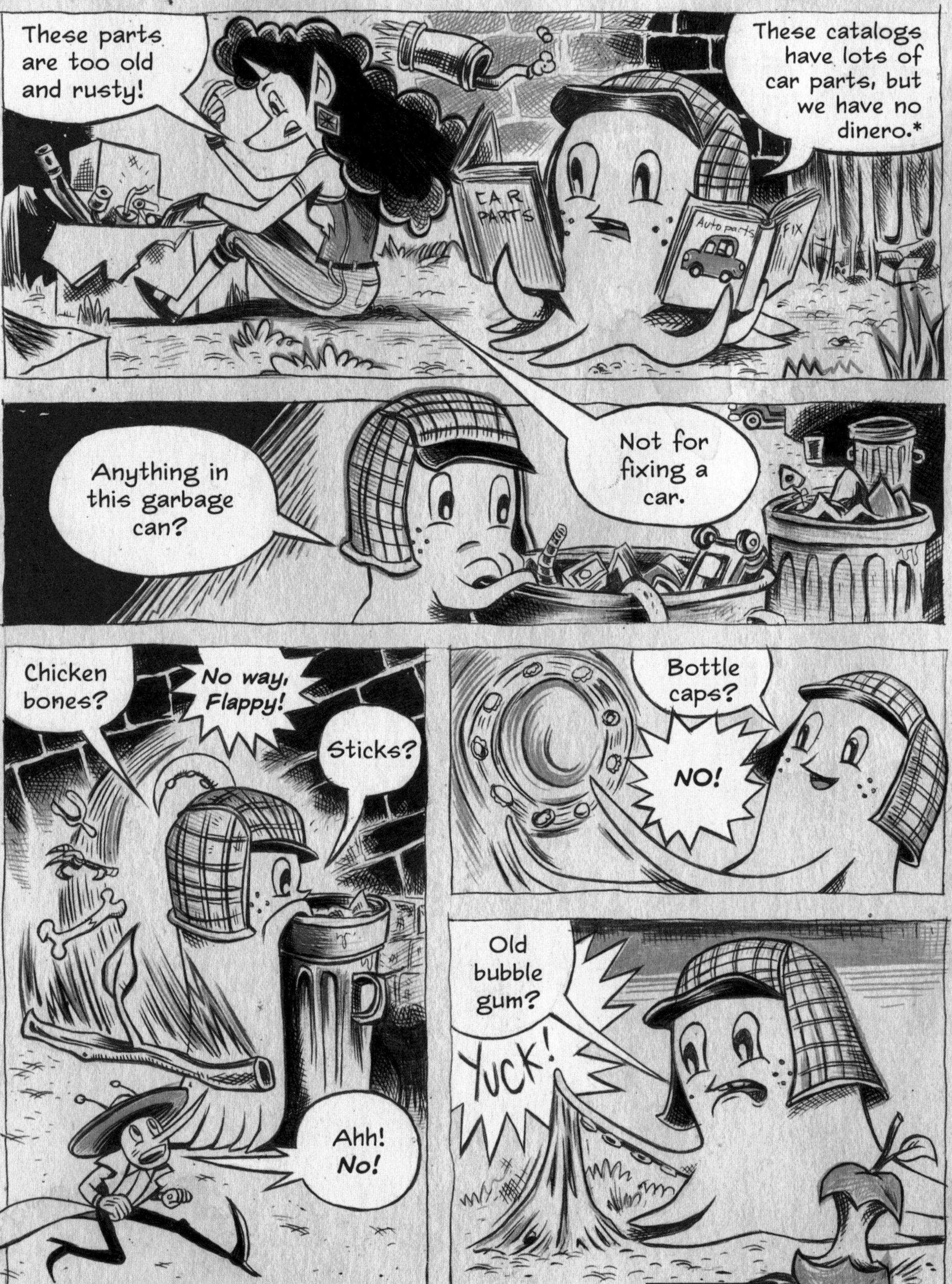
These parts are too old and rusty!
These catalogs have lots of car parts, but we have no dinero.*
CAR PARTS
Auto parts
FIX
Anything in this garbage can?
Not for fixing a car.
Chicken bones?
No way, Flappy!
Sticks?
Ahh! No!
Bottle caps?
NO!
Old bubble gum?
YUCK!

* MONEY

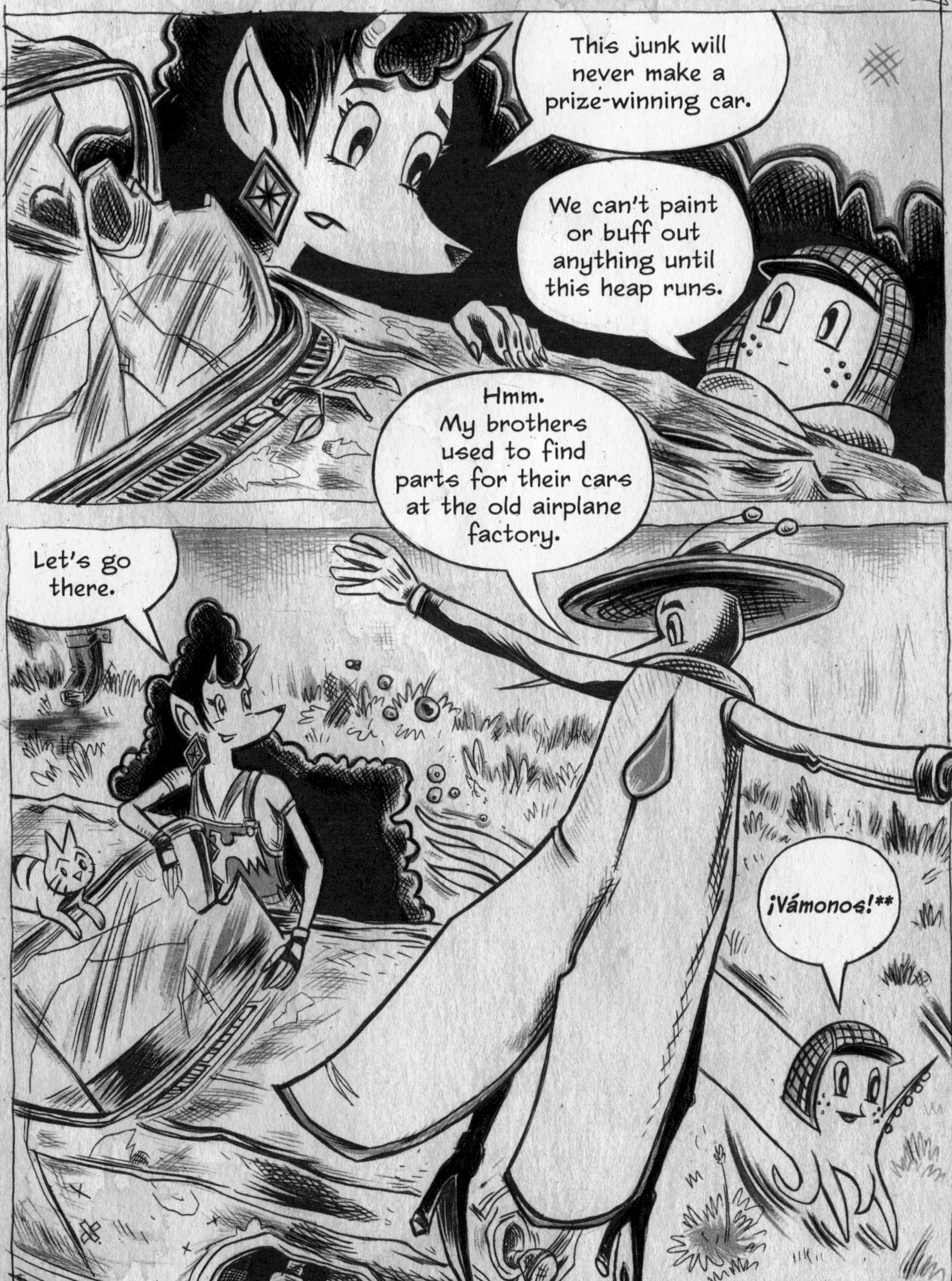
This junk will never make a prize-winning car.
We can't paint or buff out anything until this heap runs.
Hmm. My brothers used to find parts for their cars at the old airplane factory.
Let's go there.
¡Vámonos!**
** LET'S GO!

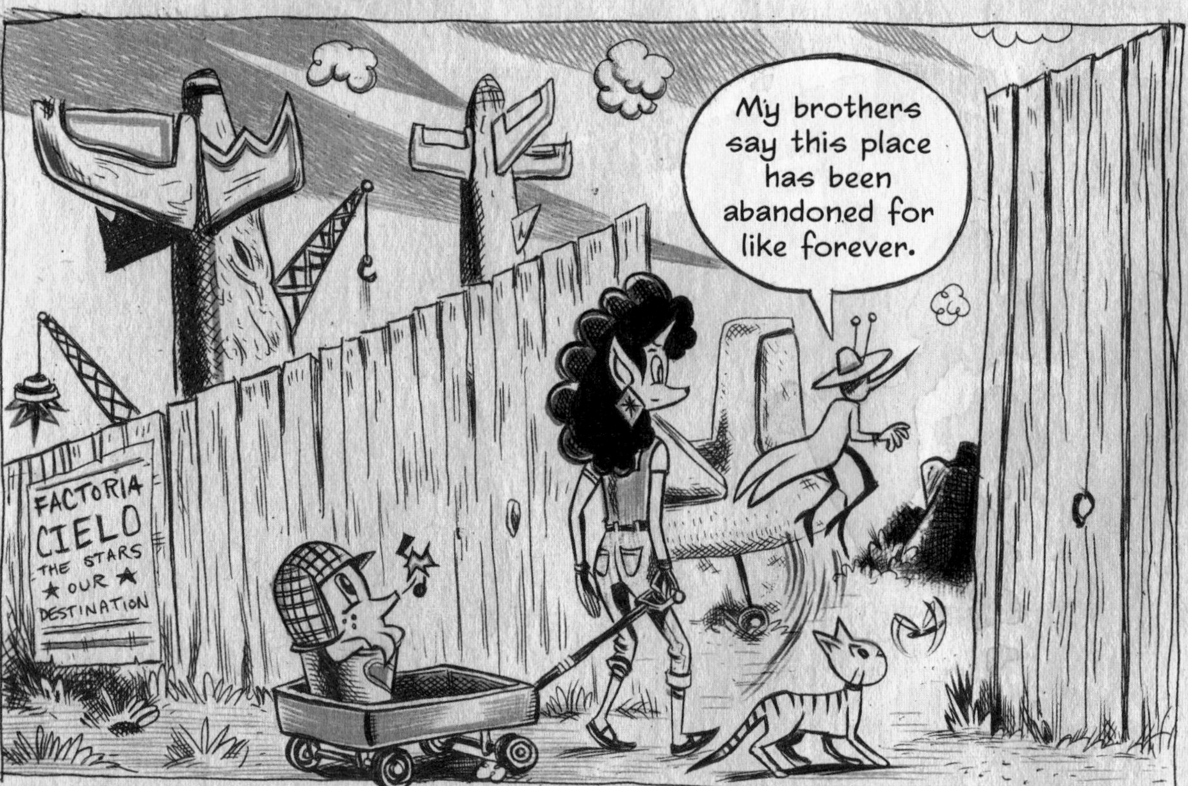
FACTORIA CIELO
THE STARS ★ OUR ★ DESTINATION
My brothers say this place has been abandoned for like forever.

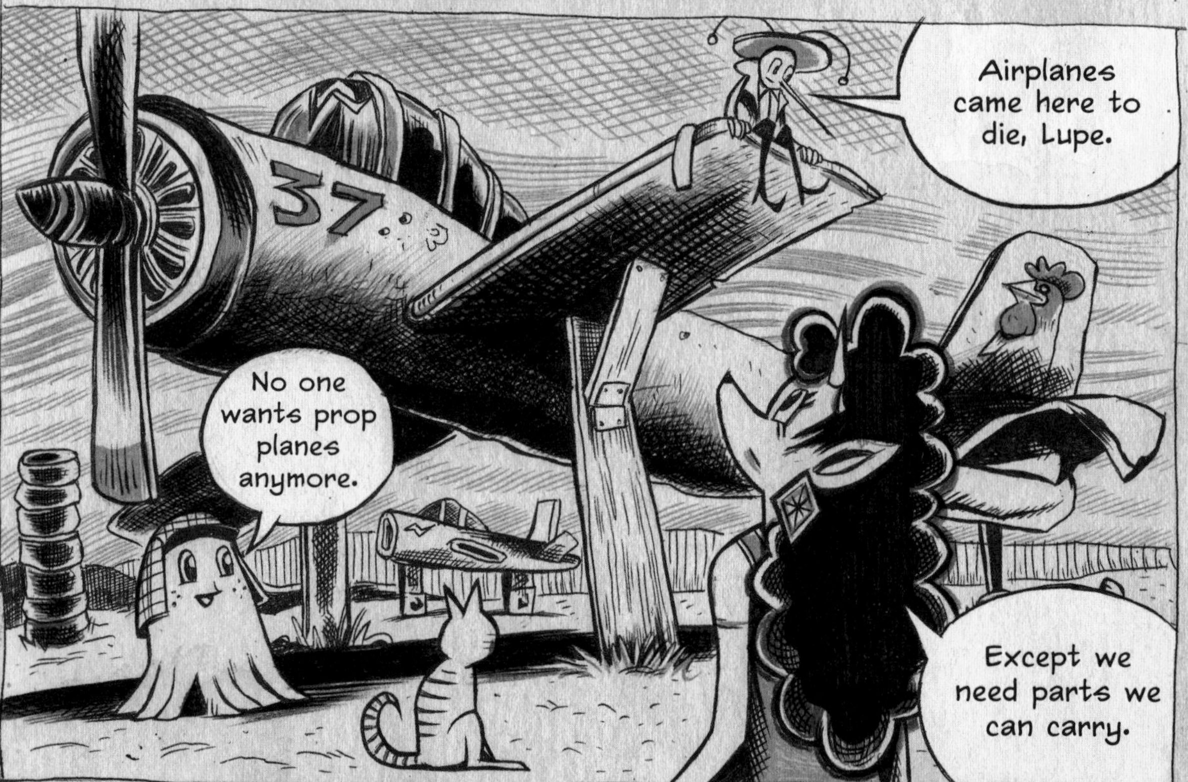
37
Airplanes came here to die, Lupe.
No one wants prop planes anymore.
Except we need parts we can carry.

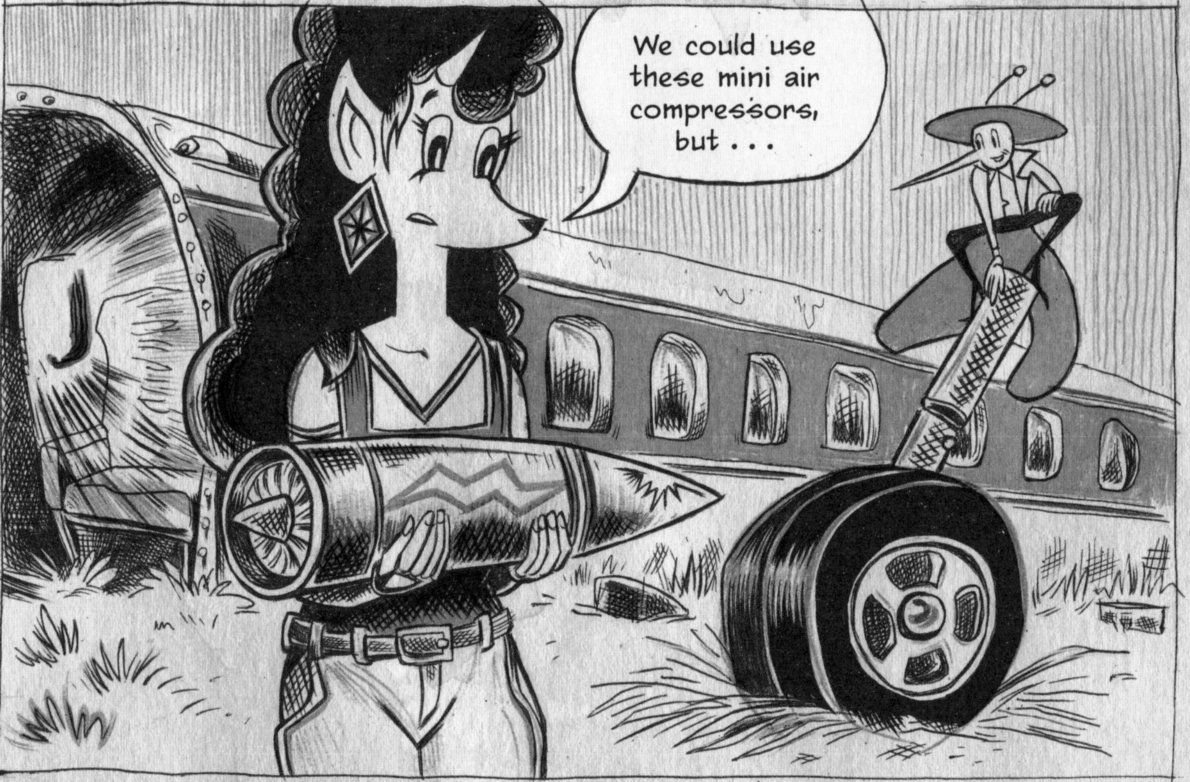
We could use these mini air compressors, but . . .

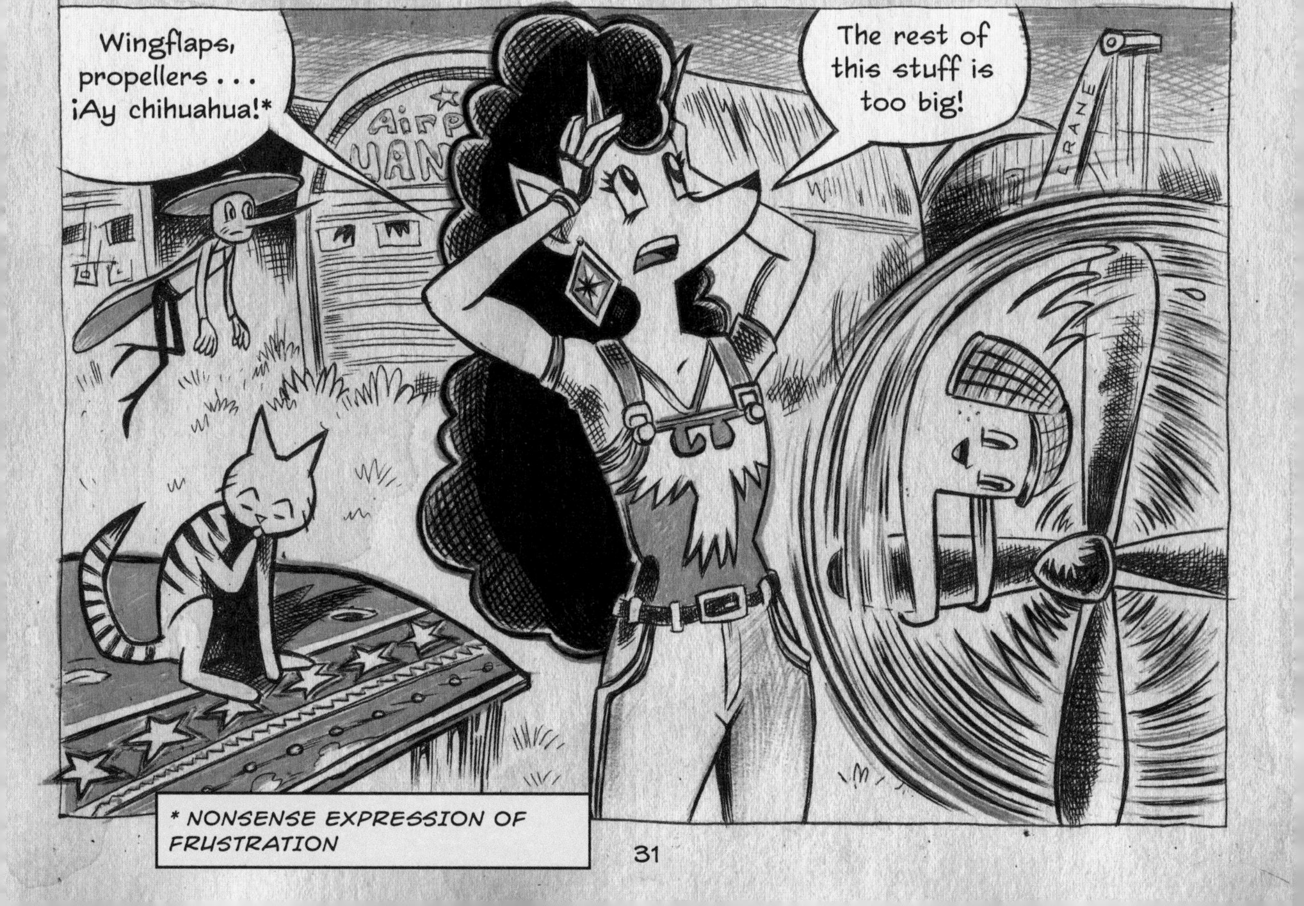
Wingflaps, propellers . . . ¡Ay chihuahua!*
The rest of this stuff is too big!

* NONSENSE EXPRESSION OF FRUSTRATION

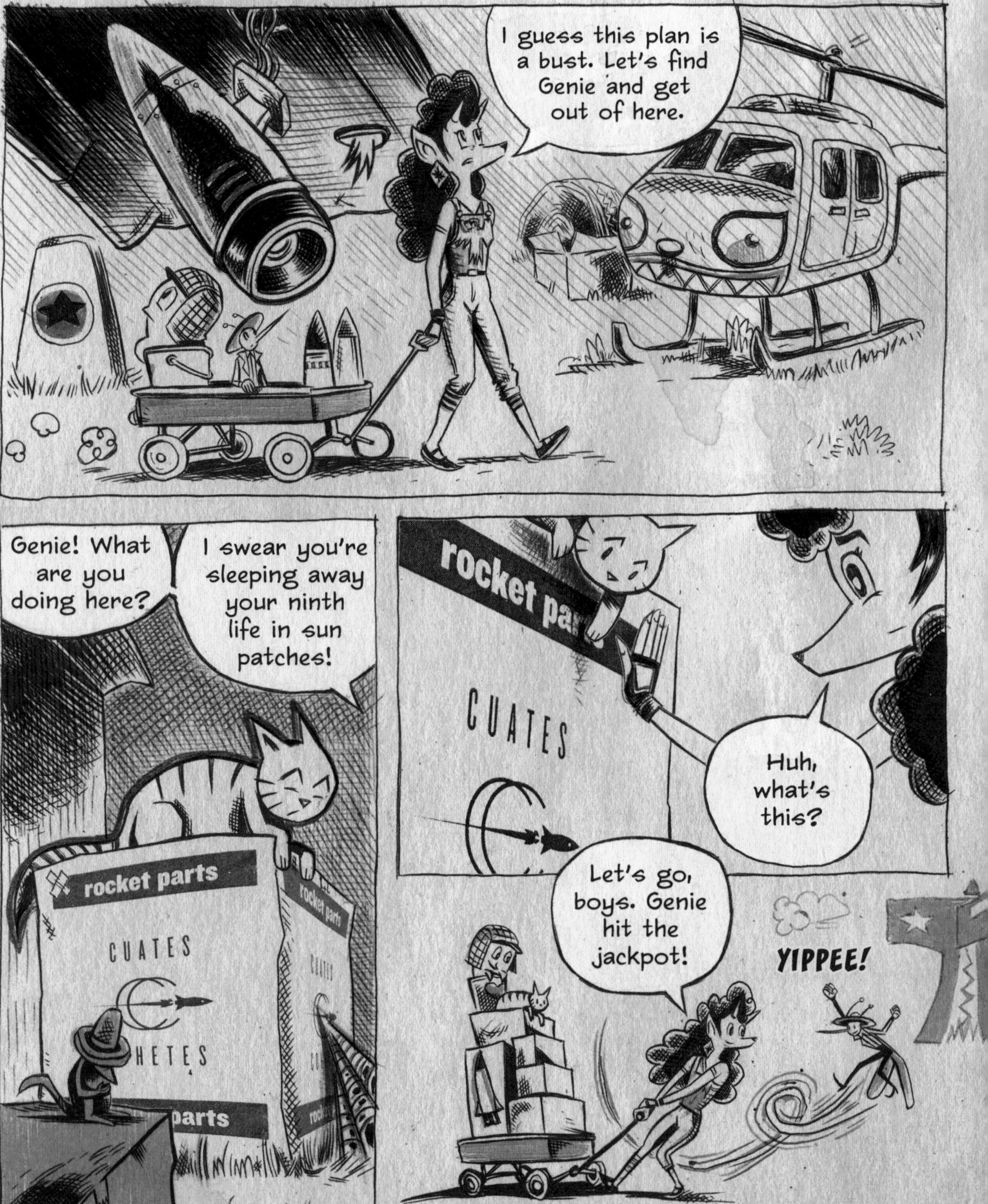
I guess this plan is a bust. Let's find Genie and get out of here.
Genie! What are you doing here?
I swear you're sleeping away your ninth life in sun patches!
rocket parts
CUATES
rocket parts
CUATES
Huh, what's this?
Let's go, boys. Genie hit the jackpot!
YIPPEE!

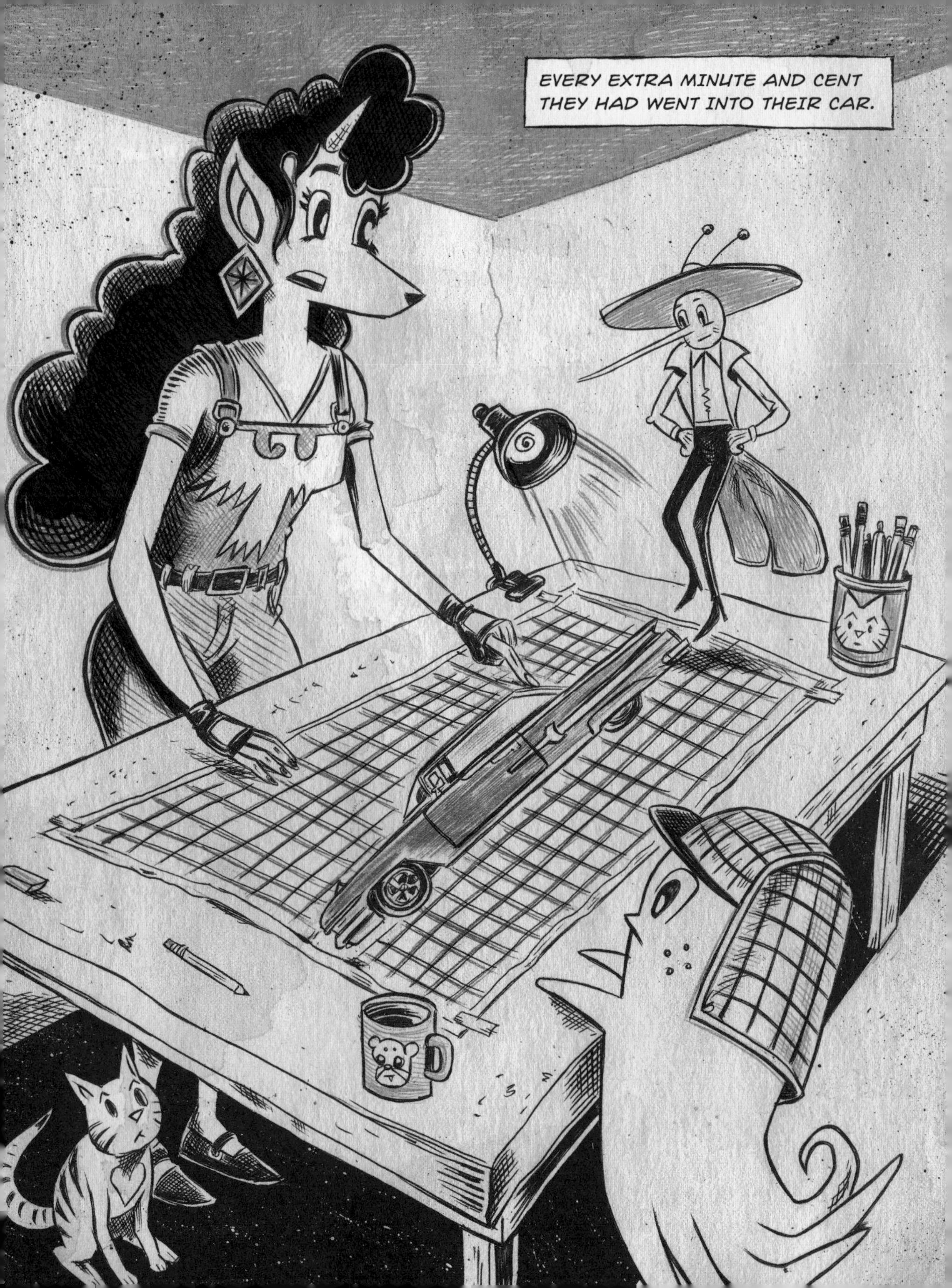
EVERY EXTRA MINUTE AND CENT THEY HAD WENT INTO THEIR CAR.

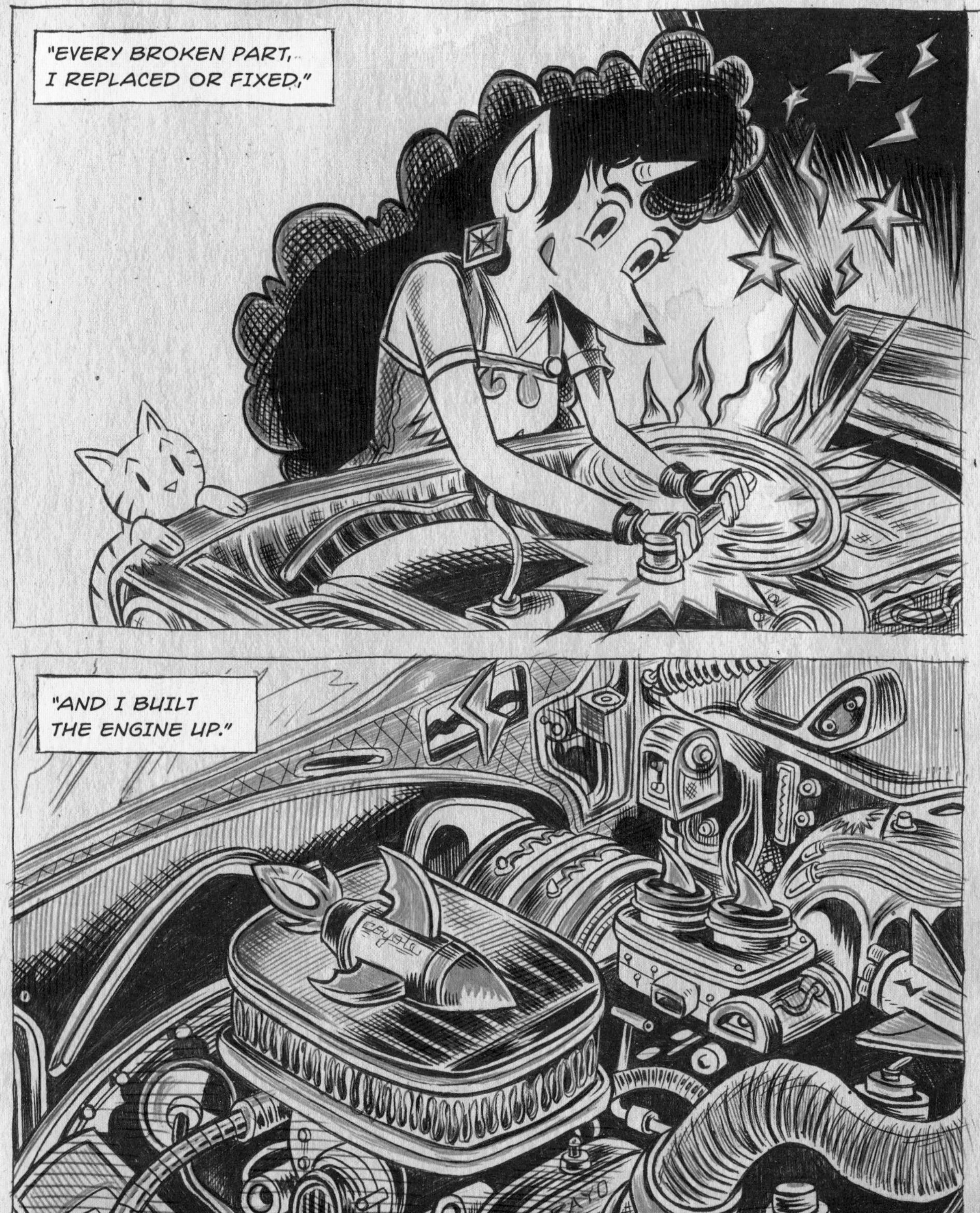
"EVERY BROKEN PART, I REPLACED OR FIXED."
"AND I BUILT THE ENGINE UP."
RAYO

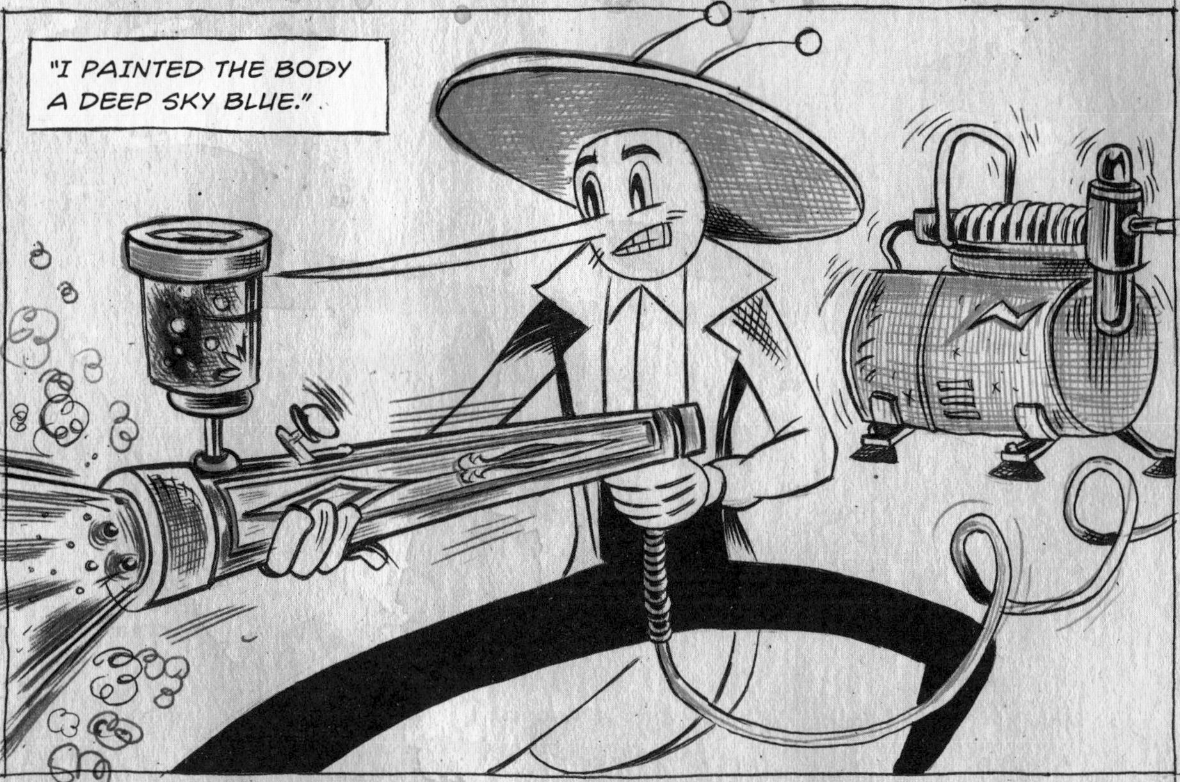
"I PAINTED THE BODY A DEEP SKY BLUE."

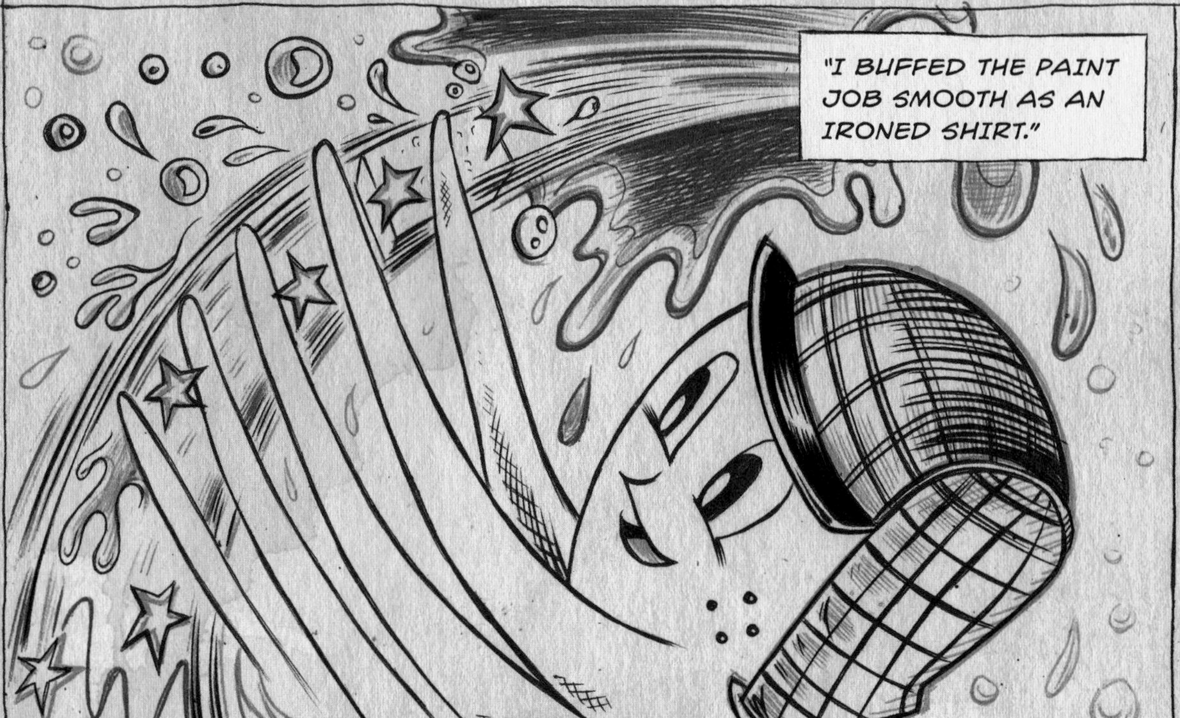
"I BUFFED THE PAINT JOB SMOOTH AS AN IRONED SHIRT."

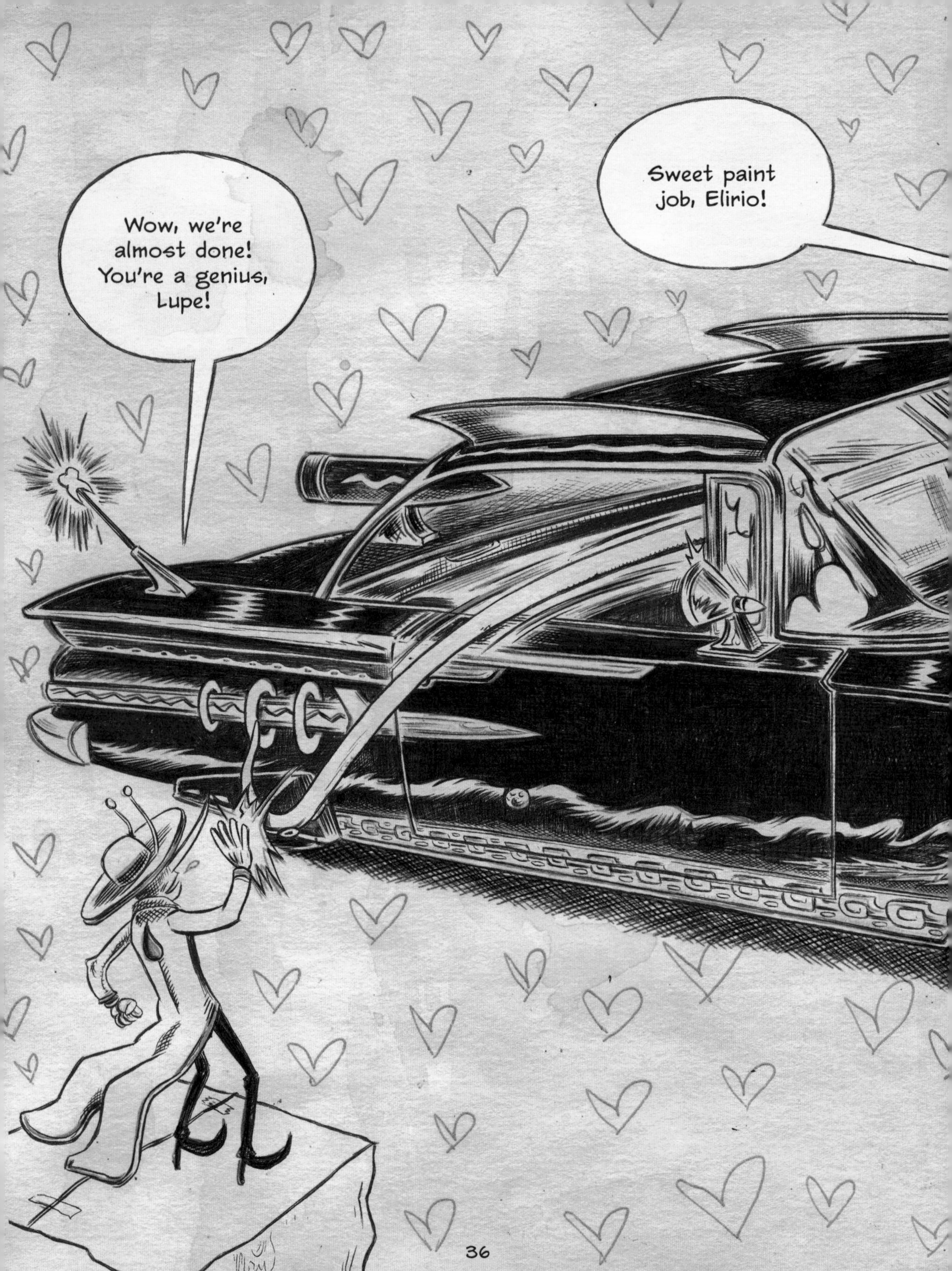
Wow, we're almost done! You're a genius, Lupe!
Sweet paint job, Elirio!

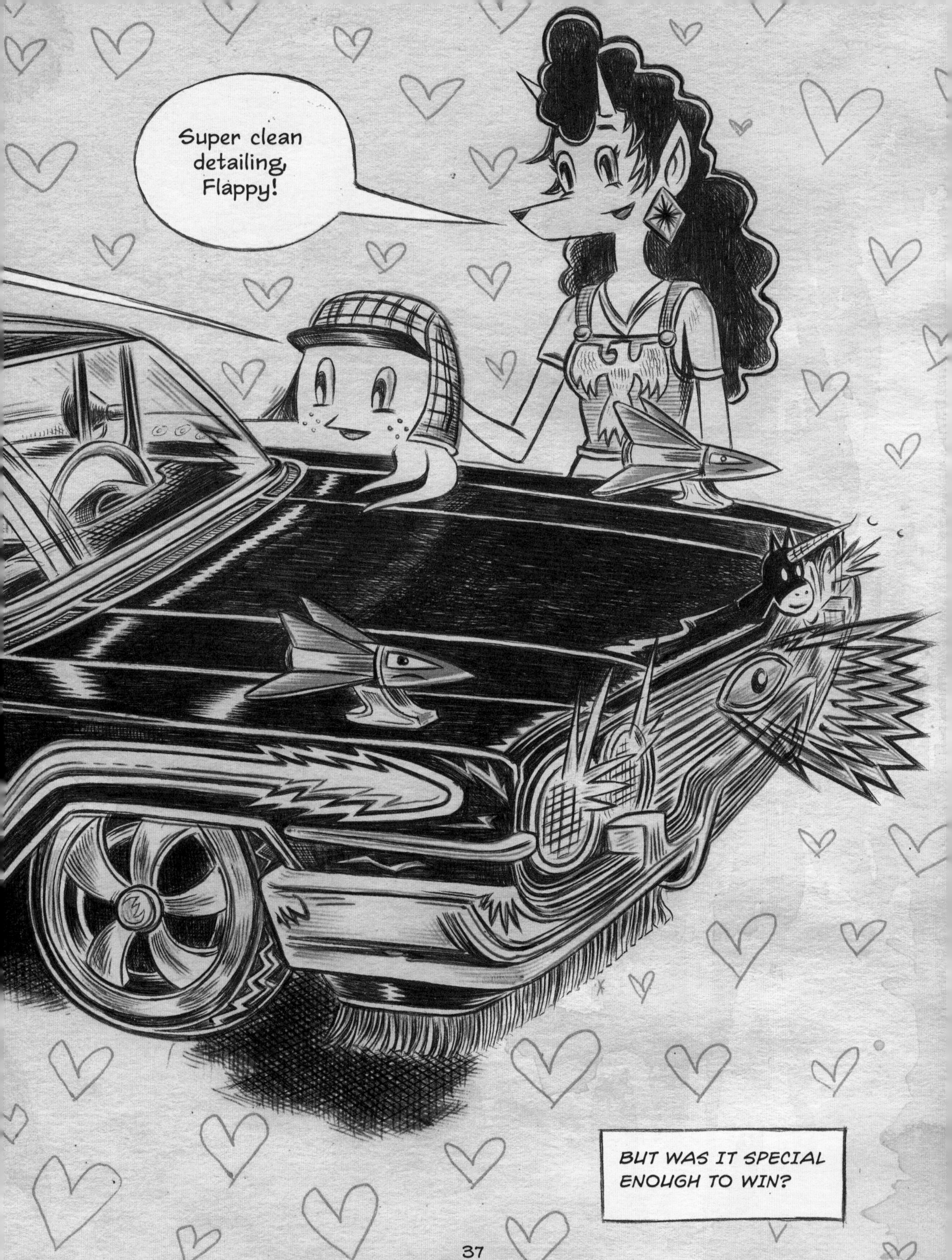
Super clean detailing, Flappy!
BUT WAS IT SPECIAL ENOUGH TO WIN?

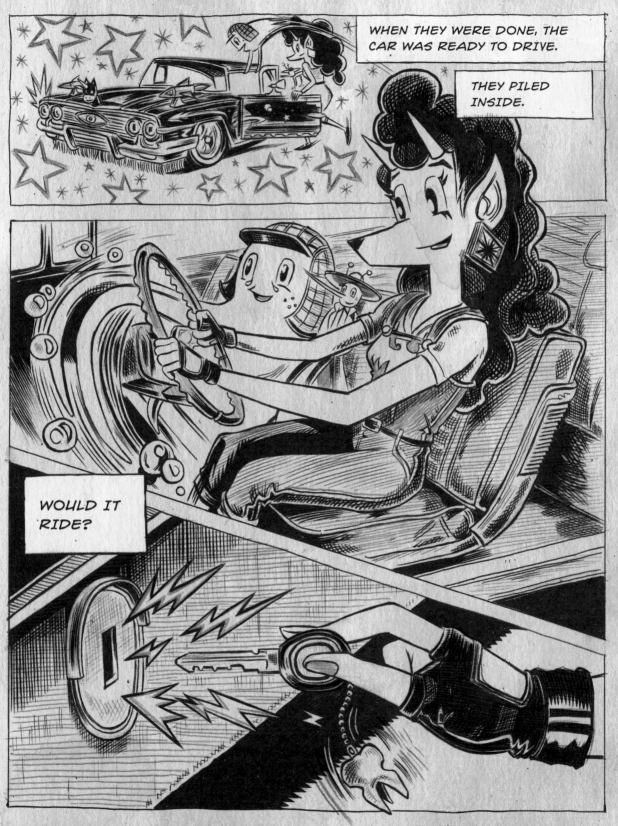

WHEN THEY WERE DONE, THE CAR WAS READY TO DRIVE.

THEY PILED INSIDE.

WOULD IT RIDE?

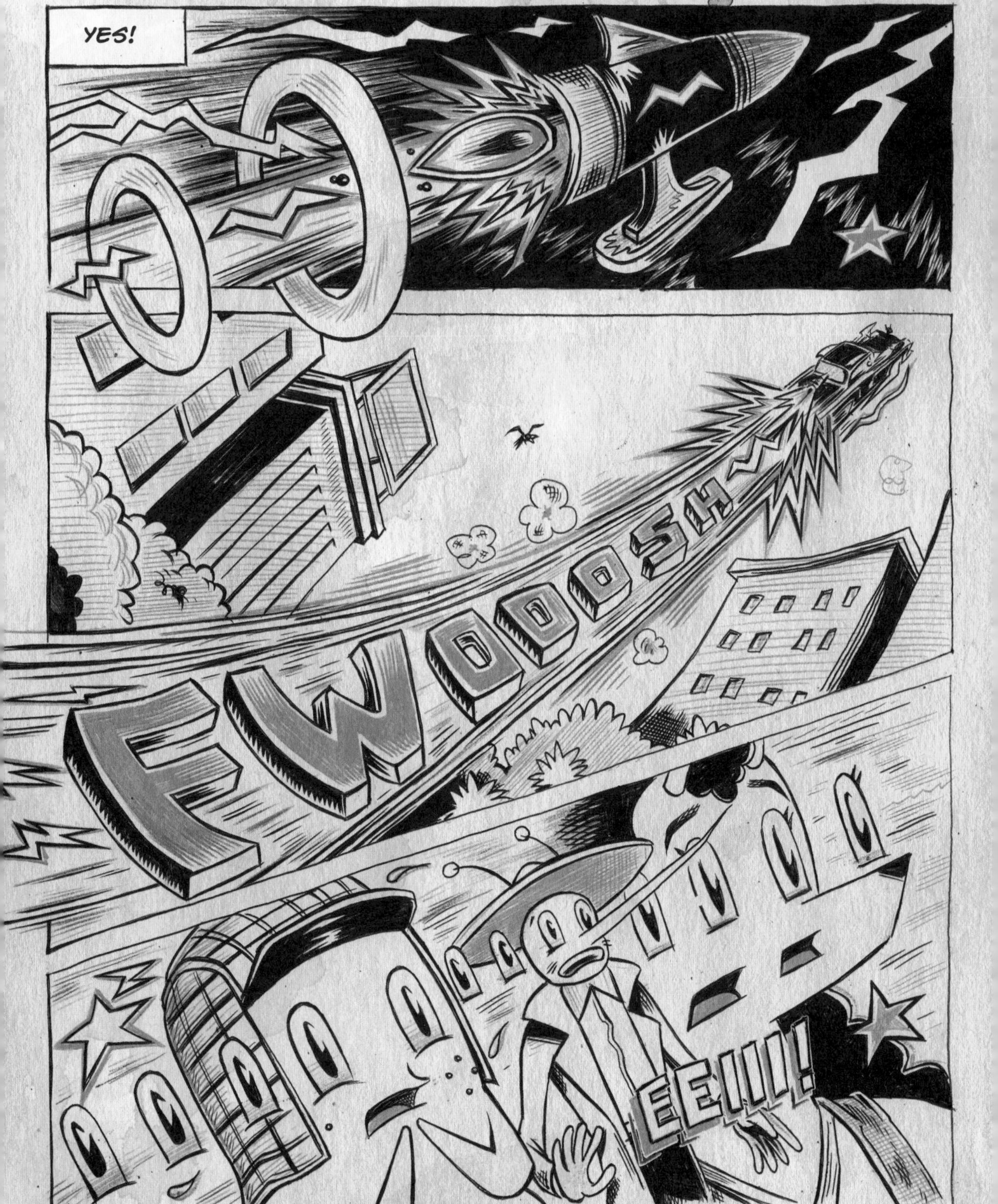
YES!
FWOOOSH
EEIII!

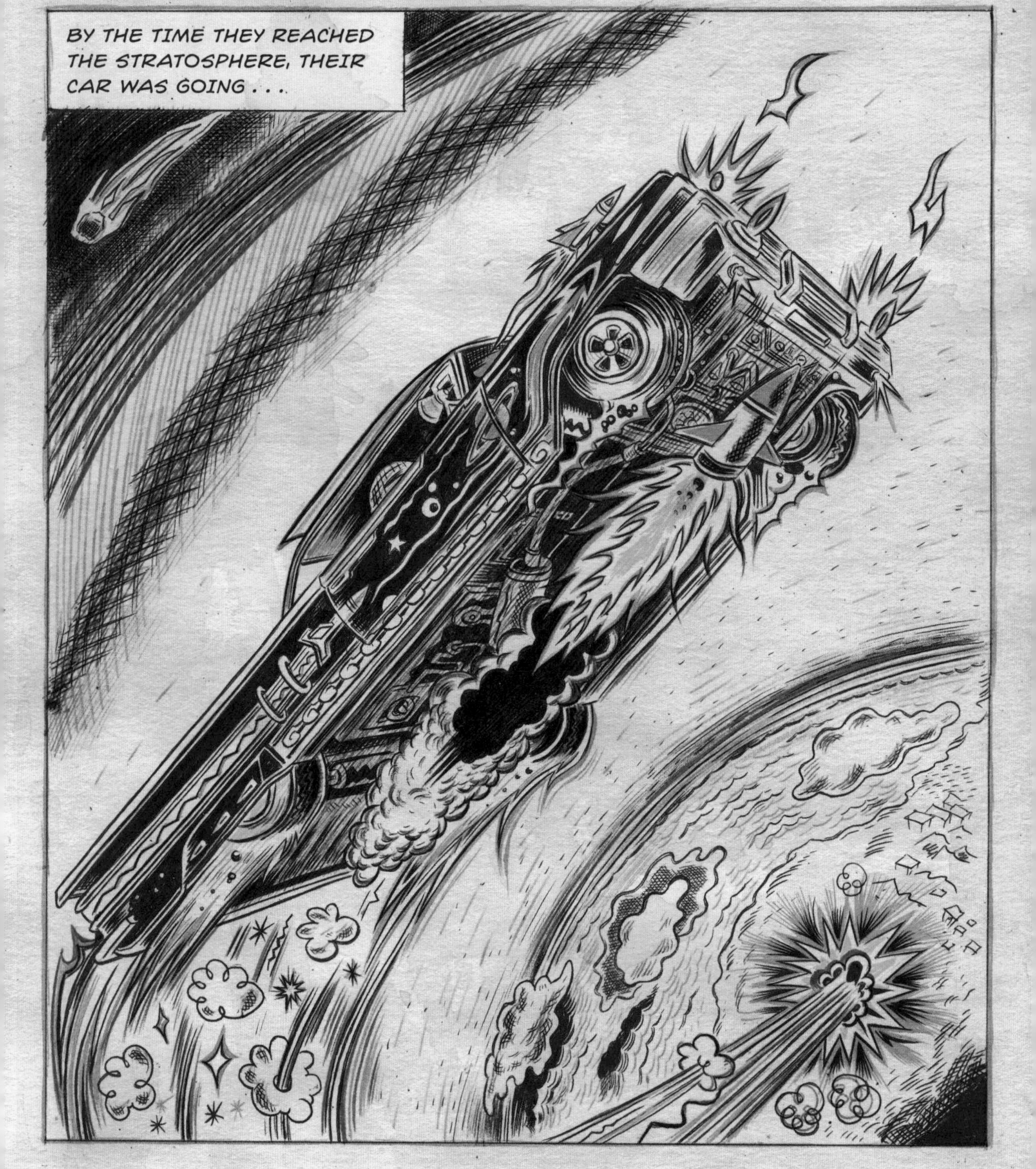
BY THE TIME THEY REACHED THE STRATOSPHERE, THEIR CAR WAS GOING . . .

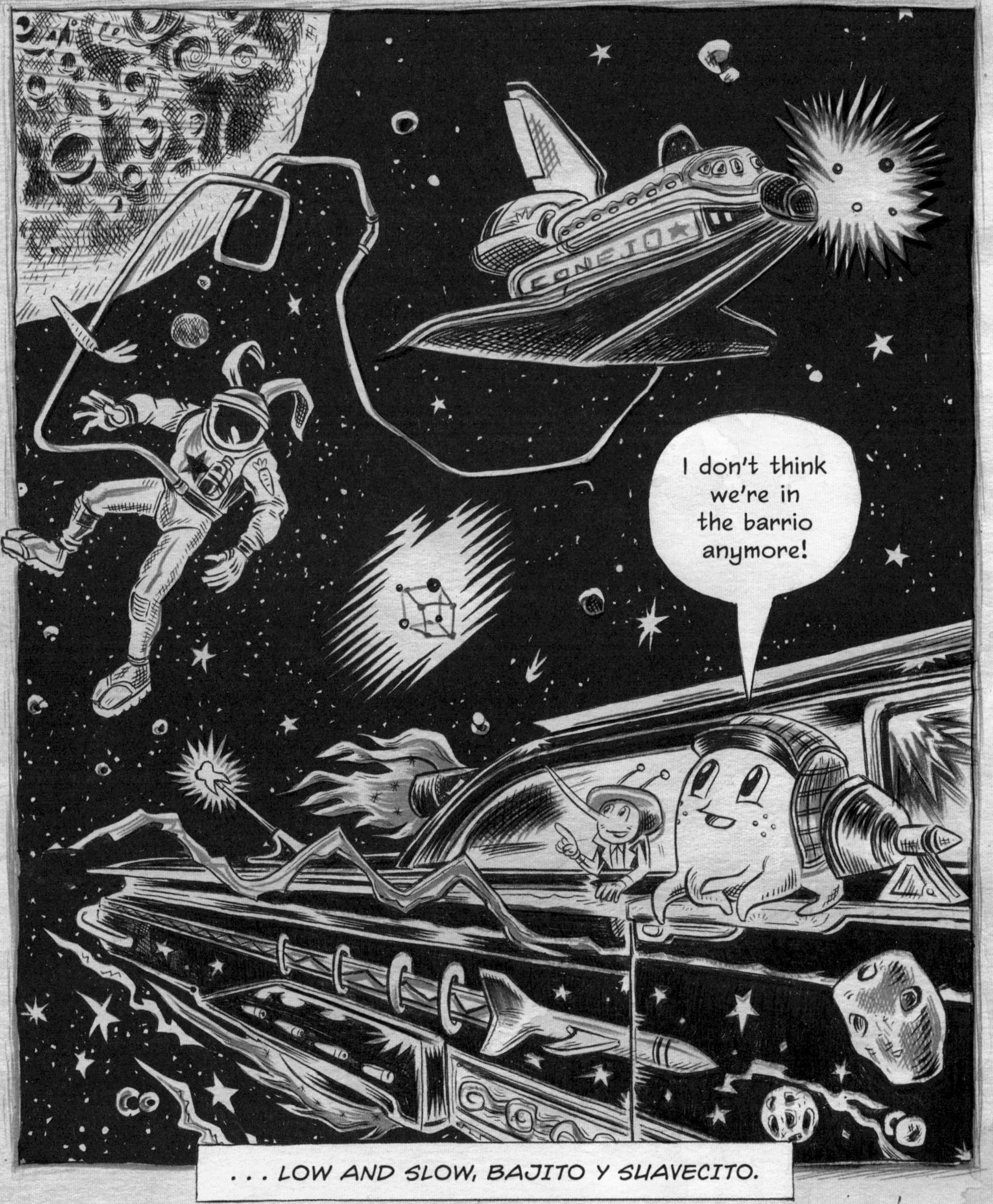
CONEJO
I don't think we're in the barrio anymore!
. . . LOW AND SLOW, BAJITO Y SUAVECITO.

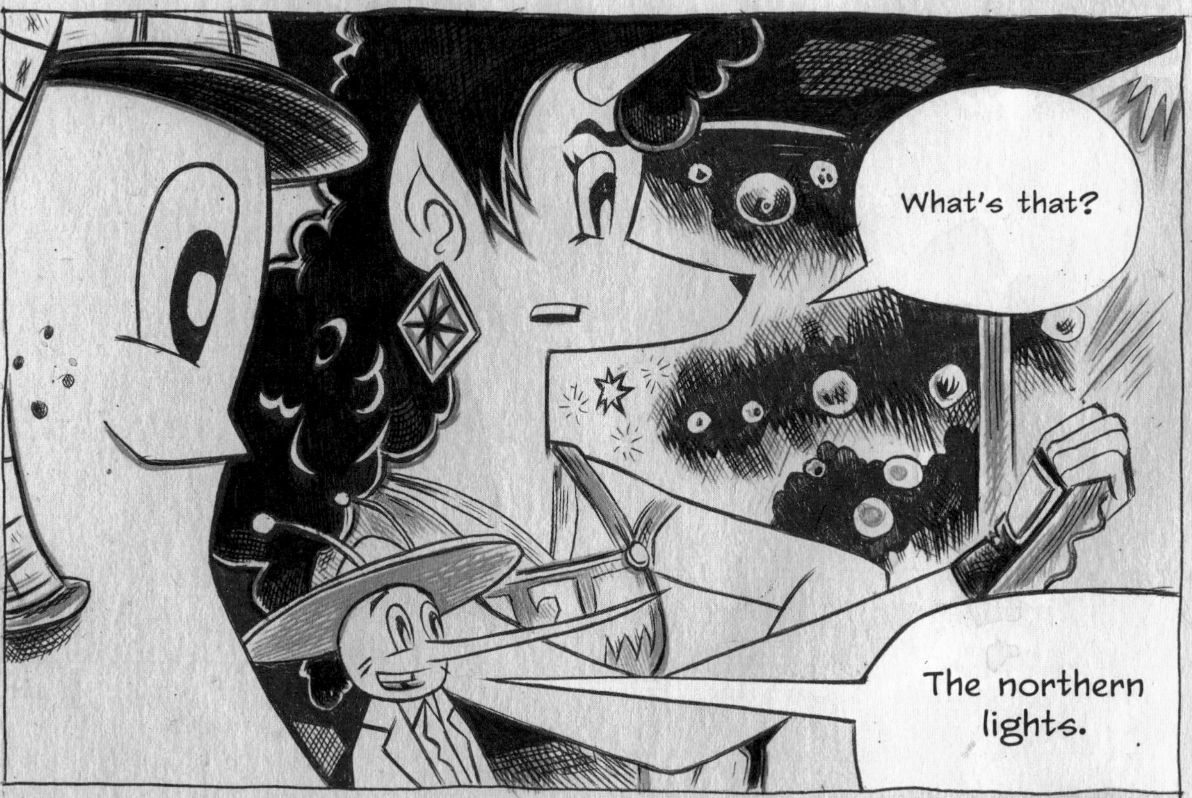
What's that?
The northern lights.

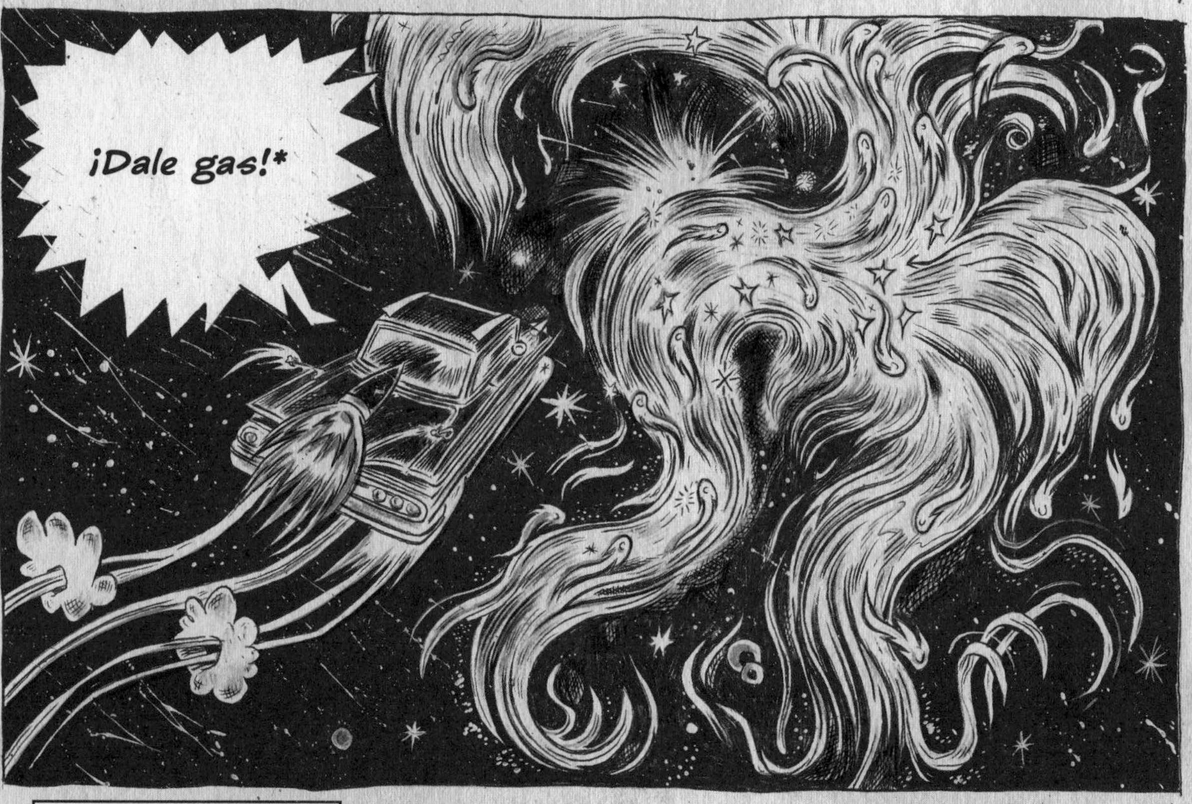
¡Dale gas!*

* GIVE IT SOME GAS!

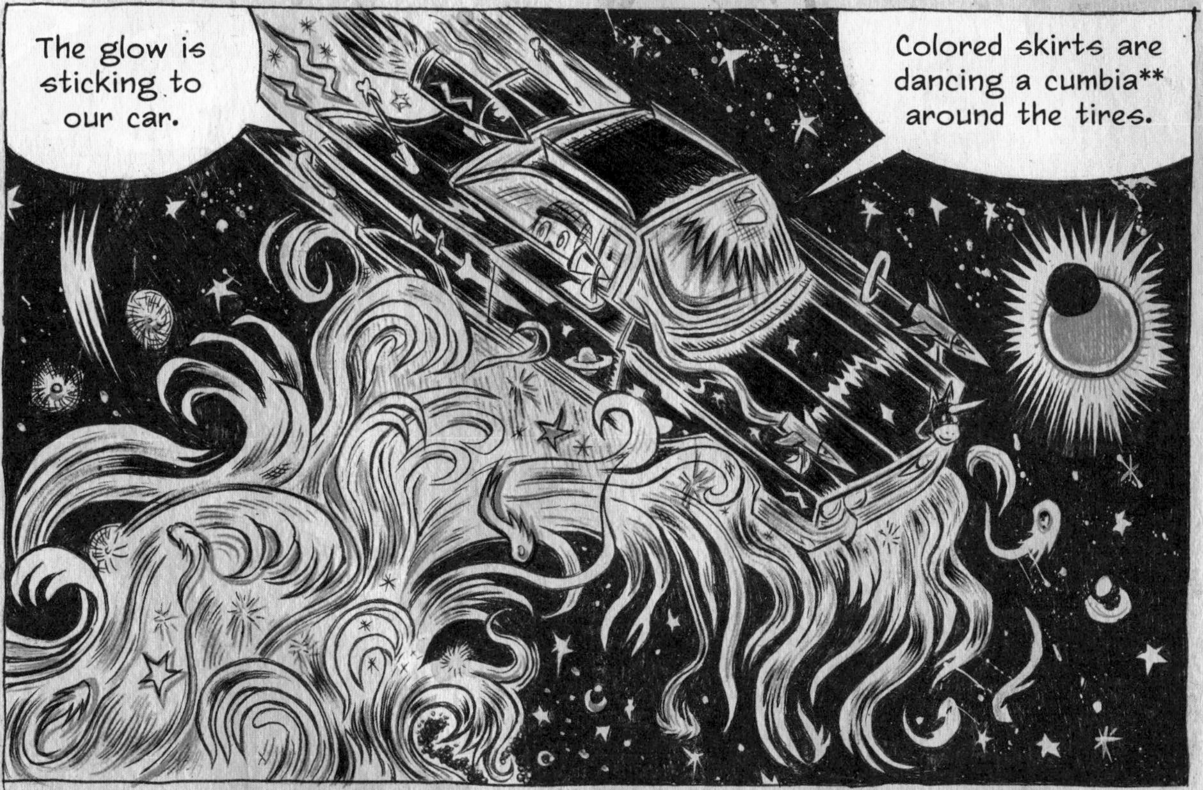
The glow is sticking to our car.
Colored skirts are dancing a cumbia** around the tires.

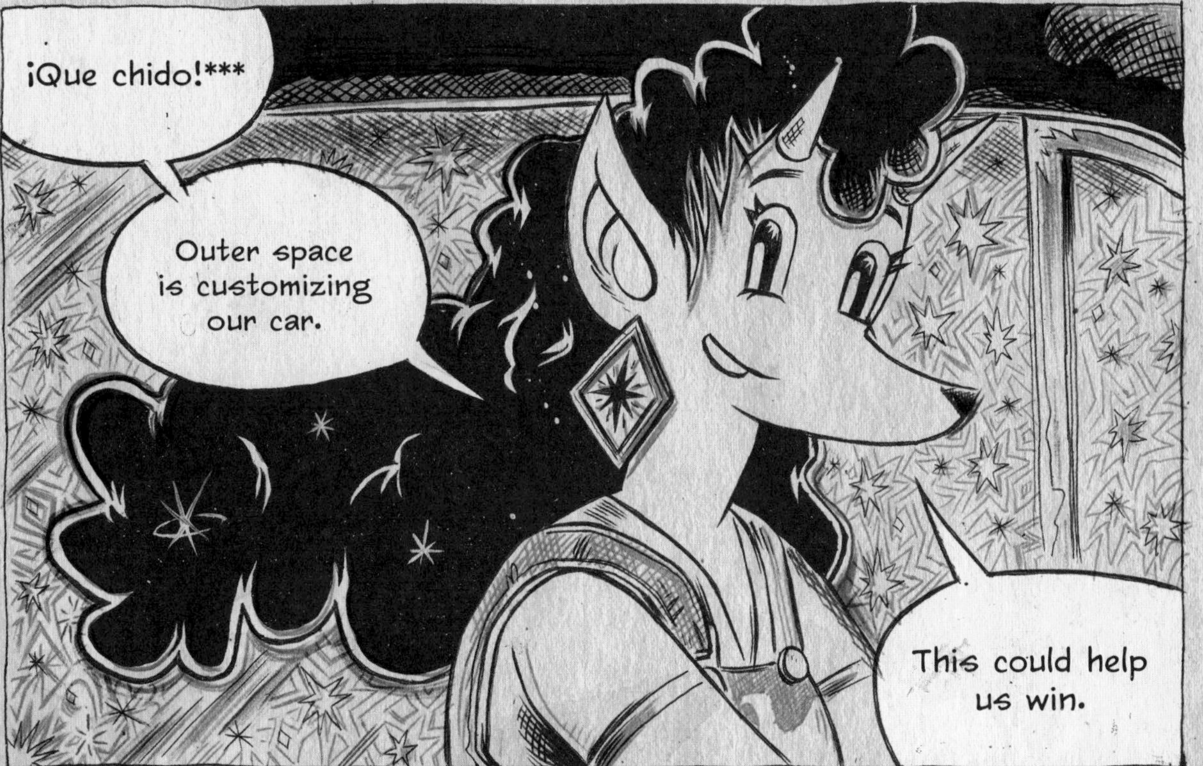
¡Que chido!***
Outer space is customizing our car.
This could help us win.

** A DANCE FROM COLOMBIA *** COOL!

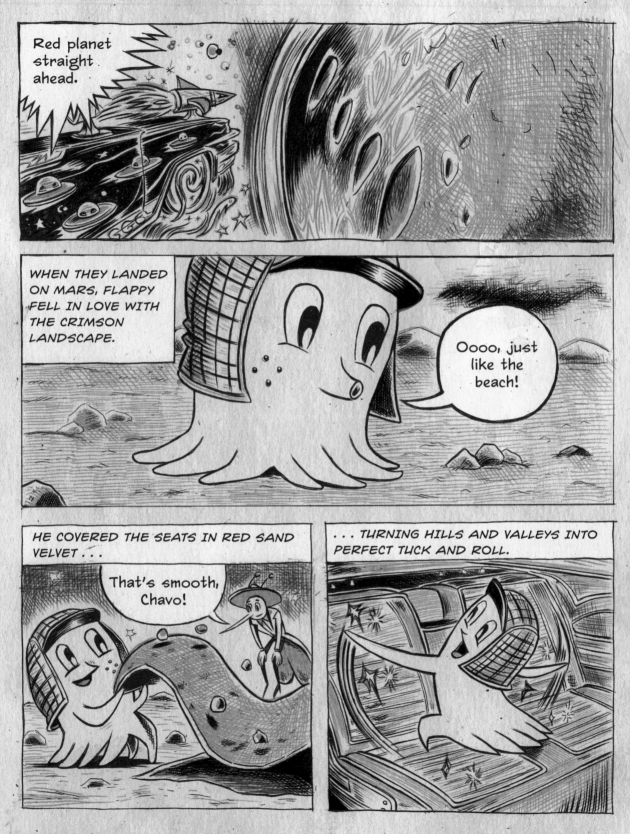

Red planet straight ahead.

WHEN THEY LANDED ON MARS, FLAPPY FELL IN LOVE WITH THE CRIMSON LANDSCAPE.

Oooo, just like the beach!

HE COVERED THE SEATS IN RED SAND VELVET . . .

That's smooth, Chavo!

. . . TURNING HILLS AND VALLEYS INTO PERFECT TUCK AND ROLL.

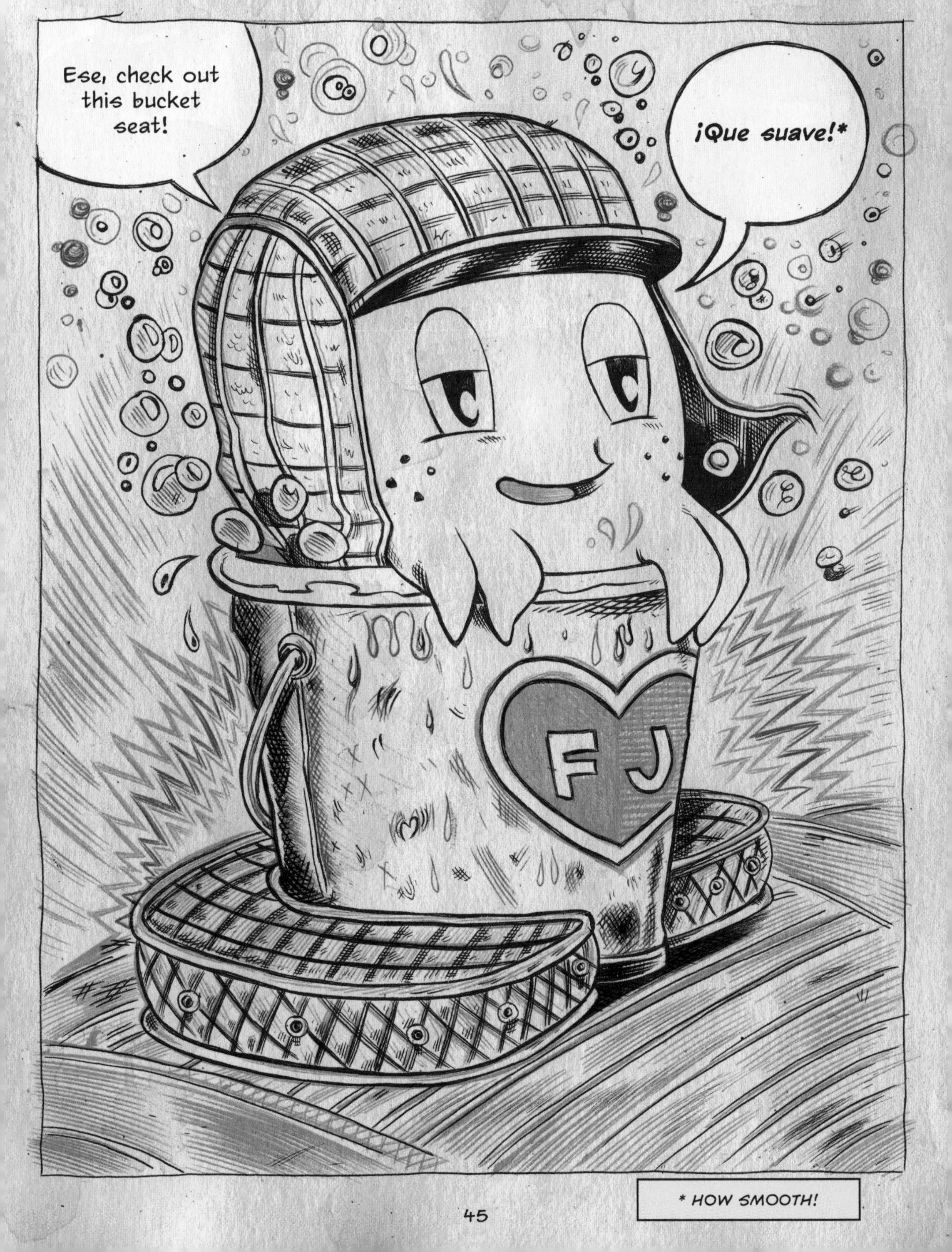
Ese, check out this bucket seat!
¡Que suave!*
FJ

* HOW SMOOTH!

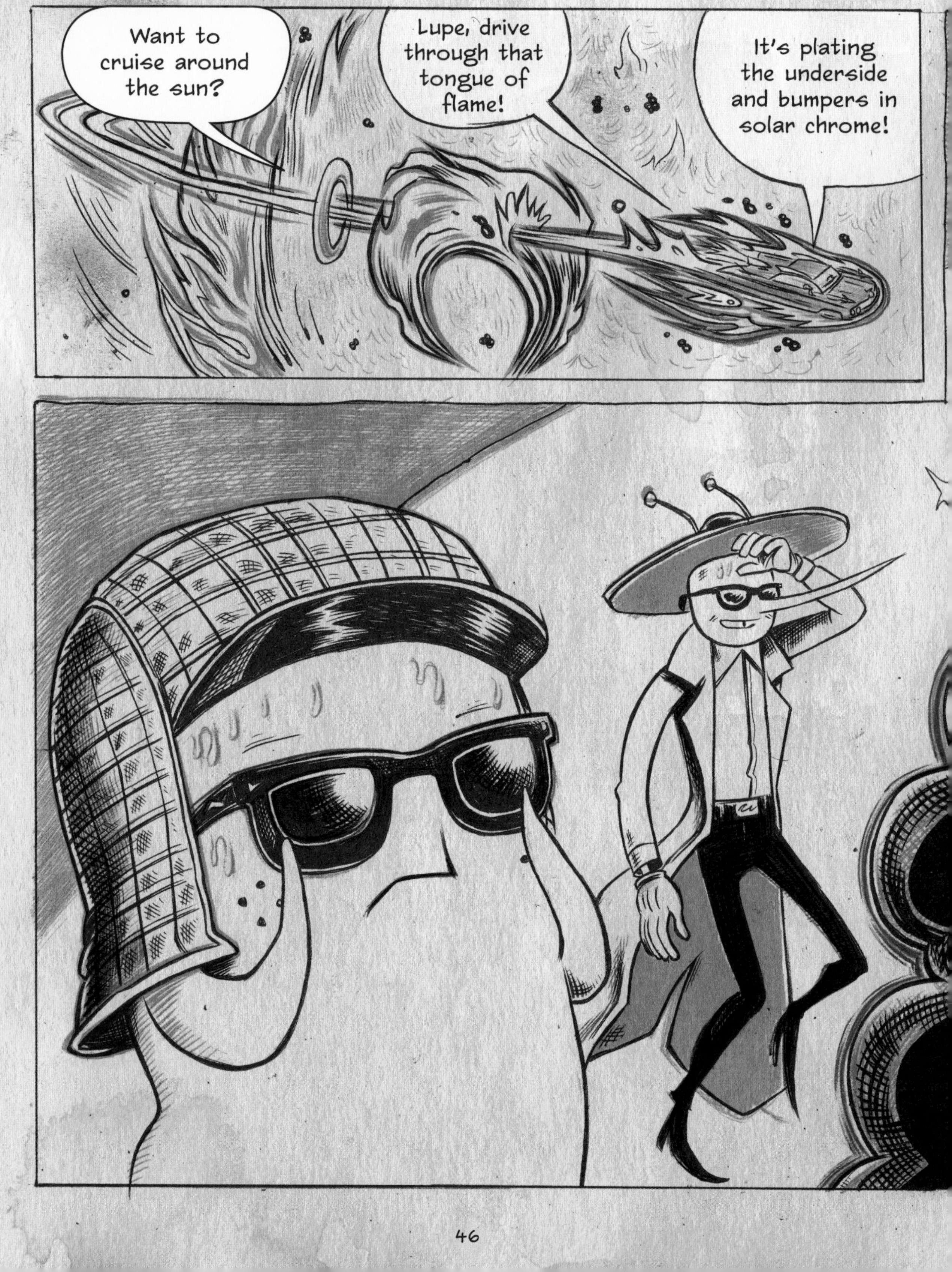
Want to cruise around the sun?
Lupe, drive through that tongue of flame!
It's plating the underside and bumpers in solar chrome!

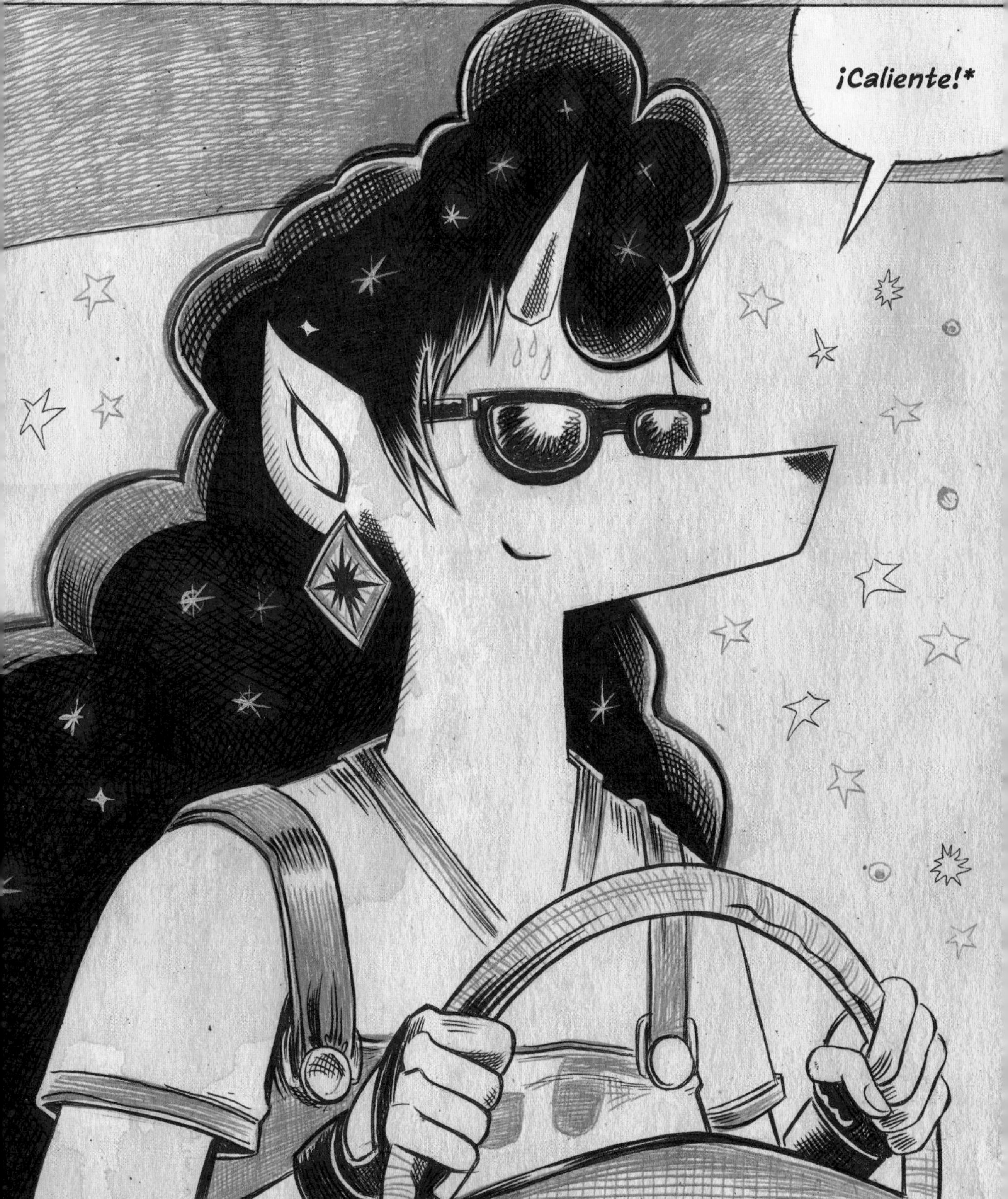
¡Caliente!*

* HOT!

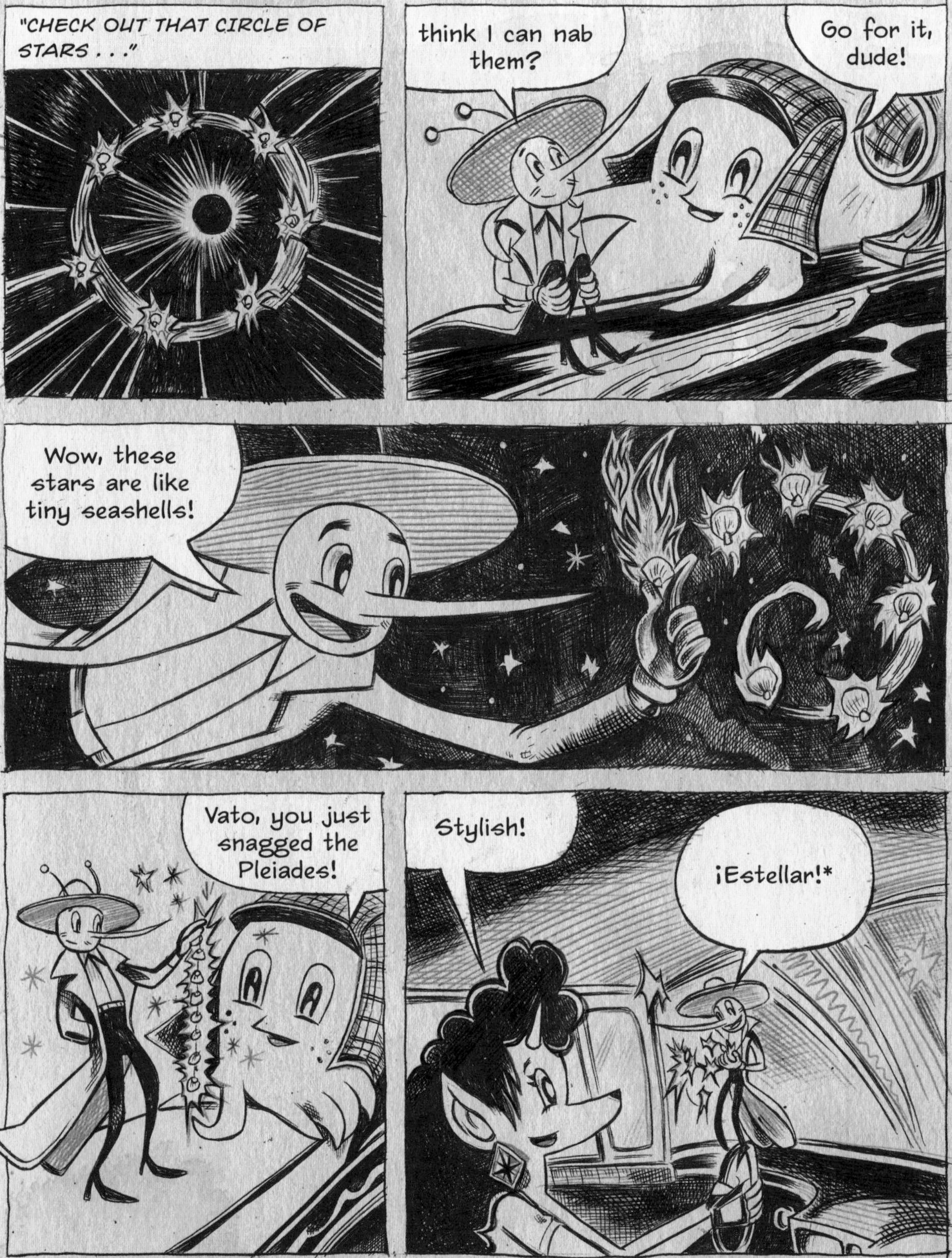
"CHECK OUT THAT CIRCLE OF STARS . . ."
think I can nab them?
Go for it, dude!
Wow, these stars are like tiny seashells!
Vato, you just snagged the Pleiades!
Stylish!
¡Estellar!*

* STELLAR!

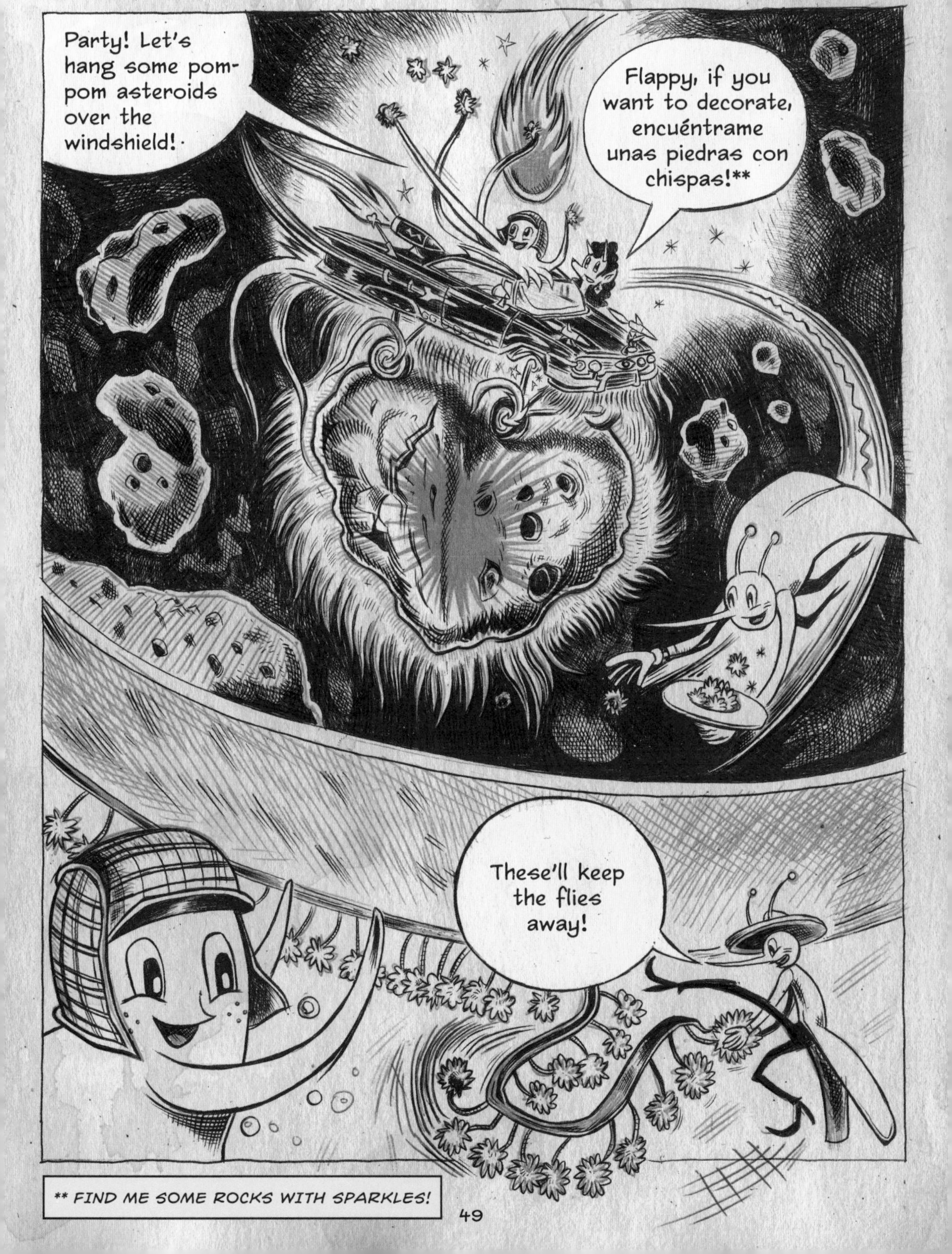
Party! Let's hang some pom-pom asteroids over the windshield!
Flappy, if you want to decorate, encuéntrame unas piedras con chispas!**
These'll keep the flies away!

*** FIND ME SOME ROCKS WITH SPARKLES!*

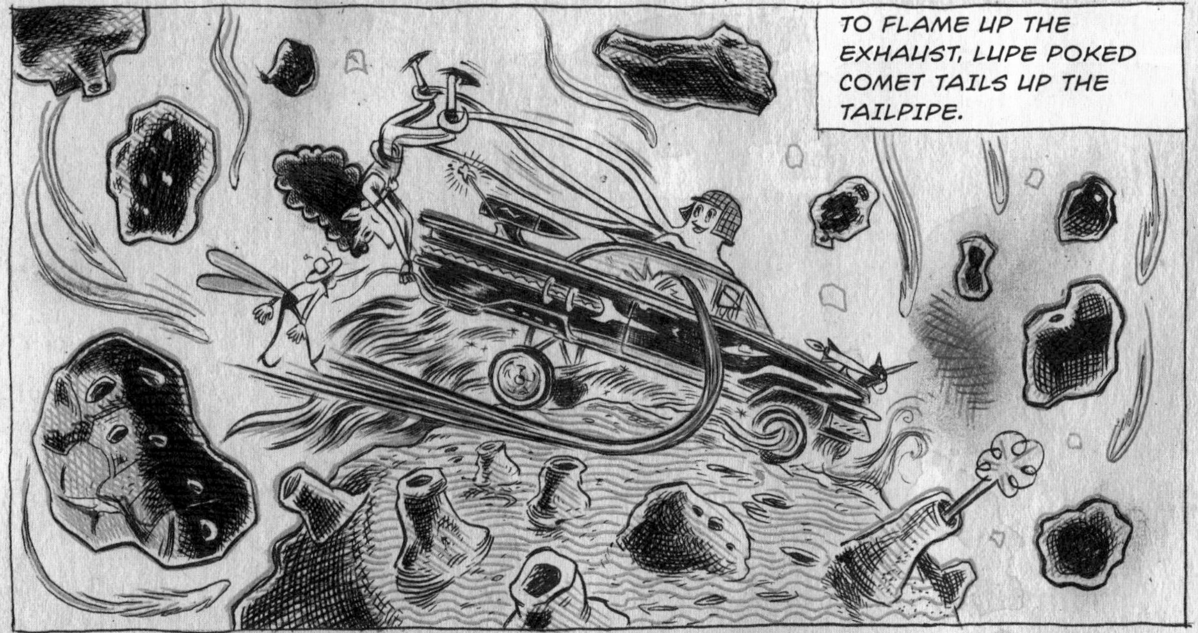
TO FLAME UP THE EXHAUST, LUPE POKED COMET TAILS UP THE TAILPIPE.

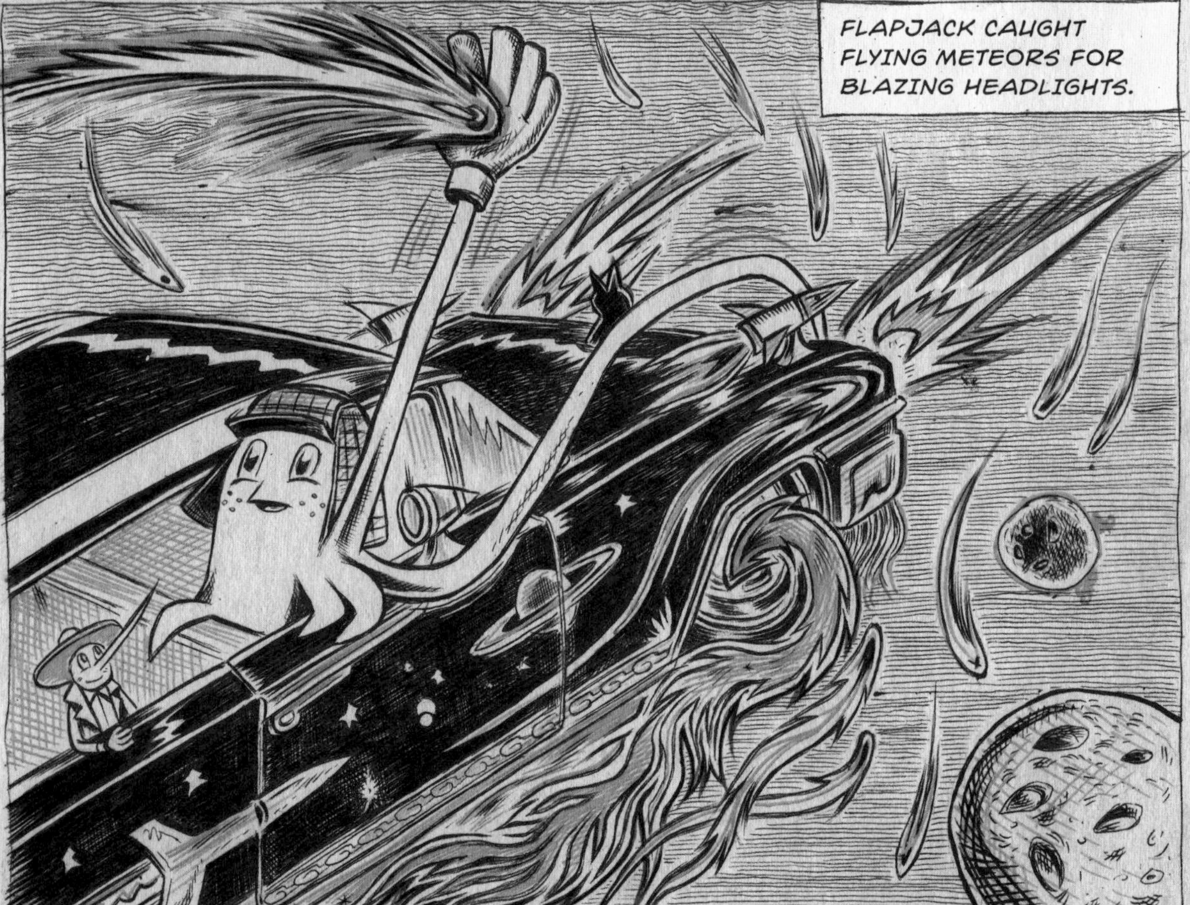
FLAPJACK CAUGHT FLYING METEORS FOR BLAZING HEADLIGHTS.

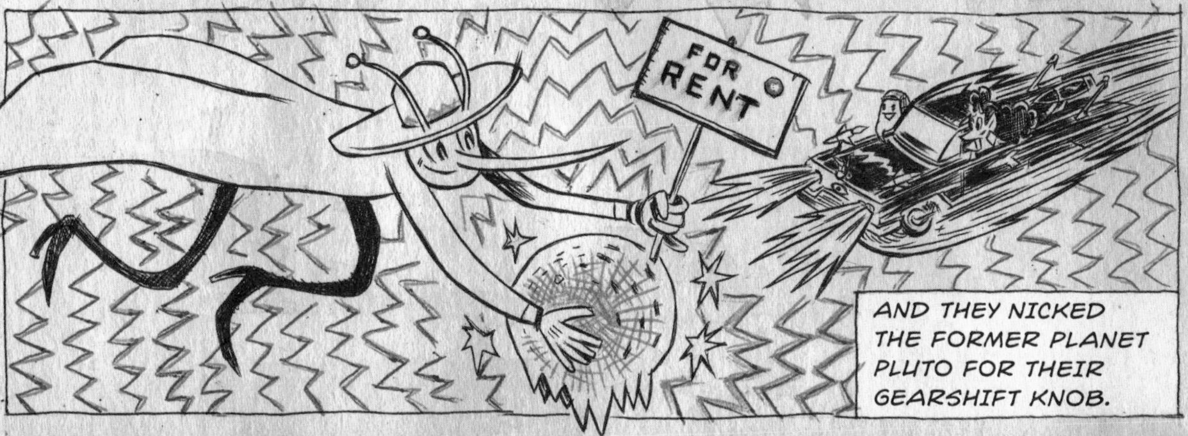
FOR RENT
AND THEY NICKED THE FORMER PLANET PLUTO FOR THEIR GEARSHIFT KNOB.

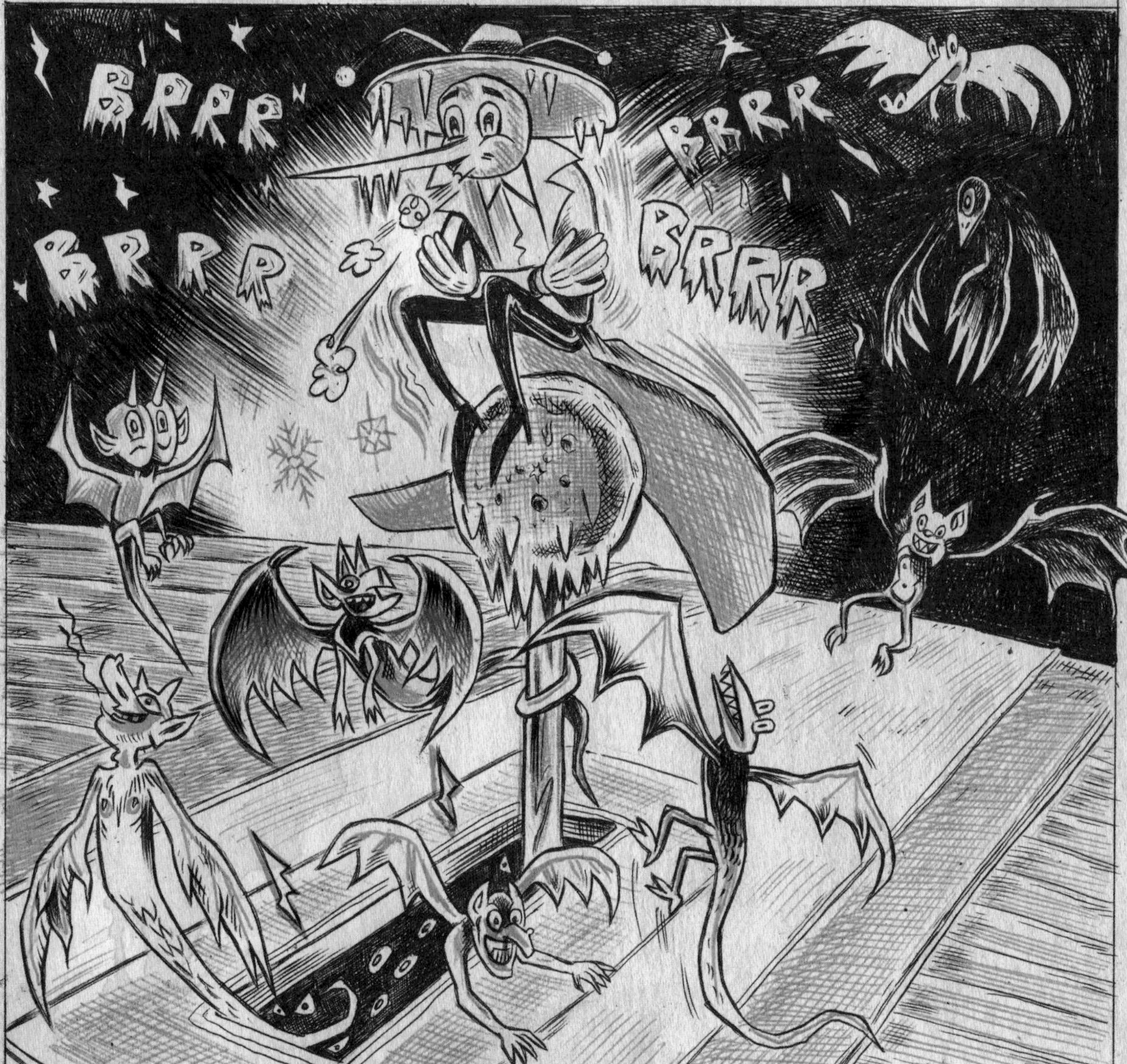
BRRR
BRRR
BRRR
BRRRR

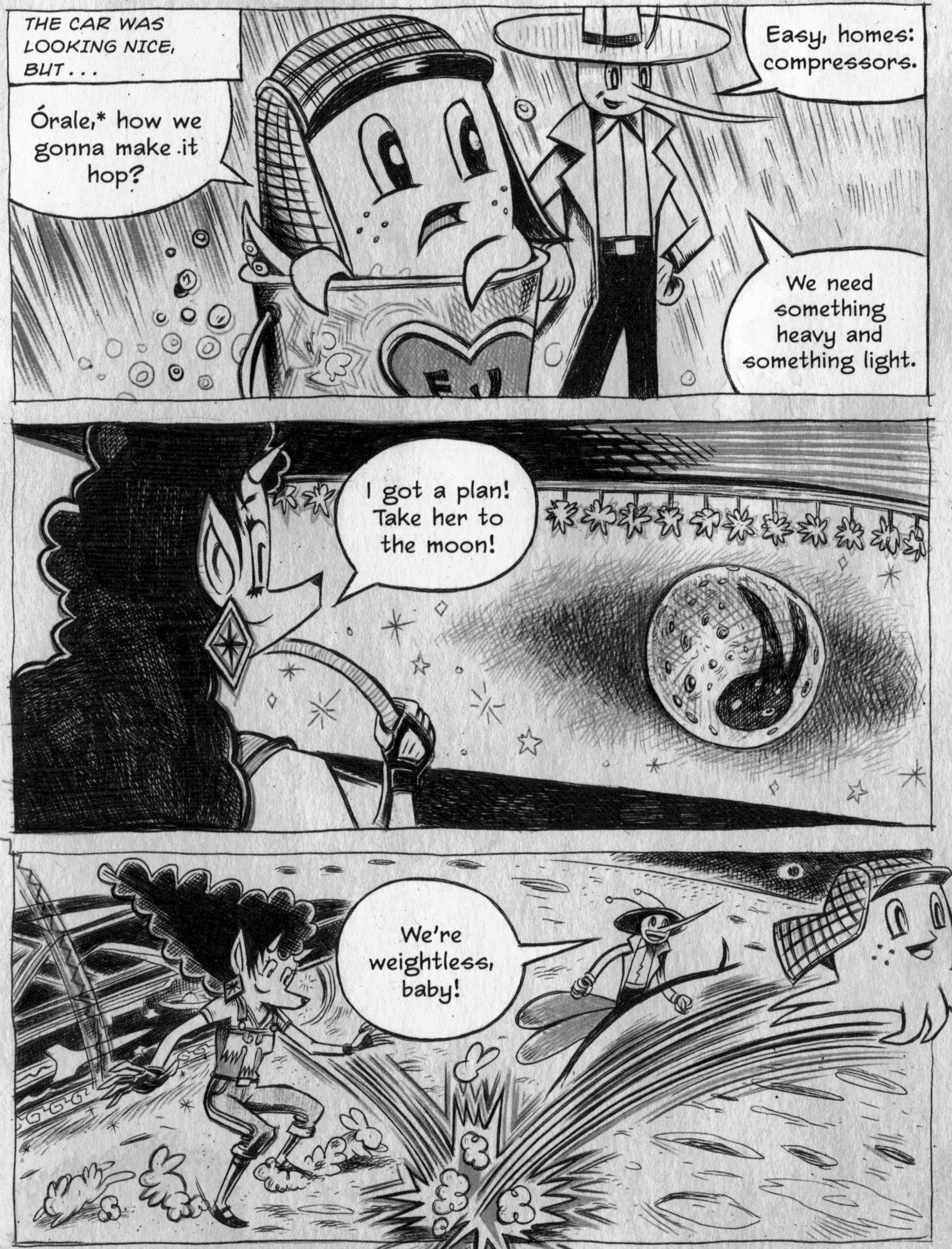
THE CAR WAS LOOKING NICE, BUT . . .
Órale,* how we gonna make it hop?
Easy, homes: compressors.
We need something heavy and something light.
I got a plan! Take her to the moon!
We're weightless, baby!
* ALL RIGHT

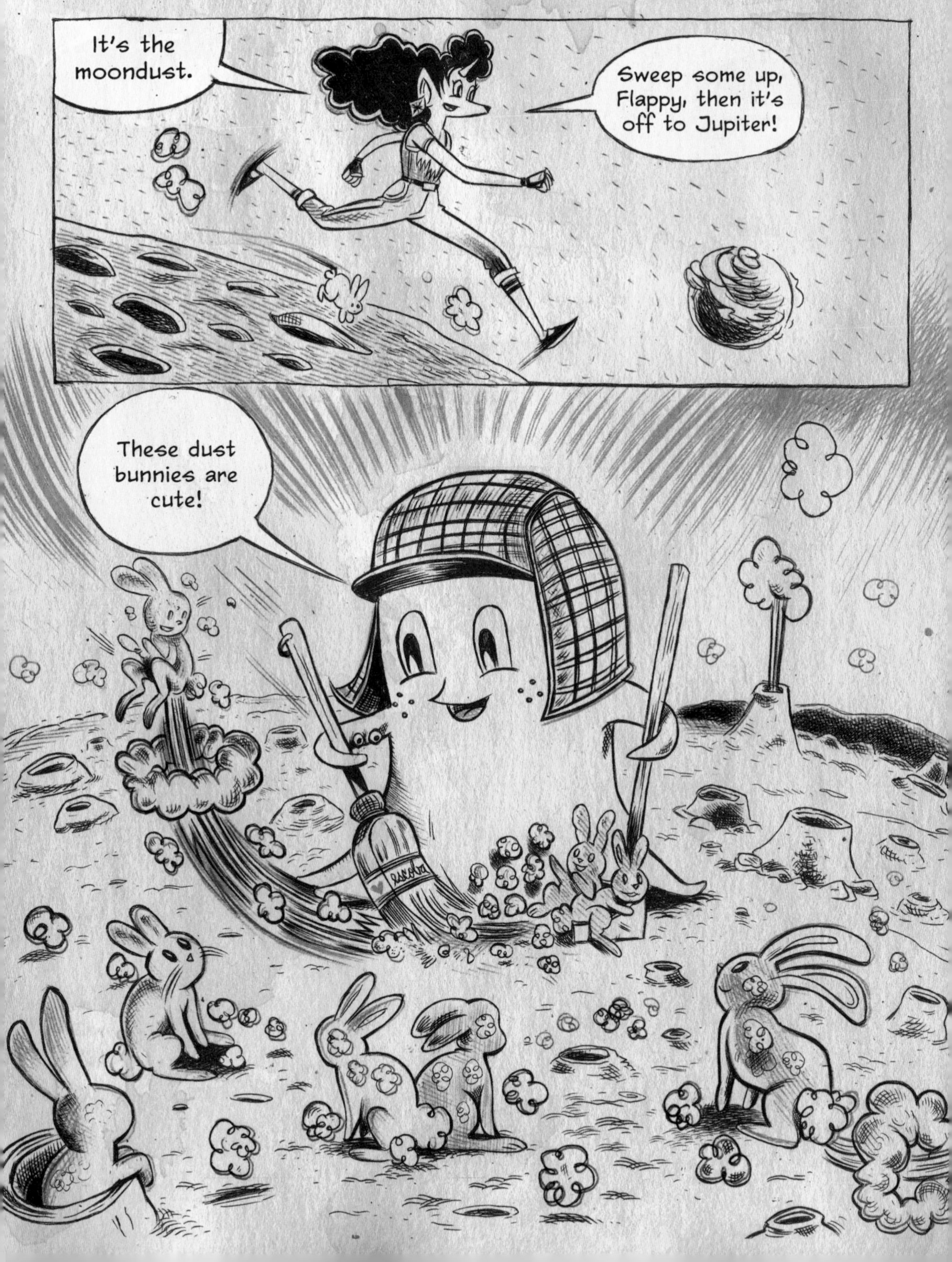
It's the moondust.
Sweep some up, Flappy, then it's off to Jupiter!
These dust bunnies are cute!

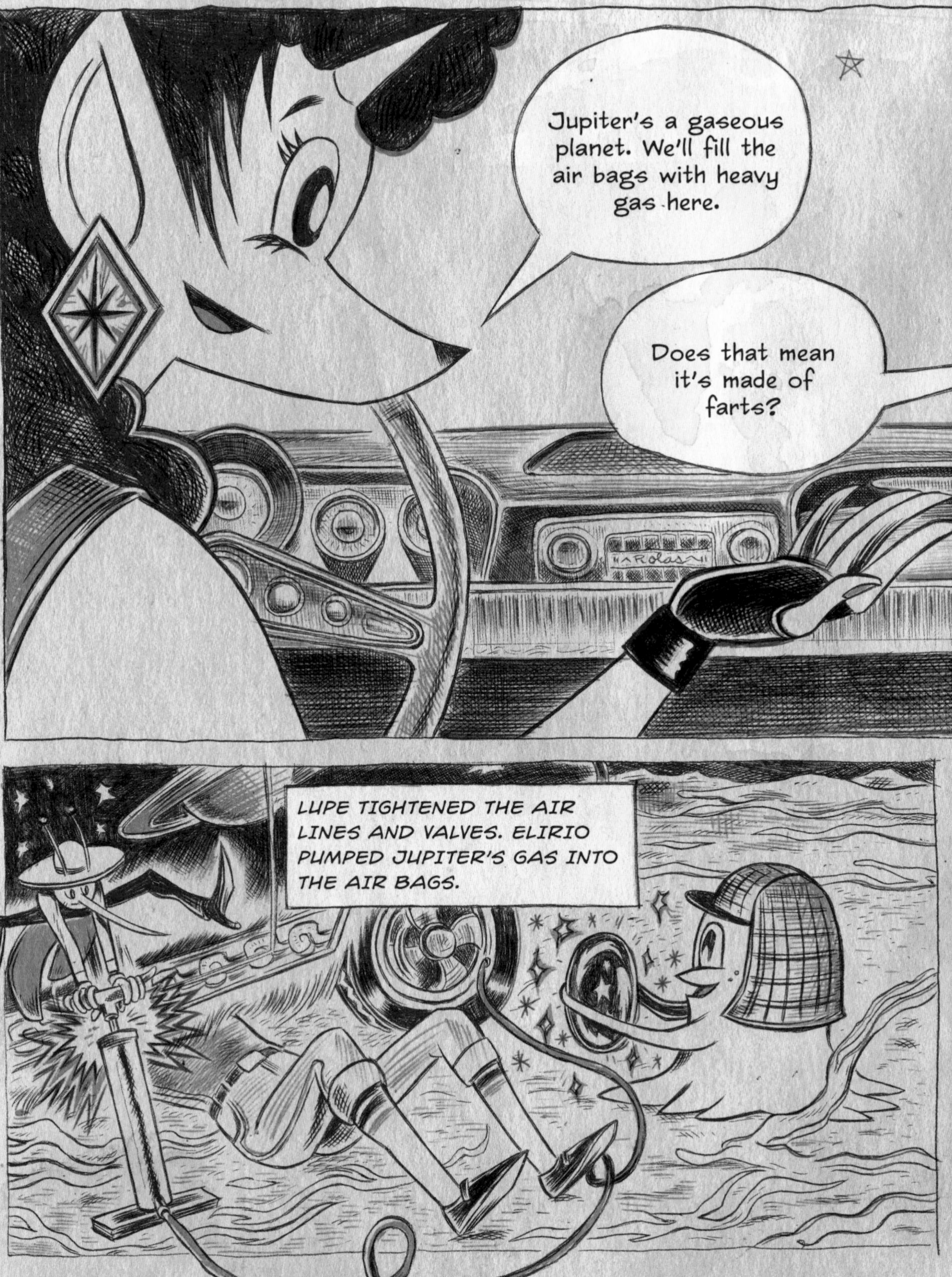
Jupiter's a gaseous planet. We'll fill the air bags with heavy gas here.
Does that mean it's made of farts?
LUPE TIGHTENED THE AIR LINES AND VALVES. ELIRIO PUMPED JUPITER'S GAS INTO THE AIR BAGS.

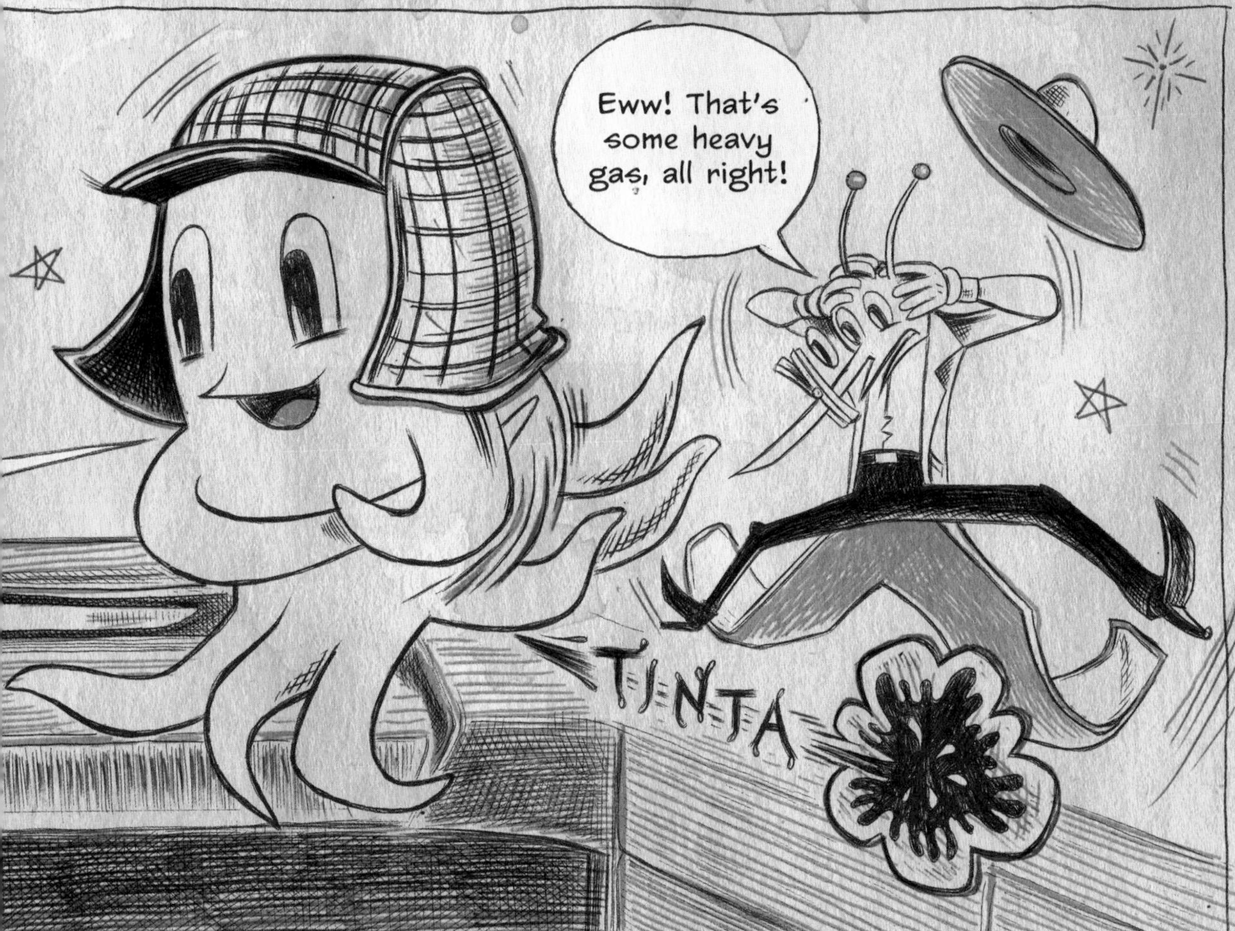
Eww! That's some heavy gas, all right!
TINTA

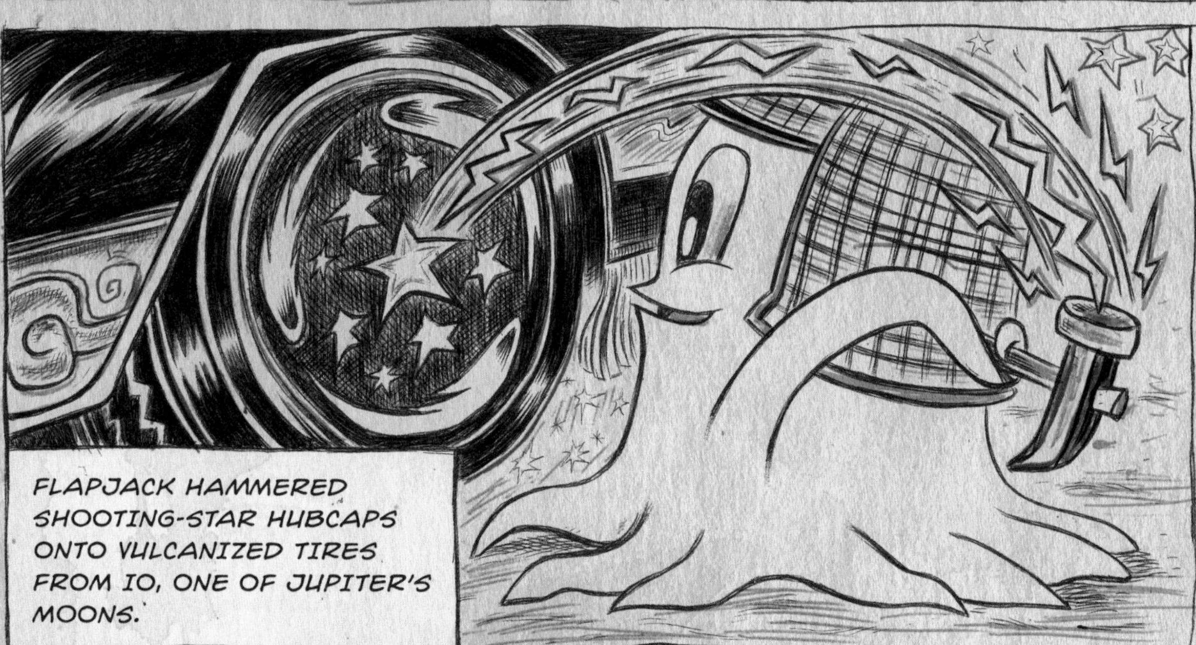
FLAPJACK HAMMERED SHOOTING-STAR HUBCAPS ONTO VULCANIZED TIRES FROM IO, ONE OF JUPITER'S MOONS.

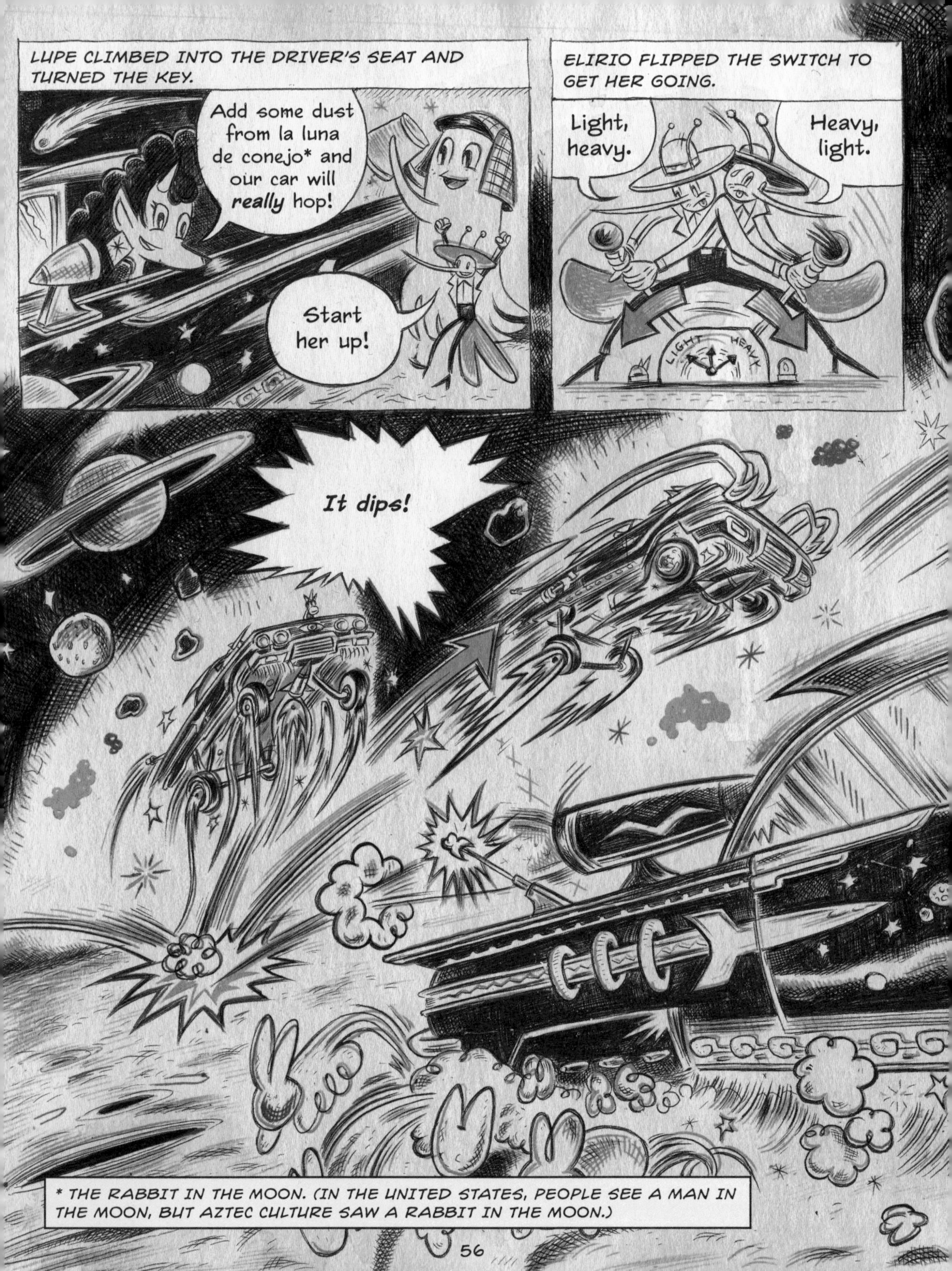

LUPE CLIMBED INTO THE DRIVER'S SEAT AND TURNED THE KEY.
Add some dust from la luna de conejo* and our car will *really* hop!
Start her up!
ELIRIO FLIPPED THE SWITCH TO GET HER GOING.
Light, heavy.
Heavy, light.
LIGHT HEAVY
It dips!
* THE RABBIT IN THE MOON. (IN THE UNITED STATES, PEOPLE SEE A MAN IN THE MOON, BUT AZTEC CULTURE SAW A RABBIT IN THE MOON.)

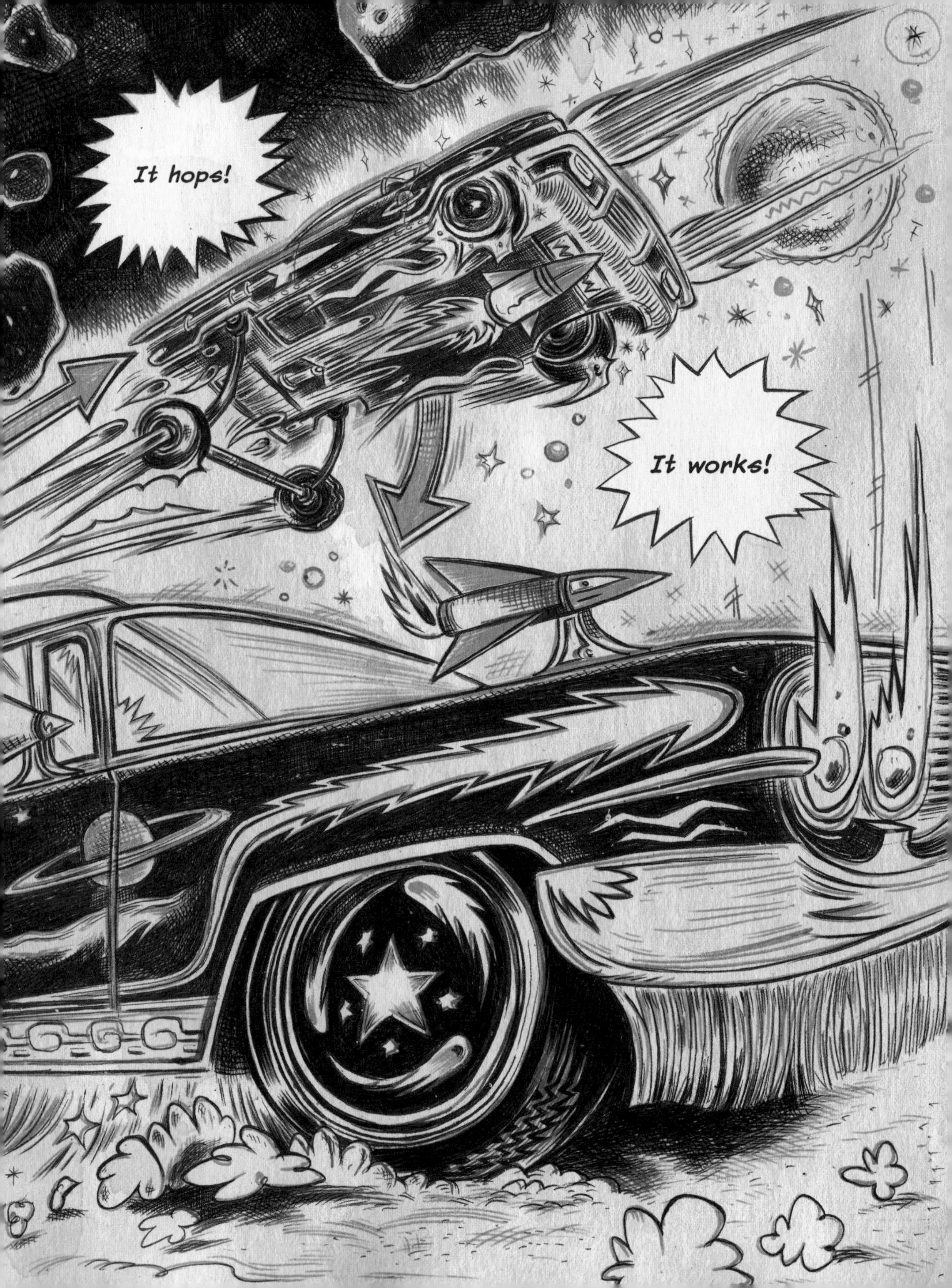
It hops!
It works!

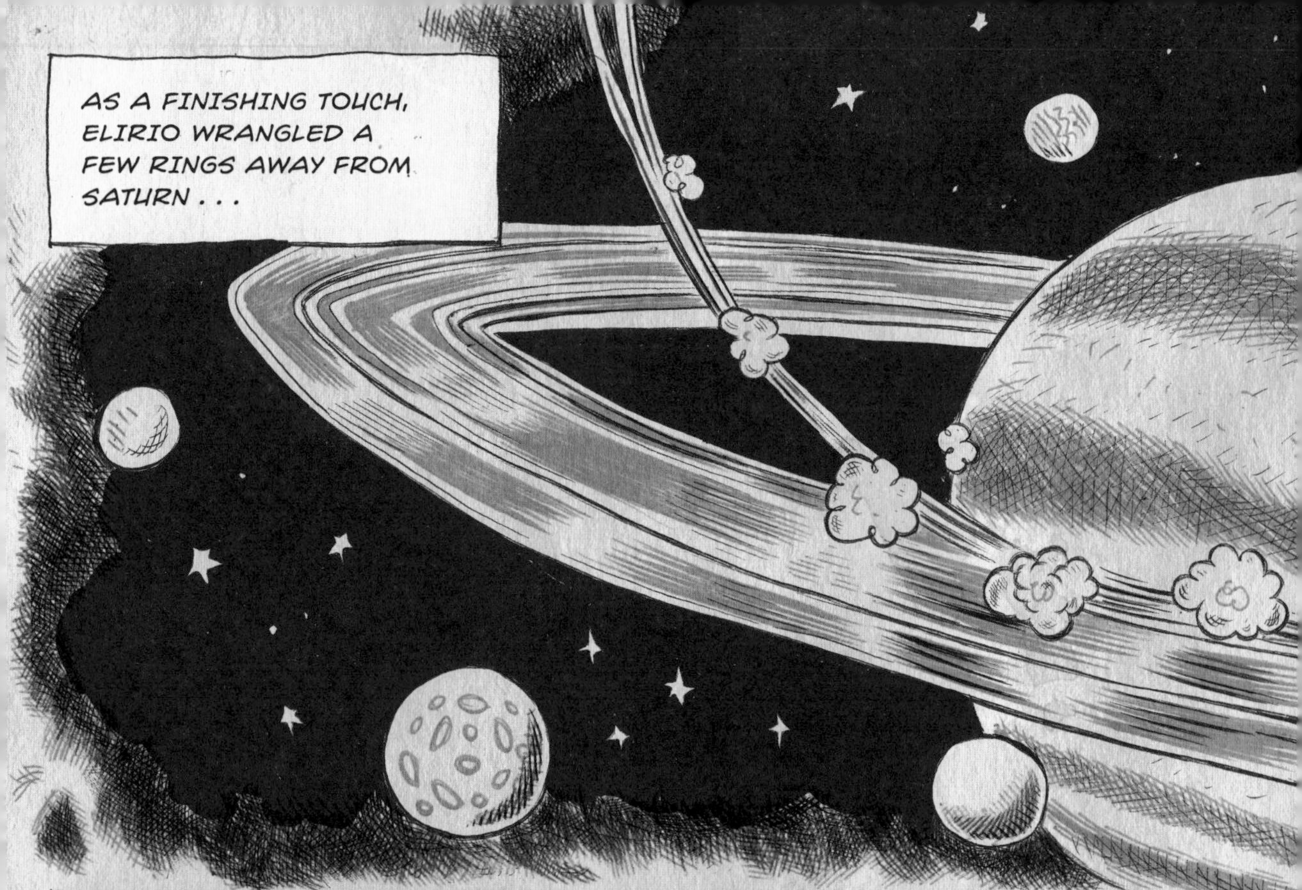
AS A FINISHING TOUCH, ELIRIO WRANGLED A FEW RINGS AWAY FROM SATURN . . .

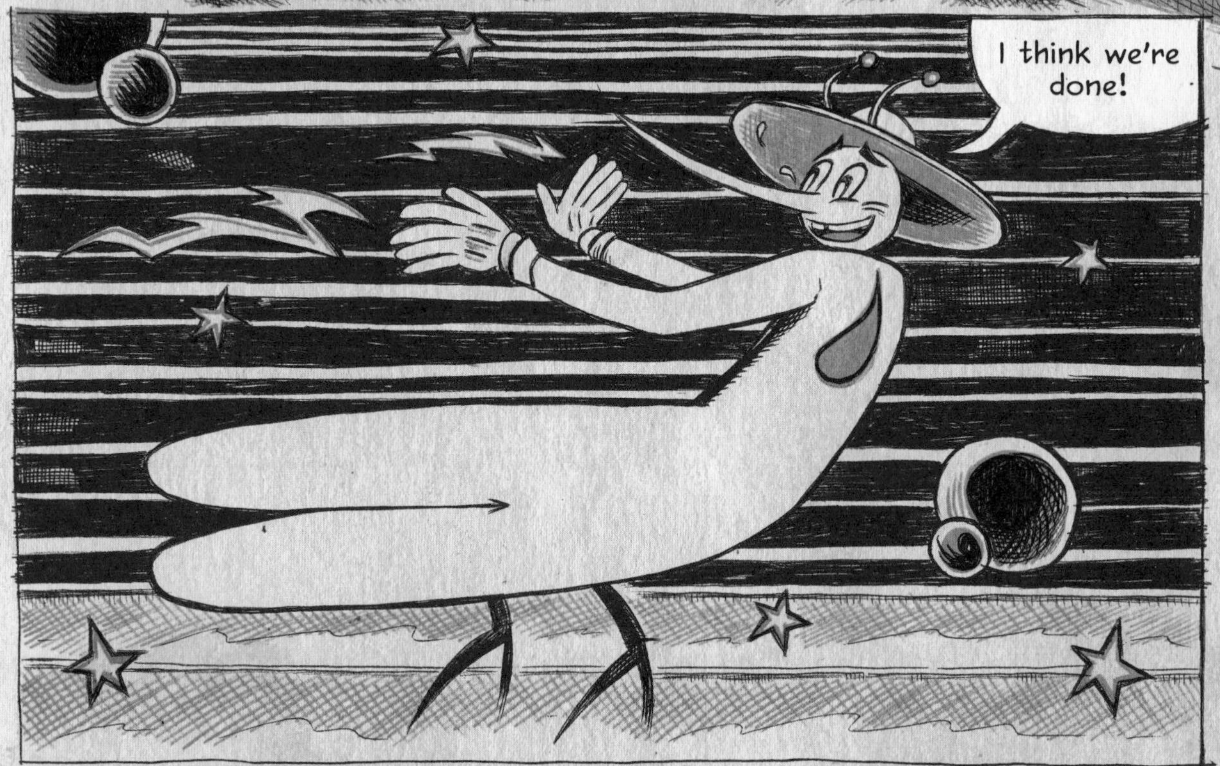
I think we're done!

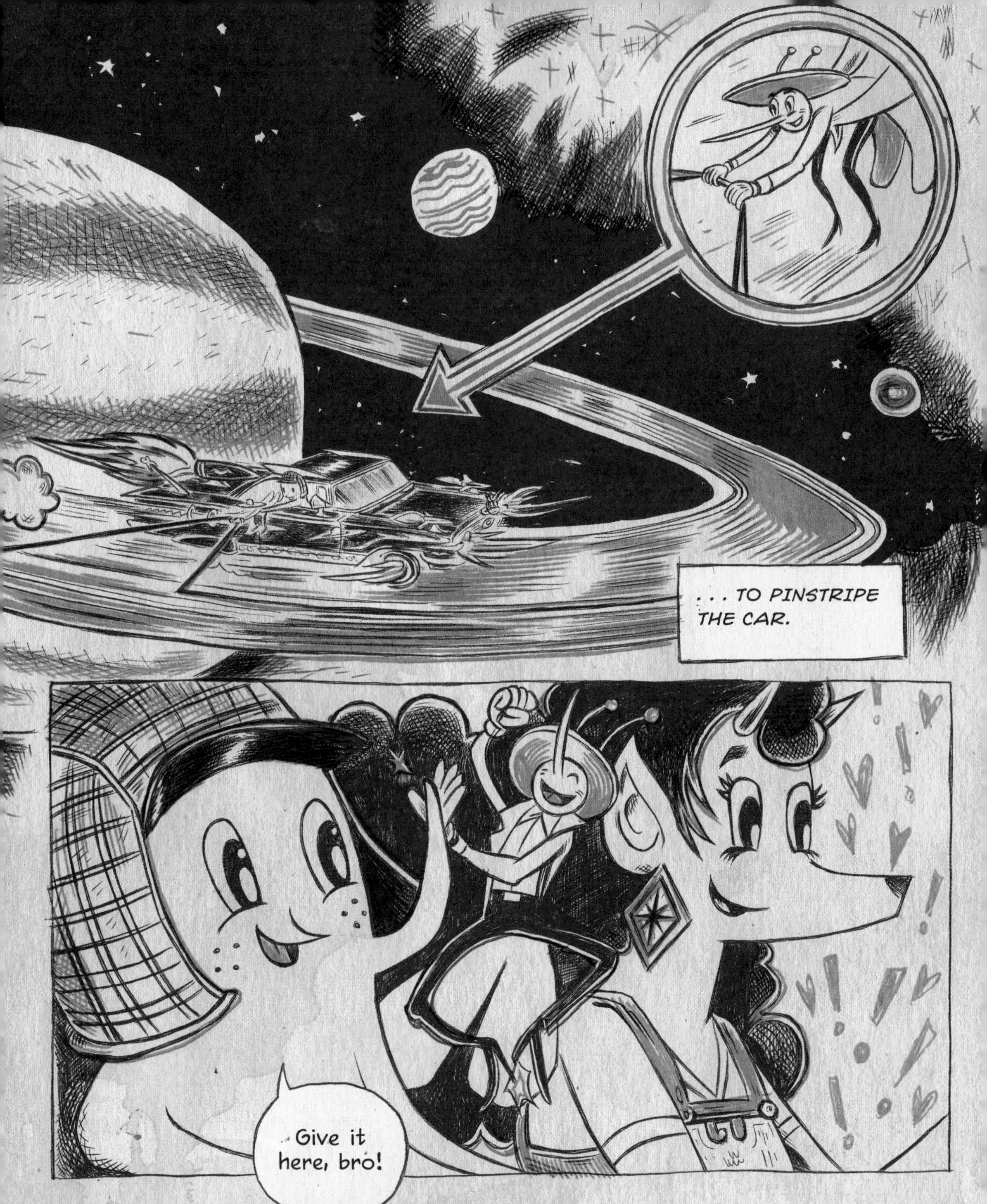
. . . TO PINSTRIPE THE CAR.
Give it here, bro!

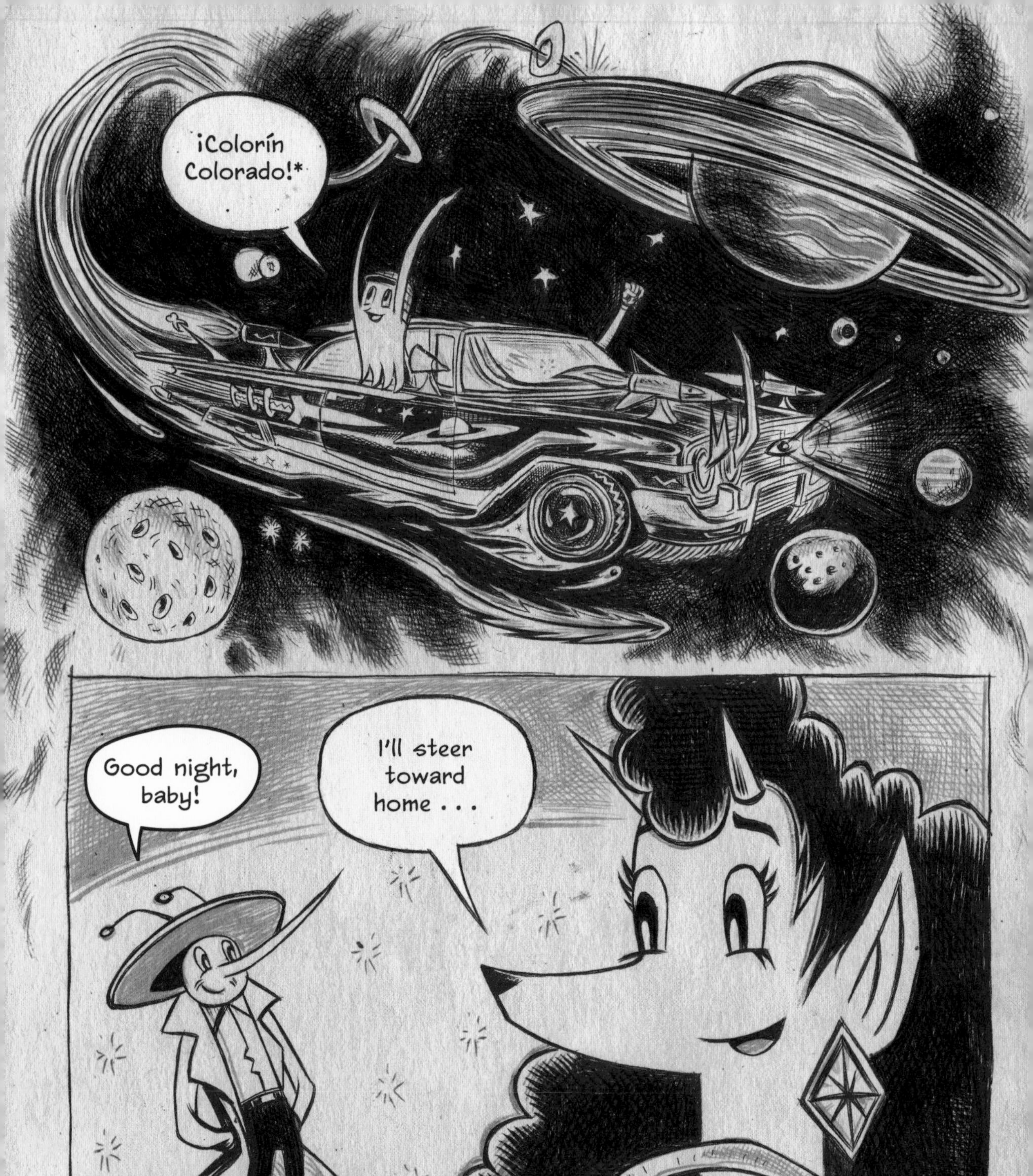
¡Colorín Colorado!*
Good night, baby!
I'll steer toward home . . .

* JUST AS YOU BEGIN A STORY, "ONCE UPON A TIME . . . ," THESE ARE NONSENSE WORDS THAT MEAN IT IS THE END OF THE STORY.

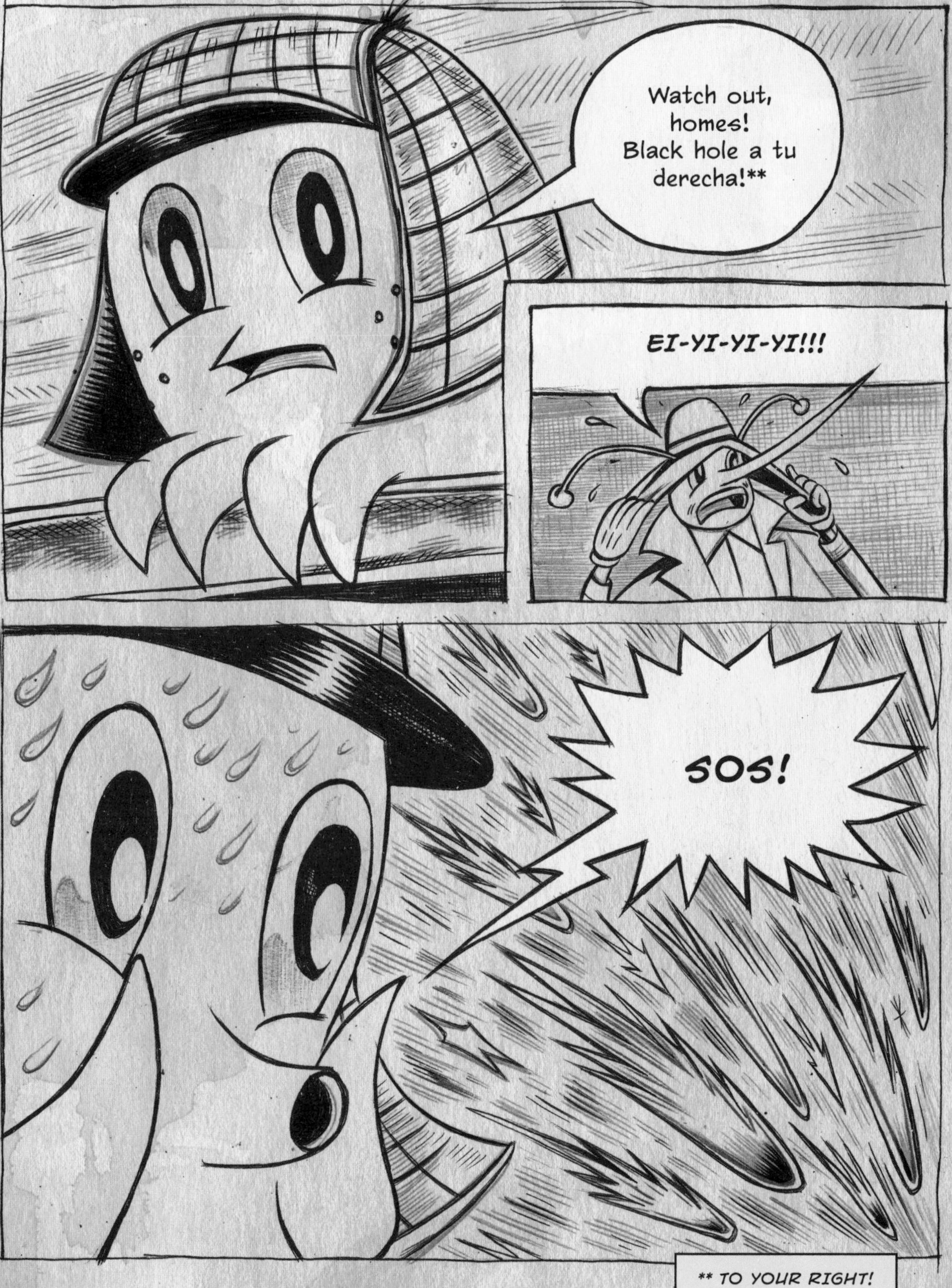
Watch out, homes! Black hole a tu derecha!**
EI-YI-YI-YI!!!
SOS!
** TO YOUR RIGHT!

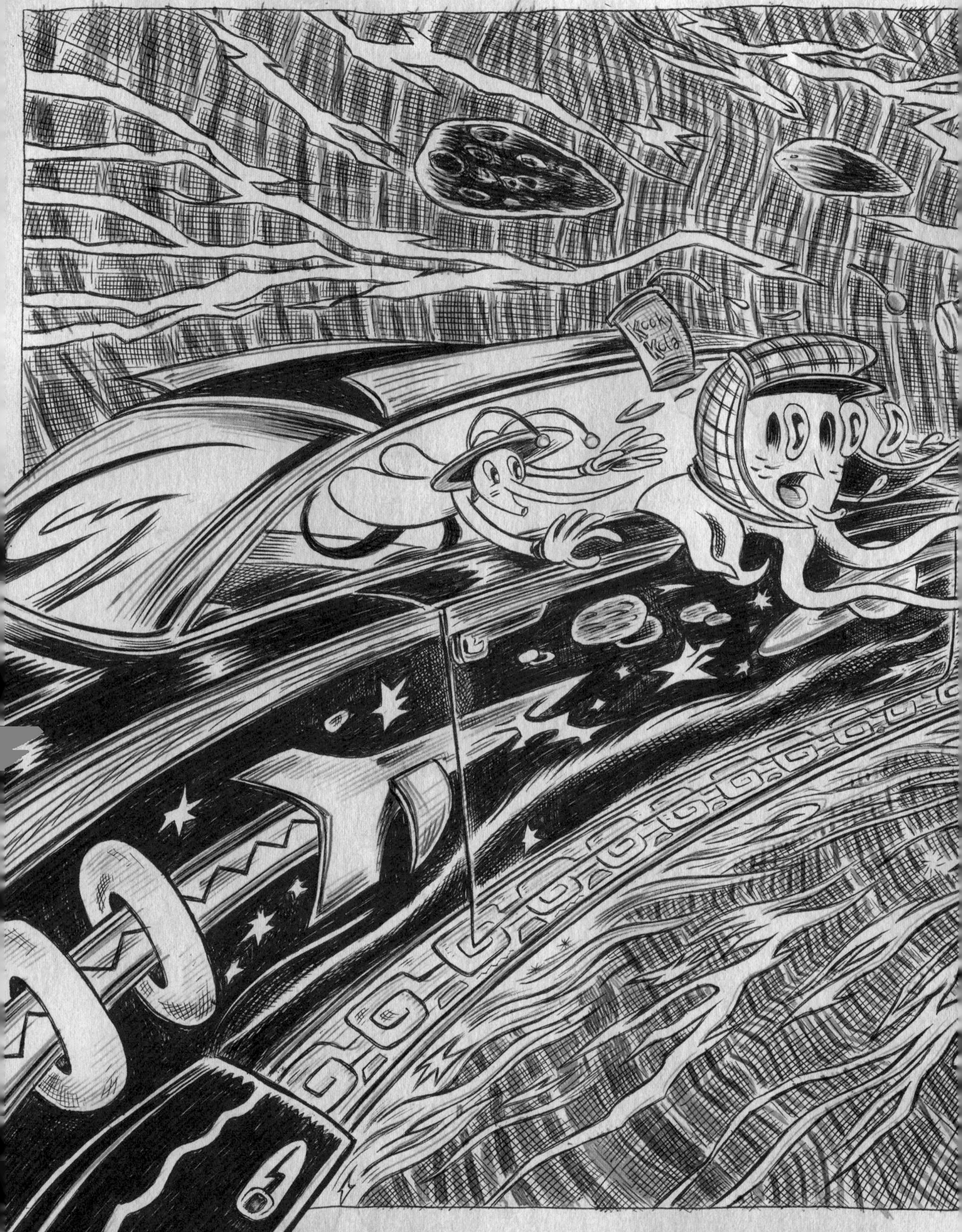
Kooky Kola

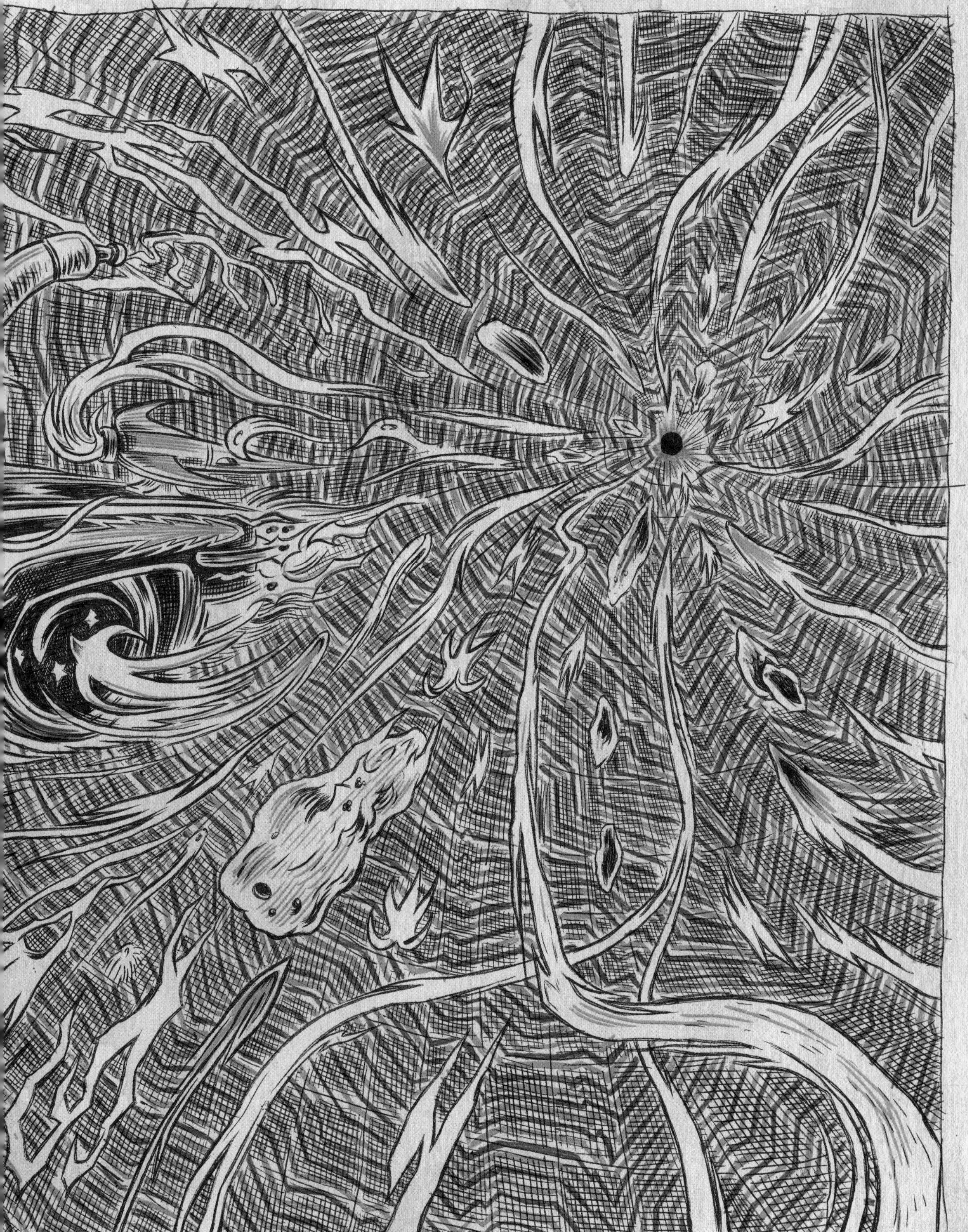

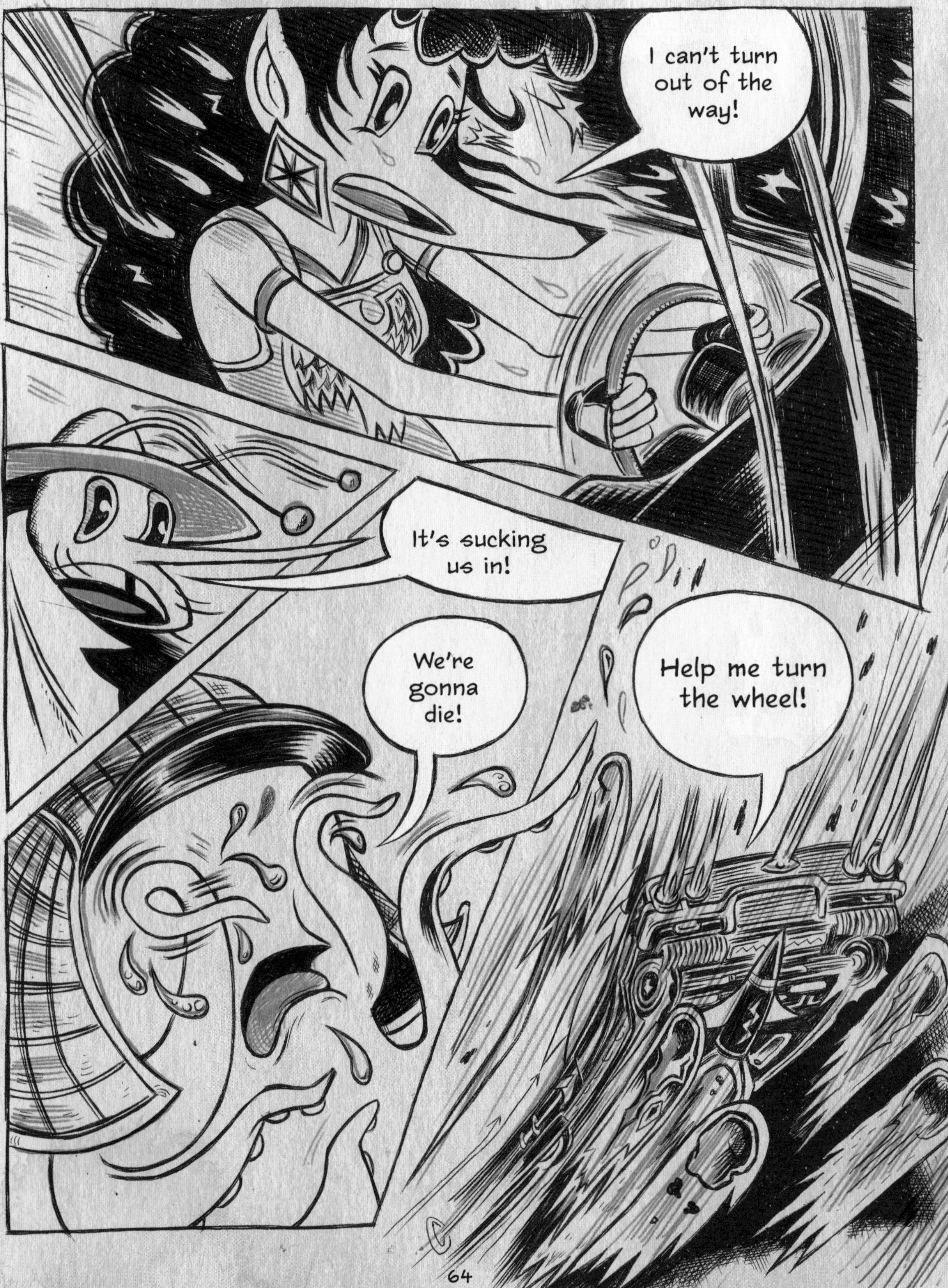
I can't turn out of the way!
It's sucking us in!
We're gonna die!
Help me turn the wheel!

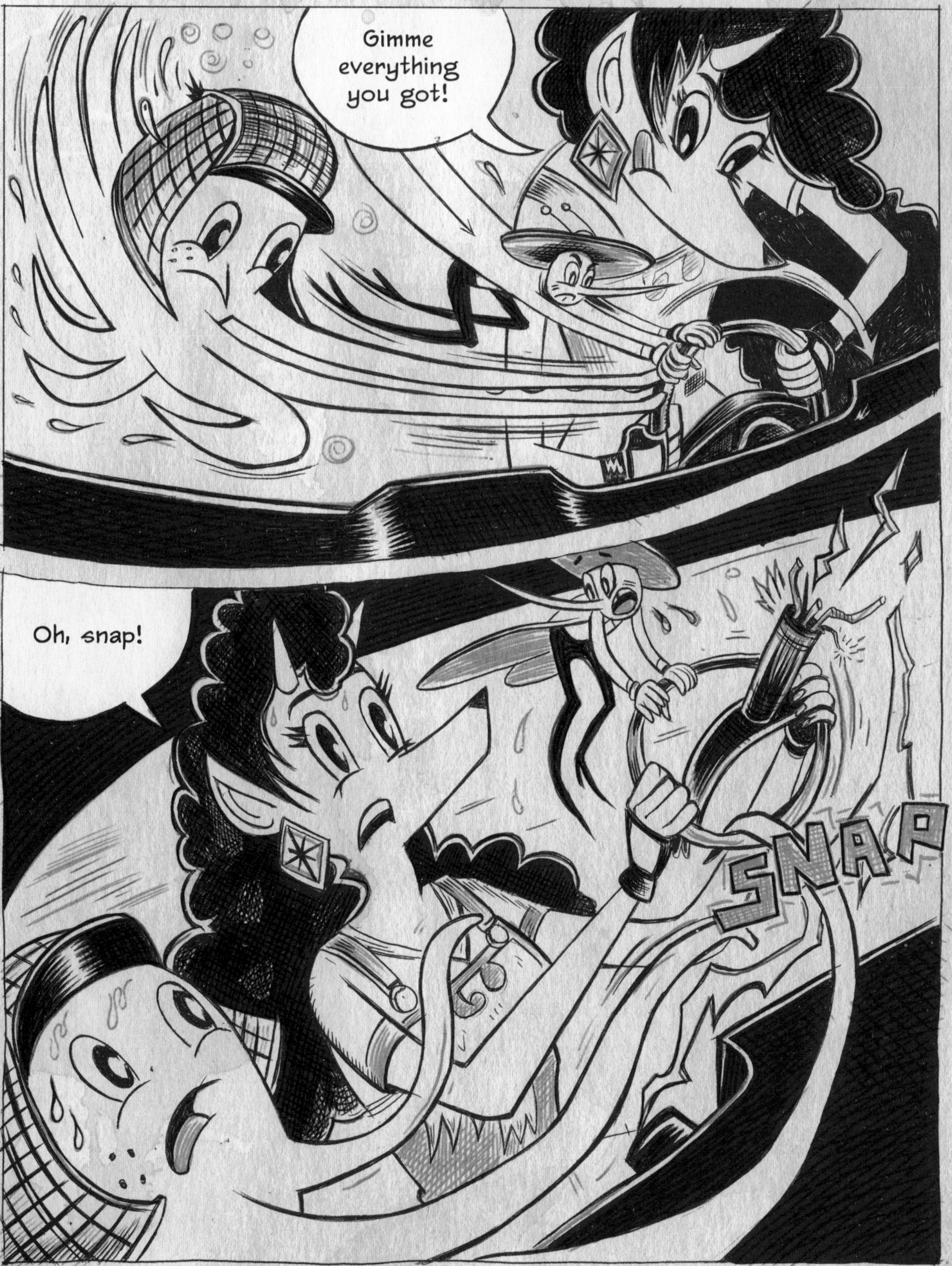
Gimme everything you got!
Oh, snap!
SNAP

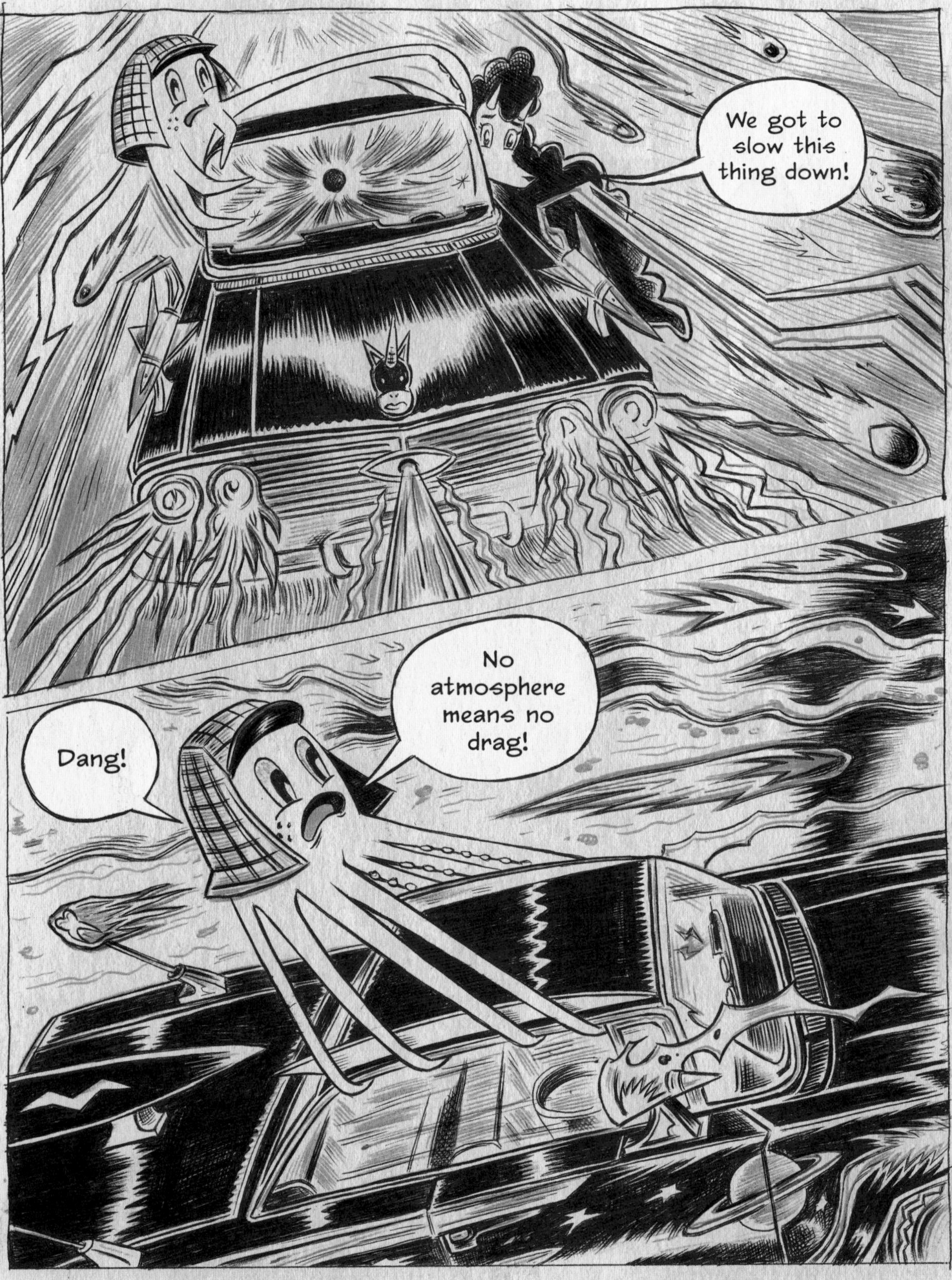
We got to slow this thing down!
Dang!
No atmosphere means no drag!

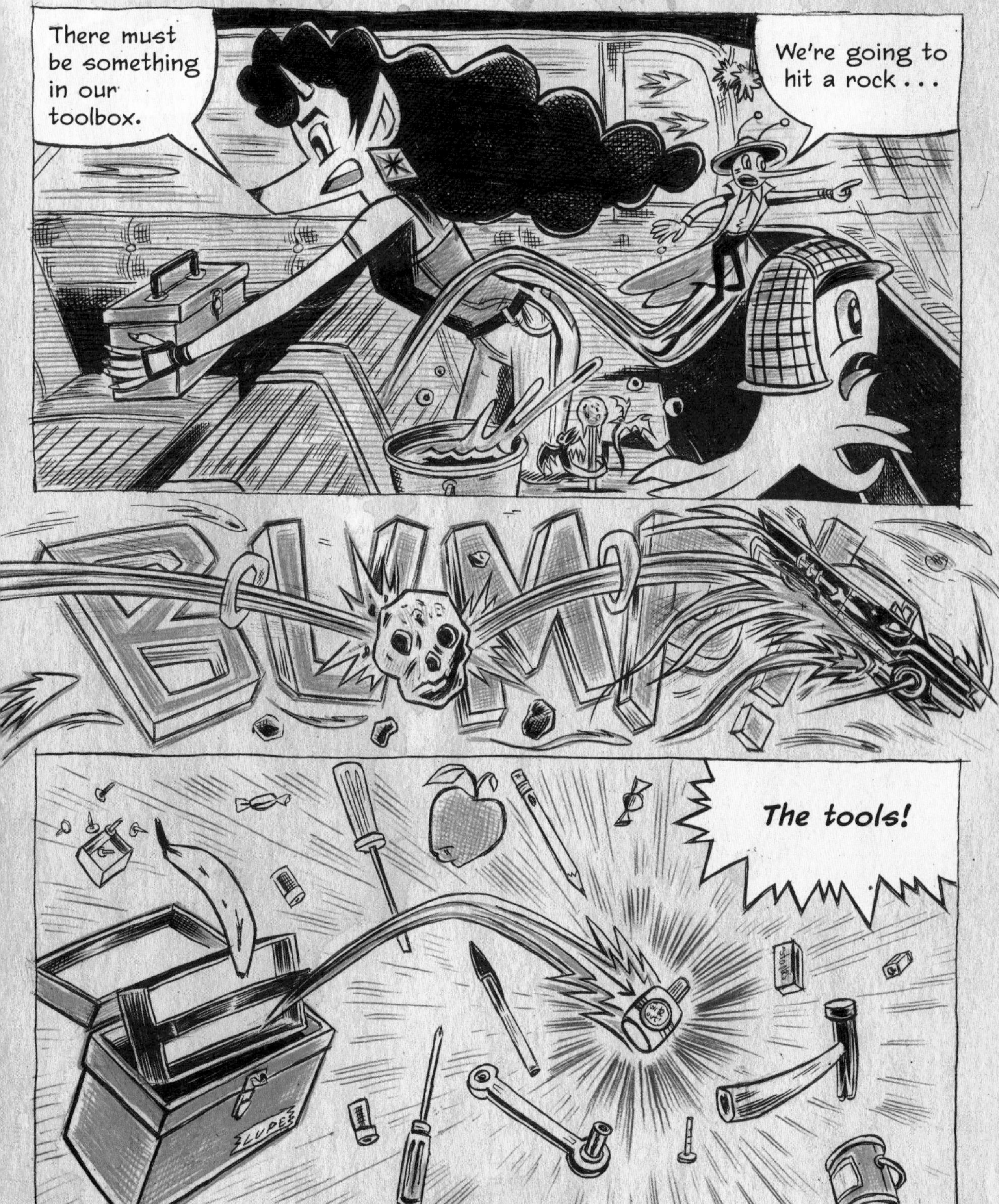
There must be something in our toolbox.
We're going to hit a rock . . .
BUMP
The tools!
LUPE

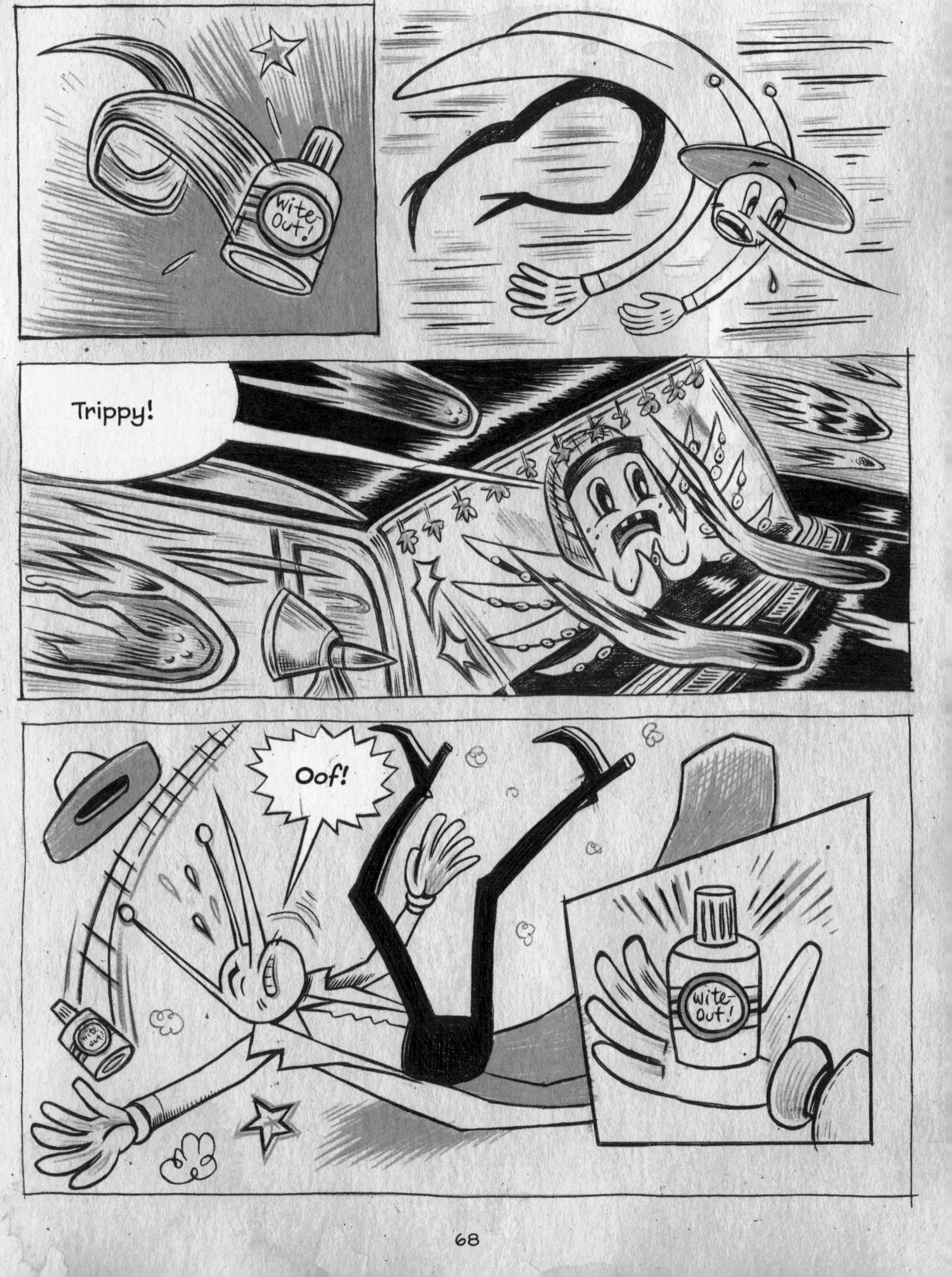
wite-out!
Trippy!
Oof!
wite-out!
wite-out!

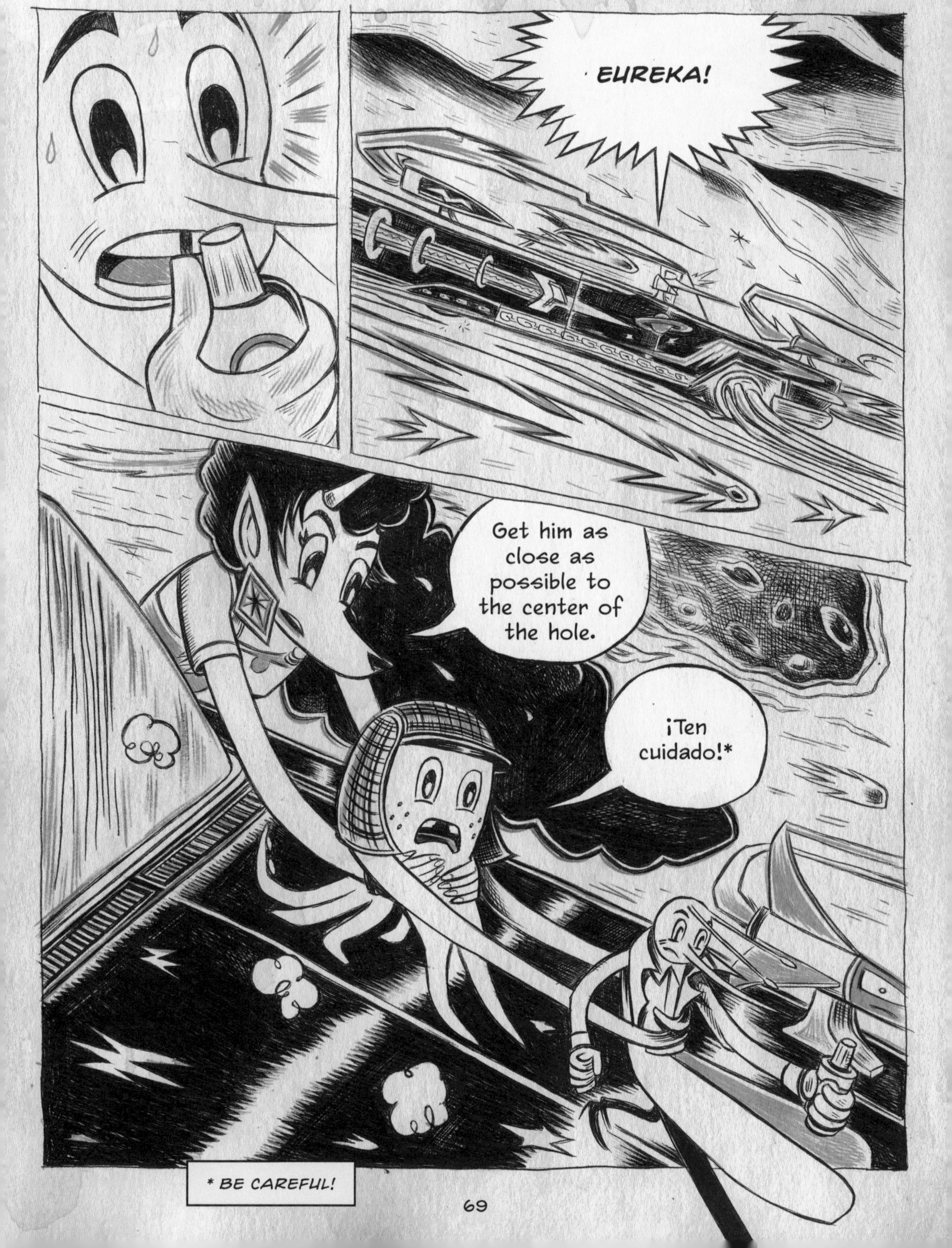
EUREKA!
Get him as close as possible to the center of the hole.
¡Ten cuidado!*

* BE CAREFUL!

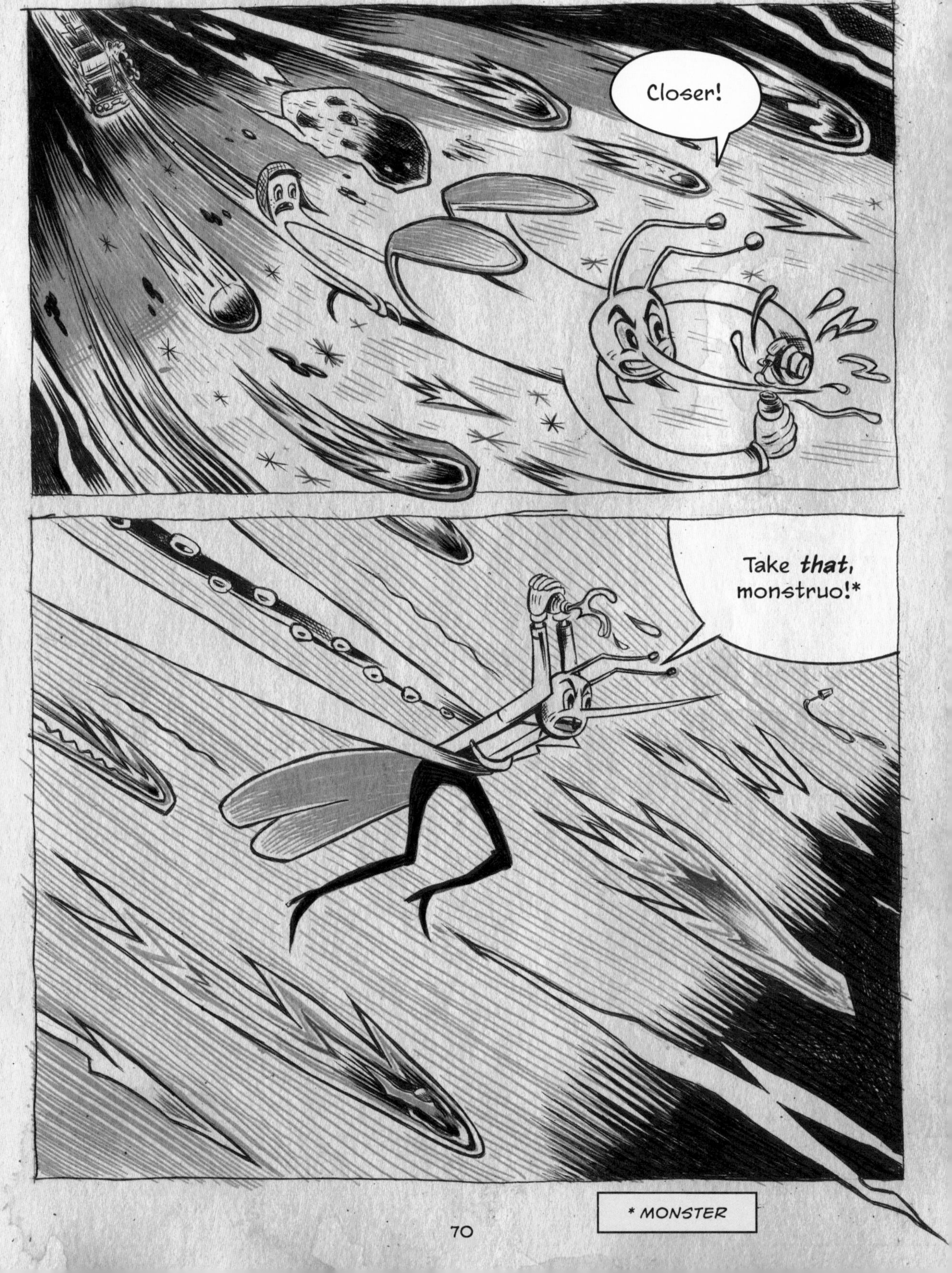
Closer!
Take *that*, monstruo!*

* MONSTER

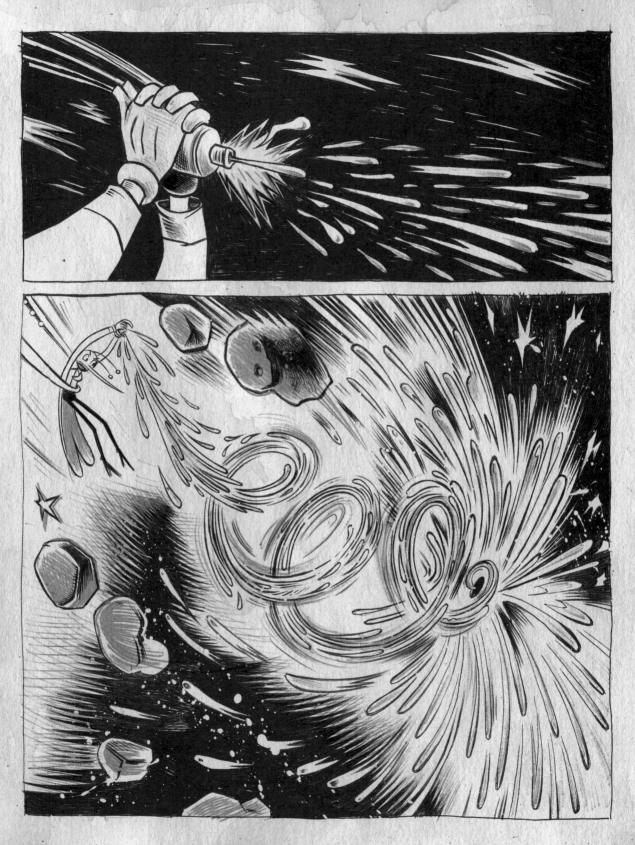

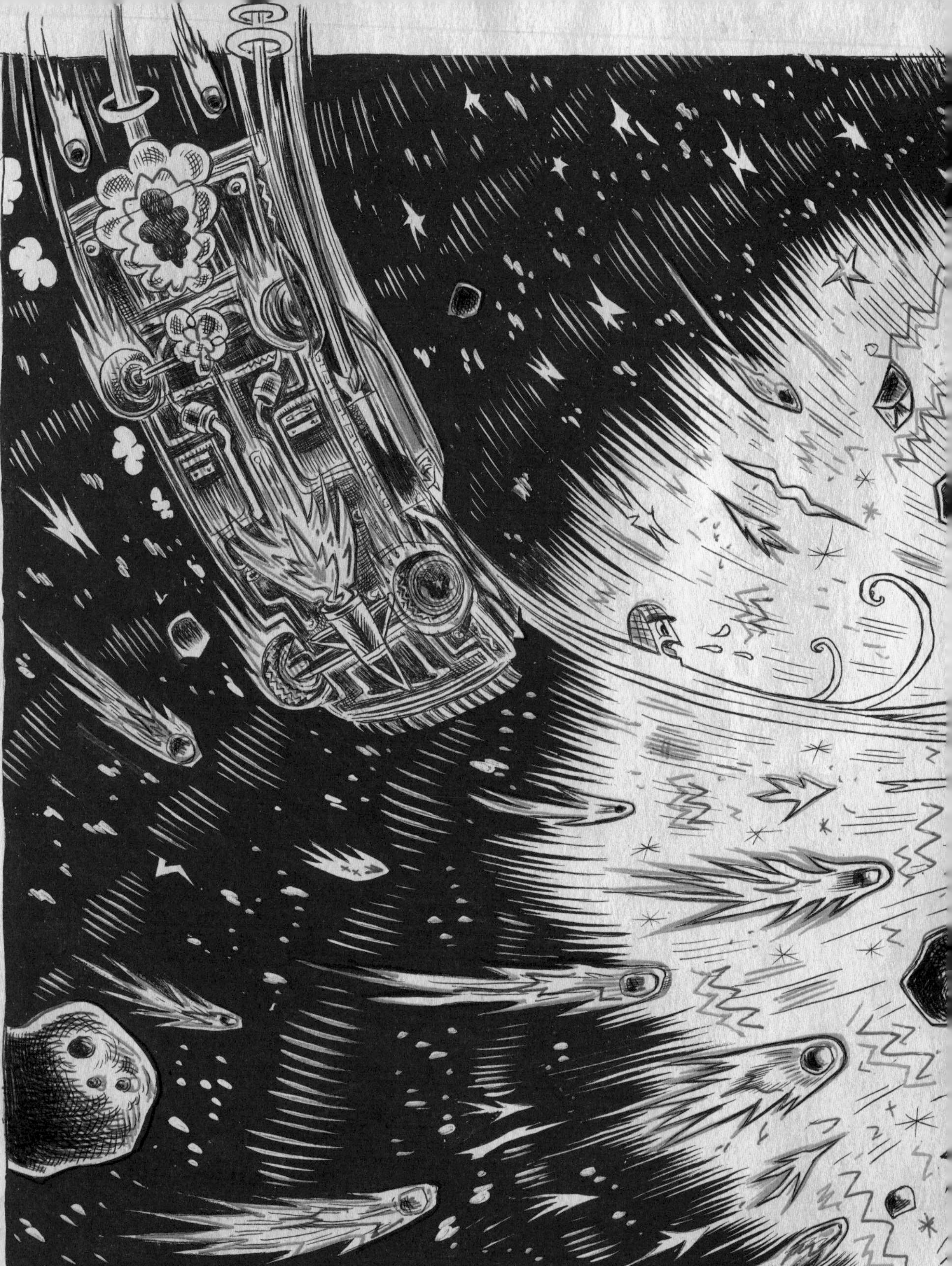

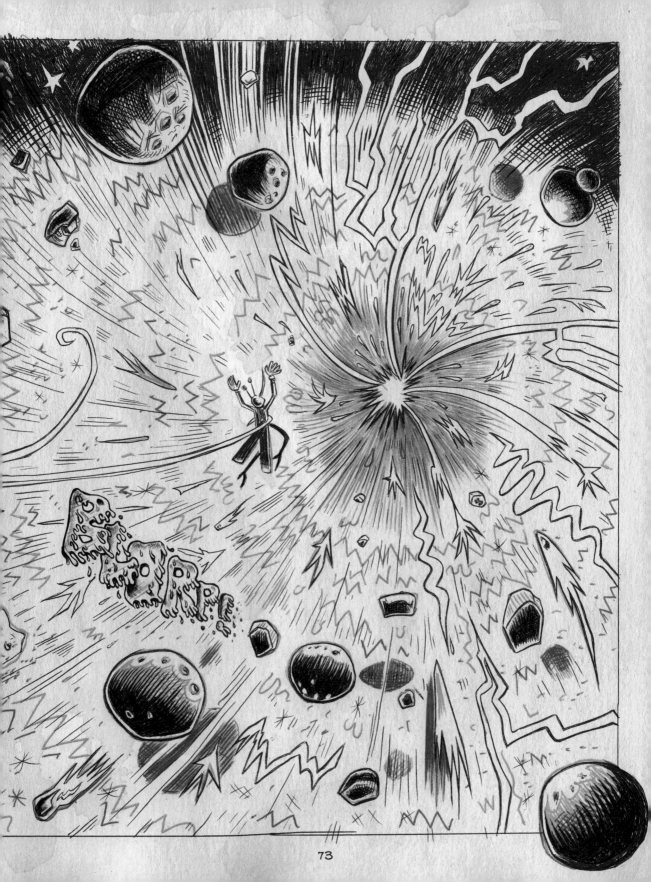

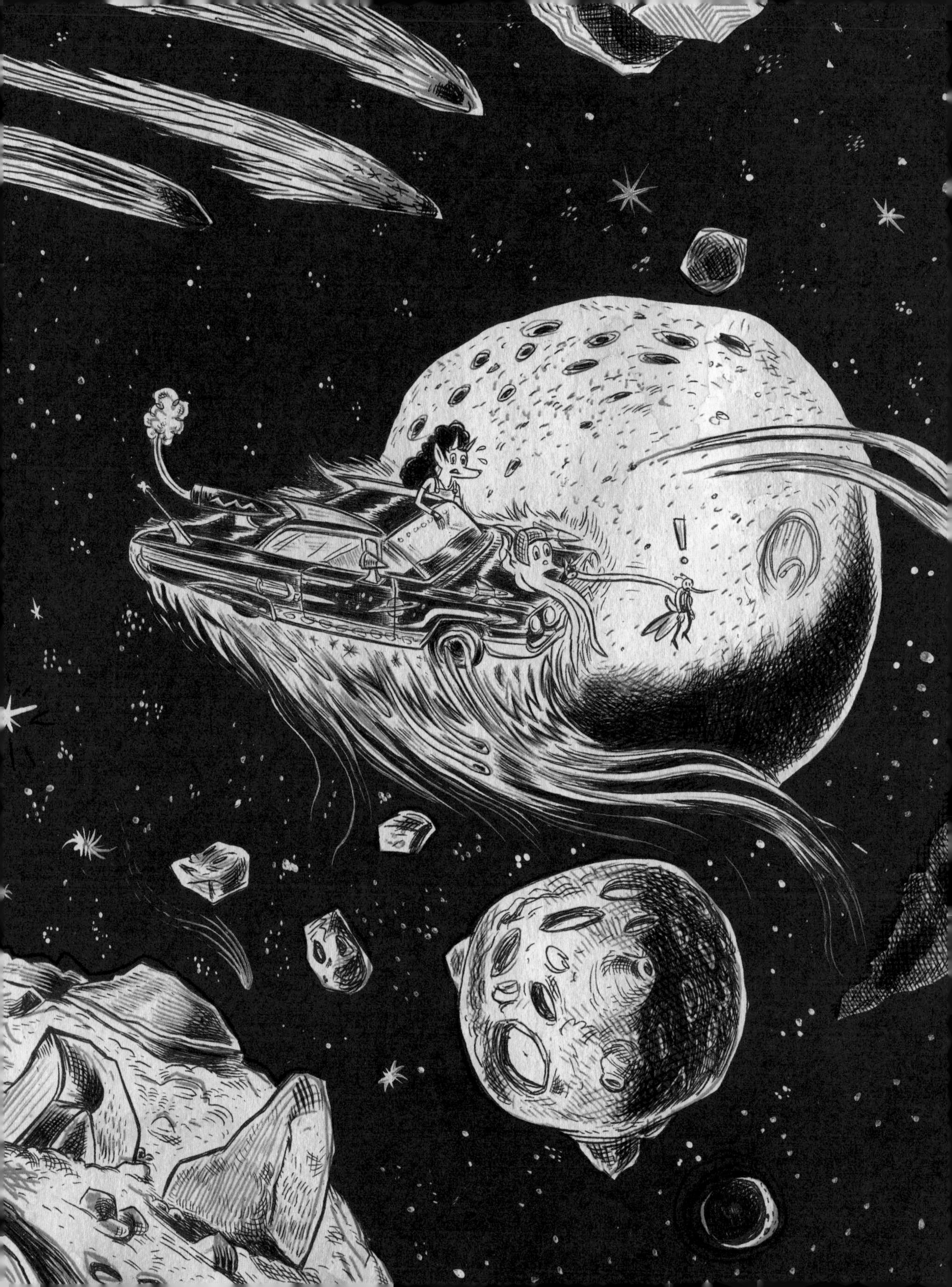
!

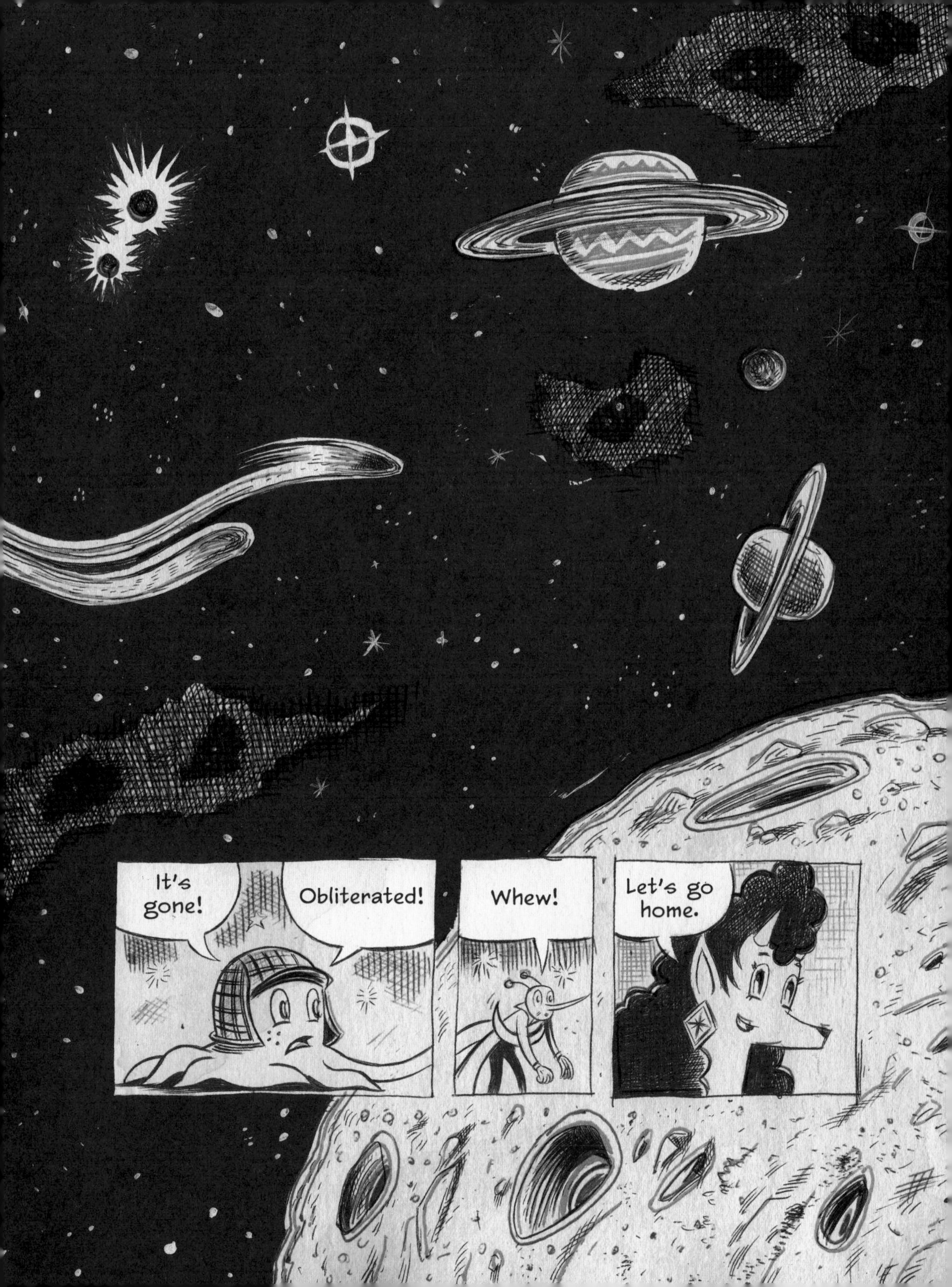
It's gone!
Obliterated!
Whew!
Let's go home.

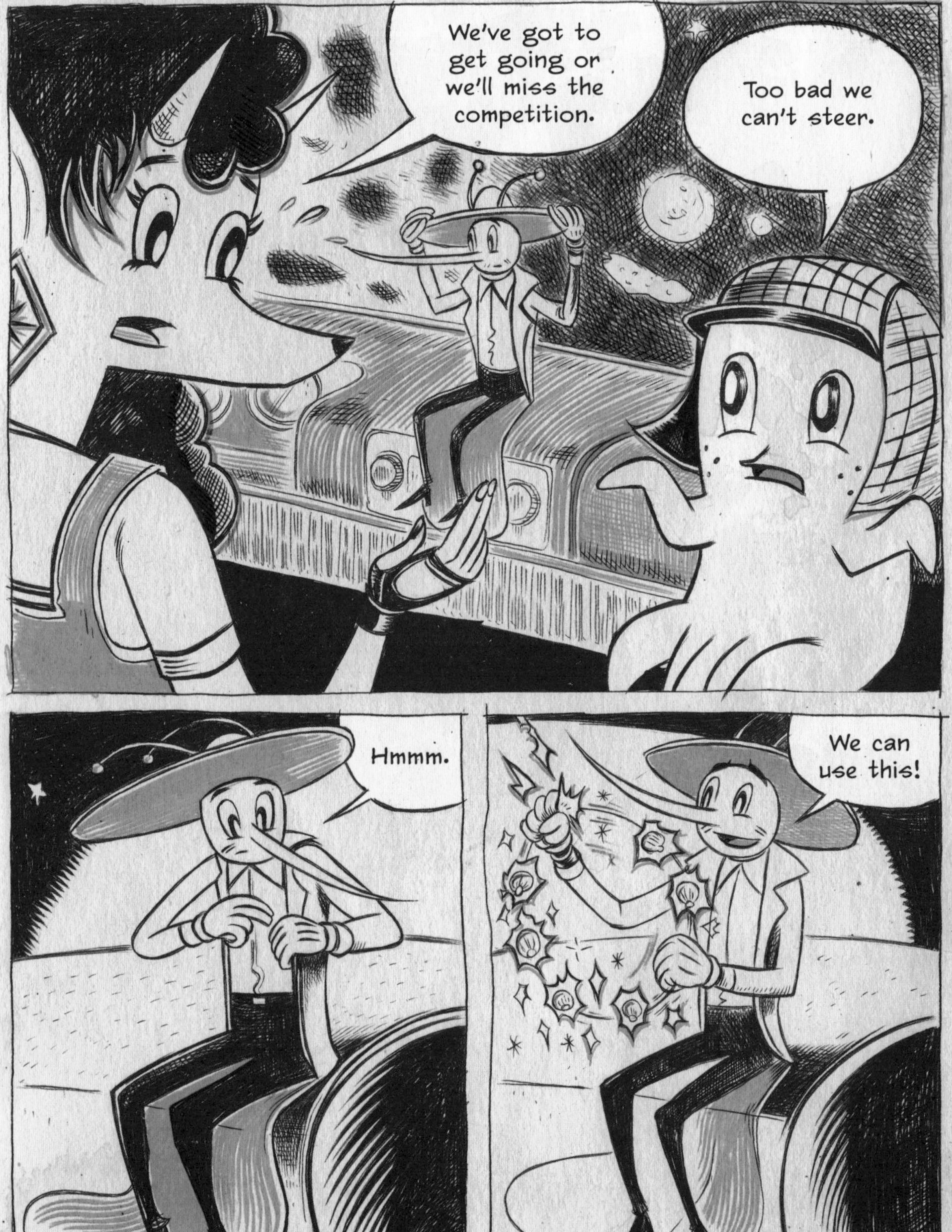
We've got to get going or we'll miss the competition.
Too bad we can't steer.
Hmmm.
We can use this!

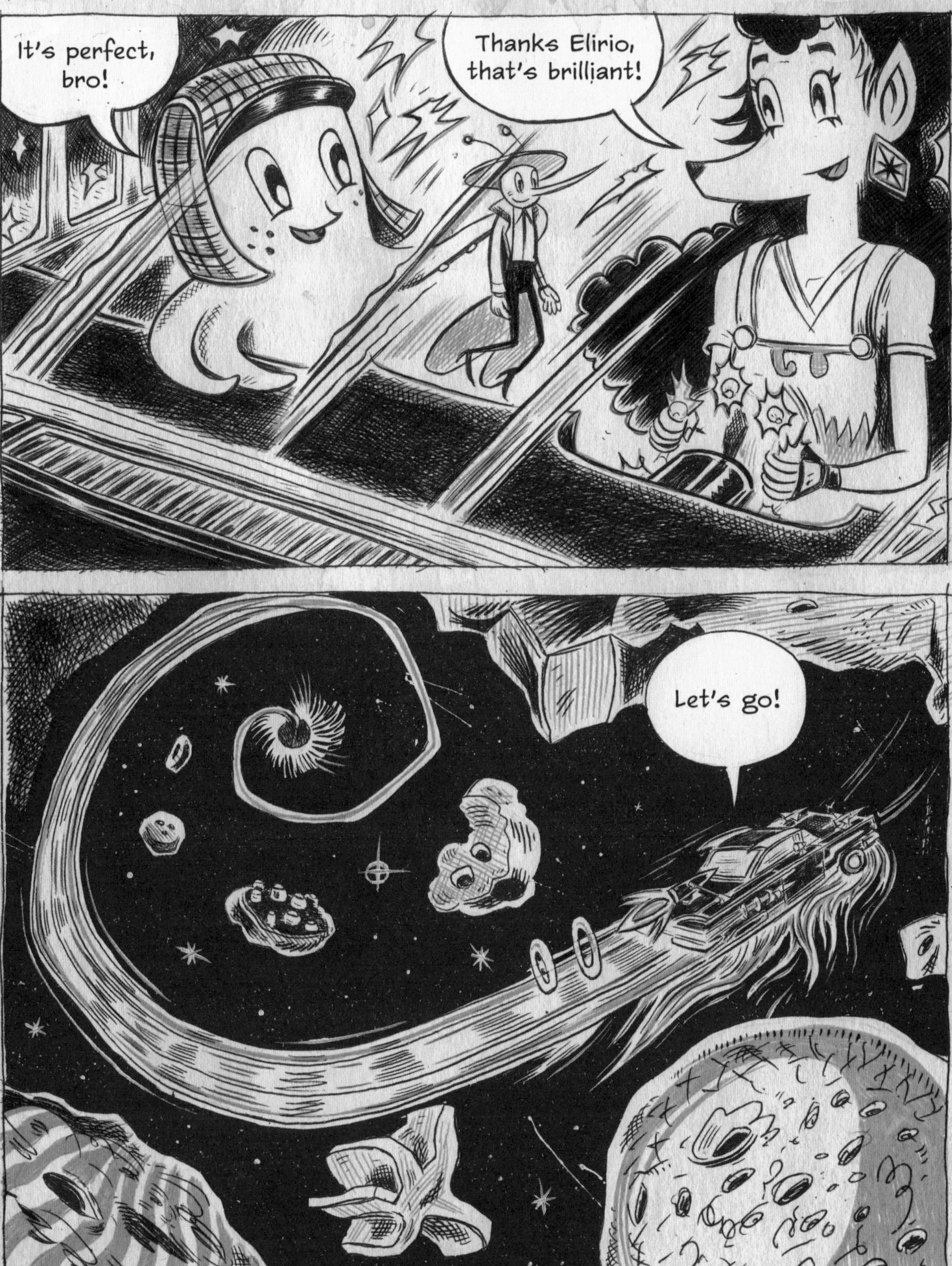
It's perfect, bro!
Thanks Elirio, that's brilliant!
Let's go!

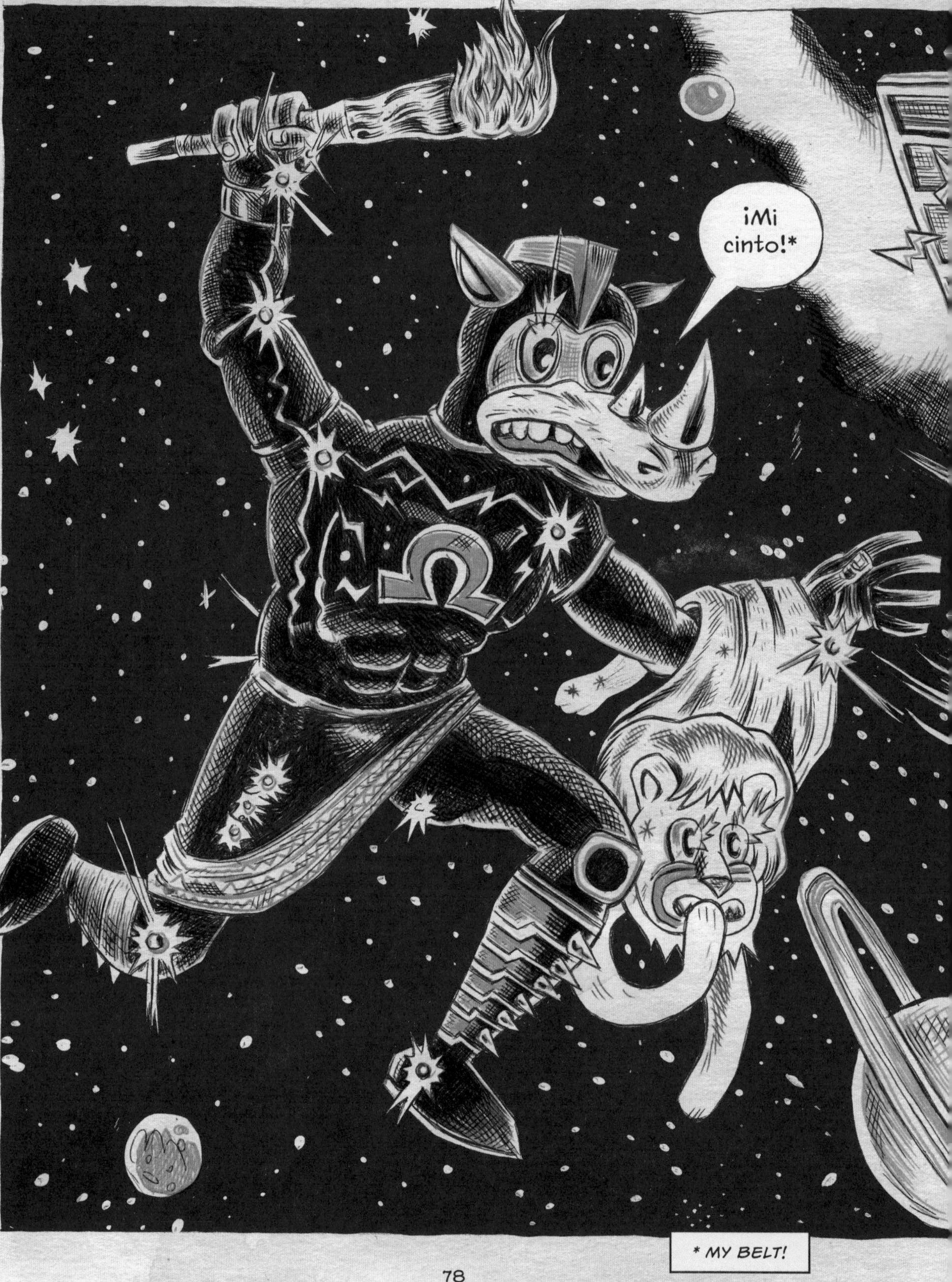
¡Mi cinto!*

* MY BELT!

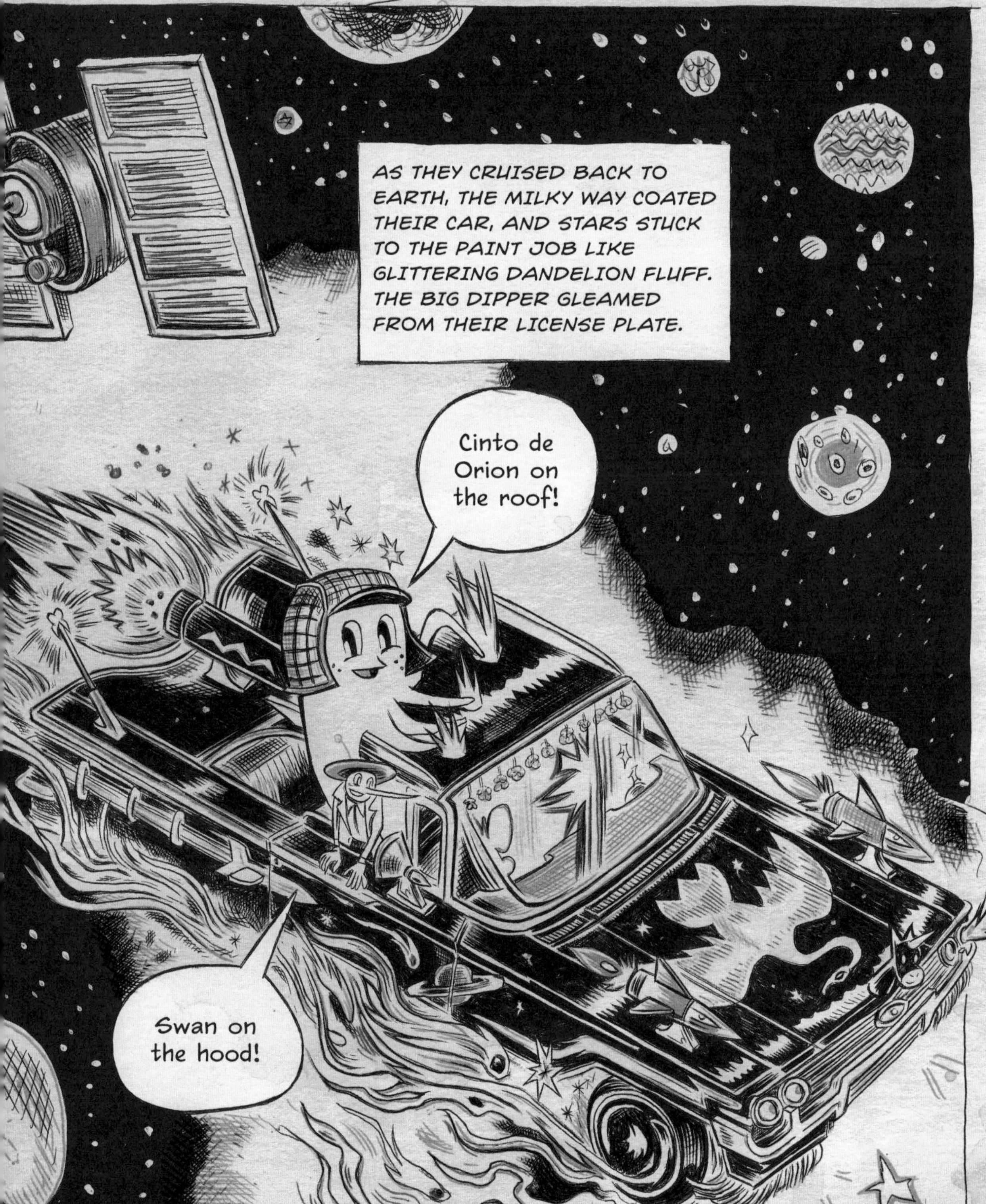
AS THEY CRUISED BACK TO EARTH, THE MILKY WAY COATED THEIR CAR, AND STARS STUCK TO THE PAINT JOB LIKE GLITTERING DANDELION FLUFF. THE BIG DIPPER GLEAMED FROM THEIR LICENSE PLATE.
Cinto de Orion on the roof!
Swan on the hood!

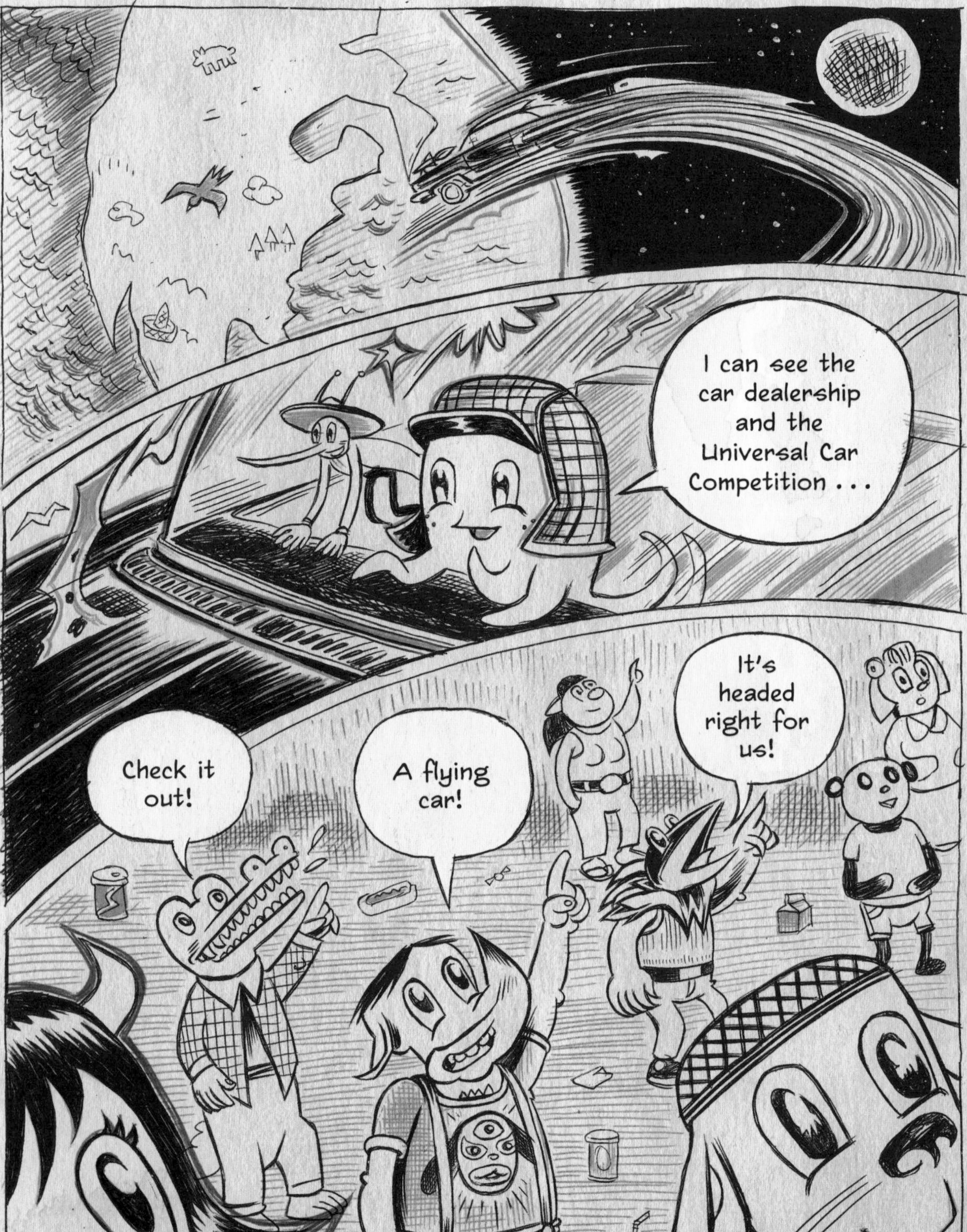
I can see the car dealership and the Universal Car Competition . . .
Check it out!
A flying car!
It's headed right for us!

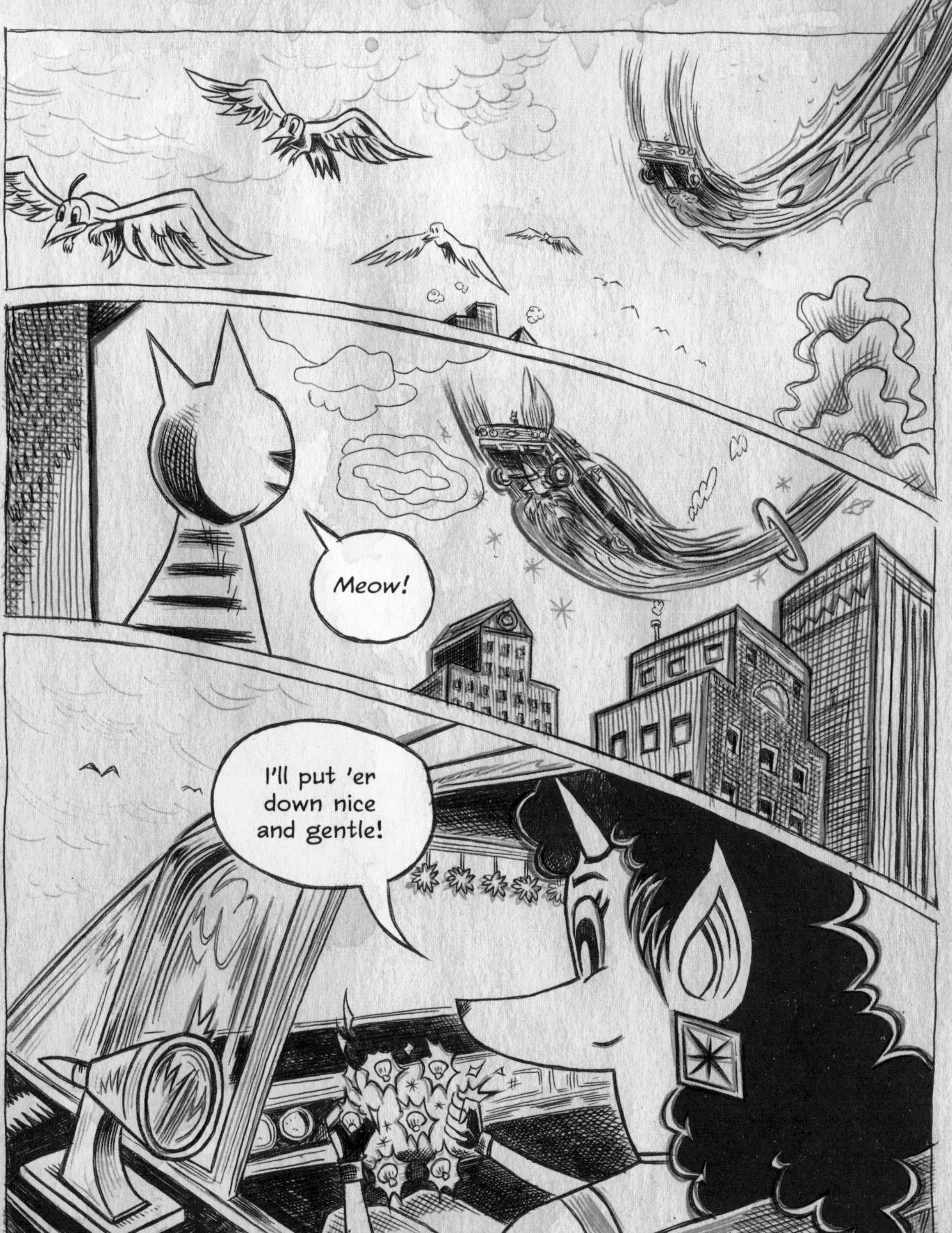
Meow!
I'll put 'er down nice and gentle!

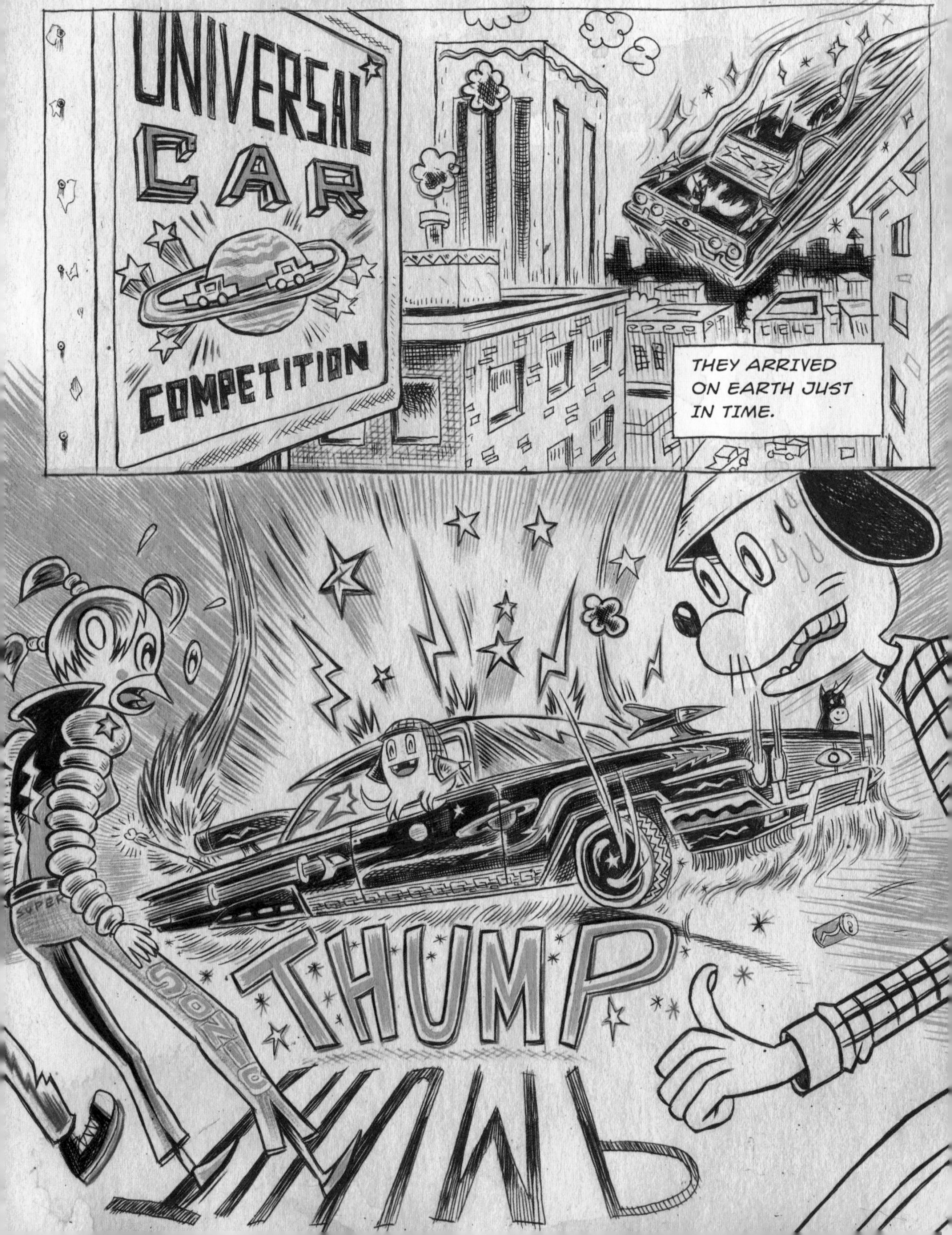
UNIVERSAL
CAR
COMPETITION
THEY ARRIVED ON EARTH JUST IN TIME.
THUMP

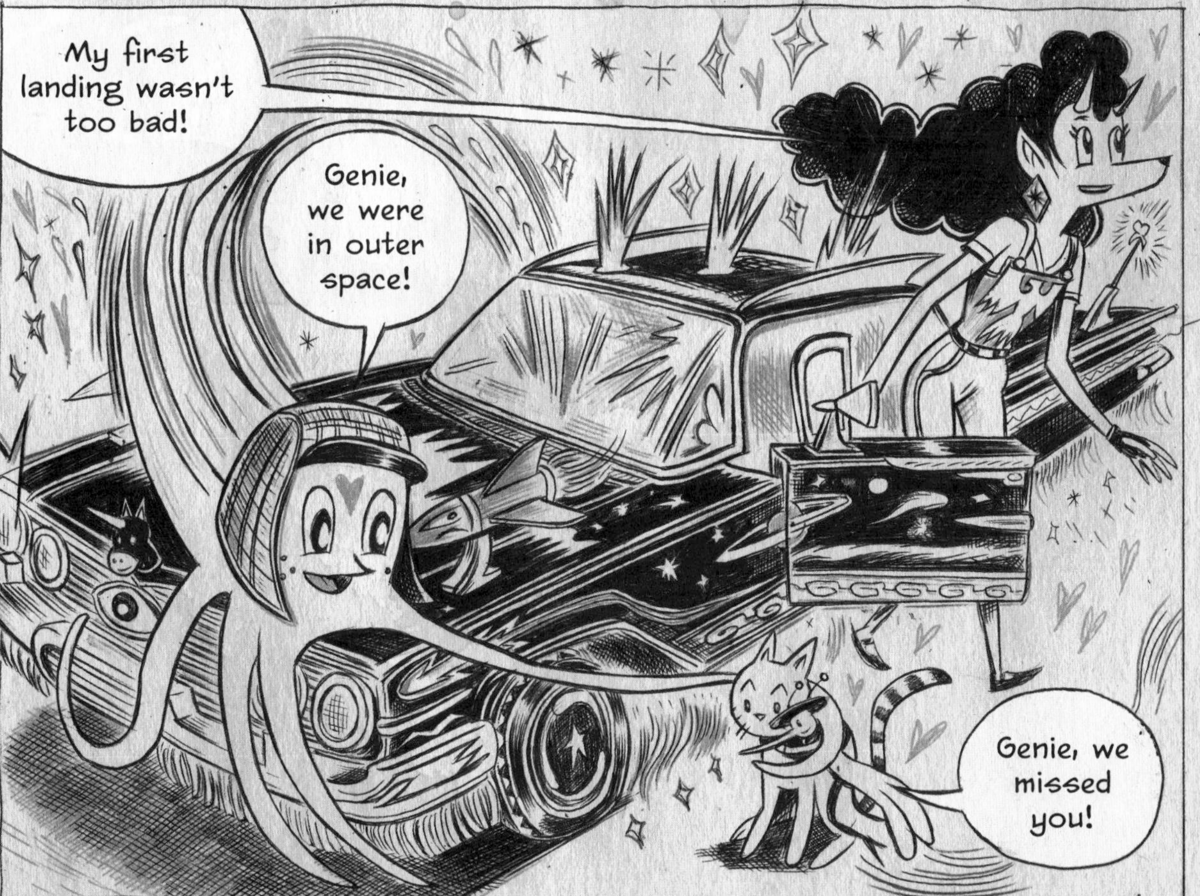
My first landing wasn't too bad!
Genie, we were in outer space!
Genie, we missed you!

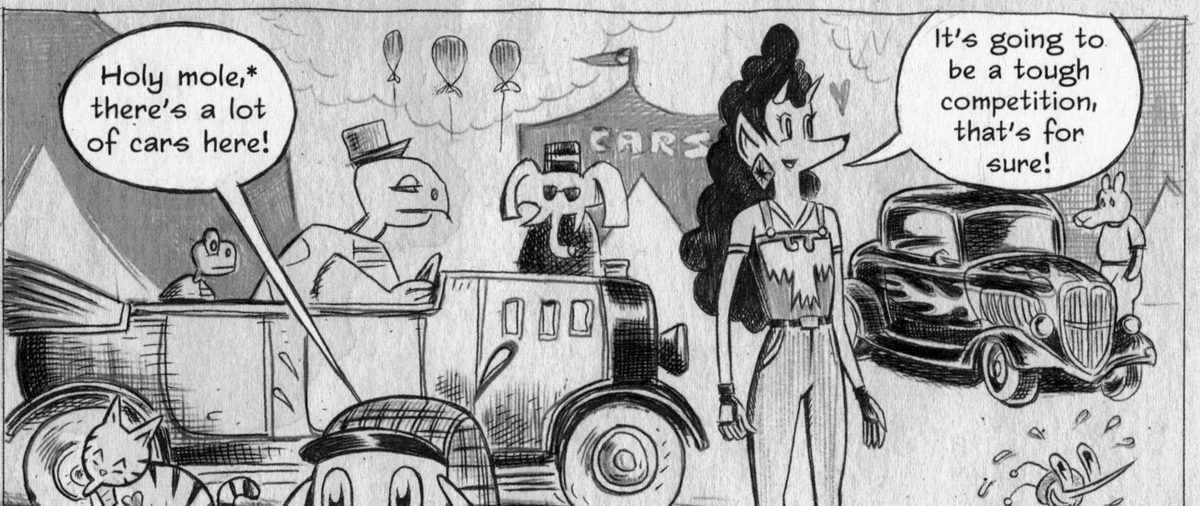
Holy mole,* there's a lot of cars here!
It's going to be a tough competition, that's for sure!
CARS

* THICK MEXICAN SAUCE FOR MEAT MADE OF MANY INGREDIENTS, INCLUDING PEPPERS AND CHOCOLATE

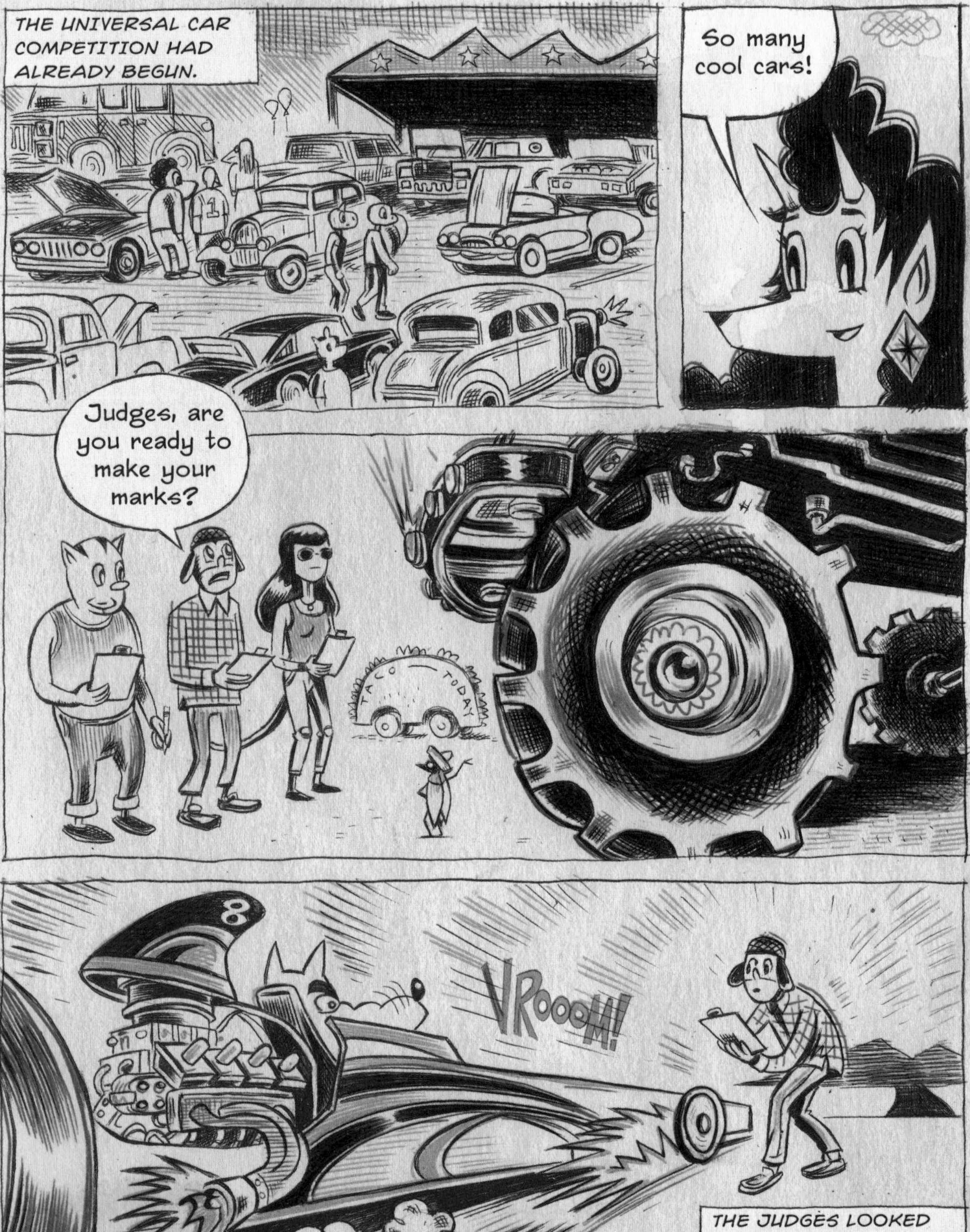
THE UNIVERSAL CAR COMPETITION HAD ALREADY BEGUN.
So many cool cars!
Judges, are you ready to make your marks?
TACO TODAY
8
VROOOM!
THE JUDGES LOOKED AT CARS THAT BLASTED BY FAST,

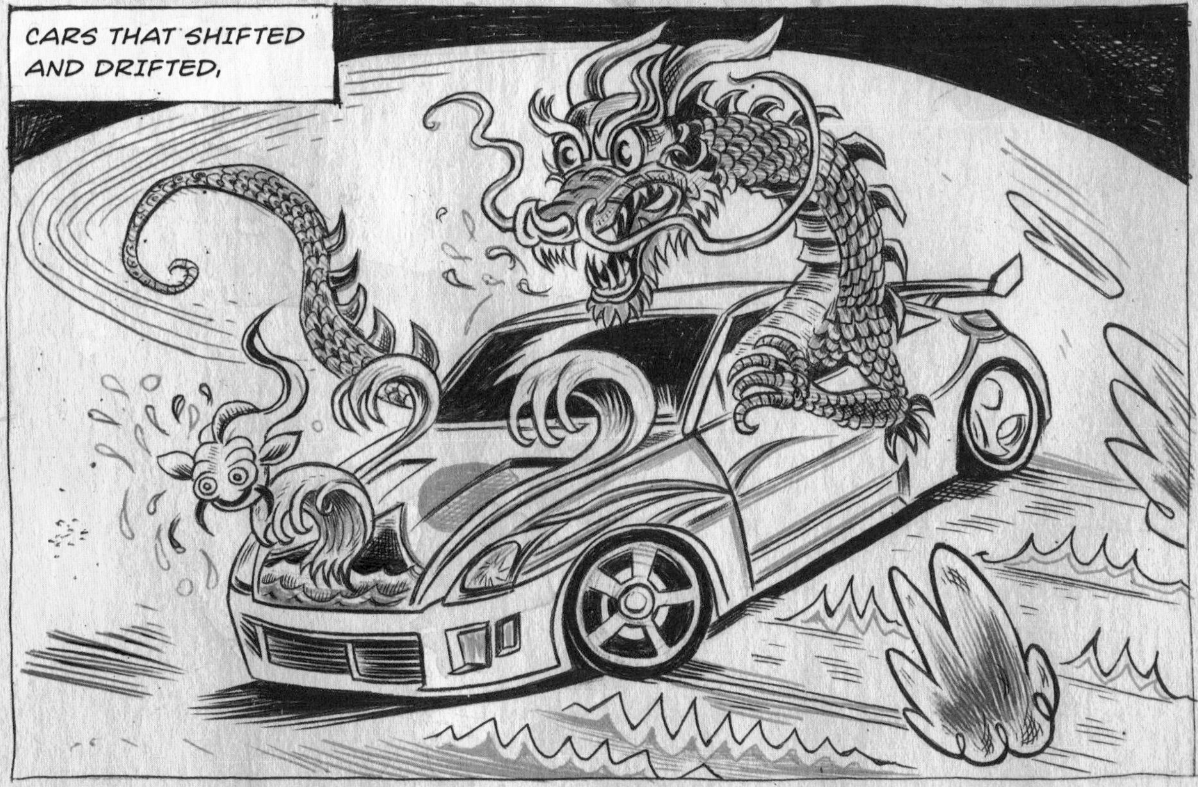
CARS THAT SHIFTED AND DRIFTED,

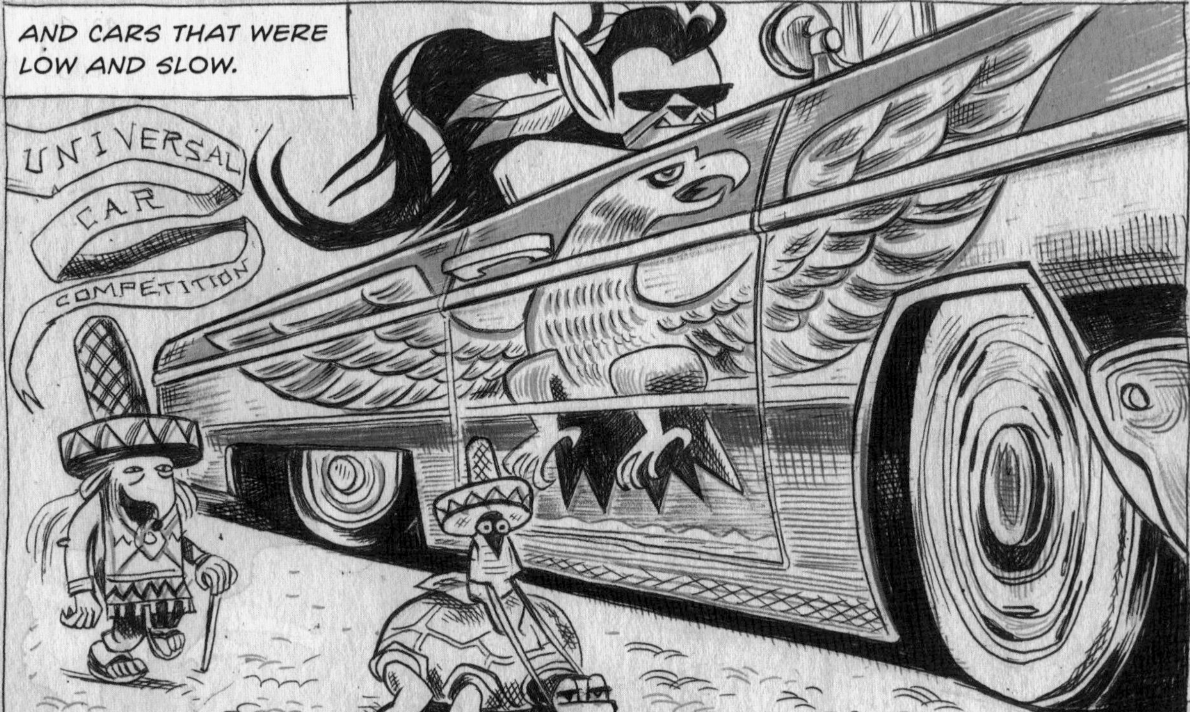
AND CARS THAT WERE LOW AND SLOW.
UNIVERSAL
CAR
COMPETITION

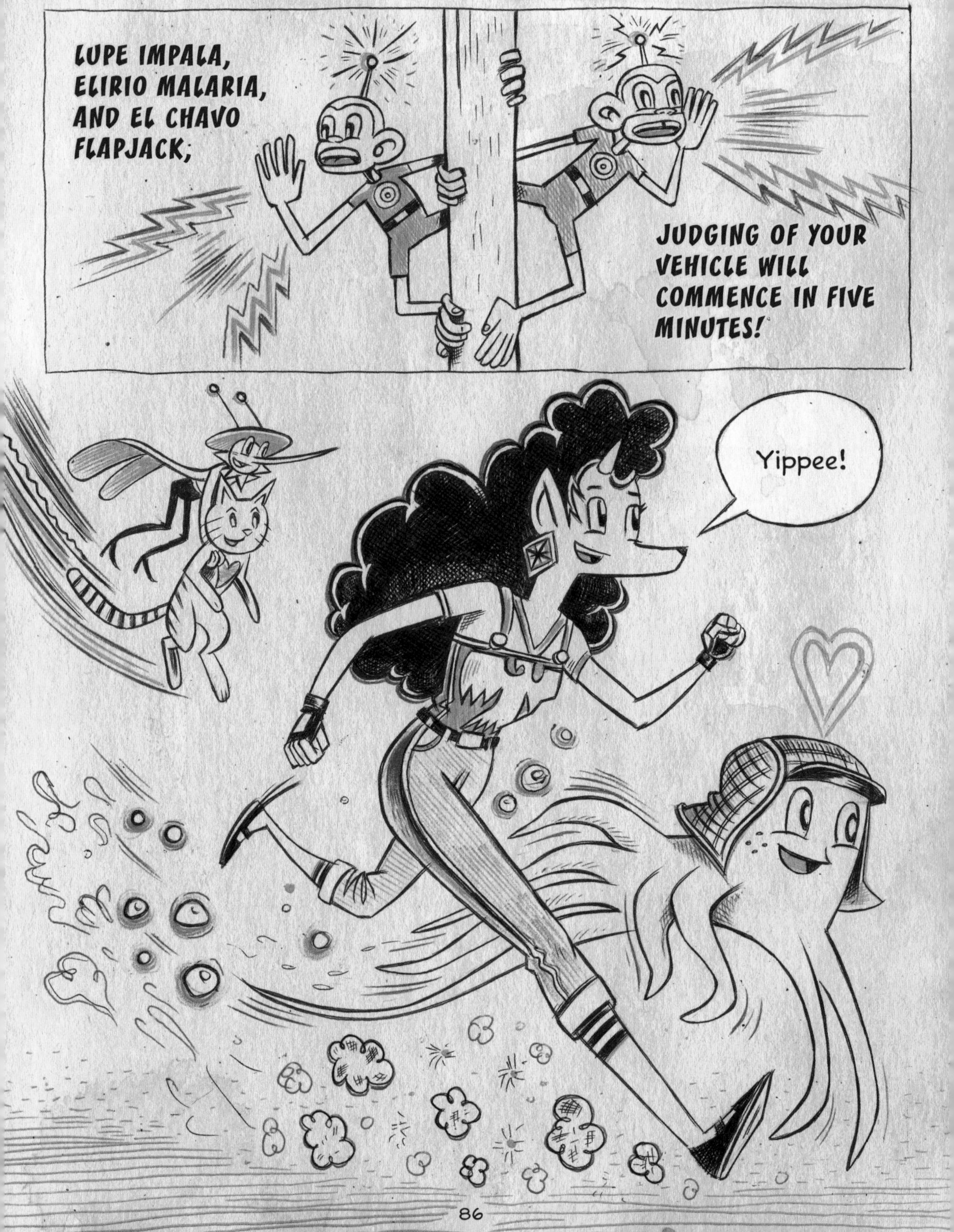
LUPE IMPALA, ELIRIO MALARIA, AND EL CHAVO FLAPJACK;
JUDGING OF YOUR VEHICLE WILL COMMENCE IN FIVE MINUTES!
Yippee!

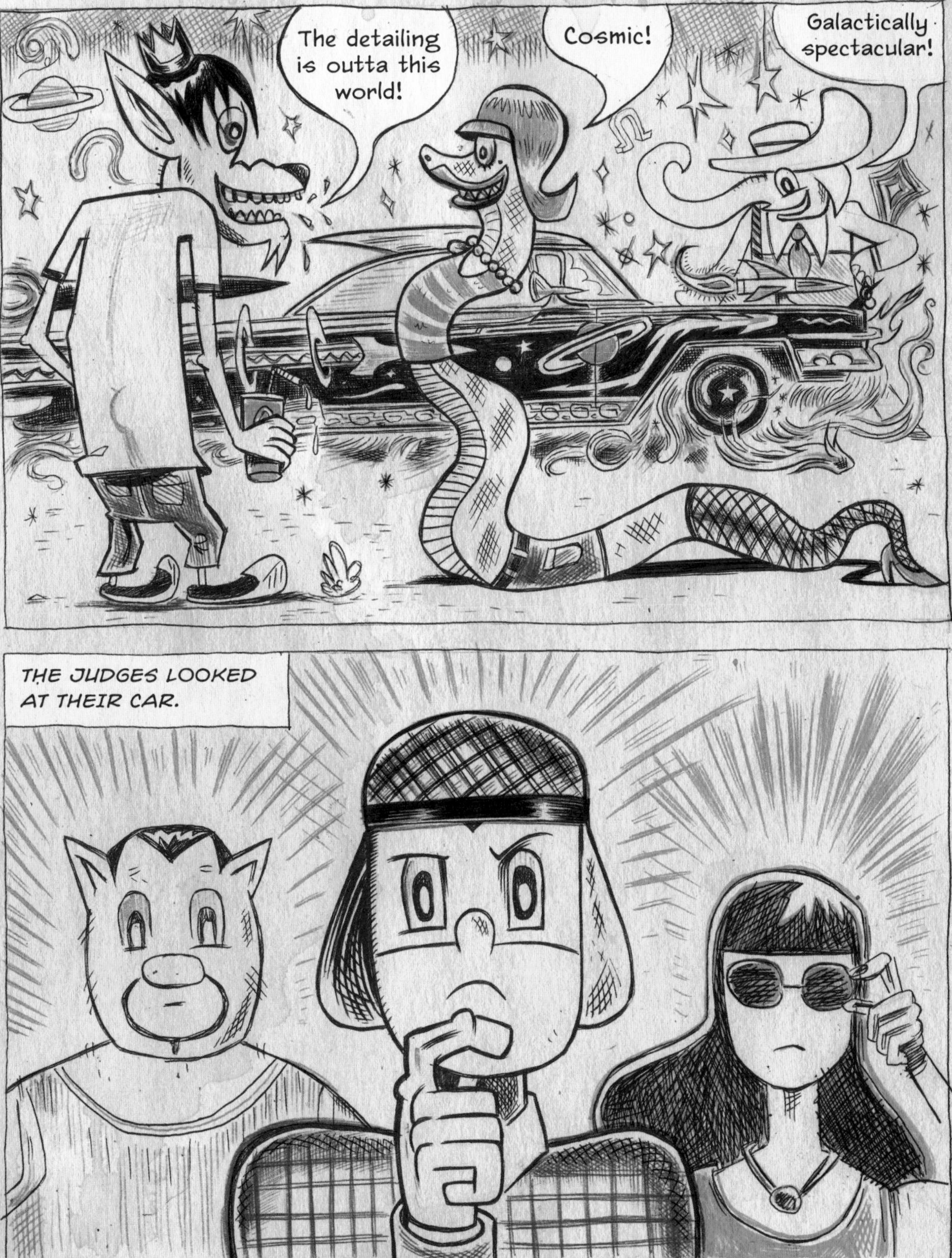
The detailing is outta this world!
Cosmic!
Galactically spectacular!
THE JUDGES LOOKED AT THEIR CAR.

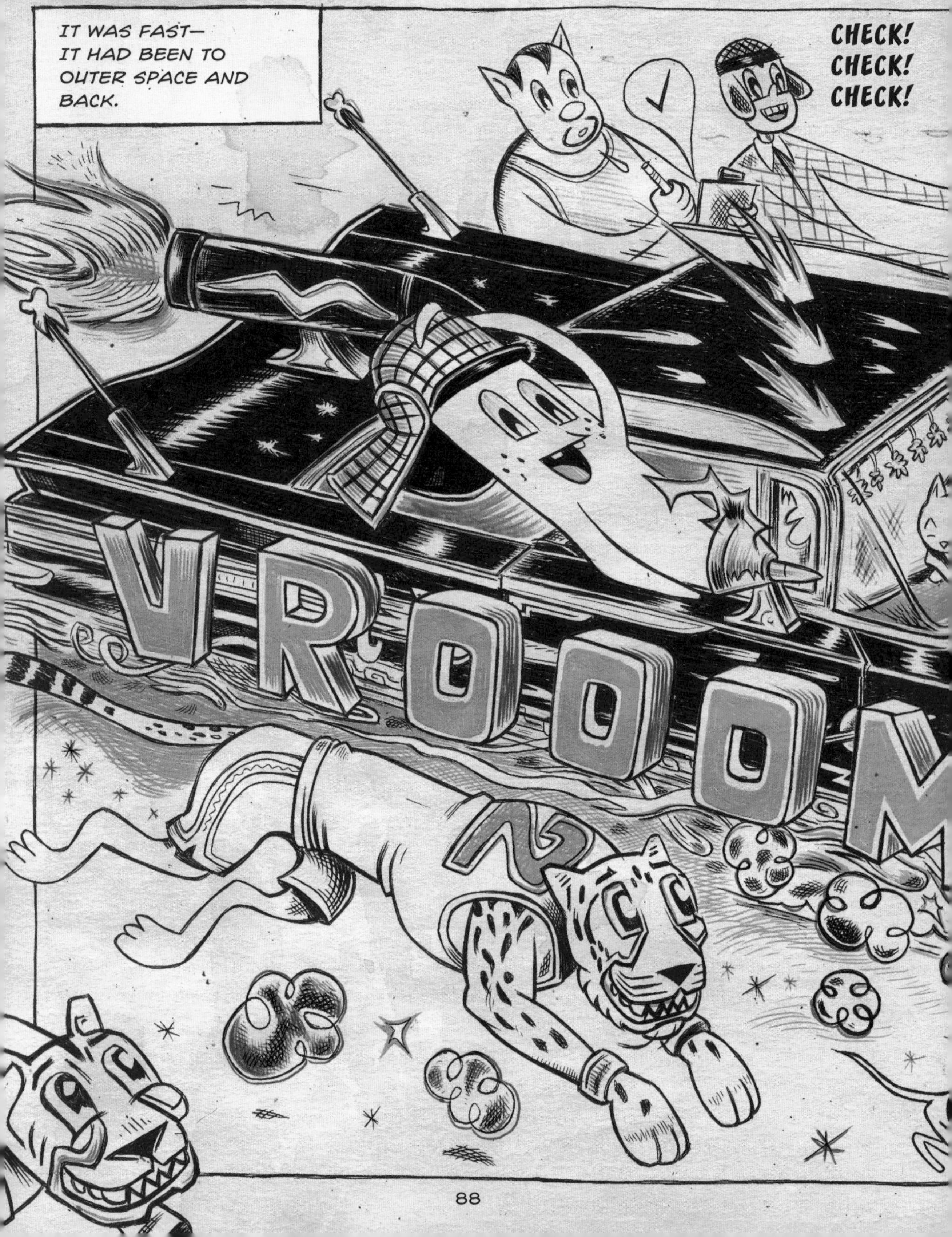
IT WAS FAST— IT HAD BEEN TO OUTER SPACE AND BACK.
CHECK! CHECK! CHECK!
VROOOM

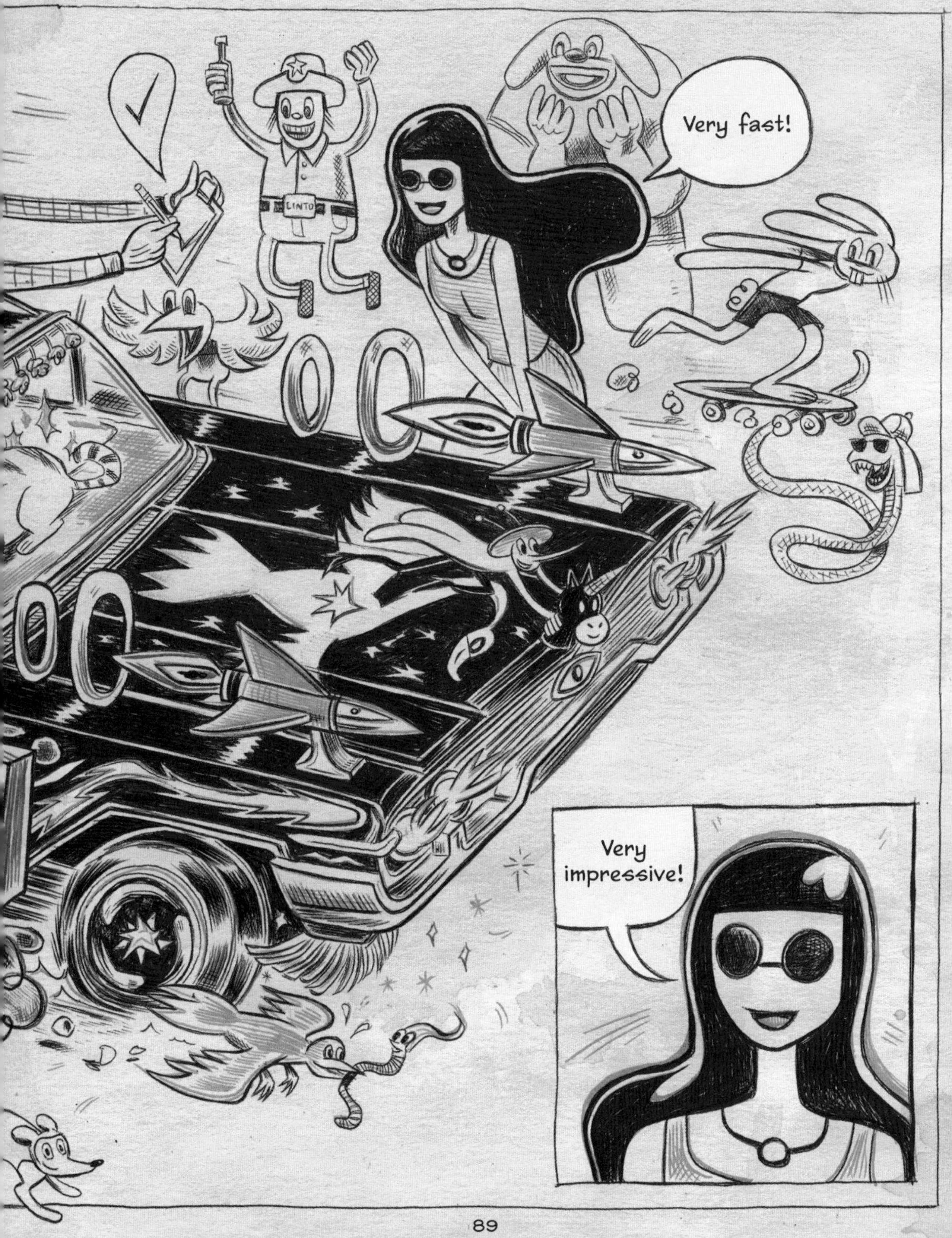
✓
LINTO
Very fast!
Very impressive!

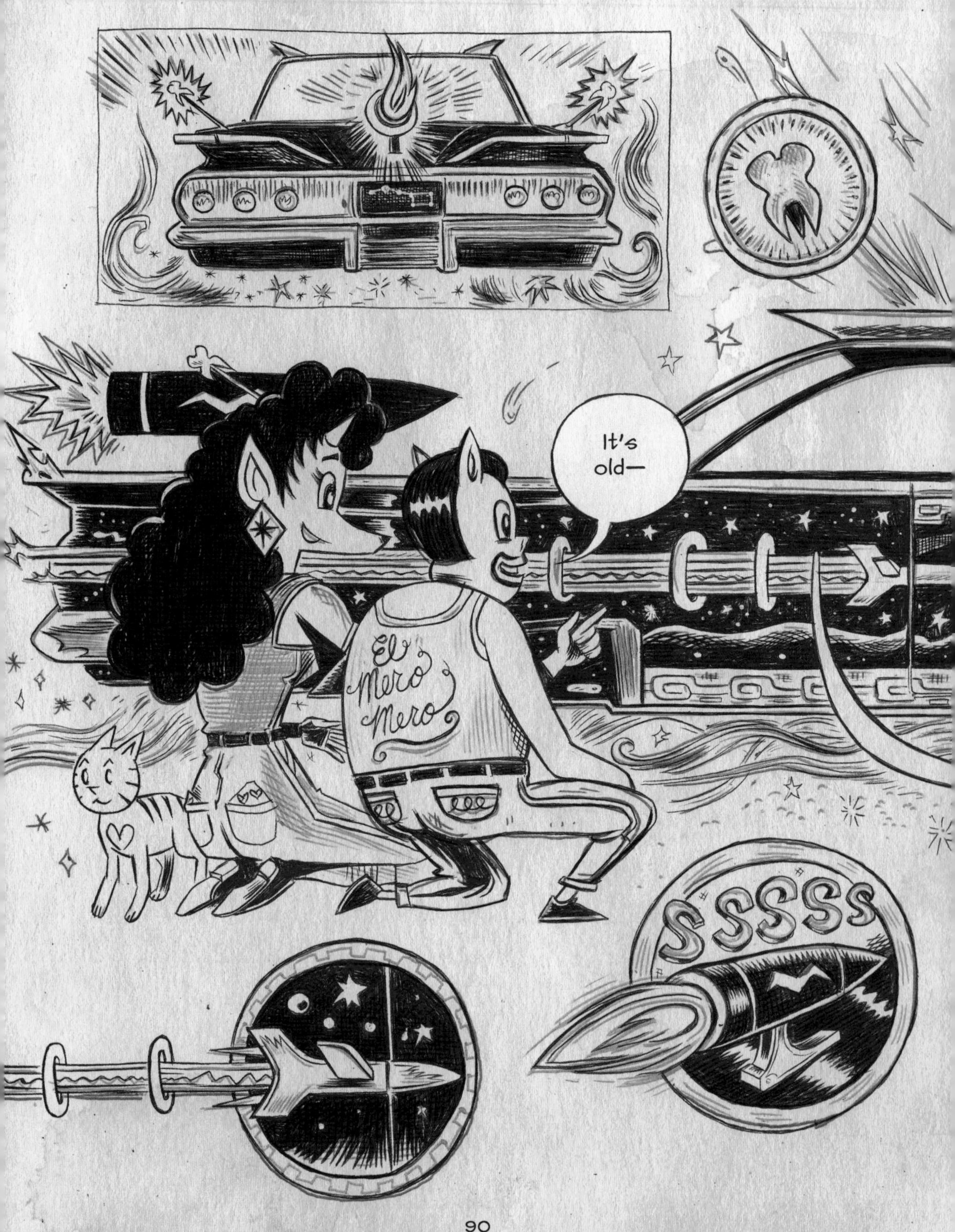
It's old—
El Mero Mero
SSSSS

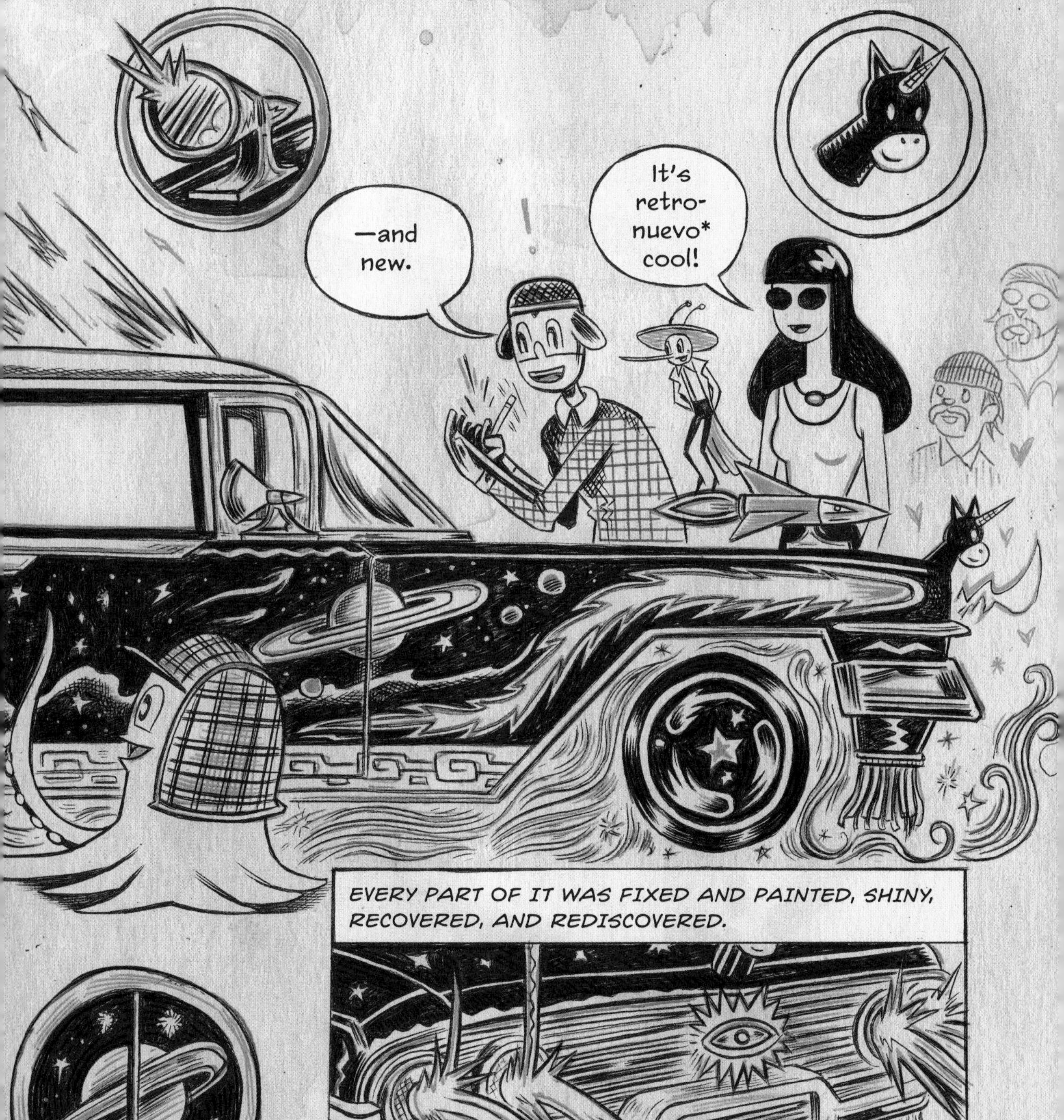
—and new.
It's retro-nuevo* cool!
EVERY PART OF IT WAS FIXED AND PAINTED, SHINY, RECOVERED, AND REDISCOVERED.

* OLD AND NEW

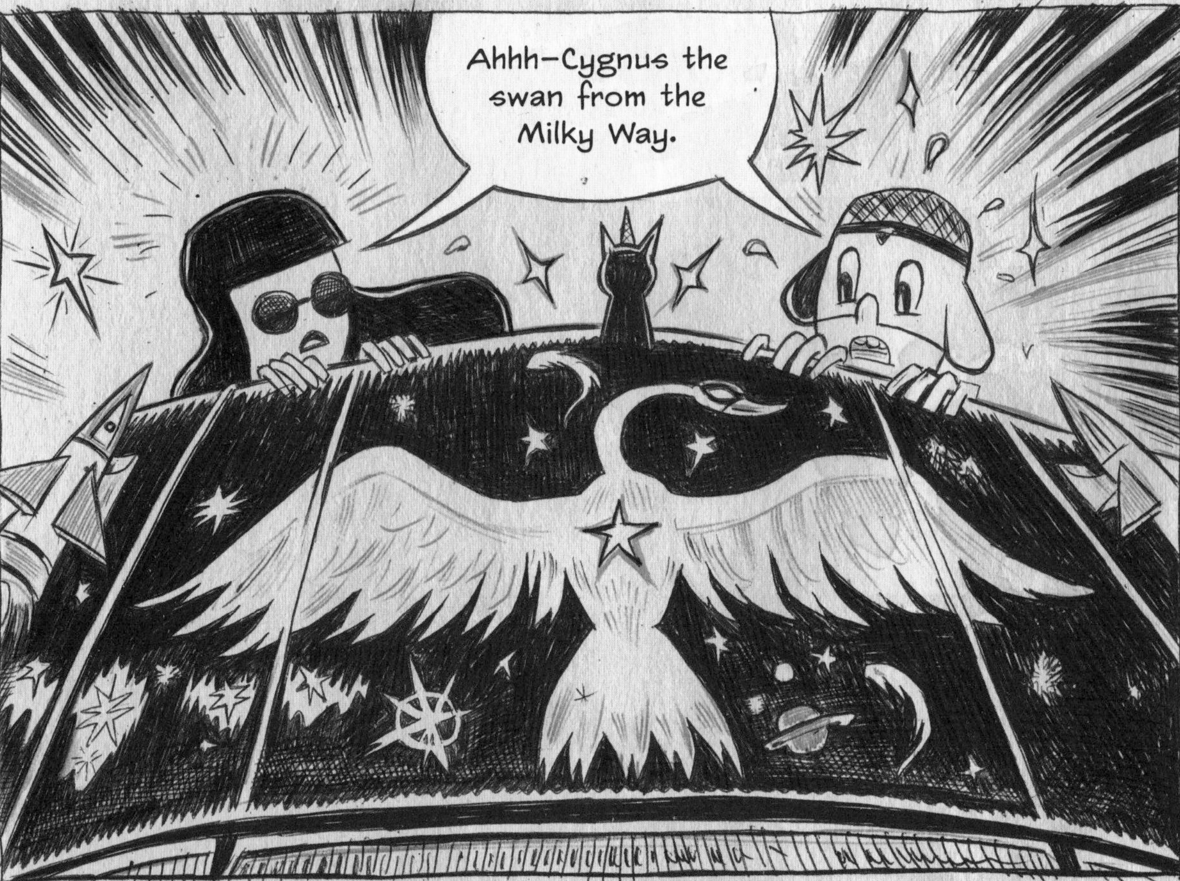
Ahhh–Cygnus the swan from the Milky Way.

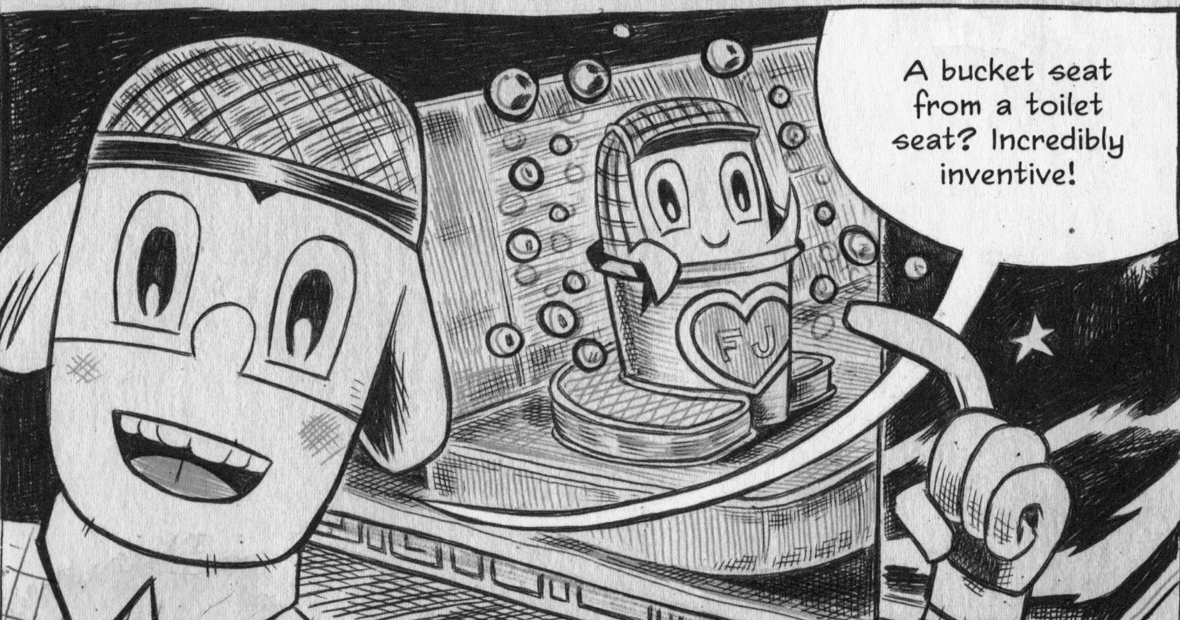
A bucket seat from a toilet seat? Incredibly inventive!
FJ

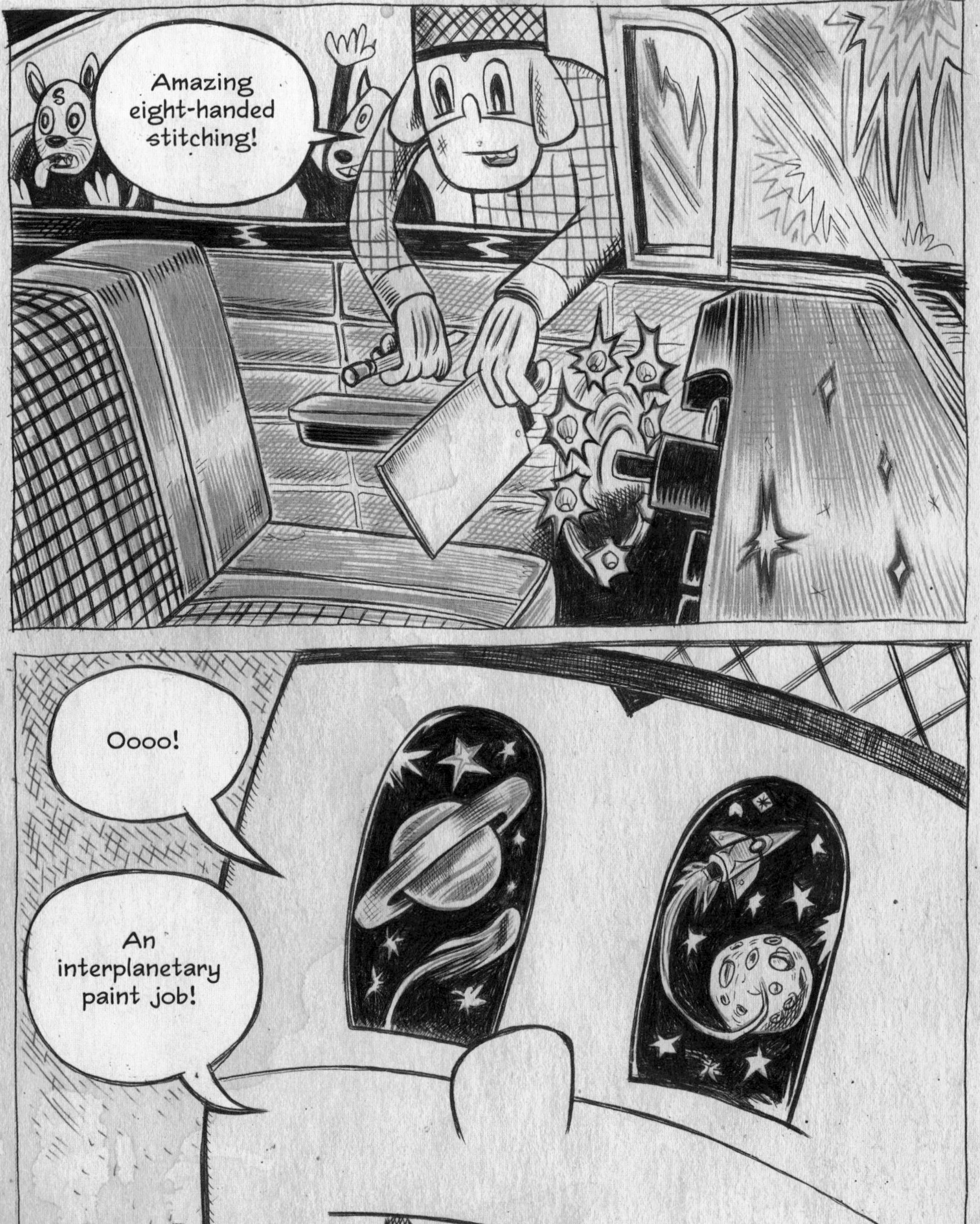
Amazing eight-handed stitching!
Oooo!
An interplanetary paint job!

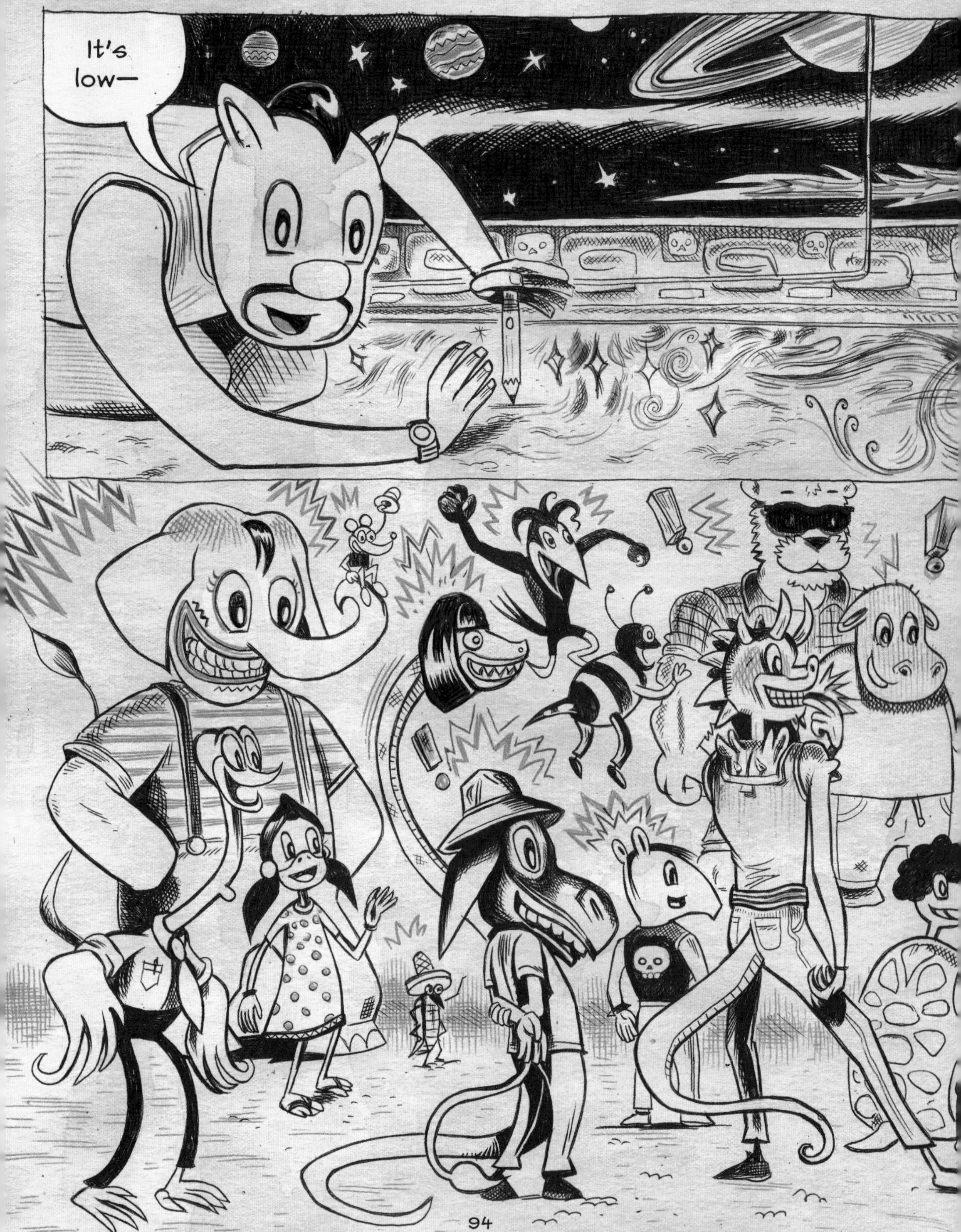
It's low—

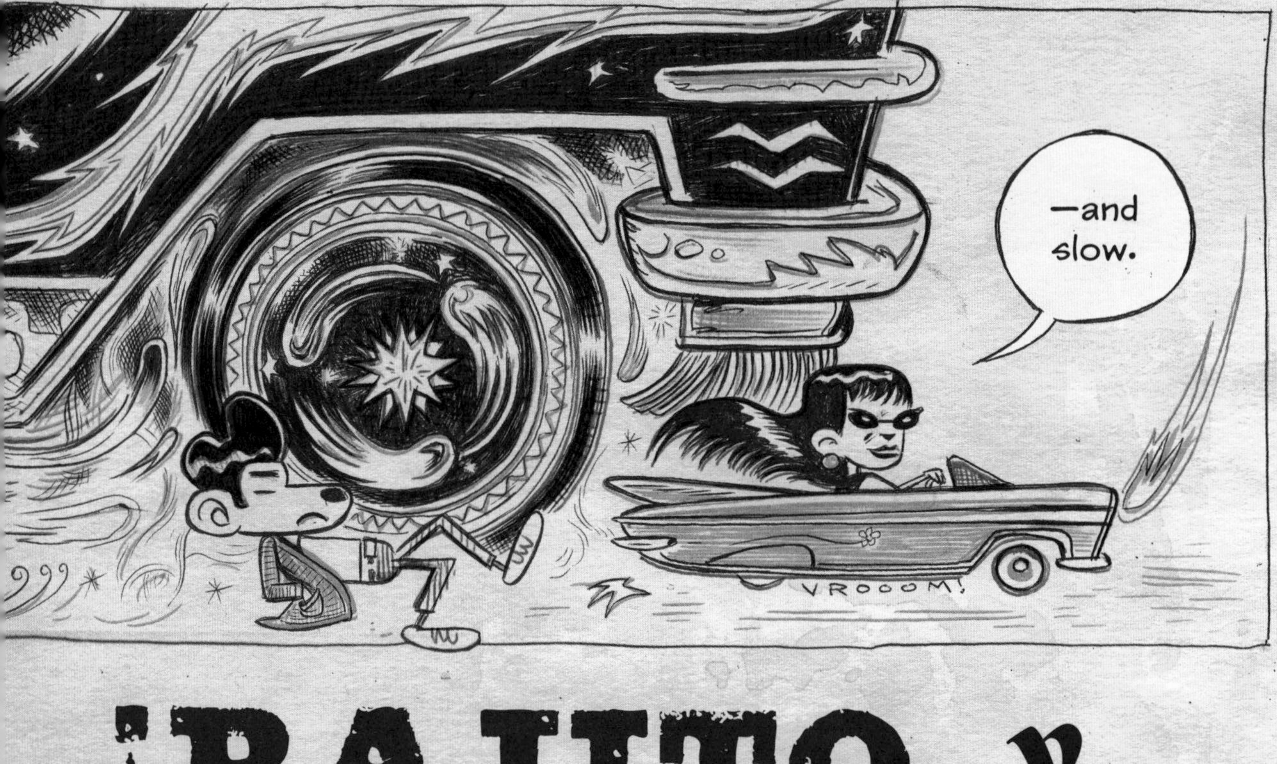
—and slow.
VROOOM!

¡BAJITO y

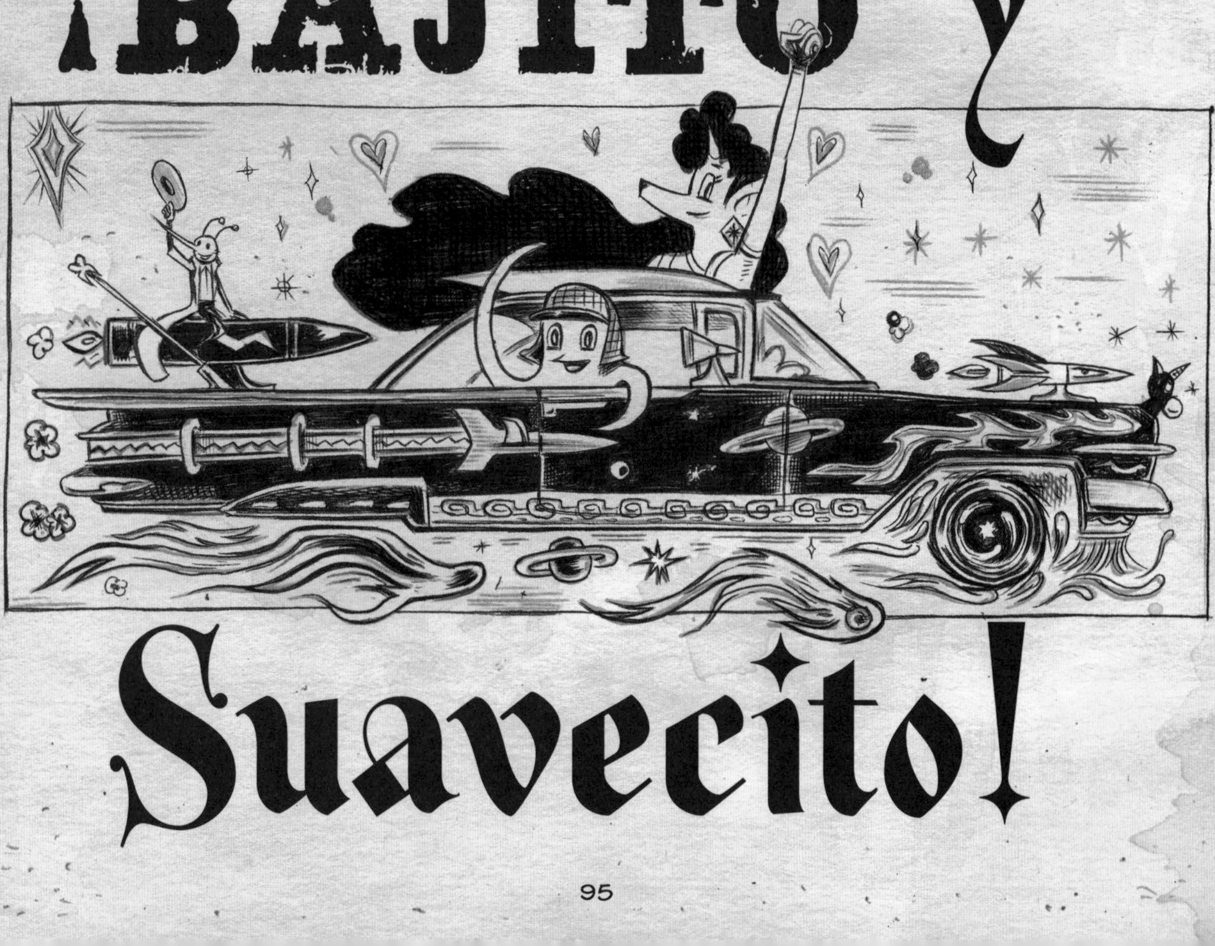

Suavecito!

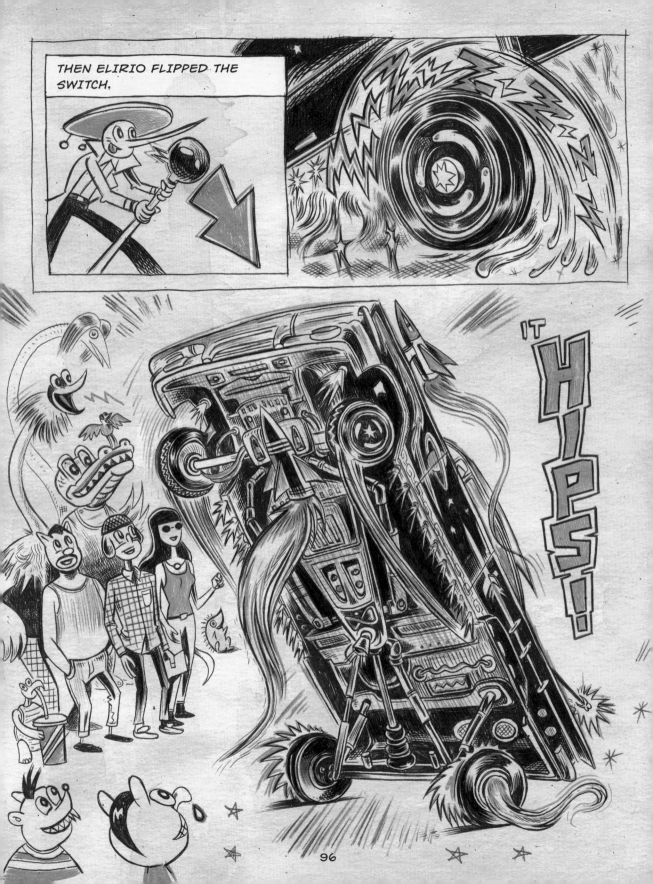

THEN ELIRIO FLIPPED THE SWITCH.

IT HIPS!

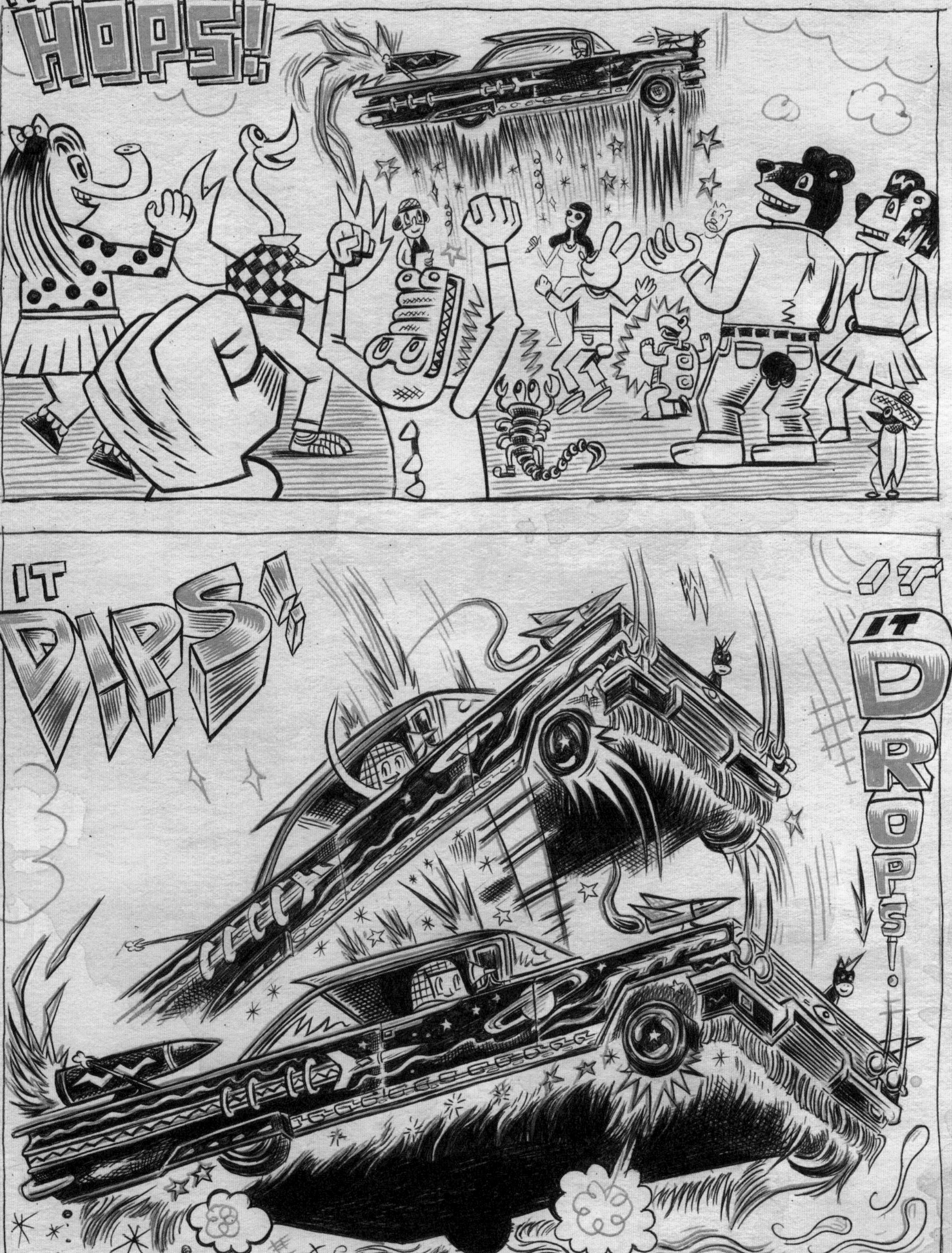
IT HOPS!
IT DIPS!
IT
IT DROPS!

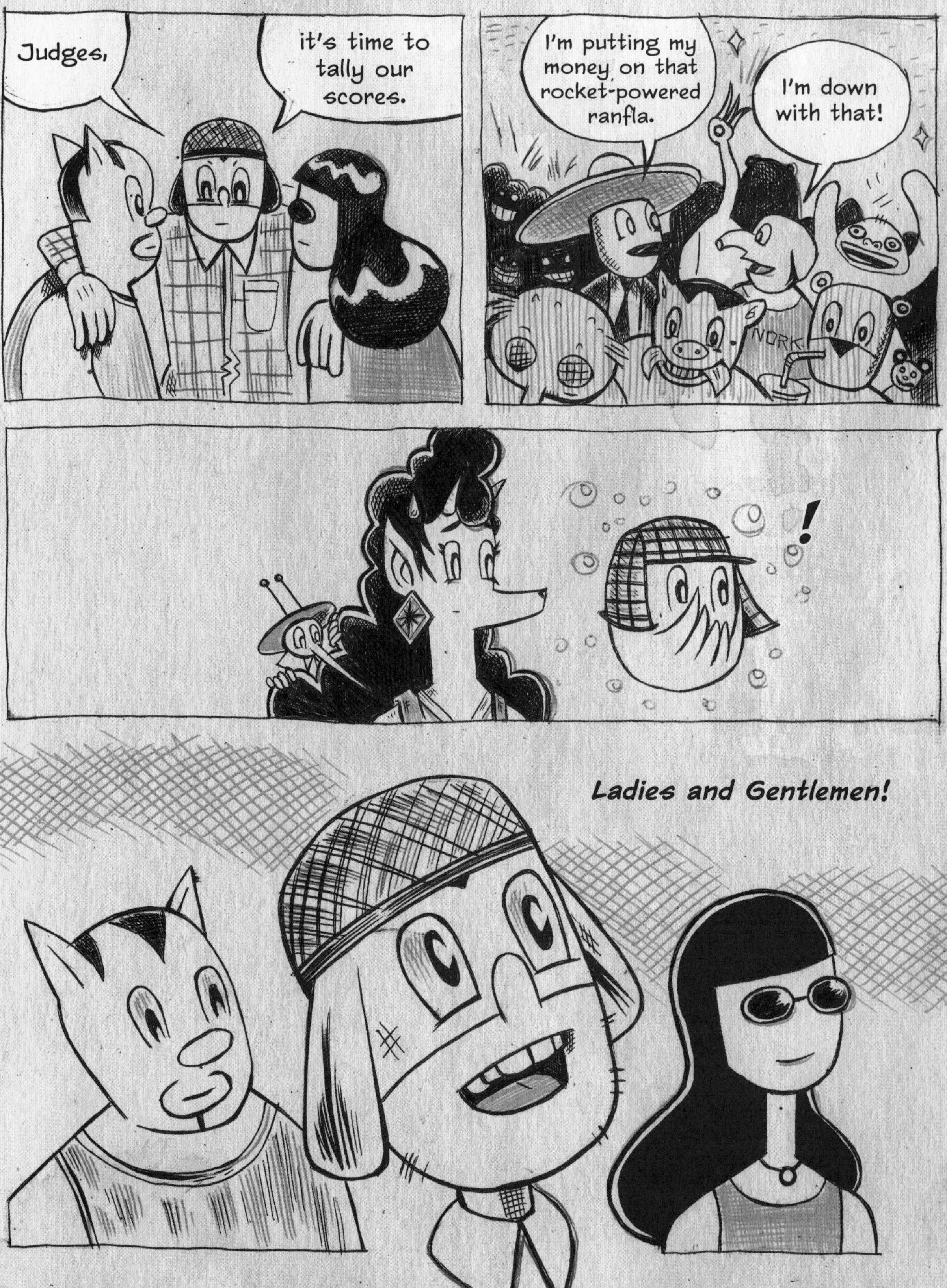
Judges,
it's time to tally our scores.
I'm putting my money on that rocket-powered ranfla.
I'm down with that!
!
Ladies and Gentlemen!

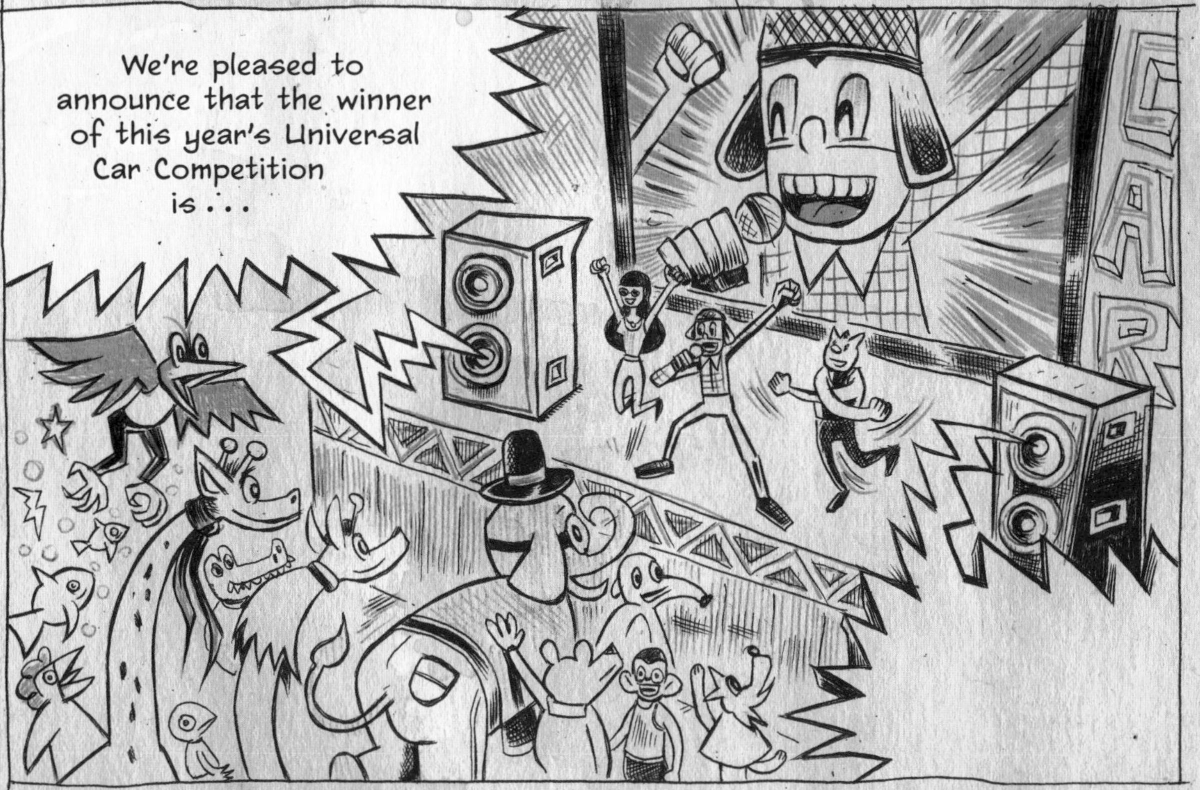
We're pleased to announce that the winner of this year's Universal Car Competition is . . .

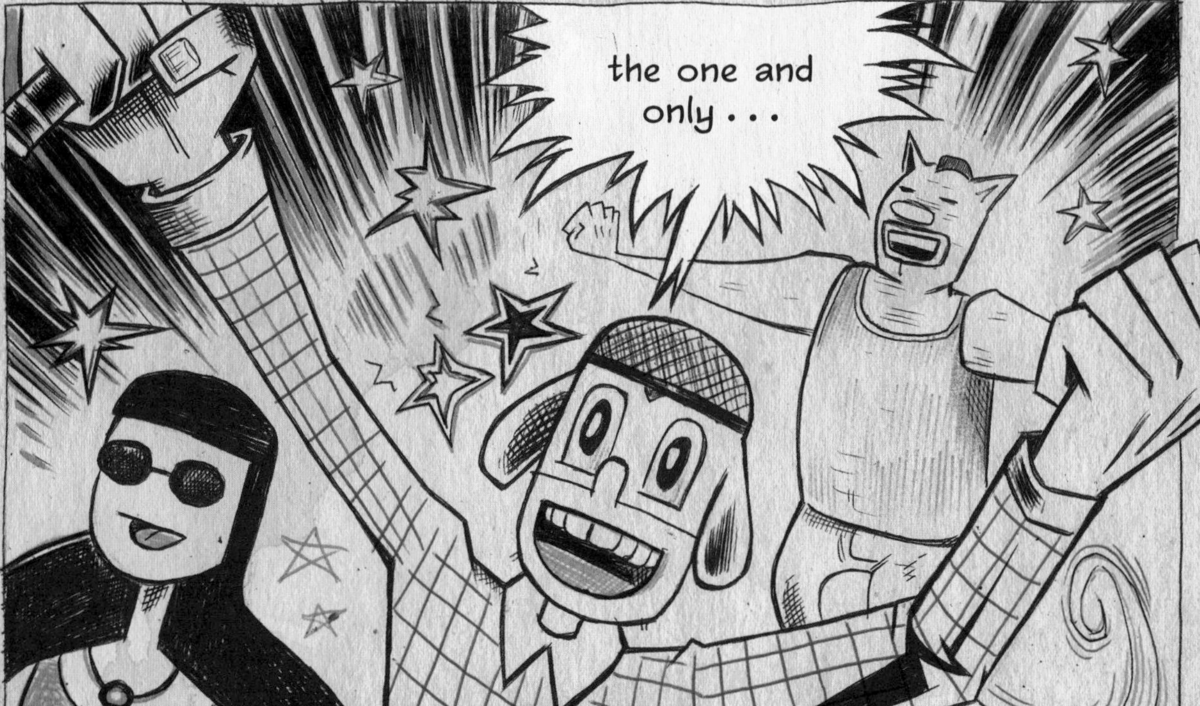
the one and only . . .

LOWRIDERS in SPACE!

Lupe Impala!
Elirio Malaria!!
El Chavo Flapjack!!!

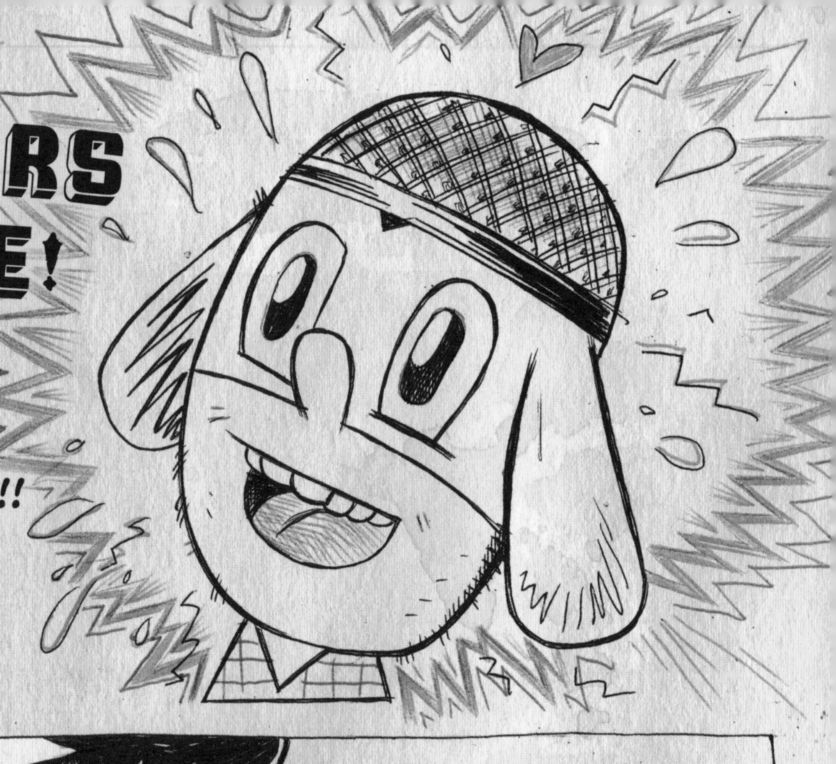

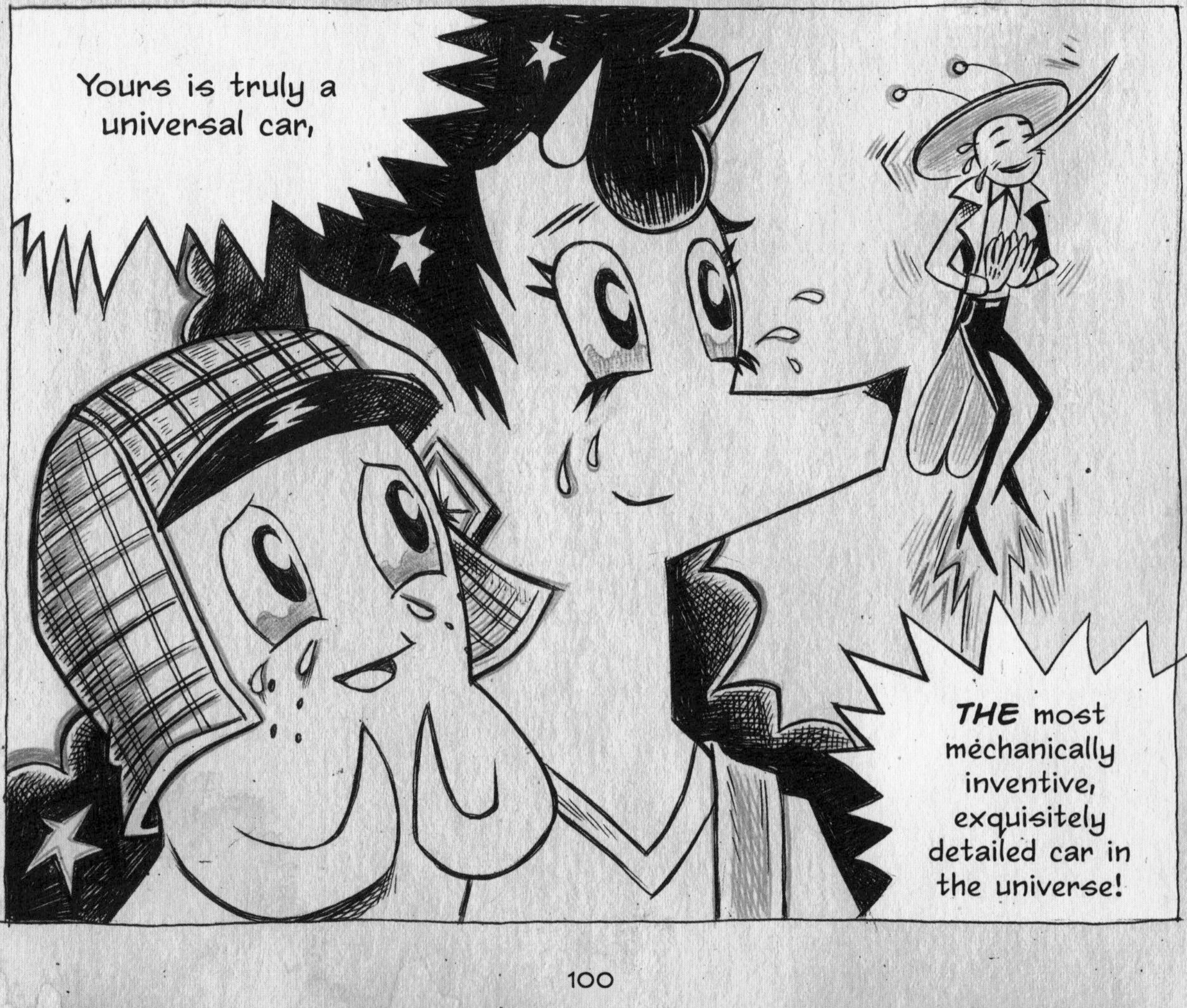

Yours is truly a universal car,
THE most mechanically inventive, exquisitely detailed car in the universe!

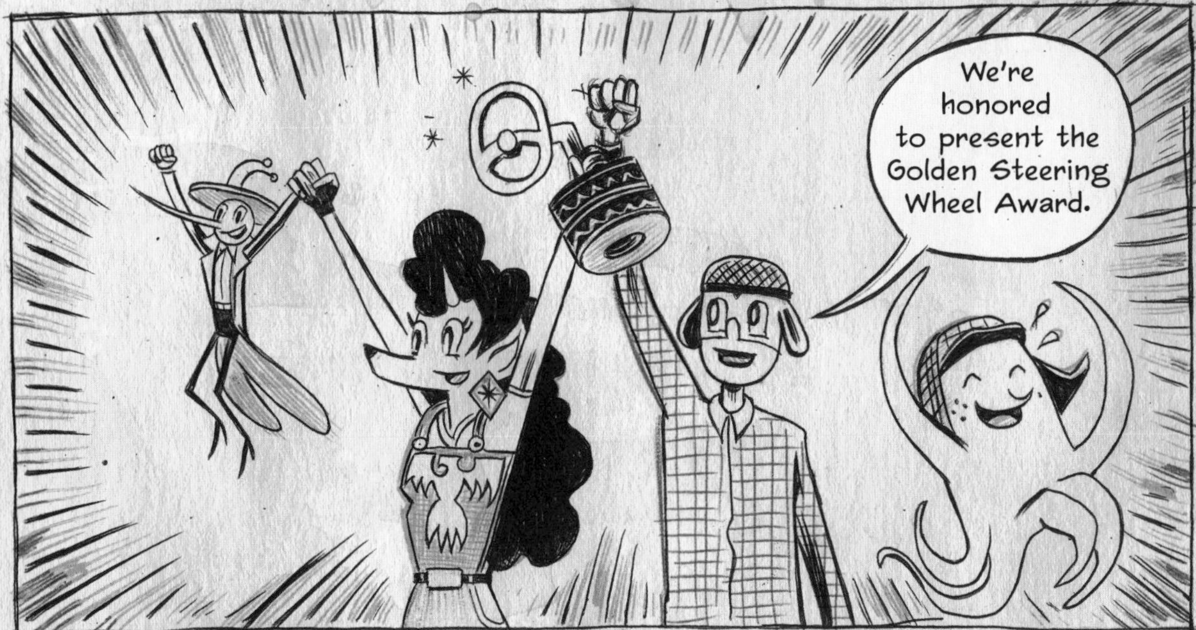
We're honored to present the Golden Steering Wheel Award.

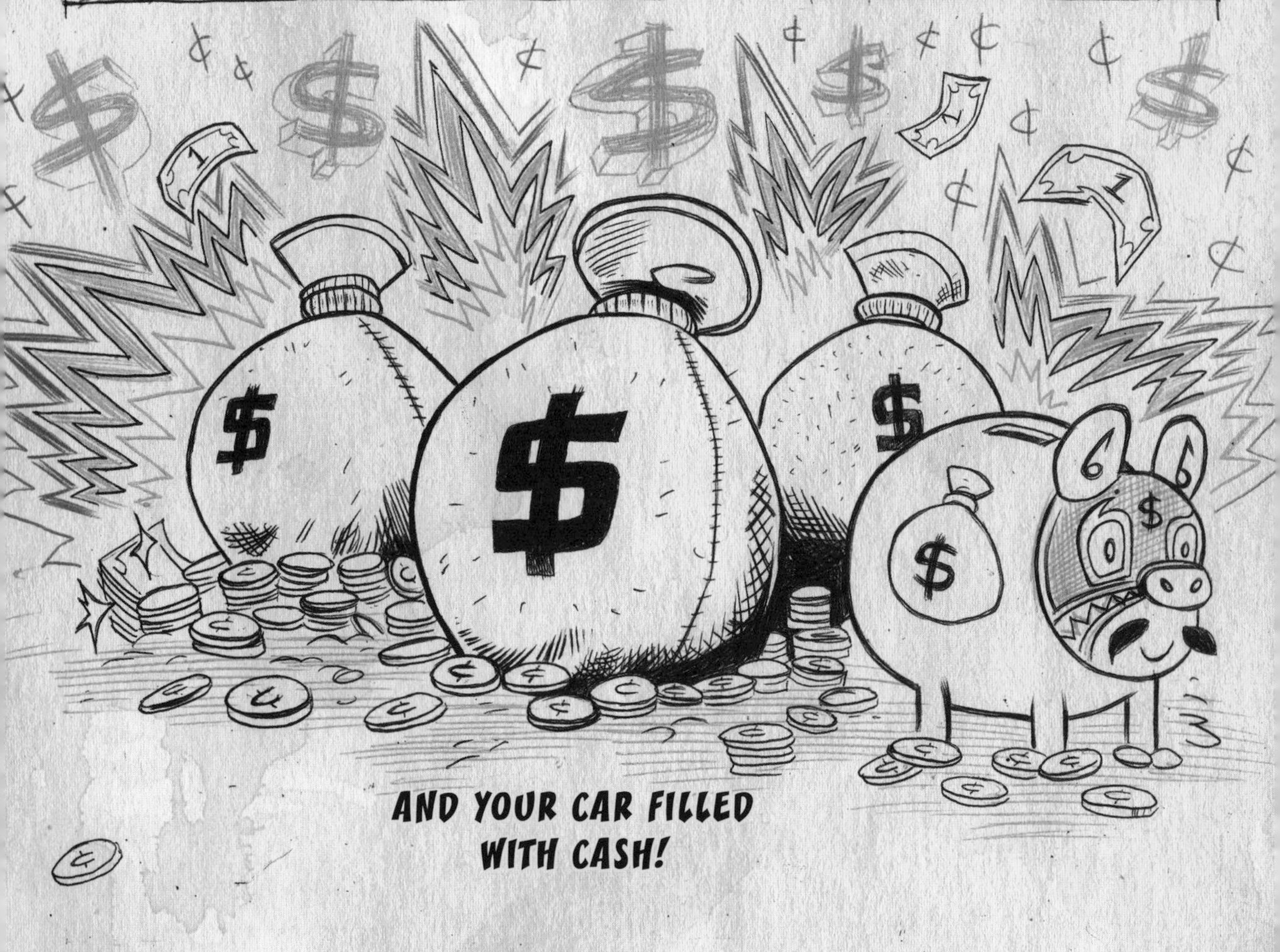
AND YOUR CAR FILLED WITH CASH!

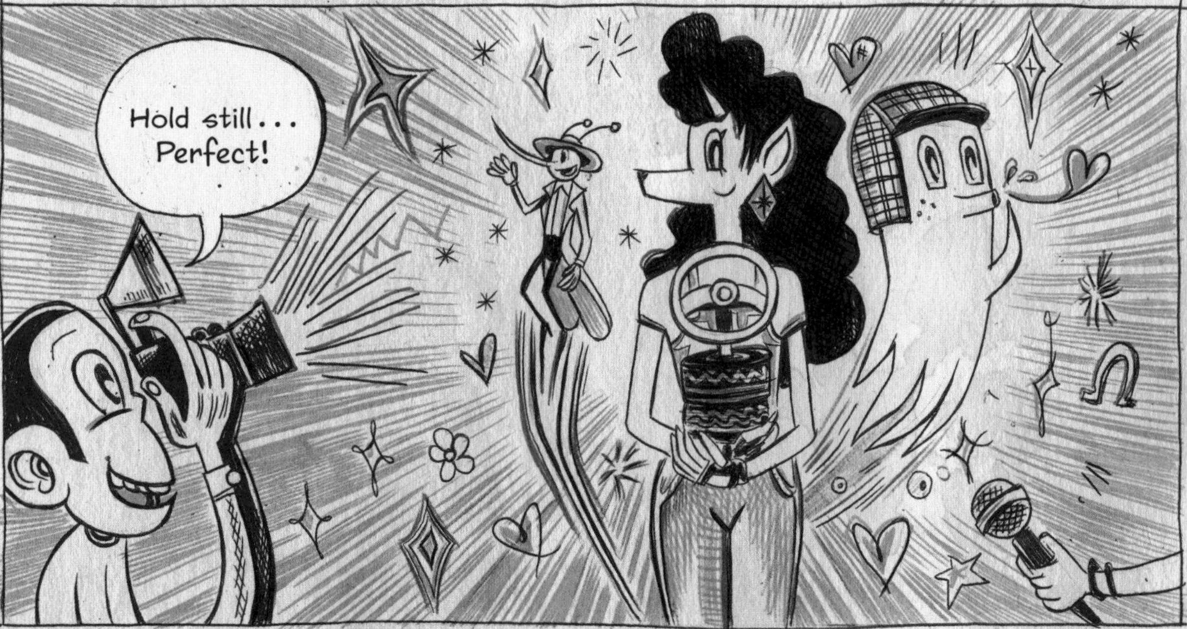
Hold still . . . Perfect!

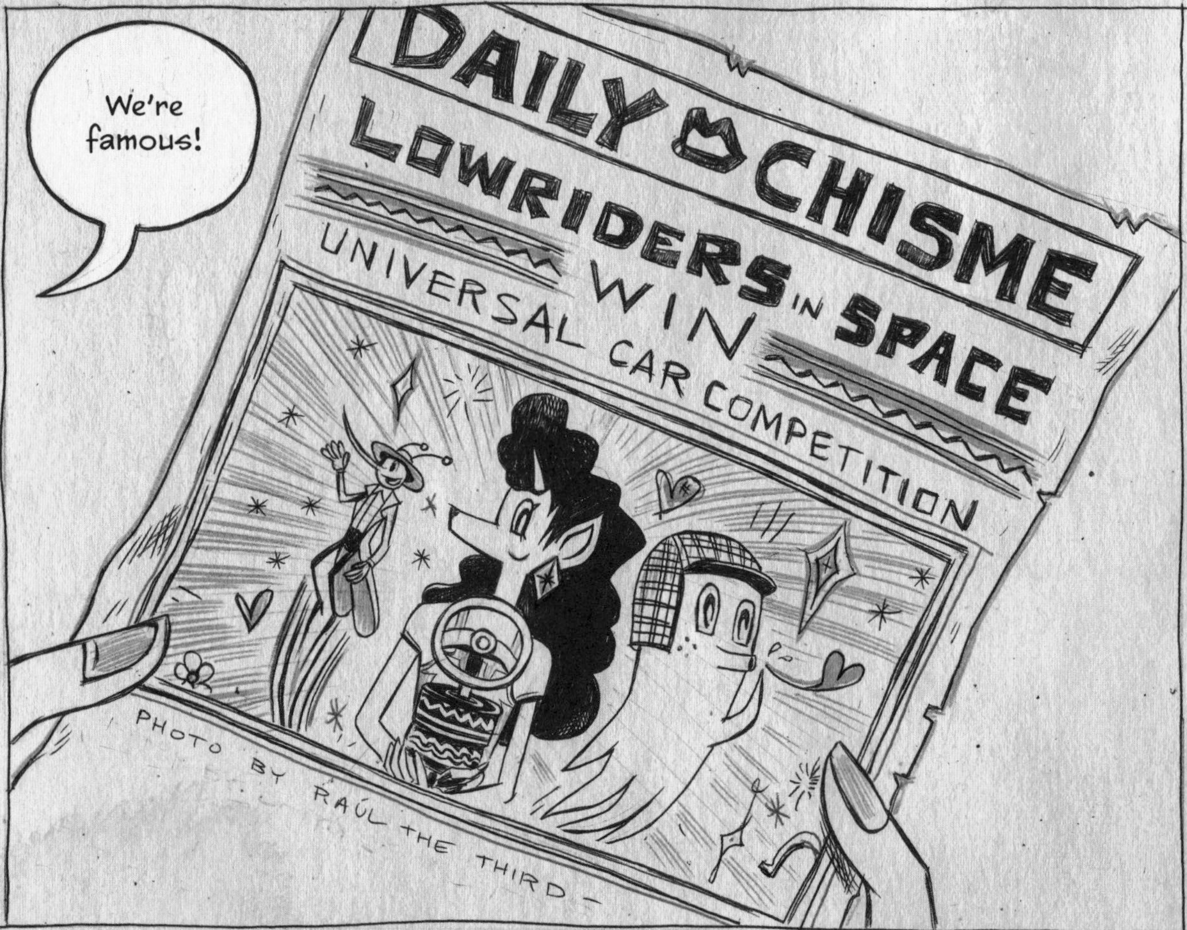
We're famous!
DAILY CHISME
LOWRIDERS IN SPACE WIN UNIVERSAL CAR COMPETITION
PHOTO BY RAÚL THE THIRD

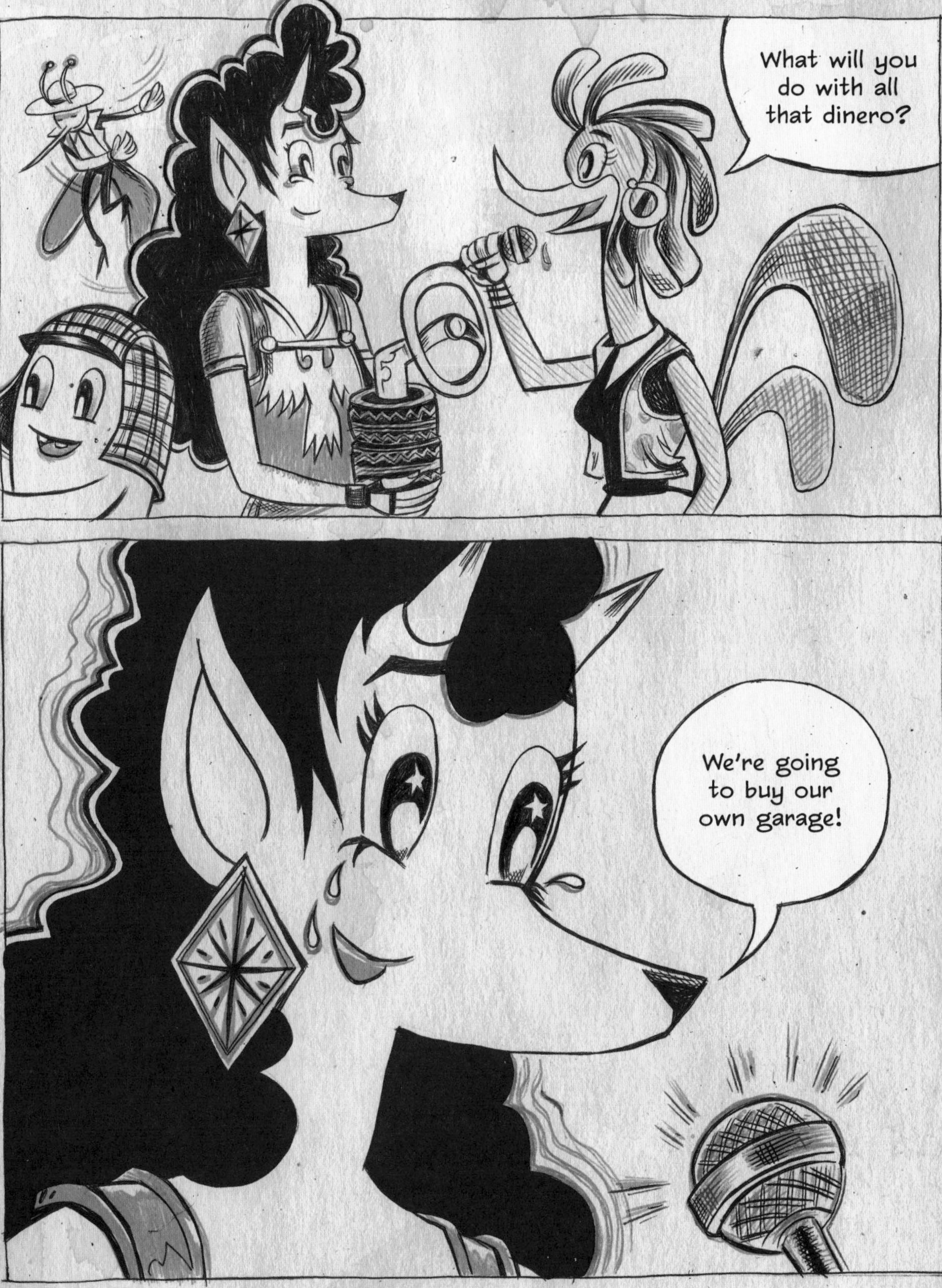
What will you do with all that dinero?
We're going to buy our own garage!

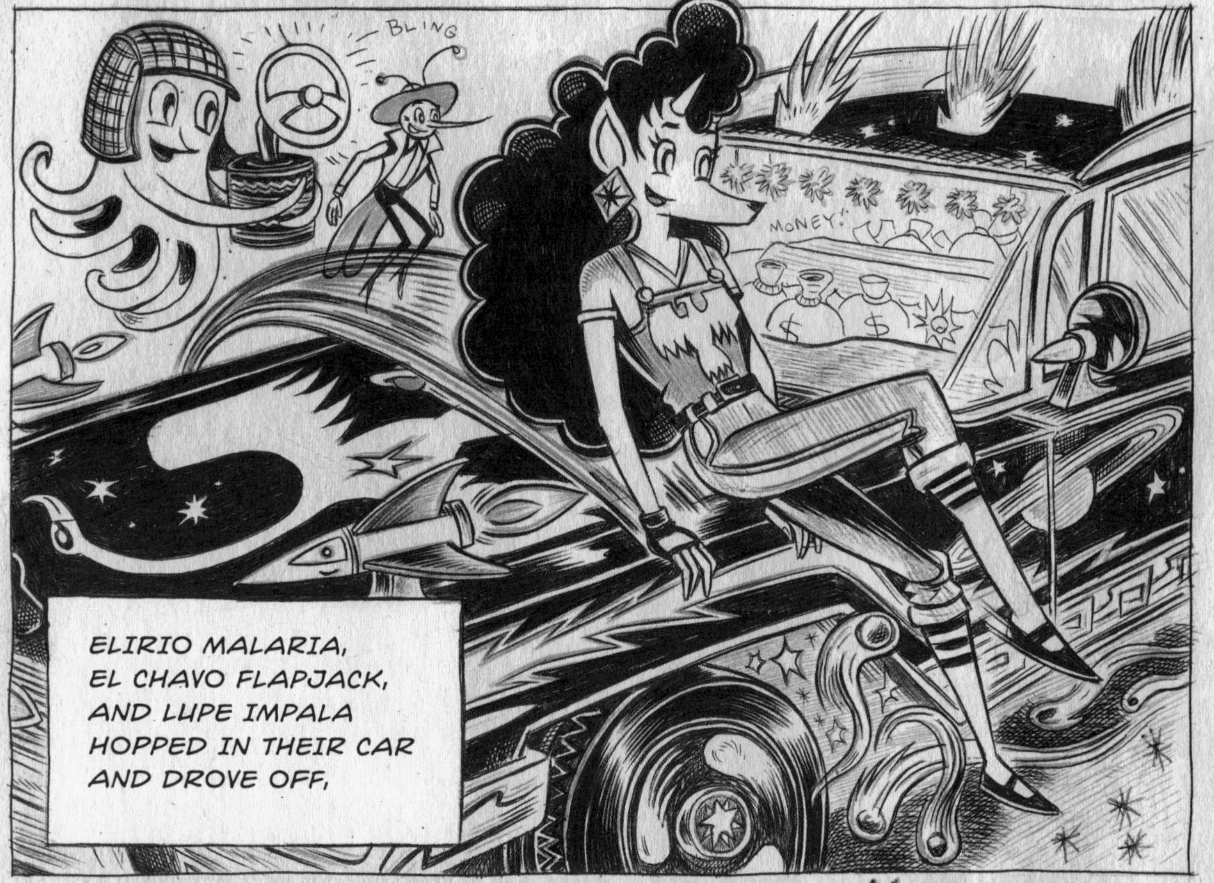
BLING
MONEY!
ELIRIO MALARIA, EL CHAVO FLAPJACK, AND LUPE IMPALA HOPPED IN THEIR CAR AND DROVE OFF,

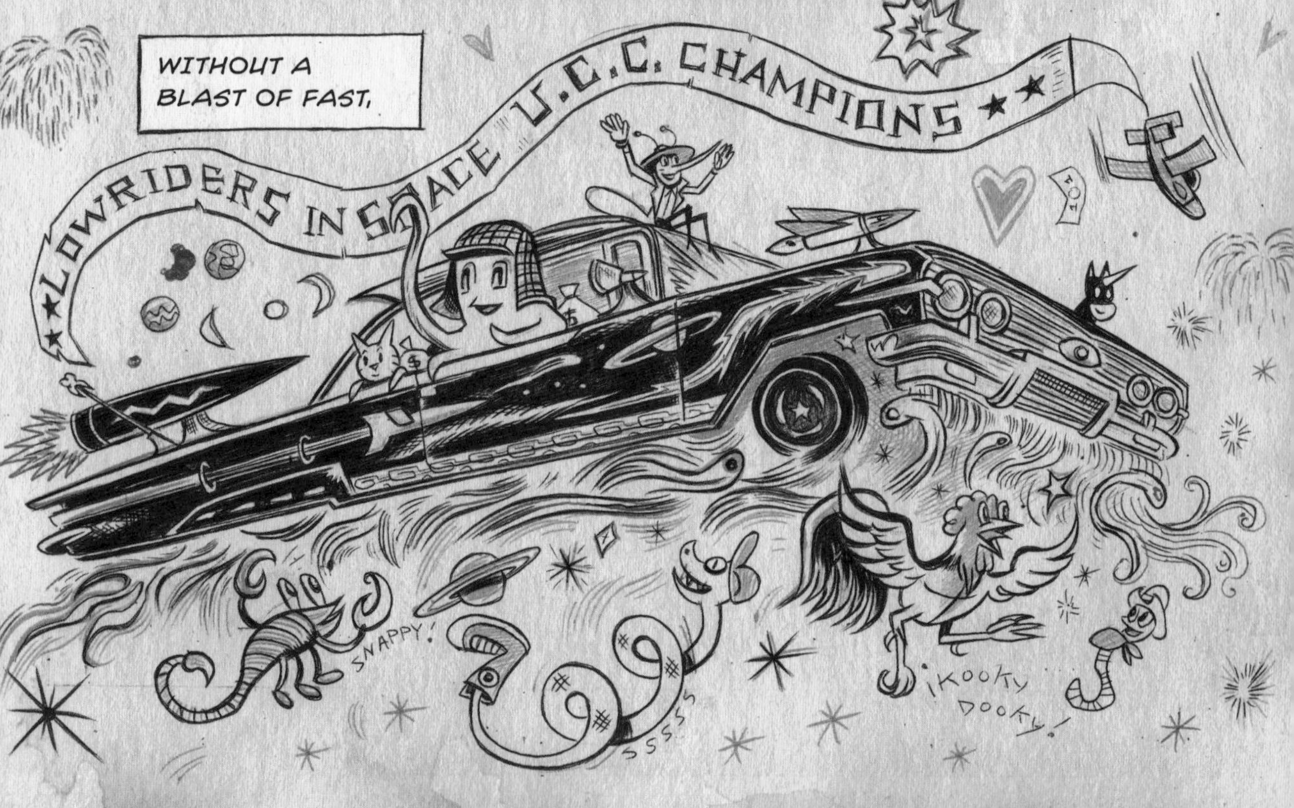
WITHOUT A BLAST OF FAST,
LOWRIDERS IN SPACE U.C.C. CHAMPIONS
SNAPPY!
SSSSS
¡KOOKY DOOKY!

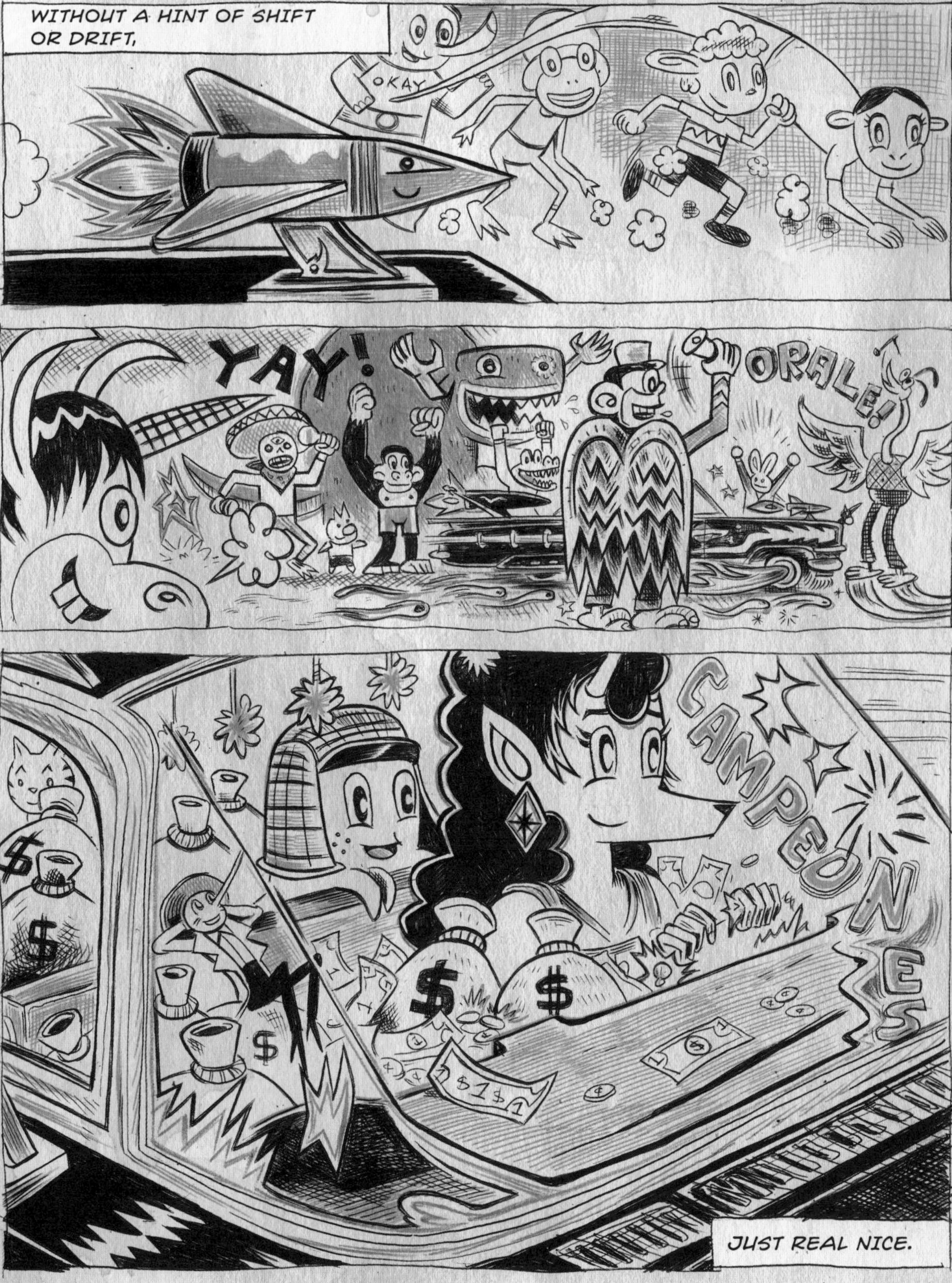
WITHOUT A HINT OF SHIFT OR DRIFT,
OKAY
YAY!
ORALE!
CAMPEONES
JUST REAL NICE.

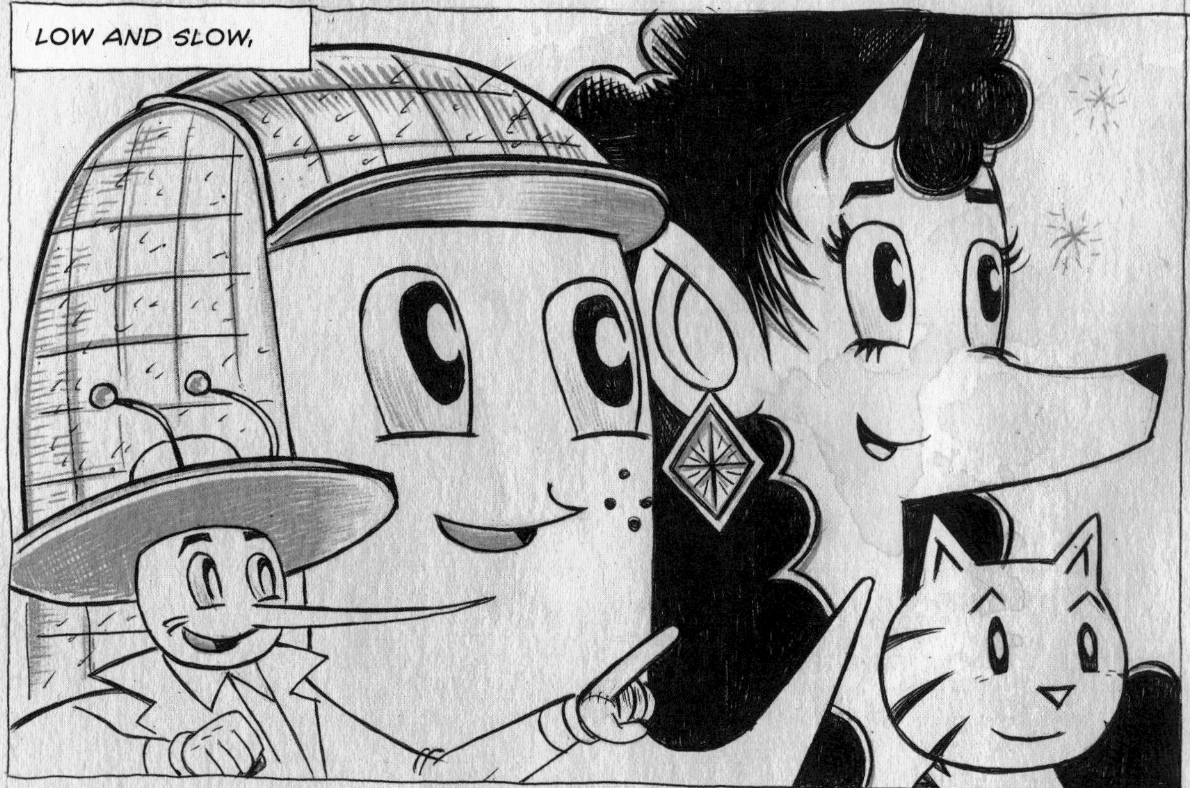
LOW AND SLOW,

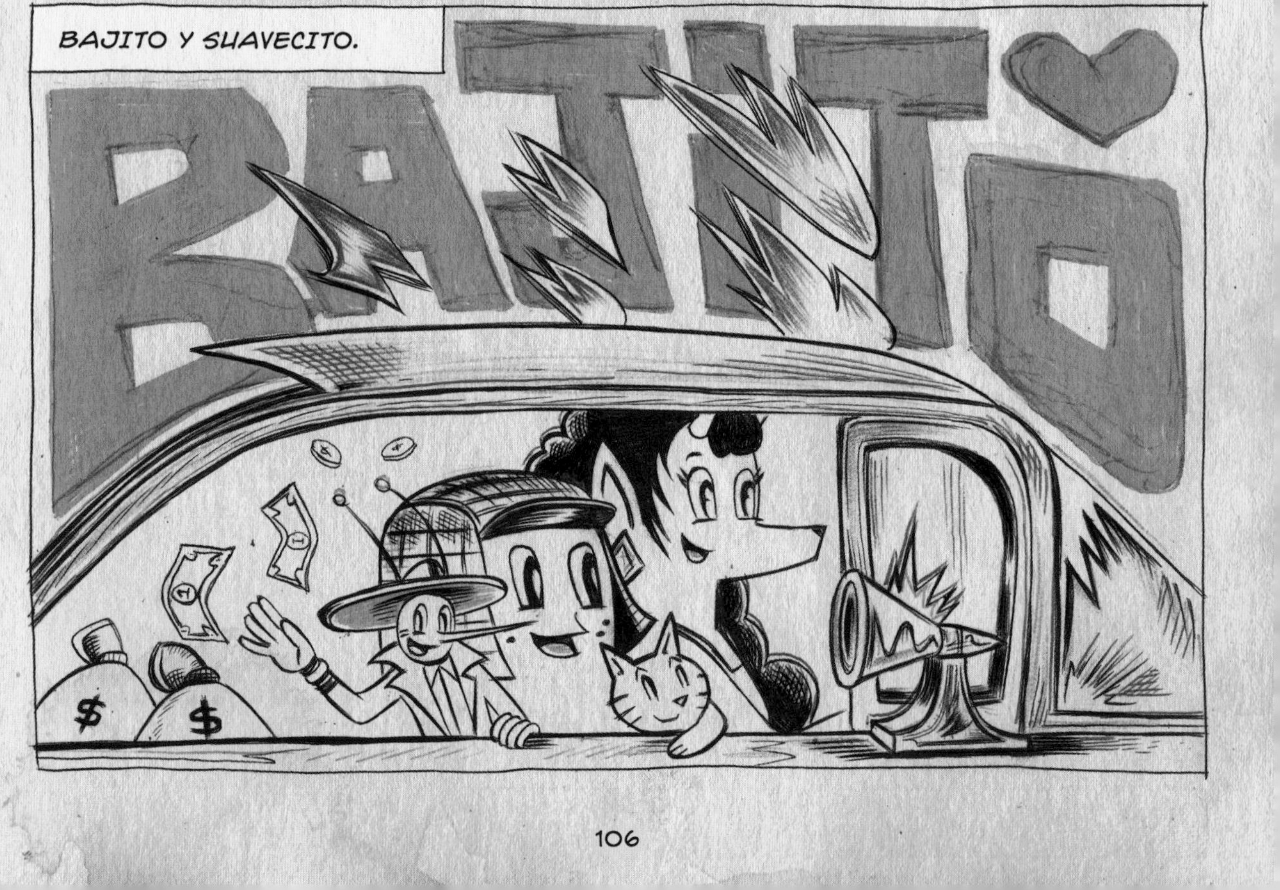
BAJITO Y SUAVECITO.
BAJITO

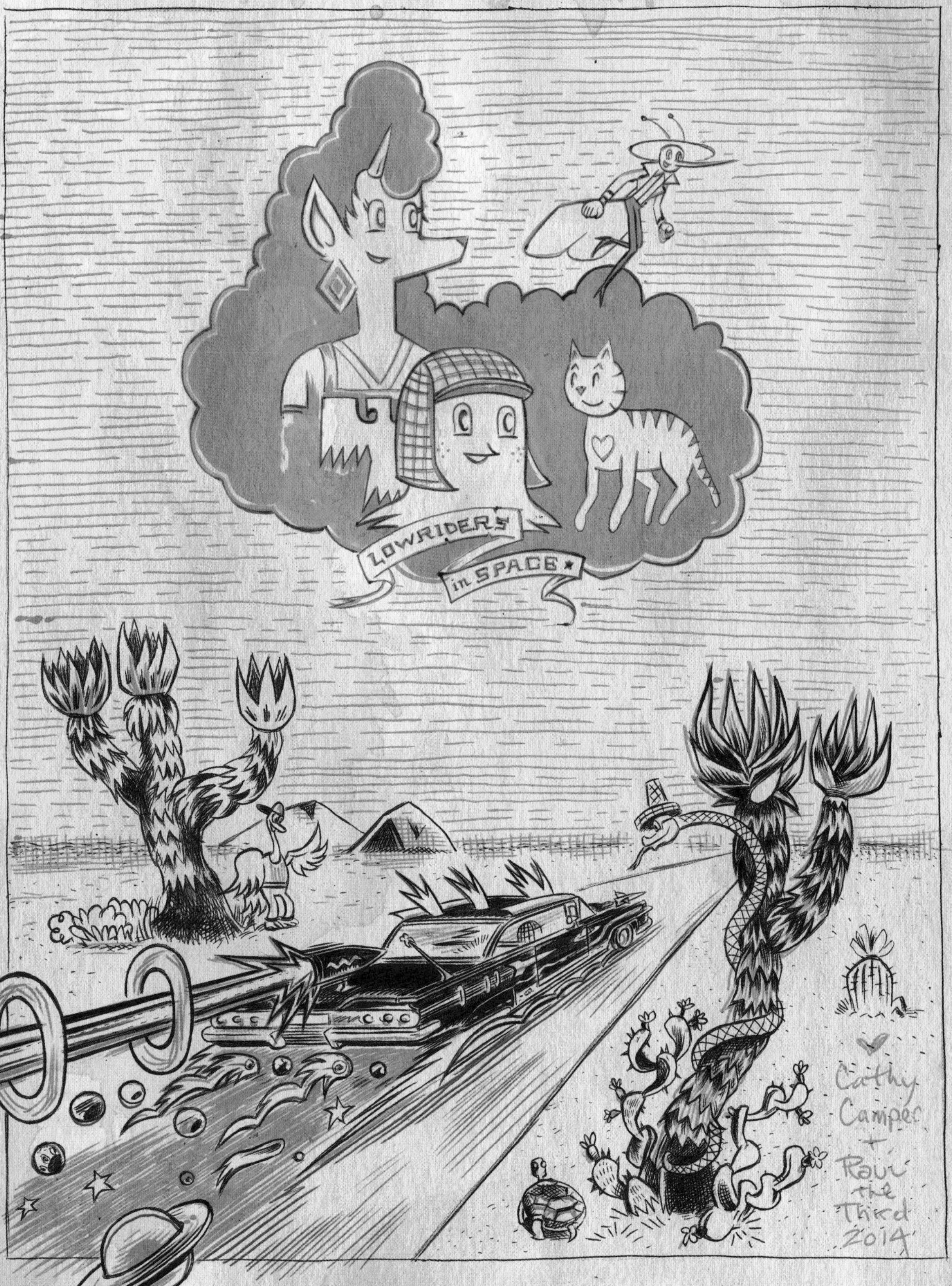
LOWRIDERS in SPACE
Cathy Camper + Raul the Third 2014

A NOTE ABOUT LOWRIDERS

Lowriders were created by Mexican Americans, and originated in Southern California after World War II. The first customized cars were street racers and hot rods, built by Anglos and Mexican Americans alike. Both groups thought their cars looked cooler when they were modified to ride lower to the ground.

Anglos continued to build hot rods while Mexican Americans developed their own vehicles that rode low and slow, which made them good for cruising neighborhood streets and hanging out with friends and family. And of course, both groups used their cars for flirting and for competing over who could build the best car.

Many Mexican Americans couldn't afford new cars, so they modified old ones to create cars that drew respect. They often chose Chevys over Fords because Chevys were readily available and were considered more reliable and better-looking. The Chevy Impala remains a lowrider favorite.

Old-school lowriders, called bombs or lead sleds, rode low to the ground and were decorated with extra chrome, sirens, fender skirts, and spotlights. The original lowriders put bags of sand or cement in their cars' trunks to lower the rear ends. "Torching" was another method of lowering the car, where the springs were heated until they were red-hot, making them sag and the car ride lower.

But once these cars were lowered, they stayed low. Preferable methods were ones that allowed drivers of lowriders to raise and lower their cars to avoid run-ins with the law for driving vehicles that scraped the pavement.

After World War II, there were plenty of spare parts from the aircraft industry in the junkyards of Southern California. Ron Aguirre, a California lowrider, came up with the solution to use aircraft hydraulic cylinders to raise and lower his car. Another method of raising and lowering a car's body uses air bags for each tire, and an air tank and compressor to empty and fill the bags.

Accessories make a lowrider. Exquisite upholstery, chrome, fog lights, mirrors to show off the engine, sound systems, TVs, neon underlighting, pinstriping, and airbrush paintings are all ways owners make their rides look good. Steering wheels are also important. Some of the most popular are small wheels made of chrome chain links, known as "fat man" wheels because they allow more space for a large driver's belly.

This book was written to celebrate the artistry, inventiveness, mechanical aptitude, resilience, and humor that are all part of lowrider culture.

A NOTE FROM THE ARTIST

I have been drawing for most of my life, and I love it because anyone anywhere can do it. Drawing requires the simplest tools—cavemen used sticks with burnt tips to create detailed drawings of the lives they lived, directly onto the walls of their caves!

When I was a young boy, I would spend hours dreaming up worlds using ballpoint pens on paper bags or newsprint. I didn't have "professional tools." I didn't need them. Ballpoint pens can be found just about anywhere. Sometimes I found mine on the sidewalk, or local businesses gave them away for free with their names written along the side. I still get them this way.

I decided to draw *Lowriders in Space* with red, blue, and black ballpoint pens to revisit the excitement I felt as a kid whenever I drew. Where do you get your ballpoint pens, and what kind of drawings do you like to make? —**Raúl the Third**

WHAT DOES IT MEAN / ¿QUE SIGNIFICA?

These words include Mexican-American slang, car, and astronomy terms.

a tu derecha—to your right

airbrush—a way of painting that uses air to spray the paint in a fine mist onto the car

asteroid—Smaller than a planet, asteroids are made of rock, metal, and ice. Many can be found in the asteroid belt between the planets Mars and Jupiter.

¡Ay chihuahua!—nonsense expression of frustration

bajito y suavecito—low and slow (the motto of lowriders everywhere)

barrio—neighborhood

biblioteca—library

¡Caliente!—Hot!

campeones—champions

chrome—the shiny metal on bumpers, mirrors, and other metal car parts

¡Colorín Colorado!—Just as you begin a story, "Once upon a time . . . ," these are nonsense words that mean it is the end of the story.

compressors—devices that pump air from an air reservoir (a storage container) into air bags, which when filled, raise the car, and when emptied, lower the car.

cuate—buddy

cumbia—a dance from Colombia

customize—to make something just how you want it

¡Dale gas!—Give it some gas! *or* Let's go!

dinero—money

detail—to clean and keep up your car; to remove dirt and scratches to make your car shine

El Chavo Flapjack—Flapjack's nickname is a reference to the classic Mexican TV character El Chavo del Ocho, who wears the same kind of hat as Flapjack and sits in a barrel instead of a pail.

el jefe—boss

¡Encuéntrame unas piedras con chispas!—Find me some rocks with sparkles!

ese—buddy, dude, pal

¡Estellar!—Stellar! *or* Awesome!

gearshift—a lever in the floor of the car that lets the driver change the car's gears to go faster or slower

¡Gracias!—Thank you!

homes—short for "homeboy," something you call a friend or person you know.

homies—plural of homes

hubcap—metal covers for the center part of a car's wheel

impala—a fast-moving African antelope. Also, Chevrolet Impalas are one of the favorite lowrider cars.

interesante—interesting

Io—one of the planet Jupiter's moons, which is known for its volcanoes

la luna de conejo—the rabbit in the moon. (In the United States, people see a man in the moon, but Aztec culture saw a rabbit in the moon.)

¡Mi cinto!—My belt!

Milky Way—the galaxy, or group of stars, that surround the Earth and the solar system. When you look up overhead at a very dark sky, and it appears milky with stars, you are looking at the Milky Way.

miren—look

mole—thick Mexican sauce for meat, made of many ingredients, including peppers and chocolate

monstruo—monster

northern lights—colored lights that appear near the North Pole. They are often white, blue, green, or pink and appear to dance like a light show. They are caused when charged particles from the sun bump into gas particles of Earth's atmosphere. Northern lights are also called aurora borealis.

órale—all right, right on, OK, what's up?

Orion—a constellation in the northern sky shaped like a giant hunter. It's easy to spot the three stars of his belt.

pinstripe—a thin stripe that decorates a car

Pleiades—a little cluster of seven stars named after the seven daughters of Atlas (from the Greek myth), who were placed in the sky to hide from Orion. The Aztecs drew the stars as shells in their codices (the writings of their beliefs).

Pluto—Discovered in 1930, Pluto was thought to be the ninth planet in the solar system, but in 2006, it was reclassified as a dwarf planet. It was named after Pluto, the Greek god of the underworld.

¡Que chido!—Cool!

¿Que significa?—What does it mean?

¡Que suave!—How smooth! *or* How cool!

ranfla—lowrider

retro-nuevo—old and new

Salton Sea—a large saltwater lake in Southern California that is slowly drying up into a salty desert.

¡Ten cuidado!—Be careful! *or* Watch out!

tuck and roll—a method of stitching the upholstery on car seats

V-8—a powerful eight-cylinder car engine

Vacaville—a city in Northern California

¡Vámonos!—Let's go!

vato—dude, guy

vulcanized—a way of heating up rubber to make it stronger (named after the word volcano)

¡Y hay un montón de carros!—And there's a ton of cars!

¡Y vamos a tener que echarle ganas!—And we will have to give it our best!

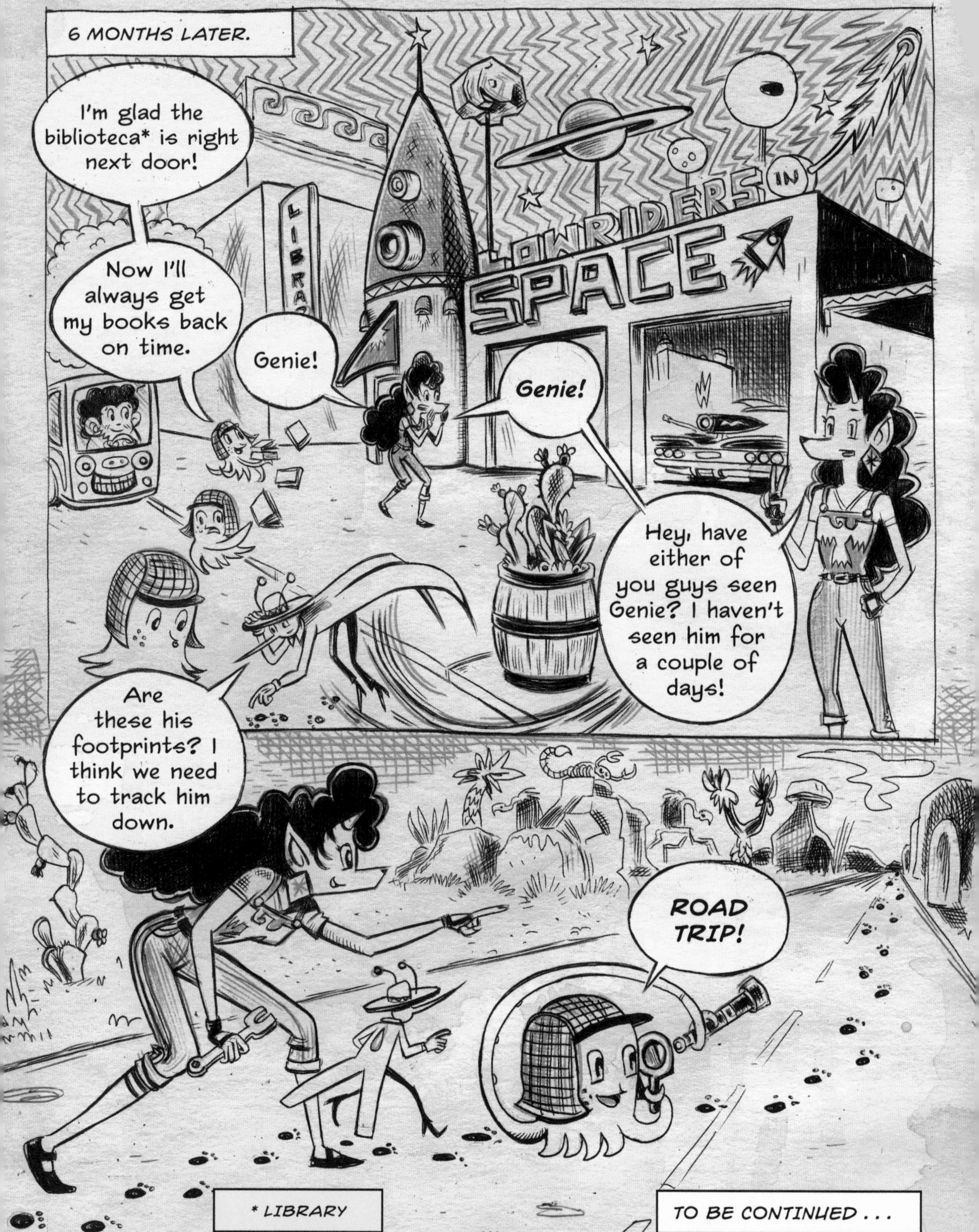
6 MONTHS LATER.
LIBRARY
LOWRIDERS IN SPACE
I'm glad the biblioteca* is right next door!
Now I'll always get my books back on time.
Genie!
Genie!
Hey, have either of you guys seen Genie? I haven't seen him for a couple of days!
Are these his footprints? I think we need to track him down.
ROAD TRIP!
* LIBRARY
TO BE CONTINUED . . .

To my family, to Matty, to Christopher Monaghan, and to Jambi—I remember you! —**Cathy Camper**

To Mama, for daily visits to the biblioteca; Dad for his stories; my two bros for playing make-believe; my wife, Elaine, for twenty years of love and adventure; and little Raulito the Fourth for being perfect. —**Raúl the Third**

ACKNOWLEDGMENTS

Thanks to: Jose Barajas, who read it FIRST!

. . . and to Matty Monaghan, Raúl Gonzalez III, Jon Scieszka, Megan McDonald, David Henry Sterry and Arielle Eckstut (The Book Doctors), Jennifer Laughran, Catherine Wynne, Ginee Seo, Taylor Norman, Neil Egan, Kevin Sampsell, Lee Montgomery, Michael Schaub, Alison Hallett, Dave Kiersh, Jo Tracy, Ana Schmitt, Delia M. Palomeque Morales, Laura Jones, Paulina Aguirre-Clinch, Rita Jimenez, Diana Nunez, Violeta Garza, Diana Miranda, Josh Rodriguez, Deborah Gitlitz, Katie O'Dell, Rob Schmieder, Ivan Velez Jr., Dylan Williams, Aron Nels Steinke, Angie Larson, Rudy Ubaldo, Byrd, Cynthia Cowen, Constance Williams, Christopher Gruener, Leonore Gordon, Myra Kooy, Karena Beuter, Rob Kirby, John Capecci, Jen Camper, VONA, Mat Johnson and my VONA graphic novel pals, Multnomah County Library staff and resources, my family, and everyone else who believed in and supported this escapade! Plus a heartfelt thank-you to *Lowrider* magazine and their car shows, Manic Hispanic, El Vez, and the magnificent Hernandez Brothers, who inspired me. —**C. C.**

Thank you to Clark Jackson for assisting me with the undercoat of the lowrider with his handy sky-blue Bic pen. —**R**

‏‏‎

Text copyright © 2014 by Cathy Camper.
Illustrations copyright © 2014 by Raúl Gonzalez.
All rights reserved. No part of this book may be reproduced in any form without written permission from the publisher.

Library of Congress Cataloging-in-Publication Data:

Camper, Cathy, author.
  Lowriders in space / by Cathy Camper ; illustrated by Raul Gonzalez III.
      pages cm. — (Lowriders ; book 1)
  Spanish words and phrases used throughout English text.
  Summary: Lupe, Flapjack, Elirio customize their car into a lowrider for the Universal Car Competition to win the cash prize that will enable them to buy their own garage.
  ISBN 978-1-4521-2155-0 (alk. paper)
  1. Lowriders—Comic books, strips, etc. 2. Competition (Psychology)—Comic books, strips, etc. 3. Friendship—Comic books, strips, etc. 4. Lowriders—Juvenile fiction. 5. Competition (Psychology)—Juvenile fiction. 6. Friendship—Juvenile fiction. 7. Graphic novels. [1. Graphic novels. 2. Lowriders—Fiction. 3. Competition (Psychology)—Fiction. 4. Friendship—Fiction. 5. Mexican Americans—Fiction.] I. Gonzalez, Raul, 1976- illustrator. II. Title. III. Title: Lowriders in space.

  PZ7.7.C363Lo 2014
  741.5'973—dc23

          2013040709

Manufactured in China.

Design by Neil J. Egan III.
Additional typesetting by Liam Flanagan and Mia Johnson.
Typeset in Comiccraft Hedge Backwards, P22 Posada, and ITC Century.

10 9 8 7 6 5 4 3 2 1

Chronicle Books LLC
680 Second Street
San Francisco, California 94107

Chronicle Books—we see things differently. Become part of our community at www.chroniclekids.com.

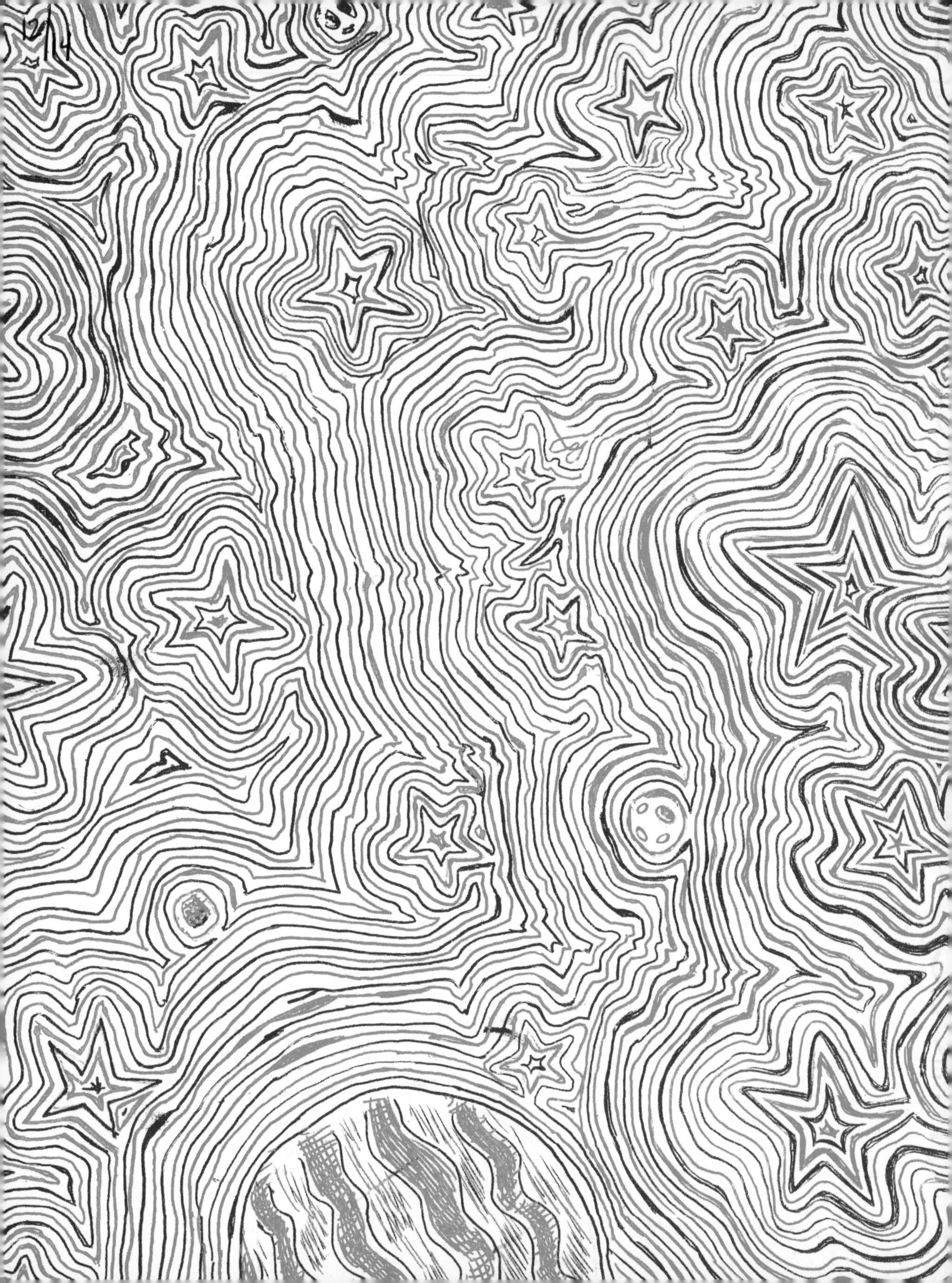
12/14